CANDACE CAMP

Scandalous

HQN™

Recycling programs
for this product may
not exist in your area.

ISBN-13: 978-0-373-77480-7

SCANDALOUS

Copyright © 1996 by Candace Camp

This edition published by arrangement with Harlequin Books S.A.

For questions and comments about the quality of this book
please contact us at Customer_eCare@Harlequin.ca.

® and TM are trademarks of the publisher. Trademarks indicated with
® are registered in the United States Patent and Trademark Office, the
Canadian Trade Marks Office and in other countries.

www.HQNBooks.com

Printed in U.S.A.

Also available from

CANDACE CAMP

and HQN Books

Scandalous

CHAPTER ONE

THERE WAS A NAKED MAN ON HER DOORSTEP.

Priscilla had been in the sitting room, curled up with a book, when she heard a thunderous pounding on the front door. She had jumped to her feet, a trifle alarmed, for it was rather late in the evening for any visitors. Moreover, the loud noise had rung with urgency. She had snatched up a candle from the table and hurried to the front door. When she swung it wide open, she had found this man standing there. He had on not one stitch of clothing, and his skin was covered with a thin sheen of sweat and decorated with a multitude of thin red scratches. He was breathing rapidly, his chest rising and falling as he took huge gulps of air.

She stared at him, for one of the few times in her life rendered speechless.

He was a huge man; he seemed to fill the tiny porch of Evermere Cottage, presenting a wide expanse of bare skin. Priscilla had never seen so much naked flesh in her life, all of it tanned, muscled and intensely masculine.

The man stared back at her. He looked dazed and exhausted as he swayed, muttering, "Help me." Then he collapsed at her feet.

Priscilla let out a little shriek of horror and reached out to grab him, but he was far too heavy, and his damp, bare skin simply slid across her palm as he crumpled to the floor of the tiny porch.

The door of her father's study opened, and Florian Hamilton stuck his head out. His graying hair was rumpled and sticking up in spikes from his habit of shoving his fingers through it whenever he was deep in thought. He frowned vaguely.

"Priscilla? What was that noise? Is there someone at the door?"

His familiar voice broke Priscilla's temporary paralysis. "It's all right, Papa," she said, in a voice that wavered only slightly from her usual brisk tone. "I will take care of it."

She turned back to the porch to survey her problem. The man now lay partly inside the house, on his side, most of his massive chest and arms on the floor at her feet, his long legs and the rest of his torso sprawled out on the stoop. It was obvious that she could not possibly move him herself.

Who was he? And whatever was he doing here—naked and unconscious? It occurred to her that it must be a jest; it seemed, in fact, just the sort of nonsense that Philip or Gid might think up. However, she could not imagine that even one of her mischievous brothers would send a nude man to his sister's door—and what man would be willing to run around stark naked? If nothing else, it was still early spring, and rather chilly. No, she concluded, it could not be a joke.

Her eyes went to the man's face. It was boldly chiseled, with a wide jaw and prominent cheekbones, a firm, full mouth and a long, straight nose. His was not a handsome face, exactly; it was too sharp and hard for perfect beauty, but there was power in it, even in slack unconsciousness—and with his eyes closed, the thick fringe of lashes shadowing his cheek, there was even a hint of vulnerability that made her heart twist strangely in her chest. She bent forward, holding her candle lower to light his features.

He was clean-shaven, his skin smooth and tanned, darker than her own milk-white color and that of most of the people she was accustomed to seeing. There was a narrow red scratch across his jaw, and another on his forehead. His hair was a thick, rich brown, and, as she held the candle closer, a glint of red shone through, like polished mahogany. A strand of it had fallen across his cheek, and unconsciously she reached out and brushed it back. He groaned and rolled over onto his back.

Priscilla's eyes moved lower, over his wide, muscled chest, lightly strewn with dark hair, and onto the flat plain of his stomach, where the hair converged in a V and swept downward....

"I say!"

Priscilla started guiltily at the sound of her father's voice, right behind her. She turned and straightened, frowning. "Papa! You startled me."

Florian paid no attention to her words. He was staring in astonishment at the man lying at their feet. "I say," he repeated. "Who is this chap?"

"I have no more idea than you," Priscilla replied. "I opened the door, and there he was."

"But what's he doing on the floor?"

"He fainted."

Florian's brows rose. "Doesn't look the sort to faint, does he? And what's he doing dressed like that?"

"Papa…"

"Oh. Sorry—of course you don't know that, either."

Florian tilted his head, considering the man's unconscious form thoughtfully. "Looks like he's been through rather a rough time, doesn't it?"

Priscilla looked back at their visitor. "It would appear that he has run through bramble bushes," she agreed. She leaned closer, noticing several dark marks that she had not noticed in the dim light of the porch. "And look, he's bruised."

"You're right." Florian adjusted the little glasses perched on his nose and leaned forward analytically to examine a bluish mark on the man's chest. "I'd say the fellow's been in some sort of fight, as well as running through the bushes." He looked at his daughter, his eyes lit with his usual scientist's curiosity. "Mysterious, isn't it? How do you suppose he got in this shape? And what's he doing here?"

"Mmm..." Priscilla replied dryly. "Just like a book."

"Yes, isn't it?" He stopped short, obviously struck by a thought. "You don't think Philip— No, surely not."

Priscilla had to grin. Her brother's mischievous ways were well-known. "No, I don't think so."

"Ohhhhh!" A gasp from the top of the stairs made both of them turn and look up. A tall, stick-thin woman stood at the top of the stairs, a vision in a long-sleeved, high-necked white cotton nightgown, a brown shawl wrapped around her thin shoulders and her hair a Medusa-like arrangement of strands tied in white cotton strips. The old-fashioned white mobcap she wore over her head at night was still tied beneath her chin, but the cap had slipped over and down to one side, dangling on a few of the strips of old bedsheets in which she tied her hair at night in a largely vain effort to put curls into it.

Her eyes were as wide as saucers, and she stared down at them wildly. "Is he—is he dead?" she hissed.

"No, Miss P., he's breathing, just out cold."

The middle-aged woman sucked in her breath, her hand flying to her chest so dramatically that Priscilla wondered how she could have looked any more appalled if the man *had* been dead. Miss P. hurried down the stairs toward them, her multitude of ties fluttering wildly. Florian, who had never before seen Miss Pennybaker in her nighttime attire, could only stare at her, mouth agape, but Priscilla, long accustomed to her former governess, scarcely noticed.

Miss Pennybaker reached them, and for the first time got a good look at the man stretched out on the floor in front of them. "Oh, my!" she said, her face flushing a deep red. "Oh, my!" She closed her eyes and averted her face. "He's…he's…"

"Yes, I know," Priscilla said flatly. "Now, don't have hysterics on us. The important thing is, what are we going to do with him?"

"But you mustn't…" Miss Pennybaker's eyes flew open, and she fixed Priscilla with a stern look. "It is not a sight for a maiden's eyes. You should come with me and let your father deal with it."

"By himself?" Priscilla countered calmly. She saw no need to point out what they all knew: that her father rarely handled anything in their household. His considerable intellect was generally employed in scholarly pursuits; he was considered an expert in several fields and received correspondence from other scientists all over the world, asking his opinion. But the small matters of daily life rarely captured his interest, and if the running of the house had been left to him, it would probably have fallen down around their ears by now. "This man is far too heavy for Papa to lift by himself."

Miss Pennybaker, who had lived with them since Priscilla was four years old, knew Florian Hamilton as well as his daughter did. Indeed, nowadays it was usually she who made sure that Florian came out of his study or workshop at least twice a day to eat, and who could be counted on to locate his pipe or his spectacles whenever he lost them. She knew as well as Priscilla that their unexpected guest might still be lying on the floor when they came downstairs the next morning, while Florian sat in his study sketching a machine designed to lift and move him.

"Yes, of course. But it isn't decent for you—" She stopped, a smile of triumph spreading across her face, and whisked off her shawl. Holding the shawl at arm's length, she sidled closer to the prone man, squinting through almost closed eyes, and dropped the garment across his lap. "There," she said with a decisive nod. "It still isn't decent, but that will have to do."

Priscilla suppressed a grin. "Thank you. Now…Papa, why don't you grab one arm, and I'll get the other, and we'll pull him inside? Penny, could you get his feet?"

The other woman looked askance at the idea of touching any part of the man's body. "But, Priscilla, do you think we should bring him in?"

"He's already half-in. It's only a question of pulling him the rest of the way."

"I mean…do you think it's safe?" She cast another brief, disapproving glance at the unconscious man. "He looks like a ruffian to me. He might murder us all in our beds tonight."

"That's true," Florian agreed. "We don't know what

sort of man he is, or anything about him at all—except that he's apparently been in a fight."

"A fight!" Miss Pennybaker gasped.

"Yes. See how he's scratched and bruised."

Miss Pennybaker ventured a closer look at their visitor. Her nose wrinkled in distaste. "He's wet, too."

"He was perspiring, I think. Although, judging from the state of his legs, he has probably splashed through a stream or two, as well," Priscilla said.

All three of them turned to look at the man's feet and calves, liberally splashed with mud and quite wet, and at the dark hair plastered to his skin. Miss Pennybaker turned quickly away. Florian peered at his feet with interest.

"You know, you're right, Pris. Always said you had an eye for detail. Looks like the watermark comes just below his knee. Something shallow, then, maybe the Slough." He bent down and plucked a wet leaf from the top of the man's foot. "Looks like he went through vinca, too. And grass."

He thought for a moment. "My guess is, he came through the woods on the east."

"But we still don't know who he is or what he's been doing," Miss Pennybaker reminded them, her hands fluttering nervously in front of her, as they always did whenever she was bold enough to dispute one of her employers. "He doesn't look like a nice person."

Priscilla looked down at the man's face. "Well, not nice, maybe…but not bad, either. Just…I don't know. Strong." She raised her head. "That's not a bad thing."

"But he's been fighting!"

"What if he were attacked?" Priscilla pointed out. "He would have every right to fight back. A man wouldn't be running about attacking people when he didn't have on any clothes, would he?"

"Not unless he were mad," Florian agreed.

Miss Pennybaker sucked in her breath sharply. "Oh, no! Do you think he's escaped from an asylum?"

Florian grinned. "More likely some insane Aylesworth cousin, kept locked up in the attic at the Court. Sounds like the sort of thing they would do, don't you think?"

Miss Pennybaker's eyes widened. "Do you really think so? You know, that's what happened to that sweet Henrietta Fairfield in *Derwood Abbey*. Lord Comfrey's mad uncle escaped from the tower room, and—"

"No," Priscilla replied firmly, grimacing. "Papa is poking fun at those books. Now, be serious, Papa. I think it's far more likely that he would have lost his clothing if he had been robbed. But then he escaped through the woods, splashed through one or two of those shallow streams down in Ridley Bottoms, and came up here. He probably saw the lights of our house and was coming for help. If he were intent on doing evil, I don't think he would have come right up to the door and knocked. No, he would have been slinking around, trying to get in an open window."

Miss Pennybaker cast a nervous look around them. "Perhaps we should lock the windows."

"He was hammering at the door," Florian admitted. "It even roused me in my study. Sounds more like someone seeking help than a robber."

"But if there *was* someone after him," Priscilla pointed out, "we had better get him inside, don't you think? Instead of standing here talking about it?"

"You're right." Florian cast a look out into the dark night. "All right, ladies, let's get to it."

Priscilla bent and grasped the man's left arm, high up, close to his shoulder. His skin was hot and slick with sweat, and when she touched him, it did odd things to her stomach. She had never touched a man's bare flesh before, unless one counted taking her younger brothers firmly by the hand—and touching this firm-muscled stranger was a far cry from that.

Her father grasped the man's other arm, and Miss Pennybaker, with an expression of distaste, went around and gingerly picked up his feet. They lifted, but could not manage to get his torso completely off the floor. They set him back down and winced as his head made an audible thud.

After that, Miss Pennybaker came around and held his head up while the other two yanked and pulled. Finally, when they had managed to work his entire torso into the room, Priscilla took his feet and lifted his legs, turning him enough to the side that they were able to close the door and bar it.

Panting, the three of them stood for a moment, looking down at the stranger. He slept on.

"What are we going to do with him now?" Florian asked.

Priscilla thought. "What about the cot in the little room off the kitchen? Where the scullery boy used to sleep."

Her father nodded. "Excellent. But surely there's an easier way to get him there. We could move him easily if we just had the right sort of leverage." He eyed the recumbent man speculatively. "What do you think his weight is?"

His eyes grew distant and unfocused as he began to consider the problem, and Priscilla hastened to intervene. "I don't think you need do any calculations right now, Papa. I'll fetch a blanket, and we can roll him onto it, then pull him in there on the blanket. That would be the easiest thing, don't you think?"

"Of course." Florian beamed at his daughter. "You are always so practical, my dear. I can't think where you got it."

"Some distant ancestor, I'm sure," Priscilla replied, with a twinkle in her eye, and hurried off to pull a blanket out of the cedar chest in the hall.

When she returned, they followed her suggestion, tugging and rolling the man onto the blanket with some effort. After that, it was much easier to move him across the polished wooden floor, though the three of them were panting by the time they had maneuvered him down the hallway and through the kitchen into the tiny bedroom. Priscilla straightened up, putting a hand to her aching back. She looked from the stranger to the cot, then to her father. How could they possibly lift him up onto the cot?

"I think we'll leave him on the floor for now," Florian said, echoing her own thoughts. "Perhaps he will come to and be able to get there on his own."

Priscilla nodded, but a worried frown creased her forehead. "Did he seem...rather warm to you?"

"Yes." Florian frowned, too. "Perhaps he has a fever. He could be ill."

"Maybe he's been wandering about in a delirium," Miss Pennybaker put in. "That could even explain why he's, well, in, uh, an unclothed state."

"I suppose...if he were out of his head with fever,

he might have ripped off his clothes thinking it would make him cooler."

"A brain fever might make one do anything," Miss Pennybaker assured her. "He might have left his bed and gone running out into the night, thinking heaven knows what."

"Well, if that *is* the case, we need to get him a doctor," Florian said. "Perhaps I should go get Dr. Hightower."

"No," Priscilla protested quickly. "If there's someone or something dangerous outside, you don't need to be out there with it." As her father began to bridle, she quickly amended her first, heartfelt concern, adding, "And Miss Pennybaker and I would be left alone here with no protection. What if someone tries to break in to get this man?"

"Hmm... You are right."

"Pennybaker and I have taken care of Philip and Gid through countless fevers. I expect we can manage this one, as well. If he gets worse, you can go for the doctor."

"All right. Perhaps I ought to check the windows... make sure we're locked up good and tight."

Priscilla nodded absently, already sinking down onto her knees on the floor beside the stranger. She felt his forehead; it was burning-hot. Miss Pennybaker brought in the oil lamp from the kitchen, and in the better light Priscilla could see that the man's face was flushed. He moved restlessly, turning his head to the side, and she saw now that the back of his hair was sticky and clotted with something.

"Blood!" She felt carefully along the back of his skull, finding a knot in the midst of the sticky blood. "I knew it! There's been some sort of foul play here. Someone hit him on the back of the head—hard. Penny, get me water and a cloth. We need to clean his wounds."

"Oh, my. Oh, my." Miss Pennybaker shook her head, sending the myriad of curls fluttering absurdly. " I don't like this at all."

"Of course not. It is obvious someone has mistreated this man. Why, Pennybaker, look!" Her eyes had fallen on the man's wrists, and she lifted his arm so that her former governess could see it better. "See those red marks around his wrist? His skin has been rubbed raw there. Rope burns, I should think. There's another on the other wrist, in the same place. And look, his ankles, too. He has been tied up."

Miss Pennybaker stared at her, aghast. " Priscilla! How do you know such things!"

Priscilla grimaced. "That is the way Gid's hands looked that time he was playing pirate and slid down a rope from the roof. Remember?"

"True." The older woman cast an uncertain look at their uninvited guest. "But being tied up— Priscilla, things like that only happen in books."

Priscilla shrugged. "Well, they must happen to real people sometimes, don't you think? It certainly seems to have happened to this man."

"Yes, but I mean—not to the sort of people one *knows*. It makes me nervous. I'm sure he's a ruffian."

"He is a ruffian who is out cold right now, and running a fever, as well. Surely we can manage to subdue him if he tries to attack us."

Miss Pennybaker took a look at Priscilla's wide gray eyes, dancing with humor, and sniffed. "All right. Go on. Think I'm an old fuddy-duddy. But mark my words—"

Priscilla chuckled. "Come now, Penny, how many times has the dashing hero been rendered unconscious and his sweetheart has had to nurse him back to health? Where is your romantic spirit?"

"But never in his—his altogether! Heroes are always gentlemen. This one looks much too rough."

"We shall find out, I suppose, whether he's a villain or a stalwart hero. But whichever he is, I think we need to see what we can do to make him well, don't you? Bring the tincture of echinacea, too, will you?"

Miss Pennybaker agreed, albeit reluctantly, and went into the kitchen, returning a few moments later with a bowl of water and supplies for cleaning a wound. Priscilla dipped a cloth in the water and carefully began to wash the back of the stranger's scalp. The man winced and moaned at her ministrations, but he did not waken. Priscilla dampened a small square of cloth with several drops of the healing tincture, then gently applied it to the wound.

"Goddamn it!" The man's eyes flew open, and his hand wrapped around her wrist like a steel band.

Priscilla froze, staring down into his eyes. They were bright green, the color of new leaves lightened by the sun, clear and penetrating, and it seemed to Priscilla as if they stabbed right through her into her soul. She sat utterly still; once more, he had left her bereft of words.

His eyes narrowed. "Who the devil are you?" he snapped.

"Let go of her!"

Priscilla had forgotten about Miss Pennybaker's presence until she shrieked out these words. Her eyes flew to the woman, who was standing now on the other side of the man, the bowl of water held threateningly in her hand, her whole body so taut that she was trembling. The multitude of white cotton strips that decorated her head fairly quivered.

The unknown man's gaze went to Miss Penny-baker also, and his mouth dropped open in astonishment as he gazed at the apparition. "Holy hell! I'm in a madhouse!"

His hand dropped from Priscilla's wrist, and he surged to his feet. Miss Pennybaker backed up with a shriek, sloshing water everywhere, and Priscilla jumped up after him, crying, "No!" and reaching out to restrain him.

His face immediately went pale, and he wavered. Then his eyes rolled up in his head, and he crumpled.

This time Priscilla was quicker, and she wrapped her arms around him. He collapsed onto her, and for an instant she was enclosed in his heat and his smell, the hair-roughened skin of his chest pressed against her cheek, his head bending down over her and his arms around her. But she could not hold him up; her knees gave way beneath her, and together they slid to the ground.

"Priscilla! Oh, my love, are you all right?" Miss Pennybaker put aside her weapon and rushed to them.

"Yes." Priscilla tried to squirm out from beneath his weight. "Help get him off of me."

He was lying on top of her, pressing her against the floor, but it was less the feeling of the hard stone beneath her than the strange sensation of his body pressing into hers that disturbed her. There was a peculiar tingling all over her, and her loins were suddenly hot and melting. They were sensations she had never experienced before, and they were unnerving, even though they were at the same time strangely exciting.

Miss Pennybaker grabbed the man's arm and shoulder and tugged, while Priscilla pushed from beneath, and they managed to roll him off her and back onto the blanket. Priscilla sat up for a moment, recapturing her breath and letting the flush in her cheeks subside.

"Are you sure you're all right?" Miss Pennybaker queried anxiously, gripping her gown with nervous fingers.

"Yes. I'm fine." Priscilla brushed back a strand of hair and picked up the roll of bandages Miss Pennybaker had brought in earlier. "Just hold his head and let me wrap this bandage around it."

A little tentatively, Miss Pennybaker did as she said, and Priscilla wrapped the narrow strip of cloth around his head a few times and tied it, pleased to see that her hands were steady. She went on to wash his wrists and his ankles, steadfastly ignoring the rest of his naked body, and covered them with tincture-soaked bandages. This time he flinched but did not open his eyes when she laid the potent mixture upon his wounds.

"There, now." She stood up and shook out her skirts, looking down on her charge. "I've done everything I can think of. He'll need another blanket, of course, to cover him."

She picked up the bowl of water, now stained pink from his blood, and went into the kitchen, Miss Pennybaker trailing along behind her.

"I think we need to keep watch over him to see how his fever is progressing," Priscilla told the other woman.

"Yes, and to make sure he doesn't come to and decide

to murder us all in our beds," Miss Pennybaker added dramatically.

Priscilla smiled. "I think we could lock our doors and prevent that. However, he may need medical care. I think I will sit up with him."

"Not by yourself!" Miss Pennybaker gasped. "Think of what could happen! What he might do! Remember what he just did."

"Well, he didn't attack me. In fact, it was we who threatened him, as I remember."

"He grabbed your arm."

"I was hurting him. I should think it would be only natural to try to stop the pain. He was not in a clear state of mind."

"No. You must not. It's too dangerous." Miss Pennybaker squared her shoulders. "I will stay with you."

"Don't be silly. I shall keep a weapon handy—a rolling pin, say, so that I can knock him over the head if he comes to and tries to strangle me."

"Priscilla, this is no time for joking!"

"I'm not. I promise, I will keep a rolling pin at hand. Better, I think, than a knife, because, you know, I have a fairly good swing, but I haven't any experience with stabbing anyone."

"Priscilla…" Miss Pennybaker wrung her hands, her face twisted with worry. "At least let me stand guard with you."

"But you can't. You must get some sleep so that you can watch over him during the day tomorrow."

"Priscilla!" The older woman's hand flew to her throat.

"Don't worry. If he hasn't tried to attack me in the night, I think it unlikely that he would try it in the light of day. Besides, Mrs. Smithson will be here tomorrow, and Papa will be around, as well."

"Then your father can stay with him tomorrow, and I will remain with you tonight."

Priscilla rolled her eyes. "Papa would be useless in a sickroom. Why, within five minutes, he'd be thinking about some experiment or theorem or something, and the poor man could expire without him even noticing."

Miss Pennybaker, having been acquainted with Florian Hamilton for so many years, was forced to see the wisdom of that argument. Still, she protested futilely for several minutes more before she finally gave in to Priscilla's arguments and left for bed. Priscilla, casting a glance at their patient, who was sound asleep on the floor, walked with Miss Pennybaker upstairs to take two more blankets from the chest in the hall. As she was closing the lid, there was a knock on the front door.

She whirled and hurried down the stairs, but her father got to the front door before her this time. Florian swung the door open, revealing two of the most unsavory-looking characters Priscilla had ever seen. One was tall and angular, with longish, unkempt hair and a sharp-feature face. His eyes were narrow and sly, and they darted around the room, peering unabashedly into the house behind Florian. His companion was short and square. His chest and arms bulged with muscles, and his nose looked as if it had been broken more than once. His face was an oafish blank.

Priscilla hastily dropped the blankets behind the stairs, where they would not be seen, and moved up to stand behind her father. If ever there were people who looked bent on no good, it was these two. Moreover, as she drew close, she realized that one or the other of them, perhaps both, reeked of alcohol. She sincerely hoped that her vague, pleasant-tempered father did not decide to trust them. It also occurred to her that it would be quite comforting if she had that rolling pin in her hand right now.

"Yes?" Florian asked, his voice icy with hauteur. "My good man, do you realize what time it is? Rather odd to be calling on people at this time of the night, don't you think?"

Priscilla almost sagged with relief. Obviously her father had taken the same immediate dislike to these two men that she had. He was usually quite egalitarian in his dealings with everyone, but he could, if he chose, fall back into the aristocratic tone and stance that generations of breeding had instilled in him.

His words obviously had the desired effect on the men on the porch. The shorter one squirmed and looked aside, and the tall one quickly pulled off his cap, bobbing a sort of bow toward Florian.

"Sorry to disturb you, guv'nor. But it's an emergency, like."

"You don't say." Florian's voice dripped with disbelief.

"Yessir. We're chasing a man…a bleedin'—er, I mean a bloomin' bedlamite. We was thinking 'e might 'ave come 'ere."

"A lunatic? Here? Unlikely."

"Well, er, 'e, that is, we was takin' 'im back 'ome, to 'is family, see, and 'e conked Mapes 'ere over the 'ead." His companion turned to him with an indignant expression, but the speaker quelled him with a black look and hurried on, "We 'as to catch 'im, sir. 'E's right dangerous. Crafty, you see."

"I see. Well, he obviously caught *you* napping, at least," Florian said to the smaller man.

"It weren't my fault," the shorter man protested, and rounded on his cohort. "It could've 'appened to you."

"Yeah, well, it didn't now, did it? And I 'adn't emptied a bottle of gin, neither."

His words effectively silenced the short man, who scowled and looked away. Florian gazed first at one man, then at the other, as if he were studying some curious form of insect life, letting the silence build until both men were fidgeting uncomfortably.

"Well," Florian drawled finally, "I fear that I cannot help you with your problem. You shall have to take your search elsewhere."

The tall one, the apparent leader of the duo, persisted. "You ain't seen nobody this evenin'?"

"My good man, I just said so, didn't I? Do you doubt my word?" Florian invested his voice with scorn. "I rather suspect that it is the two of you who are escaped madmen—or perhaps it's simply that you have spent too much time with your gin bottles. Now, kindly take your wild stories elsewhere—you are frightening my daughter."

Priscilla moved behind her father a little, doing her best to look timid. The tall man grimaced. He seemed reluctant to move away, but, as Florian was firmly closing the door, he had little choice. Florian shut the door and shot the old-fashioned metal bar across it. He turned, smiling down at his daughter.

"Well, my dear, was that a satisfactory performance?"

"Absolutely splendid," Priscilla replied, beaming. "You reminded me of the old Duke for a minute there."

"Actually, I was aping my father's cousin, but Ranleigh will do."

"I'm glad you decided to protect him."

"I couldn't see turning anyone over to those two. I'm not sure yet whether our guest is a villain, but it did not take much imagination to see that *they* were up to no good." He paused, looking thoughtful. "I wonder what the real story is."

"Perhaps we shall find out when our visitor awakens. He came to a few minutes ago, but he tried to stand up and sank like a stone again."

"Seems to do that rather a lot," Florian commented mildly.

"Mm…I think I found the reason—or at least one of them. He has a ferocious knot on his head. His hair was matted with blood."

"So…knocked over the head."

"I also discovered something else. He has been bound hand and foot. There are rope burns on his wrists and ankles."

Florian's eyebrows lifted. "Been held prisoner somewhere, then. This story gets more and more interesting. Who do you suppose those men are? And who is *he?* Were they cohorts who fell out? Or is he an innocent set upon by ruffians? Or could their story be true—that he's mad as a hatter and they've been hired to bring him back?"

"They don't look very truthful to me—nor the sort one would hire to look after someone."

"If he is mad and strong, one might have to choose

force over finesse." He paused. "Did he say anything while he was awake?"

"He cursed—fiercely. Then Pennybaker threatened to bash him in the head with the bowl of water. He looked at her and her curling rags all over her head and declared that he was in a madhouse. That was when he jumped up and fainted again."

Florian chuckled and ran his fingers back through his hair, as he always did when he was considering a knotty problem. "We cannot turn the fellow out into the night, though I can't like having someone we know so little in the house. Still, I suppose he can't be too much of a threat, if he faints every time he gets to his feet."

"Probably not," Priscilla agreed, walking back to the staircase to retrieve the blankets. "In any case, I intend to sit up with him tonight."

"Sit up with him? Why?"

"He doesn't just have a head wound. He is quite hot, and I think you were right about his having a fever. I need to keep an eye on him, at least for the next few hours. If he gets too serious, we may have to send for the doctor."

"Perhaps I should stay with you," Florian mused, his forehead wrinkling. "He could be dangerous."

"Papa, you said so yourself—he's too weak and sick to stand up, let alone hurt me. Anyway—" her lips curved up into a smile "—I have promised Pennybaker I will carry a weapon."

"A weapon? What sort of weapon?"

"A rolling pin was what I thought of."

"This might be more to the point." Florian reached into the capacious pocket of his jacket and pulled out a long-barreled gun.

"Grandpa's dueling pistol?" Priscilla exclaimed. "What are you doing with that?"

"I thought it best to answer the door armed, just in case."

"So you pulled down Grandpa's gun and loaded it?"

"Oh, no. It has no ammunition. I keep the guns in their case, but I haven't a clue where to find a ball and powder. It hasn't been used in ninety years. I'm not sure it would fire even if I had the powder. But it looks quite threatening."

"Yes, unless your bluff is called."

"You can always turn it around and pop him on the head with the butt. With this fellow, it should do the trick."

"Papa!" Priscilla couldn't suppress a giggle. She reached out and took the pistol, sticking it down into the long pocket of her skirt. "All right. I shall sit with it in my lap to intimidate him should he wake up."

"Still, I probably ought to stay with you." Florian's eyes darted involuntarily toward his study, where, no doubt, some fascinating tome on chemistry awaited him.

Priscilla smiled indulgently. "Nonsense," she said stoutly. "I won't hear of it. I am perfectly fine by myself, and I have this gun. And you won't be far away. I can always scream."

"That's true." Florian brightened at this easy solution to his dilemma. "I'll come running immediately."

Priscilla kissed her father on the cheek and watched fondly as he hurried off toward his study, his mind obviously already on the subject that awaited him. She turned and walked down the hall to the kitchen. Opening the door, she stepped inside.

An arm lashed out and wrapped around her, effectively pinning her arms to her side and jerking her backward against a hard male body. At the same time, another hand clamped over her mouth, stifling the beginnings of a piercing scream.

CHAPTER TWO

PRISCILLA TWISTED AND TURNED, trying to pull away, but the arm around her was too strong. She thought of the gun her father had given her, now lying useless, deep in the pocket of her skirts. She had underestimated her visitor, and she cursed herself bitterly for being so foolishly confident.

"Now!" his voice whispered in her ear. "Who the hell are you? What am I doing here? And where the hell are my clothes?"

Priscilla made an irritated noise. How did the fool expect her to speak with his hand over her mouth?

"I'll take away my hand," he went on, "as long as you don't scream. One scream, and—" His arm tightened briefly in emphasis. "I can snap your neck like a chicken's." He paused, then said, "Do you understand? Will you agree?"

Priscilla nodded. His hand loosened over her mouth, then slowly withdrew. He settled it on her throat, his fingers stretching suggestively across it. Priscilla shivered; the touch of his hot hand on the sensitive skin of her throat sent strange vibrations through her. She could feel his body, hard with muscles, pressed against hers all the way down, and she could not keep from thinking about the fact that he was naked.

"Answer me," he prodded, his breath hot against her cheek.

"I, uh..." Priscilla stopped and cleared her throat, then continued in a stronger voice, "My name is Priscilla Hamilton, and you are at Evermere Cottage. As to what you are doing here, I was rather hoping that you could enlighten me on that score."

"Hamilton?" he repeated vaguely, and she could feel his body sag a little. "I don't know you."

"No. Nor do I know you. All I'm certain of is that you collapsed on our doorstep about thirty minutes ago."

"Why?" he asked softly, but she got the impression that he was speaking more to himself than to her.

He removed his hand from her throat and brought it up to his face. He swayed a little and leaned against the wall, his arm loosening around her waist.

Priscilla knew that her moment had arrived. She stamped down hard on his bare foot with her shod one, and at the same moment lunged forward with all her strength. He let out a grunt of pain and surprise, and his arm fell away, so that Priscilla was able to break away from him. He reached out, grabbing for her, but it was too late. She pulled out the ancient dueling pistol and spun around to face him.

His mouth dropped open and he stared at the gun in her hand. "You cunning little bitch! You *are* one of them, aren't you?"

"One of whom?" Priscilla retorted, and gestured with her gun. "Move back against the wall. I am the one asking the questions now."

He leaned back against the wall, though it looked more as if from necessity than because of any command from her. His face was pale, and sweat stood out on his forehead. From the expression on his face as he closed his eyes, Priscilla suspected that his head was spinning again. Her eyes slipped a little lower. It was extremely uncomfortable standing there dealing with a man who was utterly naked. He seemed perversely unconcerned and at ease in his naked state, which somehow made her feel even more awkward.

She refused to stare at him; it would be in appalling taste. Yet it was extremely hard to look anywhere else. She could not help but notice the breadth of his shoulders or the bony outthrust of his collarbone, or the way his chest was padded with muscles. She had never seen any man naked, of course, but she could not imagine that any of the gentleman of her acquaintance would resemble this man if she was to see them in such a state. Her younger brothers' lanky, bony bodies were nothing like his, and even Alec, who was a constant and bruising rider, had a wiry build.

But this man, who was almost a foot taller than she, was anything but wiry. His body looked chiseled from granite; there wasn't an ounce of excess flesh anywhere on him. Priscilla had never realized that a man's body could be so…intriguing. Her eyes drifted lower, and she jerked them away selfconsciously, blushing. She was glad that his eyes had been closed and he hadn't seen how—and where—she was staring.

"I think it would be better if you sat down while we talked," Priscilla began stiffly. "Otherwise I'll have you back on the floor."

He opened his eyes and looked at her. "I passed out before, didn't I?"

"Mm… Twice now."

He shook his head and winced. "Damn! What is the

matter with me?" He wiped his hand over his face. "I'm sweating buckets. Things just start whirling." He looked at Priscilla as if these things were her fault.

"I suspect it's that large bump on your head. As well as the fact that you are running a raging fever. Now, I suggest you walk back that way and into that little room off the kitchen. There's a cot there." She nodded toward the blankets she had dropped on the floor when he grabbed her. "There's a blanket I brought for you."

He turned and looked at them, bent carefully and picked up one of the blankets, then wrapped it around his shoulders, holding it closed in front. He walked through the kitchen and into the side room, moving slowly but with carefully precise movements. When he sank onto the cot, he had to stifle a groan, and his head dropped to his hands for a moment. Priscilla couldn't keep from feeling a pang of sympathy.

"I am sorry," she told him. "I would give you something for the pain, but that's not really a good idea with head injuries."

He raised his head and looked at her, puzzled. "I don't understand. Why did you bring me this? Why did you bandage my head?"

"Why wouldn't I? You were obviously hurt and… and, well, you needed a blanket. Anyone would have done the same."

"But you…aren't you working with them?"

"Who is 'them'? I am not working with anyone."

"I don't know their names. The two that had me tied up. The drunk, and the other one."

"A tall fellow? Thin? With a scar?"

"Yes, that's the one. What is he to you?"

"Nothing. He and a short man who struck me as

having imbibed too freely just came to our door, looking for you."

He continued to stare at her in confusion. "You didn't give me to them?"

"No. Papa told them no one had come here tonight. He thought they looked a proper pair of ruffians, and they did."

"So you aren't working with them." He relaxed. "Thank God. Then why are you holding a pistol on me?"

"May I remind you that you were the one who attacked me as I entered the kitchen? I thought a gun seemed an excellent idea, actually."

"You're right." He wiped his hand across his forehead again. "I apologize. My behavior was...exceedingly impolite." A long shudder racked him. He pulled the blanket closer around him. "I feel very strange."

"You have a fever. How long were you tied up? And were you, uh, dressed that way the whole time?" Priscilla asked, blushing.

He looked down at himself, puzzled. "Yes. I think so. I don't remember when— That is, I woke up, and I was like this, only bound hand and foot. They were there, on guard, and they changed sometimes. First one and then the other. But it was terribly hard to keep track of the time. I think it was days—it seemed forever. But I think there were just two nights and two days—after I came to, of course. I have no idea how long I was there before that."

Another shiver shook him, and he said, "Is it cold in here? I feel quite cold."

"I'll get you the other blanket." Priscilla got up and went out into the kitchen. She was no longer really frightened of the stranger; he seemed too weak at the moment to harm her, anyway. But she was careful not to turn her back to him, even so. She returned and tossed the blanket to him, also careful not to get close enough for him to grab her arm.

He seemed to have no interest in doing anything like that, anyway. He wrapped the other blanket around himself and sat, shivering. Yet his face was flushed, and sweat was pouring off him. "Do you mind? I think—I think I have to lie down."

He lay down on his side on the cot, his eyes fluttering closed.

"But, wait. Sir…" Priscilla moved closer, bending down to peer at him. "You have not told me yet. What happened to you? Why are those men after you?"

"I—I don't know." His teeth chattered, and he curled up into a tight ball. "It's so cold."

Priscilla hesitated. Then she stuck the empty pistol back into her pocket and hurried out of the kitchen. She returned a few minutes later with three more blankets, cautiously opening the door and peering into the room before she entered. Her guest was nowhere in sight.

She found him lying on his cot, but he had turned over onto his back and now slept with all his covers thrown off and his arms flung wide. Priscilla moved closer hesitantly. His skin was red with heat, and sweat dampened his body. He had obviously gone from a chill back to a fever. Still, he should have cover. Priscilla edged closer, feeling strangely reluctant and guilty.

It was foolish to feel guilty, she told herself, though she knew why she did. It was because she was tempted to look down, to let her eyes drift lower, past their visitor's flat stomach, down to the nest of hair and the…

thing that lay there. The very male thing that she had been trying to avoid looking at from the moment she first answered the door this evening, yet which she could not keep her eyes from straying to now and then before she caught herself and pulled them back.

It was just that she was curious. She had never actually seen one of *those*. No woman of decency had, unless she was married, and Priscilla wasn't really sure one did even then. It was something she was not supposed to know about, and true ladies, she had been told when she was a child, would not even be curious about such things. However, Priscilla had decided some time ago that she probably did not have the soul of a true lady. She found most ladylike endeavors boring, and the thing she loved to do, and which brought her much needed income, was not considered a fit occupation for a lady, either.

Her secret love was writing—and not ladylike diaries or accounts of travels, or the sort of bad poetry young women were supposed to scribble, but full-blooded, hair-raising adventure stories. There was nothing she loved like a foreign setting, a stalwart hero and plenty of dangers to overcome. She had grown up reading the Gothic horrors of the Brontë sisters and the sweeping heroic tales of Sir Walter Scott. Books had carried her away to lands she dreamed of and knew she would never see, had introduced her to brave and wonderful people, the sort she knew must exist somewhere.

Her entire life she had lived a quiet existence, but in her head she had seethed with excitement. Reading the stories had not been enough; other stories danced in her head, compelling and intriguing her. So she had begun to write, traveling to exotic locales in her mind, creating the sort of perfect, adventurous men who lived only in her imagination. Men who did not stay on their estates, growing old and chasing foxes, perhaps traveling to London for a treat, men well content to be who and where they were. The men in her mind, the ones who flowed out of her pen and onto paper, were adventurers all, most of them brave and noble, some of them villainous, but all of them seekers—of treasures, of truth, of excitement. Men who risked everything.

The man who lay before her could have passed for one of those men. He looked the part: tall, handsome, strong, mysterious, and in danger. It was exactly the sort of thing a hero in a book would do, come knocking on a lady's door with men in pursuit of him—except, of course, that he would be clothed and, normally, he would fight off his pursuers. But real life, of course, could not be exactly the same as a book; real life was usually so unmanageable. This man was the closest she had ever come to one of the larger-than-life men who lived in her books. It was no wonder, she told herself, that she was curious.

Of course, one of the genteel heroines of her books would never think of looking on an unclothed man. They were the proper women that society expected, even if they did get into predicaments that no real lady would. Priscilla, however, was well aware that she was not one of her heroines. And *she* was thoroughly curious about the male anatomy.

She thought about how embarrassing it would be if he happened to wake up and catch her staring at him. But even that thought could not deter her for long. She turned and looked down his body, then quickly away, and then back, blushing furiously, but unable to keep from gazing at him.

So that was how men were built. It seemed quite strange, so different from women, and yet…there was something fascinating about it. Looking at him, she felt an odd sensation stirring deep in her loins, and she was aware of a completely improper urge to reach out and touch him. She would not, of course; even she was not that lost to propriety—or that daring.

The man stirred on the cot, and Priscilla jumped. Hastily she covered him with one of the blankets she had brought. The man was ill and needed her help, she reminded herself. She put her hand on his forehead. He was burning up.

She returned to the kitchen and got a fresh bowl of water and a new wash rag, then went back to her patient. After dipping the rag in the water, she squeezed it out and laid it on his forehead. Leaving it there, she went back into the kitchen to search for the bottle of tonic that her friend Anne had given her the last time Philip had a fever. It had worked rather well, as she remembered. She found it at last in the back of a cupboard and mixed a spoonful of it in a glass with a little water.

She returned to her patient. He was moving restlessly on the cot and had already shoved his blanket down to his waist. He murmured something unintelligible as Priscilla knelt on the floor beside him. "Mr.…." She wished she knew his name; it seemed strange to be tending someone she could not even address by name. "Sir, can you sit up? I have something for you to drink."

When he did not awaken, she prodded his shoulder tentatively. His skin felt like fire. "Sir? Please, wake up."

His eyelids fluttered open, and he turned his head. His gaze was hazy and unfocused. "What?" He ran his tongue over his parched lips. "I'm so hot. Where am I?"

"Evermere Cottage," Priscilla replied evenly. "I told you before. Don't you remember?"

He shook his head slightly and wet his lips again. "Thirsty."

"I know. You need to drink some water. But first you need to drink this. It will help you feel better. Can you sit up?"

He nodded, but made it only up onto his elbows. Priscilla put her hand behind his head to help steady it and raised the glass to his lips. He drank greedily, then pulled back, grimacing.

"What the devil! Are you trying to kill me?"

"No. It's a tonic for your fever. You need to drink it. I know it tastes wretched, but you really must drink some more."

"The hell I will!" he retorted belligerently.

Priscilla set her jaw and gave him a steely gaze. She hadn't dealt with two lively boys all these years for nothing. "Yes," she told him firmly. "You have to. Now open up."

"I want water," he replied with equal stubbornness, and the mutinous look on his face was so much that of a young boy that Priscilla almost had to laugh.

"And you shall have some…as soon as you take your medicine."

He stared at her in silence for a long moment. Priscilla returned his gaze with calm determination. Finally he grimaced, saying sullenly, "All right."

He drank the whole draft, then fell back on his bed,

his mouth twisting expressively. "Tastes like poison. Who hired you? Father?"

"No one hired me. I am trying to help you of my own free will, but I must say, at the moment you are making me reconsider my decision."

He smiled faintly at her retort, and she left to get him a glass of water. By the time she returned, his eyes were once again closed. She set the glass down on the small dresser and returned to his bedside. He was sweating profusely and had once again thrown his blanket almost completely away. Priscilla straightened it, then brought up the stool that sat in the corner of the room and sat down beside him. She washed his face with the rag, soaked it in the bowl, then washed his face again.

The cool water on his face seemed to make him a little more peaceful, but he continued to move his head and mumble something now and then, and several times he thrust the blanket down impatiently. His fever continued to rise.

When the boys ran a really high fever, she had usually sponged their chests, as well, Priscilla remembered, but she felt a little odd about doing that to a strange man. However, after a while, she decided that she had no choice. His fever was simply too high. So she dipped the wash rag in water, squeezed it out and began to bathe his chest with it, slipping it behind his head to cool his neck, as well. She brought the rag down his chest to his stomach in long, rhythmic strokes, and when it grew warm from his body heat, she dipped it in the cool water and started all over again.

The rag was thin, and through its dampness she could feel the firm shape of his muscles, the hard ridges of his ribs and collarbone. A flutter ran through her abdomen, and her breath came a little faster. She found herself watching the pulse in his throat, thinking about touching it. Finally she did, reaching out and placing a finger gently on it. His skin was blazing; it was also soft and vulnerable there, in contrast to the strength of his body, the force that she had felt in him earlier, when he pulled her back against him. His pulse beat against her finger, firm and fast; it made her own pulse accelerate to feel it.

She pulled back her hand, swallowing, amazed at the strange sensations coursing through her tonight. She had never felt a tingling quite like the one she felt when she dragged the cloth across his chest; she had never known the heat that flowered in her abdomen. It was all very peculiar and exciting and enjoyable, all at once.

She brought the cool rag from the water to his chest again and began a long, slow sweep down his body. Her finger passed over his flat masculine nipple, and she thought that it felt much harder and more pointed than it had before. Her patient moaned and turned toward her, kicking off his blanket once more. Priscilla shook her head, and was leaning down to pull it back up to his waist when her eyes fell upon the same member at which she had sneaked a peek earlier. She stopped in midmotion, staring.

It was different.

It was bigger and longer, and it seemed to be rising upward. Blinking, she drew her hand back. Automatically she began to wash his chest again, while her mind considered what she'd just seen. As she moved her hand down his chest and onto his stomach, she saw his shaft move. She stopped, amazed, then tentatively stroked his stomach again with her cloth. Again his manhood twitched and seemed to grow.

She glanced back up at his face. He was still asleep, his eyes closed, but his face looked somehow looser, and his mouth was open slightly. His breath rasped in his throat. Priscilla felt her own throat closing up, and something beginning to pulse deep between her legs. She squeezed her legs together tightly, surprised at the sensation.

He licked his dry lips again. Priscilla watched him. Then—she wasn't sure why—she dipped her forefinger into the glass of water she had brought him earlier and touched it to his lips. He pressed his lips to her finger. His hot breath seared her hand, and her stomach was fluttering as if butterflies were warring within it.

She dipped her finger back into the water and trailed her damp finger across his lips. This time his tongue snaked out, scooping the water from her finger. It was soft as velvet, hot and firm, and heat surged in her loins.

His eyes fluttered open, and he looked at her. His eyes were glazed and vague; there was no recognition, no questioning, as there had been earlier. His lips curved upward in a way that did strange things to her insides.

"Nice," he murmured. His hand came up and curved over her cheek. "How much?"

"I beg your pardon?" Priscilla looked at him blankly. The touch of his hand on her face, faintly rough and searingly hot, made every thought fly out of her head.

"For the night," he went on in a low voice. "For you." His hand slid down her throat and onto her chest, cupping her breast. "Mm…Madam Chang always knows how to pick them."

Heat flooded Priscilla when she realized, from his graphic gesture, exactly what he was talking about. He thought she was a woman of the night! Someone whose favors he could buy!

"Sir!" She pushed his hand away and started to rise, but he clamped his fingers around her wrist and held her still.

"Wait. Don't go." His other hand went to the back of her neck, cupping it and pulling her down toward him. "Don't you understand? You're the one I want."

"No! Wait! You are mistaken. You've—you're delirious." Priscilla braced her hand against his chest, but he seemed to feel the gesture was a caress, for he smiled and murmured something and pulled her even closer, until she was only inches from his face.

Then his lips were on hers, hot and demanding. She had never been kissed like this before in her life. In truth, she had been kissed only three times, and those had been mere pecks, a brush of the lips. There had not been this heat, this demand, this pounding need, radiating from the man, as there was now. His lips pressed hungrily into hers, opening them, and then, astounding her, his tongue was in her mouth, searching. She stiffened, making a surprised noise, but he did not pull away, only kissed her more fervently. Both his arms were around her now, pressing her into him. Priscilla's senses were whirling; she felt her muscles going limp as his heat invaded her. She no longer pushed herself away from him; instead, her fingertips dug into his flesh eagerly. Her lips moved tentatively against his.

He groaned deep within his throat and broke off their kiss. His lips trailed fire across her cheek to her ear.

"Take down your hair," he panted. "I want to feel it all around me."

His fingers fumbled at the knot of her hair, sending hairpins flying, and her heavy tresses tumbled down, flooding around them. He combed his fingers through it, surrounding their faces with the veil of her hair. He took the lobe of her ear between his lips, worrying it gently and sending shivers of delight all through Priscilla's body. His teeth teased at it, and she was flooded with heat. She sucked in her breath.

"No, wait," she began weakly, but his lips covered hers again, stopping her words—and all thought, as well. For the next few moments, she was lost in the sweetness of his mouth, drowning in the heat and hunger.

His hand came up once again to her breast, cupping it through her clothes and squeezing gently. The intimate touch sent excitement sizzling straight down into her loins, but it also jolted her back into reality. This stranger was touching her in a way no man should touch her. And, as if that were not bad enough, she was responding like a trollop!

Shame flooded her, and she jerked away from him. Her movement was so swift and so unexpected that he was not able to hold on to her. He lay there, looking befuddled, his arms stretching out emptily for her.

"Honey, don't go," he said plaintively. "What's the matter?" He rubbed a hand over his face, wiping away the sweat. "Damn!" His eyes wavered and closed. "I've got the money," he persisted faintly, his words growing more and more slurred. "Around here somewhere. Just wait. I'll— Where's Madam Chang? She will tell you."

He mumbled a few more unintelligible words before

he lapsed into silence. Priscilla remained standing a cautious distance from him. She put a trembling hand up to her hair. It lay loose and full all about her shoulders; just the feel of it reminded her of his fingers in her hair, his passionate words. Even now, it made her feel like melting wax inside. *And his kiss!* She had never imagined that a kiss could be like that; nothing she had ever experienced or heard about had prepared her for it. The fact that it was a stranger who had kissed her so fully, so intimately, so...delightfully made it seem all the more unreal. Surely such a kiss should pass only between those who loved each other.

There were too few hairpins for her to put her hair up again, so she pulled it back with shaking fingers and braided it, tucking the coil up into a tight bun with the two pins she found still tangled in her hair. She had to admit to herself that the fault was more hers than his. Though he had pulled her to him and kissed her forcibly, he at least had been in the throes of a delirium dream and thought she was someone else. She, on the other hand, had known full well that he was a stranger, nothing to her, yet she had kissed him back fervently. Priscilla could not imagine where this wanton streak had come from.

To make it worse, she knew that she should be deeply shamed, yet her thoughts kept running back, not to how shameful it was, but to how wonderful it had felt. She could still taste him on her lips, still smell his scent in her nostrils, and it made her shiver. Was this the way her heroines should feel about the heroes in her novels? How very odd. What she had imagined for them seemed quite tame right now.

She went into the kitchen and splashed water on

her face. It was cool against her heated skin, and she smoothed it down her face and onto her neck. She remembered his hand there, sliding like silk, like molten fire. Priscilla closed her eyes. This was not helping much. Sternly she straightened, opening her eyes, and wiped the water from her face.

She had to be practical, she reminded herself. The man in the other room was sick and needed her. She had to help him, not stand around thinking crazy things. He was a stranger to her, as she was to him. What had happened was a product of his delirium, nothing else. He had not even known who she was; he had thought she was someone else, no doubt someone from his past. Why, he hadn't even thought she was a decent woman; he had obviously thought she was a woman of the streets—talking about paying her and calling her one of some madam's girls.

Priscilla walked back to the door of his room and looked in on him. He was curled up into a ball, the blanket pulled up to his shoulders, and he was visibly shivering. His fever had turned into the chills again.

Priscilla hurried into the room and spread two of the extra blankets over him, pulling them up to his shoulders and tucking them in. He said nothing, just continued to shiver so hard his teeth were chattering. His eyes were closed, and now and then he let out a small moan. There seemed nothing dangerous about him now; his size, and the firm swell of his muscles, only made a mockery of his strength. Priscilla hovered close, frustrated by how little she could do to help him.

But it was not long before he was pushing the covers aside again, sweating and mumbling incoherently as he tossed and turned. Priscilla managed to keep him on the cot and covered most of the time, but it was a tiring task. In his delirium, he continued to try to get up, no matter how many times Priscilla planted her hands on his shoulders and pushed him back down on the bed. But at least he no longer thought she was one of the occupants of a brothel.

She poured him another draft of the tonic. It was a bitter battle getting it down him, and finally he knocked it out of her hand and sent it crashing onto the stone floor. While she was cleaning it up, he got out of bed and staggered around the room for a while before she was able to persuade and cajole him back into bed. It was a relief when he fell back into a chill and huddled in upon himself on the cot.

So it went the remainder of the night, with her patient passing from fever to chills and back again, and Priscilla worriedly watching him, forcing him as best she could to drink the draft and trying to keep him covered, as the long hours passed. Finally, when dawn was first beginning to appear on the horizon, Priscilla awoke with a start and realized that she had fallen asleep sitting up in the chair. She turned immediately to her patient.

He was sleeping, his arms flung out over the cot, and the blanket lay over him almost up to his arms. He was still, and for one horrible instant she thought he was dead. Then she saw the steady rise and fall of his chest, and she realized that, though his face was still tinged with a flush, he was sleeping peacefully. She jumped to her feet and hurried over to lay her hand on his forehead. It was warmer than normal, but far less so than it had been during the night. His fever had broken.

Priscilla let out an enormous sigh of relief and sank down onto the floor. Her knees suddenly felt like rubber.

She leaned her forehead against the cot, weak with relief. In the aftermath of tension, her muscles began to tremble, and she realized, amazed, that there were tears spilling out of her eyes.

A hand touched her head, gliding softly over her hair. Priscilla raised her head, startled, and found herself staring straight into a clear green gaze.

"Are you all right?" he asked softly, and his hand once more stroked her hair. During the night's struggles with him, her hair had once again fallen out of its pins and come loose from her braid until it lay softly over her shoulders, and she had given up trying to keep it back. She knew it was far too intimate to wear it this way around a man. Yet he did not seem at all uncomfortable with it; his hand caressed it naturally, as one might run one's fingers over a lovely sculpture or piece of porcelain.

"Yes," Priscilla replied, trying to smile at her foolishness. She quickly brushed her fingers across her cheek to rid them of the tears. "I'm sorry. I—it was relief. You have been out of your head all night, and when I saw that your fever had broken, well…"

"I see." He smiled faintly. He let her hair sift through his fingers, watching it. "You are very beautiful."

Priscilla felt a blush rising in her cheeks. "Thank you."

He frowned a little. Finally he asked, his voice puzzled, "Do I know you?"

Priscilla looked at him oddly. "No."

His words seemed to recall her to propriety, and she stood up, sweeping her hair back. "Don't you remember coming to our door last night?"

He frowned and shook his head. "I— Things are

foggy." He sat up slowly, and the blanket slid down, revealing his bare chest. He looked down, and a peculiar look crossed his face. "I haven't— Where are my clothes?"

"I don't know." Priscilla's blush intensified. "That's the way you arrived on our doorstep."

"Naked?" he asked in astonishment. "Are you joking?"

"No. I have no idea why. I don't even know who you are."

"Who I am?" he repeated vaguely.

Priscilla nodded. "Yes. That would be somewhere to start. What is your name?"

He looked back at her blankly. "I—I'm not sure." She could see panic touch his eyes. "I don't know. I don't know who I am!"

CHAPTER THREE

PRISCILLA STARED. "You don't know who you are?"

He shook his head. "I don't know my name. I—" He looked around the room, as if that would somehow give him the answer he wanted. He raised a hand to his head, saying, "Ow…my head hurts. I feel so strange. And dizzy."

"You have a large knot on your head, and it bled, as well. I would say someone gave you a nasty crack. You've also been running a high temperature, and it isn't back to normal yet. You passed the crisis point within the last hour or so."

The man eased back down onto the bed with a groan. "Does that make you lose your mind?"

"I don't know that you've lost your mind. Only your memory." Priscilla tried to sound heartening, though her own heart had sunk at his words. How could someone forget who he was or what had happened to him? "Perhaps it is a result of the fever or the knock on the head. I suggest that you go back to sleep. Get some rest, and probably when you wake up you will remember everything. You know how it is when you're sick sometimes. Things get hazy and strange."

"Not this strange," he muttered, but he did close his eyes. A few moments later, he had slid back into the escape of sleep.

Priscilla sat watching him, hoping that she was right. It sounded sensible. She remembered how once, when she was little, she had had a fever and imagined all sorts of strange things, even that there were little elves up in one corner of her room, where the walls met the ceiling, building a little house. It had been very disorienting and confusing; surely it wouldn't be all that strange to forget who one was. Once the fever was gone, and he was feeling better, he would remember.

On that optimistic note, she went into the kitchen to prepare a small breakfast and eat it. She thought about making something for her patient to eat, but she decided it would be better to let him sleep. A few minutes later Miss Pennybaker came downstairs, a worried frown on her face. Every hair was in place in a tight bun atop her head, as always, and she looked as neat and tidy as ever in her severe brown dress. However, it was obvious from her manner that inside she was a mass of nerves.

"Are you all right? Oh, my dear, I had the worst night. I tossed and turned all night. I don't think I slept a wink. I kept thinking about you. Worrying that something would happen to you. What happened?" She came to a halt breathlessly, her eyes huge and her hands twisting together in front of her breast.

"Well, he was in a state of delirium most of the night," Priscilla replied practically. "He had a high fever and chills, but the fever broke not long ago, and now he is sleeping peacefully."

Raising her finger to her lips in a gesture calling for quiet, Priscilla led her former governess to the door of the small bedroom and showed her their patient, sleeping like a child on the cot. Looking at him in the light, with his dark lashes shadowing his cheek and his face relaxed in the vulnerability of sleep, Priscilla realized all over again how attractive the stranger was. He did not, perhaps, have the handsome perfection of an Adonis, but his sharp cheekbones and square jawline were powerful and intriguing, even with the dark stubble of several days' growth of beard.

Miss Pennybaker, beside her, shivered. "How could you have stayed alone with him all night? Weren't you afraid?"

Priscilla glanced at her in surprise, wondering how the woman's only reaction to his masculine beauty could be fear. "It was rather…exciting," Priscilla answered honestly. "I mean, I was a little frightened once or twice, but when I was nursing him through his fever, it was like a battle, me against the fever." She smiled. "And I won."

"You do say the oddest things. Well, you can go up to bed now. I shall watch him." With a determined set to her chin, Miss Pennybaker picked up a chair from the kitchen table and set it down in the middle of the doorway, just outside the bedroom. With some amusement, Priscilla thought she looked more like a jailer than a nurse, but she did not comment. No doubt the woman believed herself to be facing down lions for Priscilla's sake.

Priscilla smiled to herself and went upstairs. She realized as she walked into her room how deadly tired she was. She slipped out of her clothes and fell into bed wearing her chemise and slip, not bothering with putting on her nightgown, a fact that she was sure would scandalize Miss Pennybaker if she knew it. Within moments she was asleep.

By the time she woke up, it was midday. The sun was

streaming into the room, and she blinked, disoriented for a moment. Then the events of the night before came back to her, and she hopped out of bed and began to dress. She was eager to return to her patient and find out what had happened in the hours she had been asleep, so she made quick work of getting dressed and putting up her hair.

She found Miss Pennybaker and her patient in the same positions in which she had left them, though Miss Pennybaker had been joined in the kitchen by Mrs. Smithson, who came in with her daughter daily to cook and clean for them. Mrs. Smithson was bustling about in front of the stove, where several pots were simmering, and a delicious aroma floated in the air.

Priscilla drew a deep breath. "Mm…Mrs. Smithson, it smells as if you've outdone yourself."

The cook, a short, no-nonsense woman with graying hair, turned to her with a smile. "Ah, Miss Priscilla, there ye are. I been wondering what was happening, with him in there, and herself sitting here." She turned toward Miss Pennybaker with a disdainful sniff. "Not saying a word to anybody, as if I would be going telling the whole village your business. I'm not a gossip, Miss, and you know that."

"Of course I do, Mrs. Smithson." Priscilla wanted to soothe the other woman's ruffled feathers. The cook, who had helped look after Priscilla when she was a baby, had always regarded the governess as an interloper and one who held herself above her station. *Love,* she was fond of saying with a dark look at Miss Pennybaker, *was what was important, not reading and writing and such fanciness.* "I know you would never dream of spreading gossip. But the fact is, Miss Pennybaker and I know little more than you do."

Quickly she explained how the stranger had appeared on their doorstep the night before and the subsequent appearance of the two ruffians. Mrs. Smithson listened raptly, now and then interjecting an "Ooh" or an "Ah" or a "Bless me." The two of them moved over to where Miss Pennybaker sat and looked in on the patient. He was lying with his eyes closed.

"Oh, but he's a handsome one, isn't he?" Miss Smithson whispered.

Miss Pennybaker shot her a look of disgust. Priscilla hastened to intervene. "I wonder where he's from. And what he's doing here."

"Maybe when he wakes up, he'll tell you," the cook offered.

Priscilla shrugged. She had not yet told either woman about the man's strange words last night, or his apparent lack of memory. She was hopeful that when he awoke today, his mind would no longer be muddled from the fever, and he would remember everything.

"Has he awakened yet, Penny?" she asked.

"Twice. He just looked at me. Once he asked for some water, so I gave it to him."

"Did he say anything else?"

"He asked about you. He wanted to know where the other lady was. I told him you were getting your well-deserved rest, since you'd been up all night looking after him."

Priscilla smiled faintly at her loyal friend's words. Trust Miss Pennybaker to cast her as an angel in any scene. All three women looked at the man on the cot again.

As if sensing their stares, he opened his eyes. He gazed at each one of them for a moment, his eyes narrowed suspiciously. Finally he said, his voice rusty, "Who are you?"

Priscilla stepped into the room and walked over to his bed, leaving the other two women eagerly watching the scene before them. "I am Priscilla Hamilton. Don't you remember my telling you that last night? And this is Evermere Cottage, our home."

He nodded, sitting up slowly, seemingly unmindful of the blanket sliding down to reveal his bare torso. "Yes. I remember." He looked at the two women by the door. "Who are they?"

"Miss Pennybaker and Mrs. Smithson. Miss Pennybaker helped me take care of you, and Mrs. Smithson is our cook."

The corners of his mouth twitched. "It smells as if she's a good one."

Mrs. Smithson beamed. "I'm thinking you'd enjoy some nice soup right about now, wouldn't you?"

He nodded, offering her an easy, charming smile. "You would be right about that. I feel very empty."

Mrs. Smithson bustled off happily to ladle him up a bowl of soup. Priscilla reached down and felt his forehead. It was quite a bit cooler than it had been the night before. His fever was almost gone.

"You seem to be feeling better."

He nodded. "Still weak as a kitten, though."

He turned a little and leaned back against the wall. He looked at Priscilla, then cast a wary glance toward the doorway, where Miss Pennybaker still sat, hands folded in her lap, stoically watching him. Priscilla, following his gaze, had to suppress a smile.

The man shifted a little, uncomfortably, and turned back to Priscilla. "Why does she sit there?" he asked. "And when I asked for some water, she stood as far away as she could to hand it to me. Do I have something contagious?"

Priscilla did smile this time. "I'm not sure. But I don't think that's the reason. You see, Miss Pennybaker is sitting there because she rather suspects that you are a ruffian."

"A ruffian?" He looked surprised. "Me? Nonsense."

"Are you so certain?" Priscilla raised a quizzical eyebrow.

His face shifted subtly. "Well, I…ah, I suppose you're right. I don't know whether I am or not. Strange feeling. Still, I don't feel as if I'm a ruffian."

"Then I take it you still do not remember?"

He shook his head, and his gaze turned inward, as if he were searching for something. He sighed and shook his head again. "No. Nothing."

"What are you talking about?" Miss Pennybaker stood up and took a few automatic steps forward. "Don't remember what?"

The man turned toward her. "Anything, Miss Pennybaker. I am afraid I do not know where I am from, where I am, or even what my name is."

The governess's jaw dropped. "You don't know your own name?" She looked at Priscilla. "Is that possible?"

Priscilla shrugged. "I have no idea. I suppose so. I remember that Aunt Celeste's father-in-law lost all notion of who he was—or of who anyone else in the family was, either."

"Yes, but he was eighty-four years old," Miss Pennybaker pointed out. She turned and looked narrowly at the man on the cot. "You, sir, are not."

"You have me there." He grinned at the older woman, and her cheeks pinkened. Priscilla, watching, thought that the man definitely knew how to charm. Miss Pennybaker might be suspicious now, but Priscilla doubted that it would take the man too long to have her highly romantic friend eating out of his hand. "I know it seems odd, ma'am, but it is the truth."

Mrs. Smithson came bustling in at that moment with a large bowl of soup for the patient. She set the tray down on his lap, and the man dived in eagerly. Mrs. Smithson smiled benignly at him as he ate, and even Miss Pennybaker seemed to soften at this sign of his obvious hunger. When he was through, and Mrs. Smithson had taken the tray back into the kitchen, Priscilla gently suggested that Miss Pennybaker join the cook, pointing out that it was past time for lunch. Miss Pennybaker was obviously reluctant to go, and Priscilla regretted the flash of hurt that passed briefly across her face. But she was determined to talk to their visitor alone, without Miss Pennybaker's questions, exclamations and opinions.

When the two women had left, Priscilla sat down on the chair close to the bed, where she had sat through her night watch. The man sank back into a prone position. For a moment the two of them simply studied each other. Finally Priscilla began, "Is there nothing you remember?"

"Nothing past the last few days, and those are hazy at best." He sighed and rubbed a hand across his face. "The first thing I remember is waking up in a hut. It had no windows. And I was naked. I'm not sure why." He frowned. "I was tied up, too, and it was damned uncomfortable."

"What hut? Where?"

"I have no idea. I saw the inside, mostly. The only time I saw the outside was when I escaped, and that was at night. It was simply a shack—wooden, unpainted—in the midst of some woods."

"How did you get out?"

"I managed to cut through my bonds. It took some time, but I was able to saw them upon some rough wood in the hut. It cost me a little flesh, but finally my hands were free. Then it was just a matter of untying the cord around my ankles and waiting for my guard."

"Your guard?"

"Yes. Someone came to check up on me regularly, just glanced in and looked me over to make sure I was still bound. There were two different men, actually. They seemed to take turns doing it. The short one was the one I bounced on his head."

"Honestly?" Priscilla was impressed. It sounded like the sort of daring escape her heroes were apt to make— but she had never met anyone in real life who had done such a thing.

He looked at her oddly. "Yes, of course, honestly. Why would I make up something like that?"

"I don't know. It just seems so…bizarre."

"It was. I have no idea who those men were or why they were holding me. They didn't do anything to me, just arrived periodically and looked in to make sure I was still tied up. They were not very bright. They didn't check any too closely."

"You remember nothing of how you got there?"

He shook his head. "Not a thing."

"It is certainly a mystery." Priscilla wrinkled her brow in thought. "If they had meant to kill you, I would think they would have done so immediately. And they had obviously already robbed you of whatever you had. Why keep you bound up and come in to check on you periodically? And why take your clothes?" She paused, then brightened. "Perhaps you were wearing some sort of uniform, something that would make you easily identifiable."

"That might make sense. But bound up like that, who would see me to identify me as in the military?"

"Well, if you escaped, as you did."

"You think they planned on my escaping? Intended for me to?"

"Seems unlikely, doesn't it? But perhaps they were just being very careful."

"And why would they have captured me? They're bound to have thought they would make money from it somehow."

"Perhaps they were trying to ransom you."

He nodded slowly.

"Or maybe you had to be somewhere on a certain day, and they were delaying you so that you would not make it. Someone paid them to hold you up for a week, say."

"Why?" he returned skeptically.

"Say you were going to testify at a trial. What if you knew something that would free an innocent man, and someone didn't want him freed? Or maybe you had the incriminating evidence that would put someone in jail, and he didn't want you to show up with it."

His eyebrows rose lazily. "You have a vivid imagination, I must say."

"There must be some reason for it. What happened to you wasn't exactly ordinary."

"Well, delaying me for a few days wouldn't do the trick. I could finish my task whenever they released me. Someone might have to sit in prison a few days longer or be free for another week, but the only way you could stop it for sure would be to kill me."

"Perhaps the person was squeamish. Or maybe he thought you would take this as a warning, and that now you would refuse to go. Anyway, I never said that the person was smart. Only wicked."

"I guess that's true." He smiled faintly.

"Or perhaps it would give them enough time to get out of the country, or destroy evidence, or something, and maybe that was all they needed."

"Or it could be that I am one of them, and we had a falling-out." He gave her an expressionless look.

Priscilla wondered if he was trying to frighten her. What he had said did, a little, but more because of the flat way he had said it and the blankness of his face than because of the words themselves. However, she was not about to reveal that he had rattled her. Priscilla prided herself on her calm even in the face of chaos, a state her family often seemed to find itself in.

So she merely returned his look, saying coolly, "I rather doubt it. A falling-out would have been a bit more violent, I should think. If you had stolen something of theirs, or double-crossed them, say, I shouldn't imagine they would simply tie you and up and sit around looking at you. Do you?"

A reluctant smile touched the corners of his mouth. "You have me there."

"It would seem to me that the task before us is to find out who you are and what you were doing in this area."

"Before *us?*" he repeated.

"Well, you arrived here asking for help, after all. I can hardly turn you out, unclothed and ill, to fend for yourself, especially with two blackguards after you. Anyway, as I was saying, if we can determine who you are, I think it would go a long way toward explaining why those two men are after you."

"And, how, madam, do you propose to do that, considering the fact that I have no means of identification on me and no idea who I am?"

"I can tell that you are getting tired and cranky. No doubt you ought to sleep. Just leave it to me. I shall do a little investigating."

Tired he might be—and Priscilla was sure he was, given the pale, drawn look of his face—but the hand that lashed out and grasped her wrist was certainly quick and strong enough. "What do you mean, 'a little investigating'?" he asked, his eyes narrowing. "You cannot go out there poking around with two ruffians on the loose."

Priscilla raised her eyebrows in her best grande dame manner and glanced down pointedly at her wrist. Her pose seemed to have little effect on her patient; he simply continued to hold her wrist captive and glare at her.

"I think, sir," she began frostily, "that it would be best if you released me. Now."

"Not if you're going to run out and do something foolish," he retorted.

"I rarely 'run out and do something foolish,' as

you say." Priscilla knew that wasn't strictly true; she wouldn't be a Hamilton if she always acted in a sedate and conventional manner. However, she was not about to let this man paint her as a silly little thing who would make a mess of whatever she tried to do. "I shall plan quite carefully before I attempt any investigation."

"No investigating," he responded flatly. "You could get hurt. Look at what happened to me, and I'm twice your size."

"Size is not always what's important. Sometimes it's better to be clever than huge."

His eyes widened, and for a moment Priscilla thought he was about to start raging at her subtle insult. Instead, he began to laugh, and his hand fell away from her wrist. "You have an answer for everything, don't you? Some man will have his hands full with you."

"I doubt that, sir," Priscilla retorted crisply. "I would not have a man who did not respect my capabilities."

"I'm sure of that," he agreed, still smiling faintly. "Now that I have been sufficiently rebuked for being the *large* and undoubtedly *slow-witted* creature that I am, let me point out to you that your cleverness does not change the fact that there are two rough characters about looking for me. And if you start snooping around, they may very well notice and realize that you know something about me. And believe me, cleverness doesn't stop a fist very well."

"I don't intend to go 'snooping around', as you so elegantly put it. I will not be *obvious* about it. They won't even know. I shall simply make a few calls around the village and listen to the gossip. If anyone knows of a stranger around here, I will hear about it. I won't even have to ask. Believe me, an American of your size—indeed, of any size—in Elverton is definitely fuel for gossip."

"American?" He seized on her words. "How do you know that I'm American?"

"From listening to you speak. You obviously are not from England. I have never heard anyone from any part of this country with that accent. Haven't you noticed how differently we speak?"

"Yes, I suppose I have, but I didn't pay attention to it. It seemed rather minor compared to the fact that I don't know who or where I am."

"Well, I do know *where* you are. The village of Elverton, in Dorset, England, where you obviously are not a native. Of course, you could be some other sort of colonial, but I think not. I met an American once, a colleague of my father's, and he had that same sort of flat speech."

"American," he repeated thoughtfully. After a moment, he shook his head. "It doesn't spark a memory. Boston, New York, Philadelphia…none of them make me think of home."

"Perhaps not, but it proves my point," Priscilla pointed out excitedly. "You're obviously more familiar with those cities than I. Their names came immediately to your tongue. You must be from the United States."

"Then what am I doing here? In…what did you say? Elverton?"

"Yes. My supposition is that you were merely passing through, perhaps going to or coming from a port in Cornwall, say. If anyone here had been expecting a visitor from the U.S., I would have heard all about it at least three times over. This is probably just where they happened to waylay you. But if you were in Elverton any time in the last few days, you will have been seen and speculated on, and I shall hear all about you within three minutes of calling on the vicar's wife."

He frowned. "I still don't like your walking about unprotected."

"Why would those men attack me?"

"They obviously suspected that I had come here, or they wouldn't have been knocking on your door last night. Perhaps this is the only house close to where I escaped. Or maybe they followed my trail here. God knows, I crashed through enough brush and stumbled through enough creeks to leave a track anyone could see."

"That's true," Priscilla mused. "They may still be suspicious of this house. But if that is the case, then it is you, here, who are in danger, not me. They would be trying to get into the house and seize you again, not pounce on me going to the vicarage."

"Don't worry about me," he replied. "Give me that pistol you were brandishing last night, and I'll stand firm against them."

"Doubtful. It hadn't any shot in it, you see. It's one of a pair of my great-grandfather's, and Papa only keeps them for sentimental reasons. I doubt they would fire, and we haven't any balls and powder for them, anyway."

"So you bluffed me." Again a smile played about his lips.

Priscilla shrugged. "I didn't think you intended to harm me, anyway."

"Still, I was a stranger, and out of my head. What if I had called your bluff?"

Thinking of what he had done while he was out of

his head, Priscilla had to blush. His eyes went to her cheeks, and color tinged his face, too. She wondered, wretchedly, if he remembered kissing her.

She glanced quickly away. There was a long, awkward silence, and finally, he began, "I—I hope I did nothing untoward last night in my fever. I— My memories are blurred, you see. I am not sure what I dreamed and what happened."

"Nothing happened," Priscilla assured him hurriedly, and hoped that he believed her. "You were out of your head and said a few things. Most of them I couldn't even understand."

"That's all?" His voice sounded doubtful.

"Of course. What else could there be?" Priscilla gave him a brief, impersonal smile to back up her words. Let him think it was all a dream. That would be the easiest way to deal with it.

He smoothed a hand across his face in a weary way. "Good. I wasn't sure. The dreams were so vivid…."

"'Tis often that way in a fever, I think. Now, I think you should go back to sleep. You are looking rather tired."

"Yes, perhaps I will." His slight smile was tinged with embarrassment. "I feel a perfect fool—worn out by a few minutes of talking."

"You will be better soon, I imagine."

"Why don't you wait until I am? Before you go visiting, I mean. Then, at least, you'd have some protection."

Priscilla gave him a pointed glance. "The same protection you had?"

He flushed. "Damn, but you've a wicked tongue on you. No, it would not be the same. Obviously I was not prepared for anything to happen before. This time I would be. I'm not a bad man in a fight."

Looking at his sculpted chest and arms, Priscilla felt sure that he was right. "Be that as it may," she said, "I have no wish to find myself in a fight, and since you are the man they are searching for, I would think that having you with me would be the surest way to bring those two ruffians down on me. I will be much less noticeable by myself."

"You have an answer for everything."

"I try to." Priscilla grinned. There was something quite enjoyable about verbally sparring with this man. She rarely had anyone upon whom she could sharpen her wit, now that her brothers were gone. Her father, intelligent though he was, was usually too much in his own world of thought to trade quips, and Miss Pennybaker was far too easily hurt.

As she turned to leave the room, she heard the sound of her father's voice. "I say, Mrs. Smithson, have you a jar, oh, about this tall and this wide? Has to be wide at the mouth, as well."

"I might could find you something, Mr. Hamilton, providing you sit down and eat your luncheon first. It's been waiting for you this half hour or more."

"Is it that time already?" Florian advanced farther into the kitchen, until he was visible in the doorway. He was looking at his pocket watch in some amazement, as though unable to understand what had happened to the hours. "I suppose I am a bit hungry. Why don't you fix me a tray, and I'll take it out to the laboratory with me?"

Mrs. Smithson was obviously accustomed to this argument, for she folded her arms across her chest and shook her head firmly. "I know what happens then, sir. I go out later and find half the food still on the tray, 'cause you've gotten all wrapped up in them heathen experiments of yours and forgotten all about your food. If you was in charge of your food, you'd be dead within a week, and that's God's truth."

"No doubt you're right," Florian agreed pleasantly. He turned and caught sight of his daughter in the smaller side room. "Priscilla! There you are. I'd been wondering where you were. What are you doing in here?"

He advanced farther into the room, looking faintly puzzled. His hair was sticking up here and there all over his head, as usual, and there were strange yellowish smears across the front of his shirt. His fingers, too, were stained yellow, along with a few orange and black marks. His waistcoat hung unbuttoned, exposing the smudged shirtfront, and a half-tied ascot dangled loosely over one shoulder.

Priscilla glanced over at their visitor and found him eyeing her father with great curiosity.

"Oh, it's you!" Florian exclaimed, delighted at finding their late-night visitor suddenly before him. "I had forgotten you were here. Feeling better, I hope."

"Yes," the man on the cot answered, somewhat warily. "At least I'm conscious now."

"I knew Priscilla would set you to rights. She's good at that sort of thing. Always knows what to do."

"So I've found." The visitor cast a sardonic look at Priscilla.

"I am Florian Hamilton," Priscilla's father went on in a friendly manner, stepping forward to shake the other man's hand.

The stranger propped himself up on his elbow and

returned the handshake, saying, "I only wish I could return the favor and tell you my name."

Florian looked puzzled. "What do you mean? Is it a secret?"

Priscilla chuckled. "No, Papa. What he means is, he doesn't know what his name is. He can't remember anything, including who he is."

Florian's face brightened. "Amnesia?" He looked back at the patient with something close to glee in his expression. "Are you serious?"

When the stranger nodded, Florian beamed. "Fascinating. I've read about it, of course, but I've never actually met anyone who suffered from it." Eagerly he pulled the chair up to the edge of the bed and sat down. "Have you no memory whatsoever?"

The stranger looked somewhat taken aback by Florian's enthusiasm. Priscilla explained, "Papa is a scientist. He is interested in all sorts of phenomena."

"Oh, yes," Florian agreed. "Right now I'm concentrating on chemical reactions. But the human brain is always fascinating. Now, is there anything you do remember?" He patted his pockets and finally pulled out a sheet of folded paper, then a pen.

"Nothing before a few days ago," Priscilla said crisply, and went over to put her hand on her father's arm. "For pity's sake, Papa, put away your notes. The poor man is tired, can't you see? Let him go to sleep now. He's had a very rough night. Later you can ask him all your questions."

Florian looked pained, but he stood up, reluctantly. "Very well, if you insist, my dear." He turned away, saying to Priscilla, "But what do you think caused the amnesia, Pris? The fever?"

"Wait!" Their visitor spoke up, and they turned back to look at him. "I do have one thing I would like to discuss with you, sir."

"Really?" Florian looked pleased and started back toward the chair, reaching in his pocket again for his notes. "About your condition?"

"No." He smothered a smile as Florian's face fell. "It's about your daughter."

"Priscilla?" Florian looked perplexed. "Well, you had best speak to her about that, wouldn't you think?"

"No. I mean, I have already talked to her about it, and she refuses to listen to reason."

Florian's face cleared. "Oh. That. Well, I'm afraid you'll find that Priscilla always knows her own mind. Not much use trying to change it."

It was the other man's turn to look taken aback, but he continued gamely, "But, sir, you can't allow her to walk into danger!"

"Danger!" Florian turned toward his daughter. "Priscilla, what's he talking about? What danger?"

"There is none, Papa," Priscilla began soothingly.

The man on the cot snorted derisively. "Two men bashed me on the head, stole all my possessions and held me prisoner for days, and you say there's no danger?"

Florian's eyes widened. "All that happened to you?"

"Yes. That is the sum total of my memory—being held captive by two scoundrels, until I finally escaped. Miss Hamilton says they came here looking for me."

"Indeed they did," Florian replied. "My, I am certainly glad we decided not to tell them anything about you. Aren't you, Priscilla?"

"Yes, I am. Now, Papa, why don't we leave and let our visitor rest?"

"Wait. You haven't answered my question," Florian protested. "Why should Priscilla be in danger?"

"Because she is planning on charging out there asking questions, that's why."

"Asking questions of whom?" Florian asked. "Priscilla, do you mean to try to find those two men and question them? I must say, I do agree that that would be foolhardy."

"Indeed it would, but I have no plans to do anything of the sort. Mr.—oh, bother, it is so absurd not being able to call you anything. We really need to come up with some sort of name for you, until you can remember your real one."

"Mr. Smith?" Florian suggested.

"No. Much too common. What about Wolfe?"

Florian tilted his head, considering. "Yes. That isn't terribly ordinary. But not uncommon, either. What about a first name?"

"Oh, something plain, I should think. So we won't forget it or slip up."

"What about George?"

Priscilla shook her head. "I've never liked that name."

"Well, then, John."

"All right." Priscilla nodded. "John Wolfe."

"I think that sounds quite believable."

"Could we forget about my name and get back to the subject at hand?" their newly christened patient snapped. "Namely the danger in which you're about to place yourself?"

"As I was saying, Mr. *Wolfe* is concerned about

nothing. I am merely planning to go to the village and visit with Mrs. Whiting. Within the hour, I'll know all about Mr. Wolfe, if anyone saw him or is expecting him."

"Oh, yes, that's true," Florian told the other man. "The vicar's wife knows everything that goes on in the area. That makes me think, Priscilla, perhaps we ought to tell the vicar about Mr. Wolfe and his problem. He is a most intelligent man. And Dr. Hightower, of course. He'd know much more about amnesia than I."

"I don't know." Priscilla looked doubtful. "Somehow I feel that the fewer people who know about Mr. Wolfe, the safer he will be. I had not planned to tell Mrs. Whiting anything about him. It would be all over the village before supper. And if we tell the vicar, it's as good as telling his wife."

"Would you two stop discussing me as if I were not here?" the newly named John Wolfe said irritably. "And we were talking about *you* putting yourself in danger, not me. If those two men see you walking away from this house, they could follow you, attack you."

"To what purpose?" Priscilla pointed out reasonably. "As I told you, if they think you are in here, they are much more likely to break in. Papa, be sure to keep all the doors locked. Perhaps it would be best if you didn't go out to your laboratory this afternoon."

Florian looked shocked. "You're not serious. Not go to my laboratory? No one is going to attack me in broad daylight in my own backyard."

Their visitor groaned. "Those two would have no hesitation about attacking anyone anywhere, as long as they thought they could get away with it. And if they want me, it would be far easier to seize you, Miss

Hamilton, while you're tripping along some rural path, than to try to break into a house and take me. Once they had you, they would know I would have to give myself up to them."

He was right, of course; it was precisely what one of her own heroes would do.

"They don't know that you are in here. They could only suspect."

"They would find out if they seized you."

"Yes, but at rather a large risk. I would have seen them and could identify them. And whether they got you to give yourself up to them or not, they would know that I would go straight to the constable and tell him all about them."

Wolfe raised an eyebrow. "A dead person would not be going straight anywhere."

A chill ran through Priscilla at his words, but she stifled the frisson of fear and replied coolly, "Rather extreme measures, don't you think? Especially considering the fact that they merely held you prisoner. They had ample opportunity to murder you, and they did not. Why would they risk murdering me?"

"Why would you risk the chance that they might?" he countered coolly.

Priscilla narrowed her eyes. "You are a most infuriating man."

"You are only saying that because you know I am right."

"He probably is," Florian agreed. He wore the resigned look of a man about to sacrifice his afternoon. "I shall escort you to the vicarage. Just let me put away a few things in my laboratory."

"No, Papa, there is no need for you to do that. I am

positive that Mr. Wolfe is simply feverish. It is Mr. Wolfe and our house that are vulnerable, if there is any attacking to be done." She sighed. "I shall take Penny with me when I call on Mrs. Whiting. Surely they will not risk attacking two women. After all, Mrs. Smithson and her daughter reached our house safely this morning, and will doubtless return home this afternoon, as well."

Florian brightened. "Excellent plan, my dear. I was certain you would come up with the right thing to do."

"You think that Miss Pennybaker is ample protection?" their visitor asked, his voice rising in disbelief.

All three of them turned to look at the woman in question, who was visible at the end of the kitchen table, daintily eating her soup. She looked like a small wren in her plain brown dress. Her hair, a mousy brown streaked with gray, was pulled back severely from her face and fastened into a no-nonsense bun at the back of her head. She was at least three inches shorter than Priscilla, and quite thin. She looked as if a strong wind might blow her away.

"It is not that I think her physically capable of protecting me," Priscilla explained testily. "It is simply her presence. There is safety in numbers."

"You think they can't seize two people?"

"I'm sure they *can*. The question is whether they *will*. Miss Pennybaker and I will be perfectly safe. There is no need for you to set Papa to worrying."

"You are the most exasperating woman I know," her patient said through clenched teeth.

Priscilla smiled. "Since you cannot remember past three days ago, I would say that that means very little."

She linked her arm through her father's and led him toward the door. "Come, Papa, let's go eat our luncheon before Mrs. Smithson becomes thoroughly upset with us."

With a last triumphant glance back at "Mr. Wolfe," she swept out of the room.

CHAPTER FOUR

HE LAY LOOKING AFTER PRISCILLA and her father as they left the room, wavering between cursing and breaking into a smile. She *was* irritating; he did not need to remember his whole lifetime to know that she was more irritating and headstrong than most women. She was foolishly refusing to listen to reason—and the fact that she could make him want to laugh at the same time somehow added to his annoyance.

Well, there were two things he *did* know about himself. This episode had shown them to him. One was that he was used to being in command. His surprise at having his opinion ignored told him that, as well as the frustration and nasty sense of helplessness he felt. He was also certain that most women were more pliable than his benefactress.

He wondered whether that knowledge came from his being married. The thought brought him up short. He tried to conjure up the image of a wife or a home, but he could not. He certainly hoped he was not married. Because a third thing that he suddenly knew about himself was that he was intensely attracted to this maddening woman.

There was something about her independent air that was quite alluring. It was challenging; it made a man want to prove that he could turn that prickly attitude into a womanly softness. At the same time, it spoke of an inner passion, a wellspring of emotion far stronger than the usual feminine gentleness. He also felt a definite response to the soft curve of her breasts and hips beneath her ordinary dress. Last night, he was sure, there had been a time when she was leaning over his bed, and her hair was down, falling in a luxuriant chestnut mass over her shoulders, almost to her waist. Even in his weakened state, the sight of it had stirred him.

He closed his eyes, remembering the hot, sensual dreams of the night before. For a time, he had thought he was in a brothel in China. How had he known the place? Another bit of mystery. He had been pulsing with desire; he could almost taste the fevered kisses he had given…someone. He could not remember her face or form, could not remember anything except the honeyed taste of her mouth, the heat and hunger that had consumed him. Had it been a memory? Or merely the delusion of a fevered mind? Somehow, mixed up in the dream, there was Priscilla Hamilton, smelling faintly of roses and leaning over his bed, putting a cool cloth on his head and murmuring to him.

He groaned, wondered what he might have said or done in her presence. Had she guessed the import of his dreams? Had he spoken of the desire that gripped him?

He told himself he could not have, or she would not have spoken to him so straightforwardly this morning. She was, after all, a proper lady—a proper British lady, which he knew meant even greater gentility. She would have been far too shocked and outraged to even speak to him again, he thought, if he had been talking of brothels and prostitutes and passions.

With a groan, he turned over onto his side. Just think-ing about such things, especially in connection with Priscilla Hamilton, was beginning to heat his blood.

It was absurd. He was sick, he could remember noth-ing of his life—yet the uppermost thing in his mind was a woman who stirred his desire. It would make far more sense to try to remember who he was and what in his life might have brought about his capture by those two men. And what was he going to do? He had no clothes, no money, no identity. Even once he was feeling better, he hadn't the slightest idea what he would do or where he would go. Obviously, he could not continue to impose on Priscilla Hamilton and her father forever.

He closed his eyes. On a wave of such thoughts, he drifted into a troubled sleep.

THOUGH SHE WOULD never have admitted it to him, her guest's vehement warnings made Priscilla glance cautiously around her when she and Miss Pennybaker walked out of the house. Everything looked the same, from the garden well to the unstirring lilac bushes to the trees down the lane from their house. She could see no sign of anyone lurking, watching their house.

Still, she gripped the handle of her umbrella tightly as they set off down the lane, and her eyes flitted from one side of the road to the other, on watch for the flut-ter of a garment behind a bush or a glimpse of a head peering out from around a tree. No matter how much she had argued against her visitor's admonitions, she could see their wisdom, and she knew that if his pre-dictions proved true, she would have to fight for Miss Pennybaker, as well. Priscilla wanted to be prepared for whatever might happen. Indeed, deep in her soul of souls, where some strange part of her craved excitement, she was almost hoping that something *would* happen.

It did not. Her walk into the village was entirely un-eventful. And after fifteen minutes of chatter from the vicar's wife about this person's liver complaint and that one's runaway pig, she was sorry that she had ever had the idea of calling on her. It was obvious that no one in the whole town had spoken about a visitor from Amer-ica, either seen or expected, for such an event would have taken precedence at least over the pig.

The only bright spot was that her friend Anne Chal-comb also chanced to visit Mrs. Whiting that afternoon, and she and Penny walked home with her. Anne was quite a bit older than Priscilla, but she did not think or talk like a middle-aged woman. She was interested in women's suffrage, as was Priscilla, and she was well-read and able to talk on a variety of subjects. Though Priscilla knew that Anne must be fifty years old, she did not look it. Her figure was still quite trim, and her face was lovely, despite the lines that had begun to form around her eyes and mouth.

It seemed to Priscilla that an indefinable air of sad-ness clung to Anne, even when she smiled or laughed. She supposed it must be that Anne still mourned her husband, who had died almost ten years earlier. Pris-cilla could not imagine why Anne would be sad over his being gone. She remembered Squire Chalcomb as a large, sour-faced creature with a terrible temper, and she had heard more than one of the older ladies say that Anne was far better off without him. However, there was no accounting for love, Priscilla knew; perhaps there had been something in the man that only Anne could see.

They walked to Priscilla's cottage, chatting about a

letter that Priscilla had received from Mrs. Pankhurst, describing some of her travails while in prison for the cause of women's suffrage. At the gate to Evermere Cottage, Priscilla stopped and turned to say goodbye to her friend while Miss Pennybaker went on up the path to the cottage. However, Priscilla found to her surprise that Anne had turned off the road with her, as if to follow her into the yard.

"I thought I would pop in and get Mrs. Smithson's recipe for elderberry wine," Anne explained. "She promised to give it to me last time I visited you."

"Oh." Priscilla thought of the man in the room off the kitchen. She did not want anyone to know about him, not even her good friend, but she could hardly refuse to let Anne come in, either. So she smiled, thinking that she would simply have to make sure that the door to his room was closed. "Of course. I'm sure Mrs. Smithson was quite pleased that you asked."

Anne followed her around the house to the kitchen door at the rear. Priscilla opened the door and stepped in quickly, but she stopped short, brought up abruptly by the sight of "Mr. Wolfe," sitting at the table, taking tea with Mrs. Smithson.

"What are you doing here?" she snapped without thinking.

His eyebrows rose lazily at her words. "Well, good day to you, too. I knew you would be glad to see me so improved. Mrs. Smithson's soup has worked wonders."

The cook beamed at him.

Anne came around to stand beside Priscilla. She stopped and gazed at the man in amazement. He was, Priscilla had to admit, a sight to stare at. Mrs. Smithson had evidently dragged out some old clothes of one of her brothers' for him to wear. Priscilla supposed it accomplished the purpose of keeping him decently covered—but only barely. The muscles of his arms bulged against the lawn sleeves, and the shirt could not be buttoned for several buttons down, leaving a fair expanse of his chest exposed. Both trousers and sleeves were too short, and his thighs filled the legs of the trousers in a way that was almost obscene. Priscilla wondered that he could sit in them without cutting off his breath.

He gazed blandly at the two women with his clear green eyes. It irritated Priscilla even further that he hadn't even the grace to look abashed at being caught here, and in such attire. Anne turned curiously toward Priscilla, and Priscilla grappled for some explanation.

"Uh, Anne, I—I forgot to tell you. My cousin is visiting us."

"Your cousin?"

"Actually, a quite distant cousin. From America," Priscilla improvised wildly. "His grandfather was related to mine, but he sailed to the United States when he was a child. Cousin John was kind enough to look us up while he was visiting Britain."

"How nice," Anne murmured in their visitor's direction, but Priscilla could see the faint puzzlement in her friend's eyes. Nothing she had said explained what he was doing here in this condition.

"Unfortunately," she went on rapidly, "Cousin John had a slight accident on his way here. He, uh, got sick, and his luggage was, uh, lost."

"Yes, I arrived on their doorstep in a fever, and without a bag in sight," the man added easily. "I am most fortunate that my cousins were willing to take me in."

Anne smiled. "Priscilla is the soul of kindness."

A devilish glint sparked his eyes, and the corner of his mouth twitched. "Yes, I have found her to be so. A veritable…saint among women."

"No. Please." Priscilla shot him a dark look. "You are flattering me. Anyone would have done the same. But I am rather surprised to see you up so soon. I think you should have stayed in bed. You must not overdo."

"I can feel my energy returning. I have a sound constitution, you know."

"No, actually, I don't," Priscilla retorted dryly. "There are so many things about you I don't know."

"I feel the same way." Now a full-fledged grin curved his mouth. "About you, dear cousin."

Priscilla glared at him. He gazed blandly back.

"I am glad you find your situation so amusing," Priscilla told him sourly.

"Come, come, Cousin Priscilla," he said, slightly emphasizing the familiar name in a way she found vastly irritating. "You are too serious. One must look at oneself with some sense of humor. Otherwise, things become far too bleak."

He rose and walked toward them, his careful steps betraying the fact that his muscles were still somewhat weak and shaky from his illness. "Pardon me, madam," he said, addressing Anne. "I am afraid that my cousin was so surprised by my improvement that she forgot to introduce us."

"Oh." Priscilla colored. "I'm sorry. Anne, this is John Wolfe. Cousin John—" she had to force the name out "—this is my dear friend and neighbor, Lady Anne Chalcomb."

"I am pleased to meet you," Anne said warmly, and moved forward to meet the stranger, holding out her hand. She stopped abruptly, suppressing a gasp. Suddenly the color fled her face.

"Anne?" Priscilla looked at her, startled, and started forward to take her arm. "What's the matter? Are you all right?"

"What?" Anne looked at her vaguely. "Oh." She glanced back at John, who had stopped a foot away and was looking at her with some uneasiness. "I—I'm sorry. It was silly. For a moment there, I— But no, it's impossible. Ridiculous."

She forced a smile and held out her hand to John. "Pardon me. You will think I am a befuddled old woman."

"Never that, my lady," he answered smoothly, taking her hand and bowing over it.

"You are very kind." She smiled at him and turned toward Priscilla. "But now I must be on my way. I want to reach Chalcomb Hall before the sun sets."

"Of course. But what about your recipe?"

"What? Oh." Anne colored, embarrassed. "You're right. I am sorry." She turned toward the table, where the cook still sat. "Mrs. Smithson, you had promised me your delicious recipe for elderberry wine."

"Right you are, my lady," Mrs. Smithson said, promptly getting up and bustling across the kitchen.

Anne followed her and took the slip of paper Mrs. Smithson gave her, then turned to Priscilla and John and gave them a perfunctory smile. "I must go now. I— If you'd like, I could bring over a few of Henry's clothes for you, Mr. Wolfe. He was a large man, also. It would do better than Gid's things, I am sure, until you recover your own trunks."

"Yes, my lady." He smiled engagingly. "I am sure it

would be a good deal better. As it is, I am hardly fit to be seen."

Anne took her leave of them quickly. Priscilla watched her friend go, puzzled by her behavior, then abruptly decided to run after her.

"Anne!"

Anne was through the rear yard and almost to the path leading to Chalcomb Hall, but she stopped and turned at Priscilla's cry.

"Anne, did you—did you recognize Mr. Wolfe?" Priscilla asked when she drew even with Anne.

Her friend looked startled. "Recognize him? Why, no, how could I? I have never met him before."

"But you—when he came closer to you, you reacted oddly."

Anne shook her head, looking embarrassed. "Please, no, it was nothing, really. It was just that for a moment he looked…rather like someone I used to know. But it's impossible. It was long ago, before your cousin was even born, I imagine. And he wasn't an American, anyway."

"Who was it?" Priscilla pressed on, intrigued.

"No one. I mean, well, no one that you would know. It was merely a trick of the mind, anyway. My—my friend hadn't the same coloring, even. It was just an expression, something about his eyes. It was only for an instant, then it was gone. 'Tis of no consequence, anyway."

"Oh. Well, I wanted to ask…that is, it would be better perhaps if you did not mention that you had met Mr. Wolfe. He is, uh, still not well enough to see visitors, and you know how everyone would come at the mention of a stranger."

"Of course." Anne smiled. "I shan't say a word."

Priscilla let Anne go on her way and turned her steps back to the house, still a little confused by Anne's behavior. Mrs. Smithson was back at work at the stove, but "John Wolfe" was sitting at the table again, waiting for her.

"Well?" he asked. "What did you find out?"

Priscilla shrugged. "Little enough. Other than what you are not. The vicar's wife mentioned no one who was expecting a visitor, nor any sighting of a stranger passing through town."

"No. I meant with your friend just then. Lady Chalcomb. I thought you had gone after her to question her about the odd look she got when she saw my face up close."

"Oh. That. Yes, I did. But that was no use, either. She said that for an instant you reminded her of someone. But it was much too long ago to have been you, and he was not an American."

He tilted his head to one side, considering. "And do you believe her?"

Priscilla looked astonished. "Of course I do. Anne Chalcomb is a good woman, honest and kind. Why would she lie? If she had recognized you, I am sure she would have said who you were."

"Not if she had something to do with my disappearance."

Priscilla grimaced. "You can't be serious. Anne would never have anything to do with such a crime. I know her—she is my friend. And you could not find a more decent human being."

"Miss Pris is right about that," Mrs. Smithson chimed in from the stove, not bothering to hide her eavesdropping. She turned around and spoke to them again, waving her spoon for emphasis. "She hasn't a bad bone in her body. Only a saint would have put up with that husband of hers. Most women would have shoved him down the stairs when he was drunk—which was most of the time, so I've heard."

Priscilla suppressed a smile. Mrs. Smithson was free with her opinions, and unfailingly blunt. It was one reason why she had come to work for the Hamiltons and stayed there so many years. She could have gotten more money from another, wealthier household, but she had never been able to hold her tongue and had been dismissed from every other house in which she worked. Only the amiable, freethinking Hamilton family was willing to put up with a servant such as she.

John did not bother to hide his smile. He grinned and leaned forward, propping his elbow on the table and his chin in his hand, clearly delighted with the cook's speech. "Sounds like a rounder to me," he said encouragingly.

"That he was. The best thing that ever happened to her was him dying. It's just too bad that she never found another husband after he died."

"Maybe Squire Chalcomb soured her on all men," Priscilla suggested.

"It wouldn't surprise me." Mrs. Smithson nodded her head. "I wouldn't think it's for lack of interest on men's part."

"No. I think Mr. Rutherford is quite fond of Lady Chalcomb. I have always been a little surprised that she did not encourage him more."

John yawned and rubbed a hand across his face tiredly, distracting Priscilla from her gossip. "I think it's time for you to get back in bed," she told him. "You are not nearly as strong as you would like everyone to believe."

"Yes, ma'am," he replied with mock meekness. He rose and started back to his room, then stopped and turned to Priscilla. "I was glad to see you return this afternoon."

His words made Priscilla feel unaccountably warm. She had been planning to point out to him how wrong he had been about her being seized, but she found that she no longer wanted to.

"I looked all around as we walked to the vicar's," she told him. "But I didn't see anyone. Don't you think they might have left the area?"

He shrugged. "It's possible. I hope not, though. I should like to find one of them when I'm back to myself again. Then we might get some answers." His face tightened, and he clenched his fists unconsciously.

"I imagine we might," Priscilla murmured. She would not want to have to face this man when he was feeling well—and was bent on revenge.

He returned to his bed, and Priscilla went upstairs. She spent the rest of the evening, except for a brief break for supper, trying to write. She had gotten little work done today, what with caring for John Wolfe all night, and she wanted to get her book finished soon. They were always in need of the money she earned with her writing, even though it was scarcely a massive sum. It was her writing money that had put Philip at Eton and allowed Gid to pursue his dream of being an officer rather than spending his life as a clerk. Her father's small inheritance and occasional fees for lectures or scholarly articles were barely enough to maintain their house and two servants.

However, try as she might, the words would not come this evening. Her mind kept straying to their visitor and the puzzle he presented. It seemed far more intriguing than her novel, and just as fantastical. For once, instead of writing or dreaming about it, she was living an adventure, and Priscilla found that much more interesting.

Finally she gave up and went downstairs, where she found John Wolfe sleeping soundly in his room. Miss Pennybaker, darning socks in the kitchen, informed her that he had awakened once and eaten, then gone back to sleep. It was her opinion that he was healing rapidly, and the tone of her voice indicated that she felt this fact was an indication of a lack of gentility.

Priscilla suppressed a flicker of disappointment at not finding Mr. Wolfe up and able to bandy words with her. It was, she reminded herself, more important that he get well.

Miss Pennybaker put up her darning and walked up the stairs with Priscilla to her room. She warned Priscilla darkly that she would be better off locking her door, then went into her own bedroom and shut the door, driving home the bolt with a resounding click. Priscilla, smiling faintly, went into her own room and dressed for bed, but when she retired, she did not lock her door. Instead, she opened it partway, so that she might hear more clearly. She was not foolish enough to dismiss John's warnings about his captors breaking into the house to get him. Miss Pennybaker might think they needed protection from Mr. Wolfe, but Priscilla was more inclined to think that *he* was the one who needed protection.

She was not sure how long she had been asleep when she awakened with a start. She lay still, her heart pounding, listening to the quiet night and wondering what had awakened her. She heard a creak, then the scrape of a chair leg upon the floor.

Priscilla sat bolt upright and flung aside her covers. She moved with instinctive silence to the fireplace and snatched up a poker, then glided out of the room. She paused at the top of the stairs, but she could see and hear nothing below. After a moment, she started cautiously down the stairs, gripping the handle of the poker tightly.

She was almost to the bottom when a movement to the right caught her eye. She stopped dead still and peered into the darkness below her. A large shape was gliding along the wall with a caution to equal hers. It walked in darkness and silence; she could make out nothing except the bulk and the stealthy movement. Her heart thudded in her chest, and for a moment she was frozen with fear.

There was a rattle from the direction of the kitchen, and the shape jumped forward. Its movement seemed to release Priscilla from her paralysis. She thought of John Wolfe and the fact that he lay asleep in a room off the kitchen, precisely where the ominous shadow was going.

Priscilla hurtled down the stairs and around the newel post into the dark hall. The shadow she had seen earlier whipped around at the sound of her approach, but before it could turn completely, she raised her poker and flung herself at him, bringing the poker down hard on the man's back.

CHAPTER FIVE

THE AIR WENT OUT OF THE MAN with an audible *whoomp,* and he crashed to the floor, but as he did so, he reached out and grabbed the end of her poker, yanking it from her grasp. Priscilla staggered and fell on top of him. They rolled across the floor, wrestling and struggling. Priscilla's hands grasped something that felt like a wool blanket; she could see almost nothing, for her face was pressed against the man as she struggled. She kicked out and was rewarded with a grunt when her foot connected with hard bone. The man's grasp slackened, and she was able to pull away a little, turning and scrabbling to get up.

But then his arms went around her from behind. His hand slid across her chest, and he went still. His hand returned and cupped her breast. Priscilla drew in a sharp gasp.

"Damnation!" The voice and accent were familiar.

Priscilla turned and found herself looking into the face of John Wolfe, only inches from hers.

"Oh."

"Yes, oh!" he retorted sarcastically. "What the devil are you doing here? And why, in God's name, did you try to break my back?"

"I didn't! I was trying to protect you." Priscilla sat up, pulling away from him. "I heard a noise downstairs, so

I picked up the poker and came down. I thought those men had returned and were trying to get you."

"They had and they were," he replied in a disgruntled tone, and rolled to his feet, his hand going instinctively to his back, where the poker had landed a solid hit. "Damn! You have a swing like a longshoreman."

"I'm sorry."

"I was going to turn the tables on them. But after all this clatter, they are probably halfway to London by now." He bent down and picked up the poker. "I think this is a more effective weapon than mine." He gestured toward the kitchen knife stuck in his belt.

He moved quietly but swiftly through the hall to the kitchen door. Priscilla followed right on his heels. He shot her an exasperated glance but said nothing. Pushing open the door carefully, he peered inside. It was somewhat lighter here, for moonlight shimmered through the windows. He moved farther in, poker at the ready, eyes scanning the dark shadows lurking in the corners and beside the stove.

When he reached the table, Priscilla took the lamp that sat there and lit it, casting the room into its pale yellow glow and revealing its emptiness. There was no sign of a human being anywhere. The back door stood open. Wolfe sighed and went to close it. Just to be safe, he checked the small pantry and the side room, where his cot lay. Neither revealed a person hiding.

"Damn." He turned and scowled at Priscilla. "Why the devil did you have to come down just then? I would have had them."

"Or they would have had you," Priscilla retorted tartly. "There are two of them, and obviously they managed to subdue you once before."

His scowl deepened. "That was only because I wasn't expecting any danger. This time I was ready for it."

"Yes, and still woozy from a fever and a blow on the head. I could hardly leave you down here alone to be abducted again—or worse."

"Well, whacking me with a poker certainly helped me out."

"I didn't know it was you," Priscilla replied frostily. "I couldn't very well say, 'Excuse me, are you a villain or our patient? I wouldn't want to hit the wrong fellow.' And all I could see in the dark was a big shape."

She looked at him. He had wrapped himself in a blanket. Only his front was visible. He wore the shirt he had had on earlier, but he had left it unbuttoned to sleep in, and it hung open, exposing a wide expanse of muscled flesh. Mr. Wolfe, Priscilla thought, was all too comfortable in a state of near nakedness.

At that moment Priscilla recalled the fact that she herself was clad in nothing but her nightgown. She had not stopped to pull on a dressing gown before she hurried to Wolfe's rescue. Her nightgown was high-neck and long-sleeve, a simple, unadorned cotton gown with little allure. However, it was far thinner and more conforming to her shape than the usual petticoats and dresses she wore. He could, she was sure, see the swell of her breasts beneath the gown; there was even a possibility that he could see the darker circles of her nipples. Her nipples tightened at the thought, surprising her. Right on the heels of that thought came the realization that she was standing between him and the lamp on the table, which meant that the light would shine right through her nightgown, exposing the shape of her body to Mr. Wolfe's gaze.

Her cheeks flamed high with color, and she moved quickly to the side. She stole a glance at Wolfe to see whether he had noticed, and found his gaze focused on her breasts. She blushed even more furiously, yet, amazingly enough, there was a strange tingling warmth deep in her abdomen.

She turned away, desperately searching for something to divert their attention. "Uh, where did they come in? How did they enter the house?"

He straightened, tearing his eyes away from her. "I thought the noise came from that direction." He pointed.

"Papa's study? Oh, no, I hope they didn't hurt any of his work! Papa would be so distressed."

She picked up the lamp and started out of the kitchen. Wolfe caught up with her, grabbing her arm. "Wait! Do you always go charging off like this?"

"Actually, this sort of thing rarely happens to me."

"Well, one of them might be there still. Let me go first."

She stepped back with exaggerated obedience, waving him through the kitchen door ahead of her. He grimaced and walked past her into the hall and over to the door of her father's study. The door stood ajar, and he pushed it all the way open, revealing the darkened room, moonlight streaming through the windows. Priscilla, leaning around him, drew in a sharp gasp. One of the windows was pushed up, and it was clear that a pane of it had been broken.

"Oh, no," she murmured, holding the lamp up to illuminate the room.

Wolfe took the lamp from her hand and moved into the study, shining the light around to reveal every nook and cranny. Books lay everywhere—beside the chair, on the desk, on a side table and in the seat of another chair. Some were neatly stacked, others lay open, and others seemed haphazardly strewn about. Papers filled every other available spot. A tray of tea dishes sat precariously atop a bookcase. A circular rack for pipes sat upon the desk, but it held only one pipe. Four others were scattered around the room, as well as a few ashtrays, boxes of matches, and a pouch or two of tobacco.

Priscilla looked around and heaved a sigh of relief. "At least they didn't disturb anything."

John looked at her, quirking an eyebrow. "How can you tell?"

"It always looks like this. Papa says it is part of his creativity. I think it's laziness, myself. Mrs. Smithson and her daughter refuse to even come in here. Every so often, he will let me dust."

She went to the window, noting a pile of books before it. "I think those were knocked to the floor when they climbed in the window. Papa's more of a stacker. He claims to have some sort of obscure order to the way he sets the books."

She pulled the window shut and relatched it, then leaned closer to examine the broken pane. "Doesn't do much good to close it, I suppose, with this pane gone. I wonder how long it will take the glazier to come repair it." She stood silently, gazing at the window.

"I can tack a board across it to hold it for now, if you'll find me the nails and hammer."

"What?" Priscilla turned to look at him, as though surprised out of a reverie. "Oh, yes, of course. That will at least keep out the weather. It's rather frightening, isn't it, when you see how easily the safety of one's home can be breached?"

"Yes." He crossed the room to her and took her by the arms. "But you needn't be scared. I was watching out for them tonight, and I will continue to do so until I catch them. I won't let them harm you or your family."

"You cannot stay awake all night long," Priscilla pointed out reasonably.

"I will if I have to. I can sleep during the day. I don't think they would come then. I know you must think I'm incompetent, after the way they caught me off guard before, but I promise you, I don't usually make mistakes like that."

"How can you be so sure?" she asked curiously. "You don't remember who you are."

"I don't know how I know," he admitted, "but I am certain of it. I won't let you come to harm."

His words warmed her. She looked up into his eyes. The green was muted in the dim light, but the determination in them was clear. He was the sort of man one believed. She was reminded again of one of her heroes. In his eyes there was the light that she imagined in theirs, a look of steel and courage and more...an excitement at the thought of facing danger, a sparkle of humor and fun. Did such a man really exist outside the pages of a novel? She thought of her father, her brothers, even her friend Alec. No matter how much she loved them, she would never have thought of putting her absolute trust in them, of believing that they would keep her safe. Yet with this man, she could not help but believe that he would do as he said, that he would keep all harm from her and her family.

"Thank you," she said simply. "I feel much better."

His eyebrows rose lazily, and he smiled. "What? No witty ripostes? No questions? No reminders of my less-than-stellar past?"

"Am I really that much of a skeptic?" She smiled back at him. His smile did something funny to her insides, made her feel warm and fizzy and strangely giggly.

"No. Merely a trifle prickly." He raised his hand and brushed his knuckles against her cheek. "Personally, I find I like my women with thorns. As with roses, it makes them all the more desirable."

He gazed down into her eyes, and Priscilla could do nothing but stare back. She did not think she could have moved if their housebreakers suddenly reappeared in the window. His mouth softened. His hands, still on her arms, seared through her nightgown, igniting her skin. He lowered his head toward her, and Priscilla knew he was going to kiss her. She let out a breathy little sigh of pleasure.

Then his mouth was on hers, and it was as warm and firm as she remembered it. But this was not the hard, bruising kiss that he had given her in his delirium, the passionate claiming of a woman who belonged to him. This was softer and more tender, a seeking rather than a demand. She found it just as delightful.

She responded to him, her lips gently pressing into his. Her hands came up and curled into his shirt, holding on to him, for the world suddenly seemed to be unstable. His arms went around her, pressing her body into his, and his kiss deepened. She felt the hot tremor of his breath against her cheek, the tightening of his body, and his reactions sparked her own desire.

Finally he raised his head and looked down at her.

His face was flushed and his eyes were glittering. "This is madness."

Priscilla nodded, not taking her eyes off him. Her whole body was thrumming with new sensations. It was crazy, she agreed; they hardly knew each other. Heavens, he didn't even know *himself*. They seemed to spend most of their time arguing. But none of that mattered at the moment. All that mattered was the way she felt.

He let out a low groan and bent to kiss her again. This time his mouth was more urgent on hers, moving her lips apart, and his tongue swept inside. It was startling, but arousing. Priscilla began to tremble; heat was building within her. She had never felt this way, indeed had known nothing even remotely resembling it. Her abdomen seemed to turn into hot wax; her legs were weak, her heart was racing. And she wanted more of it, wanted it to go on and on....

She wrapped her arms around his neck, stretching up on tiptoe as she pressed her lips eagerly into his. Her own tongue tentatively touched his, and she was rewarded by the deep moan that escaped him. With the artless seduction of innocence, she stoked his passion, her tongue teasing and stroking, twining with his and slipping into his mouth to explore. His arms were like steel around her, grinding her body into his. Since she wore nothing but her nightgown, she could feel every inch of his muscled body, every curve and dip, even the persistent, throbbing hardness moving against her abdomen.

His hand moved down her back and curved over her buttocks. She jerked a little, startled, and heat blossomed deep within her. She melted into him, amazed at how good it felt to have his hand on her, to be stroked and caressed. Was this what marriage was like? Or was it only sin that was so delicious? She could not suppress a shaky little moan as his fingers dug into the fleshy mound of her buttocks.

He groaned at the sound, and his other hand went to her bottom, also, lifting her up and into him, pressing her hard against the throbbing proof of his desire. "Priscilla…" Her name was a sigh as he released her lips and began to trail his mouth down the soft skin of her throat.

"Priscilla…" For a moment, the hissing of her name blended in Priscilla's bemused mind with the low, soft moan that had just come from John Wolfe's throat. Then it came again, frantic and sharp and quite clearly in a woman's voice, "Priscilla! Where are you?"

Both of them stiffened at the sound, then broke apart guiltily and whirled around to face the door.

"Priscilla!" The name was repeated, and then an apparition appeared in the doorway. It was ghostly pale, with an enormous head, and Priscilla started before she realized who it was.

"Miss Pennybaker!" She squeaked out.

The governess's bony frame was swathed in a voluminous gray dressing gown over her nightgown, and her graying hair was caught up in an old-fashioned mobcap that ballooned out around her head like an enormous mushroom. In one shaky hand she held a candle, and in the other a black flatiron.

"Christ!" John snapped. "I've never seen such a household for weapons!"

"Priscilla! Are you all right?" Miss Pennybaker's gaze went to John and centered on the naked swath of skin between his shirt's edges. "I heard a dreadful commotion down here."

"Yes, I'm fine, Miss Pennybaker," Priscilla assured her, hurrying forward. "Do put down the flatiron. There's really no danger. John—Mr. Wolfe—and I chased the intruders away."

The older woman gasped and paled, swaying on her feet. "In-intruders? Then someone was here?"

"Yes." Priscilla reached her and deftly took the flatiron from her with one hand while she grasped the woman's elbow with the other and held her steady. "But now they are gone. It is perfectly safe."

"Oh, my." Miss Pennybaker lifted her hand, now freed from the flatiron, to her forehead in a dramatic gesture. "I knew it! I heard all that noise, and I was certain that they had come back."

"Yes, yes, but it's fine now," Priscilla said soothingly, leading Miss Pennybaker to the nearest chair, into which she sank with a moan.

"I went to your room as soon as I heard, but you were gone! I didn't know what to think! I realized, of course, that something dreadful must have happened to you."

"Of course," John agreed dryly, and plopped down with a sigh into another chair.

Miss Pennybaker shot him a look of disdain. "I suspected that he must have come in and taken you away."

"No. Now, Miss P., really, Mr. Wolfe would not harm me."

"Why do you keep calling him that?" Miss Pennybaker asked, confused. "I thought he didn't have a name."

"Well, he doesn't. At least, he cannot remember it.

But it is terribly awkward, don't you think, to be unable to call him anything? So I made up the name. I think it rather suits him, don't you?"

They both turned to look at him, and he grimaced.

"I suppose." Miss Pennybaker did not look as if she liked having to admit anything about their visitor.

Priscilla suppressed a sigh. She was used to Miss Pennybaker's odd ways, but she could not understand why the woman was so set against their visitor. Normally she would have expected Miss Pennybaker to consider his stormy and mysterious entrance the most romantic of things. Her old governess compulsively read everything she could get her hands on, but her real favorites were the gothics that Priscilla herself loved. It was she who had first put *Jane Eyre* and *Wuthering Heights* into Priscilla's hands, and there was nothing she loved like a dark and brooding hero.

Of course, Priscilla had to admit that their visitor was not really dark. Nor did he seem at all brooding, merely frustrated, but he was certainly mysterious and quite handsome. And nothing could have been more dramatic than the way he arrived, with two men chasing him and no knowledge of who he was. Why, Priscilla had been thinking ever since of exactly how to work the incident into one of her own books.

At that moment there was the sound of footsteps outside in the hall. They all swung around to face the door. Light bobbed in the hall, and a moment later Florian Hamilton stepped into the study. He, too, carried a candle and wore his dressing gown, as though he had been disturbed from his sleep, though his robe hung open, one side of the sash trailing along beside him on the floor. His hair stuck out wildly in spikes all over his head, and it was easy to see why, for he was even now plunging his hand into it as he walked along, muttering to himself, frowning in concentration. He walked with his head down, and he did not even seem to notice the people occupying the room until his daughter spoke his name.

He jumped and looked up, his eyes widening at the sight of so many people in his study. "I say! Priscilla? Miss Pennybaker? And, uh, you."

"John Wolfe."

"Yes, precisely. I couldn't remember what we were calling you. I have enough trouble remembering real names, you know."

"Yes, I know," Priscilla agreed.

Miss Pennybaker uttered a mortified groan, her face blushing furiously, and turned away from Mr. Hamilton, gathering the sides of her robe together, though little enough could be seen of her gown between them.

"Did the noise awaken you, Papa?" Priscilla asked.

"Noise? What noise? No. I just woke up. Had an idea, you see, an inspiration in my sleep. Happens sometimes, you know, and I was coming down to jot it all down before I forgot it. But why are all of you up? And why are you in my study?"

"Someone broke in, sir," Wolfe began.

"Broke in? But why would anyone—? Lot of demmed strange things going on around here, if you ask me."

"Yes, sir, there are. I can understand why you would be upset."

"Upset? No, I'm not upset. It's rather interesting, actually. There must be some sort of reason, you see, a cosmic law that causes a cluster of such things to happen at much the same time. We've talked about it often, the vicar and doctor and I, for you must admit that it seems to always happen that way. For instance, the way Mrs. Johnstone gets word that her brother has died, way out in the wilds of Australia, and not two days later, her niece's husband is hit by a runaway wagon. Coincidence, people say, but I'm not so sure. It could be the planets, I suppose, or maybe the moon…."

"I am afraid it was not coincidence this time, Mr. Hamilton."

"What do you mean? Do you have a theory about it?"

"Yes. My theory is that the same two men who were holding me prisoner, the two who were looking for me the other night, broke in tonight to try to abduct me once more."

"Ah, I see. Of course. That is entirely logical. No need to talk of coincidences, then, is there? Now, if you'll excuse me, I must write down my idea before bits of it begin to slip away." He skirted the knot of people and sat down behind his desk.

John watched him, slack-jawed, as he pulled a pen from the drawer of his desk and began to search for a blank sheet of paper. "But, sir…Mr. Hamilton…don't you want to know about the break-in? Are you not worried?"

"Worried?" Florian glanced up at him vaguely. "No. Should I be? Didn't you say you had taken care of it?"

John gaped at him. Behind John, Priscilla muffled a snort of laughter. Moving up beside him, she said, "Yes, Papa, that is exactly what we said. The men are gone now, and Mr. Wolfe will replace the windowpane they broke tomorrow. Everything is going along perfectly."

"Splendid." Florian said absently, his attention

already back on the sheet of paper. He began to write furiously.

Miss Pennybaker, assured that Mr. Hamilton's eyes were elsewhere other than on her berobed form, jumped to her feet and scurried out of the room. Priscilla took John's arm and steered him from the study after her, closing the door quietly.

Outside, in the hall, John stopped. "I don't understand. Why isn't he worried? Something might have happened to you. Could still happen to you, as a matter of fact."

"It would hardly make the situation better to have him worrying, now would it? Papa is used to other people taking care of things. He has always been, well, a bit scholarly. If he were left to himself, he would not notice whether the roof leaked, unless it damaged his papers, or whether he had eaten that day, or if his sheets were clean. And he's right. It would be a waste of his mind to apply it to such trivialities. He's much more suited to solving the larger problems of the world."

His mouth quirked up on one side. "Such as why terrible events happen to people in clusters?"

"Exactly. There are thousands of people who can solve the mundane things."

"I see." His bemused expression belied his words of understanding. "But doesn't that put rather a burden on everyone around him?"

"A burden? Oh, no. Everyone loves Papa. He's the kindest, sweetest man. There are some who find him a trifle odd, of course, but even they cannot dislike him. There is always someone there who will help him."

"Primarily you, I imagine."

"Me, and before me, my mother."

"There are some women," Wolfe pointed out as they started down the hall toward the stairs, "who would wish for more in life."

"Indeed? I find it an honor to look after a genius. He is, you know. He corresponds with some of the most intelligent people in the world, and they all respect his opinion."

"But what about a home of your own? A husband? Family?"

"Not all women are pining after a husband and family," Priscilla replied tartly. "What is that, after all, except looking after other people? I am used to my father, and he to me, and he gives me much more respect and freedom than any husband would."

They had reached the foot of the staircase, and they stopped. Priscilla faced him challengingly, her chin up. He looked down at her and smiled, his eyes smoky in the dim light.

"A husband has other things to offer," he pointed out, in a silky tone that reminded Priscilla of the kisses and caresses they had exchanged in the study, before Miss Pennybaker interrupted them.

A flush started in her cheeks, but she said only, "Ah, but freedom is the most important thing that anyone can have. Without it, all else is meaningless."

He frowned. "Even love?"

"Everything," she said firmly. "A prison disguised with sweet words and loving kisses is still a prison. Would you have been content in your captivity if they had treated you kindly?"

"No, of course not, but that's not the point. Marriage is hardly a prison."

"Not for a man, for he is free to do what he wishes. A woman is not."

"You're a suffragette!" he exclaimed. "I might have known."

"Yes, I should think you would have. It seems apparent that a woman such as I would believe in women's rights."

"And do you march for the vote and all that?" he asked with apparent fascination, crossing his arms and leaning against the newel post.

"I have not had the occasion yet. But I am quite willing."

"Provided your papa did not require looking after that day," he said, his eyes twinkling.

Priscilla arched an eyebrow. "Are you implying that I give women's suffrage lip service only?"

He grinned. "Ah, there is one I would not touch for anything. No, my dear Miss Hamilton, I would not presume to imply that. I am too much in awe of your right hand. I've experienced enough of it tonight to last me for a good while. However, it seems odd to me that you profess to dislike men when you are so loving and considerate of your father…and were so *warm* back in the study." He trailed a finger up her arm, his eyes glowing into hers. "When you were in my arms."

"Oh!" Priscilla jerked away from him, stepping up on the first stair and planting her hands pugnaciously on her hips. "You dare to throw that up to me? When you had the audacity to make advances to me under my father's own roof? After we had given you shelter?"

"Yes," he admitted, looking mock-repentant. "I was a cad, I admit. But I could not help myself. Your lips were too tempting."

"Ha! That sounds just like a man, laying the blame on the woman! As if it had nothing to do with you! Well, let me set you straight. I did not tempt you into anything. You did it of your own free will, just as I did."

He grinned. "You're right about that. And of my own free will, I would not mind doing it again." He picked up one of her hands and laid a kiss on her balled fist.

She pulled her fist away, controlling a strong desire to hit him with it. *"And,"* she went on, "just because a woman wants equality for all women, that does not make her a hater of men!"

"I am most happy to hear that," he replied, his grin growing wider.

She narrowed her eyes. "Or, at least, not a hater of *all* men."

He put a hand to his heart, as if wounded. "You have put me in my place."

Priscilla grimaced. "Must you make a game of everything?"

"What would you have me do? Make it all a tragedy?"

Since she did not know what it was she wanted him to do, this query left her speechless. She turned and stamped off up the stairs. She refused to look back, but she suspected that John Wolfe was watching her go with a big grin on his face.

CHAPTER SIX

THE FOLLOWING MORNING, Lady Chalcomb sent over a trunk of her husband's clothes for Priscilla's "cousin" to wear. The late lord had not been as broad in the chest as their visitor, nor quite as muscular in the thighs, but at least the trousers did not end absurdly several inches above his ankles, and he was able to sit down without Priscilla expecting to hear a rip from the strained material. He was also able to button his shirt all the way up the front instead of leaving a large V of bronzed skin showing, and he was able to leave the sleeves rolled down to the wrist instead of baring his forearms. All in all, Priscilla thought, it was much better, although, as Miss Pennybaker pointed out, the tight fit of the shirt and pants was not entirely "decent."

Priscilla spent most of the morning in her room, writing at her small secretary. She kept her door carefully locked, as she always did when writing, for while her father and Miss Pennybaker knew about her secret career, the rest of the village did not. She was not certain that Mrs. Smithson and her daughter would spread the news about, for they were not gossipy people. However, the temptation of something like Priscilla's writing novels of adventure and romance might be too great for them, and Priscilla was not willing to take the chance.

It was not for herself that she worried—though she

knew she would hate being the subject of gossip—but for her family. Their branch of the Hamiltons had always been considered somewhat odd and intellectual, though still, of course, of good breeding. Her father's eccentricities were accepted, because everyone knew that geniuses were different from the usual run of people. However, a female writer was an entirely different thing. Certainly, there had been a few women who wrote—Jane Austen, the Brontë sisters, Mary Shelley—but they had lived in a looser, more permissive time, and none of them had been second cousins to a baron, either. It would be a scandal if it became known that Elliot Pruett was really Priscilla Hamilton, and, added to her father's oddities and the general reputation of their branch of the Hamiltons for peculiarity, it would simply be too much. Priscilla was sure that neither of her brothers would be able to marry as well as they should, or make sufficient progress in his chosen career, if there was such a blot on their family name.

It was not, she knew, the action of a believer in women's rights to conceal her career. But, as always, her family came first. Someday, perhaps, she would reveal it, once Gid and Philip were well established. But, for now, she continued to hide it as if her occupation were some dread disease.

When she came downstairs late that morning, she found John Wolfe in the sitting room, patiently helping Miss Pennybaker untangle the skeins of yarn in her knitting bag. Priscilla stopped and pressed her lips tightly together to suppress a smile at the sight of the large and well-built man sitting on the settee, a skein of yarn looped over both hands while Miss Pennybaker hovered over him like a large gray bird, trying to work through the threads of a different color that were intertwined with it.

Wolfe looked up and saw her, and Priscilla would have sworn that a faint blush touched his tanned cheeks. When she saw that, she could hold back a chuckle no longer, and Wolfe scowled darkly at her.

Miss Pennybaker turned at the noise. "Ah, there you are, my dear. Did you finish copying your father's notes?"

Priscilla knew that her friend was signaling the lie she had told Mr. Wolfe to explain Priscilla's absence that morning, so she nodded. "Yes, I am through for the day."

"Good. I was about to start knitting a blanket for Mrs. Banks's little one, but when I pulled out my basket, it was the most awful mess." Her tone was as aggrieved as if her yarns were not in the same tangled mess every time she got out her basket. It never failed to amaze Priscilla that someone who could exercise such patience in figuring out her father's scribbled notes and recopying them could not have enough patience to roll her skeins of yarn into balls, instead of shoving them all together in the bag, loose.

"I see that Mr. Wolfe was kind enough to help you out," Priscilla commented, her eyes twinkling as that gentleman's scowl grew even fiercer.

"Oh, yes," Miss Pennybaker replied sunnily. "He has been so helpful. I was at a standstill when I looked in my bag and saw the yarn all tangled, but he came to my rescue. He picked the red out, right through all the others. You wouldn't think hands so big could be so precise and gentle, would you?"

Her remark reminded Priscilla of the way his hands

had felt on her body last night; they had been as gentle as she could imagine as they stroked over her hip and breast. It was her turn to blush now. She kept her gaze firmly turned away from John Wolfe, certain that the look on his face would be all too knowing.

"Well, it seems you have gained a friend, Mr. Wolfe," Priscilla said lightly, moving away from them to sit down in her favorite chair. She tried to keep the sarcasm from her tone, but she knew that she was not entirely successful. Wasn't it only yesterday that Miss Pennybaker had been warning her away from this man? She wondered if John had set out to charm the governess, or if his charm was simply so engrained that he could not keep from doing it.

Miss Pennybaker had the grace to look a trifle abashed at Priscilla's words. John merely gazed at Priscilla blandly and said, "Some people are easier to make friends with than others."

Priscilla wrinkled her nose but did not deign to honor his remark with a comment. Frankly, she could not think of one. Instead, she reached for her own sewing bag, tucked beneath the chair, and pulled out the small nightdress that she was embroidering for the same newly arrived baby.

She concentrated on the delicate needlework, resisting the temptation to glance over at John Wolfe. She had the definite feeling that he was watching her, but she was determined not to appear to have any interest in him. He was, in her opinion, altogether too sure of himself and of his obvious ability to charm women. No doubt, because of her behavior last night, he thought she would fall into his arms at the crooking of his finger, but he would find out that she was made of sterner stuff than that. She had never before behaved the way she had behaved last night with him; she had never felt any of those wild emotions with any other man. But now that she knew how he could affect her, she would be on guard. She would be able to control herself.

A loud boom outside made her jump, and she stabbed herself in the thumb with her needle. "Ow!" she cried out crossly, and sucked at the injured thumb.

"What the devil was that?" Across the room, Wolfe jumped to his feet, dropping Miss Pennybaker's yarn, and started across the room toward the window. Miss Pennybaker, with a little shriek, dumped her end of the yarn and followed him, twisting her hands anxiously.

Priscilla sighed. "Only Papa, I imagine." She stuck her needle into the dress and rose, joining them at the window.

They gazed across the backyard to the shed that was her father's workroom. A cloud of yellow smoke was billowing out of the open window, and a moment later the door flew open and her father emerged, more smoke gushing out after him.

Miss Pennybaker gave a loud sigh of relief, her hand going up to her heart. "Thank goodness he's alive."

Priscilla flung open the window and leaned out. "Are you all right, Papa?"

Florian turned at the sound of her voice and smiled at her, waving a hand. His teeth shone white in his smoke-smudged face. His hair stuck out wildly, and the front of his white shirt was blotched with streaks of black and yellow.

"Perfectly fine, my dear!" Florian called back. "Splendid bang, wasn't it? No, that's all right, Mrs. Smithson." He turned toward the cook, who had come bustling out the back door with a bucket of water. "No fire this time."

"Mm... Just splendid, Papa," Priscilla responded dryly.

She turned to go back to her chair and caught sight of John's slack-jawed face. She had to giggle. "Don't worry, Mr. Wolfe. It is not an unusual occurrence. Papa often blows things up."

His eyebrows vaulted upward. "Why?"

"Now that is a question that only he can answer. 'All in the name of science,' I believe he says. Personally, I think he likes to hear things go bang. My brothers often did when they were younger."

"Priscilla!" Miss Pennybaker scolded, as if Priscilla were still her pupil. Bright spots of color stood out on her cheeks. "That's not fair. Your father is one of the greatest scientific minds of this, or any other, century."

"I know, Penny, dear. But don't you find it rather awkward sometimes to live with a great scientific mind?"

"Oh, no, I consider it an honor!" Miss Pennybaker's eyes glowed with the zeal of a disciple. "To be able to witness the workings of such a mind..."

Priscilla felt a tug of sympathy for the older woman. She had suspected for years now that her governess held a much stronger feeling for her father than mere friendship or the devotion of an employee. The sad thing was that Florian Hamilton was barely more aware of Miss Pennybaker than he was of a piece of furniture. His life was wrapped up in his studies and experiments, and it was only because Miss Pennybaker had started copying his notes and papers that he paid any attention to her at all. It was not that he was cold or insensitive to her feelings, Priscilla knew; it was simply that everything and everyone else was mere background to his work. Even his children, despite his love for them, were perennially relegated to second place.

There were footsteps in the hall, and Florian soon appeared in the doorway of the sitting room. Up close, he was an even more appalling sight. Yellowish vapor drifted up from his clothing, and his face and hands were blotched. The unmistakable odor of rotten eggs emanated from him.

"Papa!" Priscilla protested, raising her hand to cover her nose.

John's nostrils flared, and he stared at Florian, seemingly stunned.

Florian smiled benignly at them all. "Pris, you should have been there. It was perfect."

"I'm sure it was, Papa." Priscilla could not help but smile at him. His innocent enthusiasm was infectious. Over the years, he had burned holes in the carpet, discolored the wall in his study and broken out the glass in several windows. That was why she had finally insisted that he conduct his experiments in the shed behind the house, paying for its conversion to a laboratory with part of her payment for her first book. But the glow of discovery that would light his face, the childlike curiosity and glee with which he approached life, the warm intelligence of his eyes, made it impossible to stay irritated with him.

"You've cut yourself!" Miss Pennybaker cried, going up to him with unaccustomed boldness and reaching out to dab her clean handkerchief upon a spot of red on Florian's cheek.

"What? Oh, yes, one of the beakers broke. But it was a minor setback. Nothing important."

Miss Pennybaker clucked over him, wiping a clean spot on his smudged face. He paid little attention to her, saying, "A really important step, you know. I must write Rigby, in Boston, and tell him. Last letter I got from him, he told me I'd blow up my whole house if I tried that combination. Guess he was wrong, eh?" He chuckled with glee over his scientific victory.

John Wolfe's eyebrows shot up at that statement, but Priscilla merely smiled, long used to her father's way of thinking. "He certainly was," she agreed, smiling. "But, Papa, you really should change clothes. You, ah, smell of sulfur."

"'Course I do," he replied matter-of-factly. "Been working with it. Anyway, I haven't the time to change now. I've got to get all this down on paper."

"I'll write down your notes for you," Miss Pennybaker volunteered.

"What?" Florian turned and looked at her, as if noticing her for the first time. "Yes, of course. That will be fine."

"Thank you, Penny," Priscilla said gratefully. In the past two years, since she had started writing, Miss Pennybaker had taken over more and more of the chores that Priscilla had done in the past for her father. Priscilla thought that she probably should not shove her burdens off onto Miss Pennybaker that way; if nothing else, being around Florian so much seemed to make Miss Pennybaker's adoration of him even worse. But, frankly, Priscilla often found her father's notes and letters rather boring, and she begrudged the time spent away from her writing. Miss Pennybaker's willingness to take over such chores seemed a heaven-sent opportunity.

Florian departed, still talking about his experiment,

and Miss Pennybaker trotted after him. Priscilla watched them go. It occurred to her that Miss Pennybaker's absence meant she was left alone with John Wolfe. She glanced over at him. He was watching her. She felt suddenly, terribly, ill at ease. She cleared her throat.

"Well...a bit of excitement."

"Yes. No wonder you took a battered stranger turning up at your door in stride," he told her. "You are obviously used to unusual events."

"Not quite as unusual as that," Priscilla assured him, a small grin curving her lips. "Your situation was unique."

She walked back to her chair and sat down, picking up her embroidery and trying to concentrate on it. She could feel his eyes on her. She wondered what he was thinking, whether he was remembering the embrace they had shared the night before. It was something *she* had a great deal of difficulty getting out of her mind.

"I know I should apologize," he said finally. Priscilla looked up at him, struggling to keep her face cool. "No doubt you think me a boor."

Priscilla shrugged. "I don't know that it is particularly important what I think about you."

"It is to me."

She regarded him for another moment, then her gaze dropped. Her heart was hammering in her chest. She didn't know what to think or say. Why did he have this effect on her?

"You have a peculiar effect on me," he said grimly, echoing her thoughts. "I am not the sort to force my attentions on a young lady."

"You did not exactly force them," Priscilla admitted in a muffled voice, avoiding his gaze.

"But I hardly exercised any control, either. Damn it!" He thudded his fist against the wall, causing her to start in surprise and look up at him. "I enjoyed it too much to say I'm sorry for it. I am not sorry it happened." His eyes gazed intently into hers. Priscilla's breath caught in her throat. She found she wanted to rise and go to him.

Finally he swung away, breaking the contact. "But I do apologize for distressing you."

"I was not distressed." She was not sure what she had been, but *distress* certainly was not the word to describe it. "Mr. Wolfe, I am not sure that we should talk about this. Last night was…" What? What had last night been? Delightful? Irritating? Scary? It seemed to her that it had been all those things and more. She had lain in bed for several hours afterward, trying to figure out what she felt or thought about it, and she never had been able to come to a conclusion. "…out-of-the-ordinary. Unusual. I am sure that neither one of us was really ourself. Why don't we agree to forget about it?"

"Forget?" he echoed. "I hardly think that is possible."

"Then put it aside for a time. There are so many things happening—those men, your inability to remember, the problem of what you are going to do—that I think it would be easier if we ignored what happened."

"Pretend it didn't happen?"

"Yes, if you would rather put it that way."

"I am not sure I can do that."

"When you don't even know who you are, you hardly need further entanglements, do you?"

They had been regarding each other frowningly, so it

surprised her when he suddenly grinned. "My dear Miss Hamilton, *need* is hardly the same thing as *want*."

"And, of course," she snapped, "you always do what you want!"

He chuckled. "Obviously, I am not sure what I always do."

Priscilla grimaced. "Must you joke about everything?"

"It makes life easier."

There was the sudden sound of footsteps in the hall, and then a young man's voice, calling, "Priscilla!"

John's eyes opened wide in question, and Priscilla muttered, "Damn!" under her breath.

"Who—?" he started to say, but was interrupted by the entrance of a young man with tousled blond hair.

His eyes were large and bright blue, with absurdly long lashes, and his face was even-featured and handsome, though it was marred at the moment by a ferocious scowl.

"She won't let me do it!" he exclaimed without preamble as he strode in the door, flinging his hat down carelessly on a table by the door. "Blast it, Pris! She treats me like a baby! I swear, when I turn twenty-one, I'm off to the army no matter what she says. Once I have my inheritance, she won't have anything to bind me with." He flung himself sulkily onto a chair, turning sideways a little and draping one long, muscular leg over the arm. He crossed his arms over his chest and glared at Priscilla.

"Alec!" Priscilla said in a reprimanding tone. "Where are your manners? I have a visitor." She nodded toward where John stood, eyeing with some suspicion the young man she had called Alec.

"Oh." Alec turned and saw Wolfe for the first time. "I say. I am sorry. I didn't see you there." He straightened and rose to his feet and made a polite sketch of a bow in his direction.

"Alec, this is my cousin from America, John Wolfe," Priscilla told him, wishing that Alec had not walked in on them. The fewer people who knew about her visitor, the better, as far as she was concerned, and she was well aware that Alec was something of a chatterbox. He would likely tell his mother, and the servants would overhear, and soon it would be all over the village. She wondered whether there was any way to persuade Alec to keep his mouth shut without making him suspicious.

"From America!" Alec repeated with interest. "I say, that's dashed interesting. I've always been curious about America, myself. Are you from the West? Have you ever seen any Indians? Have you ever shot a man?"

John blinked and was silent for a moment in the face of this assault. Finally he answered, "No, I am not from the West, nor have I ever seen an Indian. As for shooting a man, well…" He grinned devilishly. "I don't do that unless he deserves it."

Alec's eyes grew as big as saucers for an instant, but then he let out a bark of laughter. "Oh, I see. A joke, eh?"

"Afraid so."

"I didn't know you had any cousins from the States, Pris."

"On my mother's side," Priscilla replied quickly. "He's quite removed, actually. Our grandfathers were cousins, or something like that. And, Alec, don't tell everyone about his being here. We would be swarmed with visitors, and my cousin is just recovering from a fever."

"Oh, of course," Alec assured her casually, moving on to a topic that interested him more. "Where in America do you live?"

"New York."

"That's a large city, right?"

"Yes, quite big."

"Not like London, though."

"No, I wouldn't think it is much like London."

"I should like to see it. And Paris. Or India or Africa. Dash it, I'd like to go anywhere. London is the only place I've ever been—and Scotland. We've often summered in Scotland."

"I've heard Scotland is beautiful."

Alec shrugged. "I suppose. Deadly dull, though. Nothing but trout fishing or hiking up mountains. And half the time you can't understand what any of them are saying. It's like being in a foreign country, only not exciting. Have you ever been there?"

John shook his head, unable to suppress a smile at the young man's chatter.

"Well, Alec, what brings you here?" Priscilla asked cheerfully, more to lead him away from asking any more questions of John than from any desire to know. "You seemed upset. Is it the Duchess again?"

"I was. I am." He heaved a sigh and turned back to Priscilla. "Mother refuses to acknowledge that I'm a grown man. I keep telling her that all I want is to join the army with Gid." His eyes sparkled. "I got a note from him today, and he's having the grandest time. And Gid never was half the horseman I am."

"I know," Priscilla agreed, adopting an air of sympathy.

"But there he is, in the Guards, and here I am, stuck at Ranleigh Court."

"You've never met my brother Gid, I believe," Priscilla said in an aside to her "cousin," feeding him information. "He and Alec are the best of friends."

"Since we were lads," Alec agreed, looking gloomy. "But his father lets him do what he wants to, so he is an officer in the army, and I am…" He paused sourly.

"A future duke," Priscilla supplied smoothly.

"A duke?" John Wolfe looked interested. "Really?"

"Yes," Alec agreed grumpily. "A duke. Except that I'm not actually a duke, not recognized, that is. I am not even the Marquess of Lynden, when you get right down to it, though Father used to call me that."

"Oh." Wolfe looked blank. "I'm sorry."

Priscilla chuckled. "He doesn't understand, Alec. He is American, remember?" Priscilla turned toward John. "The Marquess of Lynden is the title of the heir to the Duke of Ranleigh. So the Duke's oldest son is Lynden—until the Duke dies, and then he becomes the Duke."

"I understand, I think."

"But Alec, you see, cannot be called either, even though he is probably the heir to the dukedom. There is an older son who disappeared many years ago. *He* was Lynden, but no one knows what happened to him, or where he went. He has been gone thirty years now, and everyone assumes he died. But when the old duke died a few months ago, the solicitors said they had to look for Lynden before Alec could become the duke."

"So in the meantime, Alec is in a sort of limbo."

"Exactly," Alec agreed, pleased that he understood. "It isn't as if I want to be the duke, anyway. I told Mother that. What would I want with all that responsibility—the name and the land, all the people that live on it? It's too much. All I want is to be a cavalry officer."

"But she didn't understand?" Priscilla guessed.

"Of course not. She thinks my being the duke is the grandest thing." He grimaced.

"It is a very old and honored title," Priscilla pointed out.

Alec wrinkled his nose. "I don't care about that. You know I don't. I wish they would find Lynden, frankly. Then he would have to come back and take over, and I would be free to do what I please. Father left me a fair portion."

"I'm sure he did. He loved you very much."

"I know." Alec sighed heavily. "That's why I agreed to stay here so long. I wanted to go away with Gid, but Mother kept telling me, 'No, wait until he is gone. He so wants you to be home with him. Can't you go then, after he dies?' Then I'd feel so damn low and guilty, I would agree to stay. Now he's gone, and she doesn't have that excuse anymore, but she still refuses to let me go!"

"Why don't you simply leave?" John asked curiously.

The other two turned and stared at him in surprise. He gazed back at them. "I mean, you are pretty much grown. Why don't you do as you want to?"

Alec seemed at a loss for words. Finally he said, "Mother says it isn't fitting for a duke—though it seems to me I could be a duke and still be in the army. There's the Duke of Wellington, after all, and the Duke of Marlborough."

"I believe they were given the titles after their victories as generals," Priscilla pointed out.

"Oh. Well, the Earl of Cardigan fought in the Crimea, and he was an earl to begin with."

"Very true."

"Why is it so different for a duke?"

"You do have responsibilities," Priscilla pointed out. She turned toward John, offering an explanation to him, "You see, a title carries with it certain duties and responsibilities. One cannot just do as one pleases."

"Why not? It is his title, isn't it?" John asked.

"Yes, of course, but he has a duty to future generations. For instance, he should not do anything that would bankrupt the estate."

Alec let out a short laugh. "As if the place were not falling apart already. It costs too much to keep all the houses up. The manor house in Corksey is a dead loss—wormwood got to it. The whole east wing of the Court had to be closed off. Structurally unsound, you see. It needs massive repairs. We are land-rich, cash-poor."

"And," Priscilla went on valiantly, "what would happen if you were killed in the army, Alec? You are the last, the only, son, if Lynden doesn't turn up. You cannot let the title die out."

"There's Cousin Evesham," Alec pointed out. "He would get it. I told Mother that, too, and she said she would rather die than let him become the Duke of Ranleigh. Can't blame her, in a way. He's a terrible reprobate. Father disliked him, too. But at least there is a succession. It wouldn't die out. Besides, I'm not likely to get killed. There are hardly ever any wars anymore, just little skirmishes with the natives now and then in India or someplace."

"There. You see?" Wolfe said to Priscilla, as if they had been arguing. "What's to stop him going if he wants?"

Alec screwed up his face as he tried to come up with an answer to a question he had never been asked before, indeed had never even considered. Finally he said, "Well, it's the family, you see. One doesn't go against one's family."

"But surely you don't plan to live your whole life to suit your family, do you?" John pressed. "Marry who they want you to? Live where they want you to?"

Alec looked confused. "I wouldn't marry a girl simply because she suited Mother. Might not suit me, you see." He paused, then went on, "'Course, I suppose I would not marry someone wholly unsuitable, either." He looked at John interestedly. "Would you?"

John smiled. "I haven't a title to worry about. But I can't say as I see much reason why being a duke means you have to do what other people tell you."

Alec seemed much struck by this thought. "You know, I always used to think that, too. I thought if you were a duke, you did exactly as you pleased, and it was other people who had to do as you said. It certainly seemed that way with Papa."

"You *can* do quite a bit because you are a duke," Priscilla pointed out. "I am sure a number of people would love to be in your position." She turned and frowned pointedly at John. "I suspect that my cousin, being an American, doesn't precisely understand what an important title entails."

John looked appropriately abashed. "I'm sure you are right. My American ignorance is appalling."

Priscilla made a face at him, but went on smoothly, "Now, Alec, let's talk about something more pleasant. I heard that you have bought a new hunter."

Alec immediately perked up at the mention of the horse, and all his sulkiness fell away as he sat up and began to describe his new purchase. "Oh, you should see him, Pris. A bay, sixteen hands. A sweet goer…"

THEY SPENT MUCH OF THE REST of Alec's visit discussing horses, and John contributed little to the conversation. When Alec was gone, John commented, "Poor lad. I suspect his not joining the cavalry has more to do with his being henpecked than with any ducal responsibilities."

"You are probably right," Priscilla agreed. "But it was unkind of you to encourage him."

"Unkind? I thought I was doing him a favor—you know, pointing out that he had a free will and could do what he wants. Isn't that true? Or does being English do away with one's freedom?"

Priscilla's eyes flashed. "The English were a free people with guaranteed rights before your country was even a nation! Americans think they invented the concept simply because they got rid of a monarchy. But where do you think you people got all your fine ideas about freedom? From our Magna Carta and the English Bill of Rights, that's where."

He chuckled, holding up his hands, palm out, as if in defense. "All right, all right, don't eat me. I am sure the English are a fine people, perfectly free to do as they please. That lad seems to be a different story, however."

Priscilla sighed. "He is the only son, the only heir. His mother has always overmanaged and overprotected him. His father was something of a bully, too. I imagine that's why he was forever here with Gid." She smiled fondly. "They were a wild pair, always up to some mischief or other."

John gazed at her for a moment, then asked softly, "Is he your beau?"

"My what?" Priscilla's eyes widened. "You're joking, surely."

He shook his head.

"Of all the idiotic things… Of course he is not my beau. Why, he's only twenty, the same age as Gidrey, and I am twenty-four."

John shrugged. "Many a young man has had an infatuation with an older woman."

"That is not the case with Alec and me," Priscilla said huffily.

"For you, perhaps, but I'm not so sure that the young man in question feels the same."

"You are mad. Alec thinks of me as an older sister. He brings his problems to me, but I promise you that he has no deeper affection." Priscilla returned to her sewing, jamming her needle into the cloth and pulling it through with short, sharp movements.

He watched her for a moment, a smile playing about his lips, enjoying the flush of color upon Priscilla's cheeks and the sparkle that irritation brought to her eyes. He had been teasing her, more than anything else, but he had been aware of a distinct feeling of jealousy as he watched Priscilla and the young heir talking. He did not, he realized, like the idea that another man might have feelings for Priscilla— No, more than that, what really pricked at him was the fact that Priscilla was so at ease with the lad, and so openly fond of him. Perhaps she did only look upon him as another brother, but still…

He did not like the way his thoughts were turning, so he cast about in his mind for another topic, one that would have Priscilla talking to him again instead of jabbing her needle through the cloth as if she were attacking someone.

"Tell me about this other heir," he said. "The one that has young Alec dangling."

"Lynden?" Priscilla looked up. Her tone was cool, but he could see the light of interest in her eyes. "He was Alec's half brother, the son the duke had with his first wife. I never knew the man. He left the area before I was born."

"But I suspect you know about him. There were bound to have been stories. The heir to the Duke leaves, never to return…must have caused a firestorm of gossip."

"I'm sure it did. It is one of our most famous local legends." Her eyes beginning to sparkle, she smiled with the enthusiasm of a natural storyteller. "You see, the reason he left was…murder."

CHAPTER SEVEN

"Murder!" John repeated, surprised. "He killed someone?"

Priscilla nodded. "So they say. It was never proved, of course. Never even pursued, really, once he had fled the country."

"What happened? Who did he kill?"

"Well, the story goes like this. Ranleigh's son was young, only nineteen or twenty, and a very handsome, charming young man, they say. He was up at Oxford, but he was home visiting between terms, with a friend. Apparently he was whiling away his time while home by seeing one of the local girls, one Rose Childs, who was a chambermaid at Ranleigh Court."

"Ah…"

"Quite. She had boasted to some of her friends about the handsome young lord she was seeing, saying he was head over heels in love with her. Only the weekend before, she had visited at home and hinted broadly to her mother and brother that she had 'expectations.' Her brother told her she was daft if she thought a nobleman was going to marry the likes of her, and she said that he might not have any choice. A few days later, she sneaked out of the house. No one saw her go. When dawn came, she was not back at Ranleigh Court, and it was obvious that her bed had not been slept in. But her mother and brother said that she had not gone there, either. They started a search for her. And found her dead in Lady's Woods. Strangled."

John raised his eyebrows. "Quite a story. But how did they know that it was this Lynden fellow who had done it? From what you said, it did not sound as if she had actually named him as her lover. And why would it have to be her lover, anyway?"

"No one besides her lover seemed to have any reason to kill her. They did an autopsy on her afterward, and they discovered that she was pregnant. That gave a lover a pretty powerful reason. She must have told him she was pregnant, perhaps even pressured him to marry her, from what she said to her brother, and they got into a quarrel. He wound up strangling her. And Lynden was the only handsome young lord around, except, of course, for his cousin, Evesham, who was fairly young also, but one could scarcely call him handsome. Besides, all the servants at the Court knew that Lynden had been sneaking out of the house frequently, coming and going at odd times and acting as if he did not want to be seen. It was pretty obvious that something was going on."

"Still, it hardly sounds enough to condemn a duke's son."

"I am sure the local constable was loath to arrest him. But there was damning proof, not just gossip. Near the body, they found a fragment of a ruby necklace or bracelet, as well as another loose ruby. It had obviously been torn from a larger piece of jewelry. Everyone knew about the Ranleigh Rubies."

She paused dramatically, and John smiled. "That is my cue to say, 'What are the Ranleigh Rubies?' Correct?"

"Of course." Priscilla smiled. "The rubies were a family heirloom of the dukes of Ranleigh. They had been in the family since the days of Queen Elizabeth. The legend is that the first Ranleigh, who was one of those dashing Elizabethan corsairs, seized them from a Spanish ship. They had been intended for a wedding present for some Spanish nobleman. Ranleigh gave Queen Elizabeth a lovely set of emerald earrings from the same shipment, but he never showed her the ruby necklace, bracelet and earring set. Instead, he gave them quietly to the woman he was wooing, who apparently was a proper little snob, not to mention foolish, for after they were married she wore them in front of the queen herself. The queen was furious that he had not given her the most beautiful jewels in his haul, and Ranleigh spent the next two years cooling his heels in the Tower. He was lucky he didn't lose his head. Anyway, the rubies have all sorts of stories attached to them. There is the tale of the duke during the time of Charles II who let his mistress wear them instead of his wife, and who was later mysteriously injured in a fall at his country estate and spent the rest of his life a helpless invalid, dependent upon his wife. Or the Ranleigh who gambled away almost his entire fortune in a heavy night of cards and finally used the ruby set as a wager, won the game, and subsequently won back everything he had lost and more."

"Quite a history." He grinned at Priscilla. "You know how to tell a story."

"Why, thank you." Priscilla felt inordinately pleased at the compliment. "At any rate, the rubies were very famous stones, and all the people hereabouts knew about them. So when they found the rubies beside her body, especially given the rumors about her and Lynden, the constable could not ignore the possibility that Lynden was the one who had killed her. They went to Ranleigh Court and spoke to the Duke. He was incensed, of course, that they would even suspect his son, but when they showed him the rubies, he was stunned. He recognized them, you see, though he continued to maintain that it was impossible. However, he went to the safe where he kept them and, sure enough, the ruby necklace was missing. He sent for his son, and the constable asked where Lynden had been the night of the murder. Lynden said he had been in his room alone. Yet one of the stablehands had already told them that Lynden had him saddle a horse for him that evening, that he had left and had not returned to the stable until quite early the next morning, when the stable lads were first arising. It was terribly damning."

"I can see that. So he ran away?"

"Not immediately. He protested that he was innocent, but he refused to tell them where he had been the night before. The Duke, who had a wicked temper, was practically apoplectic. Then the friend—the one who was spending the school holidays with Lynden at Ranleigh Court—stepped forward and said that Lynden had been with him the night of the murder, that he and Lynden had ridden to Harswell to play cards and drink until quite late. So he could not have killed her."

John's brows rose. "He lied for him?"

"No one knows. He maintained that they were together, which obviously was to Lynden's benefit. Since he said they were alone, there was no one else who could confirm or deny it. But with the alibi he provided, and with no more evidence than the constable had, it effectively killed the case."

"Then why did the son disappear?"

"While the old Duke was grateful for the alibi, which saved the family name from the scandal of a trial, he did not really believe the friend. Everyone says that the Duke and Lynden had an enormous quarrel that evening. He was a very strait-laced man, and very proud, and he and his son had never gotten along. Apparently they shouted and raged, and Ranleigh struck his son. Then Lynden tore out of the Court, vowing never to see his father again. And he did not. He packed his bags and rode off into the night, and he hasn't been heard from since. Not even a letter. Lynden's mother was dead, and the old Duke remarried a few years later. He was sure his son was dead, and he wanted another heir."

"Alec."

"Yes. The old Duke always referred to his oldest son as being dead, and he even insisted on calling Alec Lynden. Most people did it to please the old man, but, of course, it isn't truly his title. Nor is the dukedom, until they resolve the matter."

"How will they do that?"

"I'm not sure." Priscilla shrugged. "Through the courts, I guess—have Lynden declared legally dead or something. But that will probably take years."

"And in the meantime, poor Alec cannot inherit."

"Not the title," she agreed. "But he got the bulk of what money the old Duke had. Ranleigh left that to Alec outright. It wasn't entailed like the land, you see, so he could leave it to whomever he wished. It is not nearly as valuable nor as important as the land and title, of course. But Alec doesn't much care, really. He has enough for his horses and hounds, and he has little feeling for the land. You heard him. He would rather not have the responsibility of being the Duke of Ranleigh."

"I can understand that. It sounds as if it rather cuts into one's freedom. I don't think I should care for it much, either."

"He hasn't much choice, really."

"Mm...I guess not. Whatever happened to the other son, do you suppose?"

"No one knows. No one has heard anything from him since he left. Some say he went to the Continent, others to the colonies. Everyone suspects that he died or he would eventually have written."

"Or perhaps he got knocked over the head and has no idea who he used to be," John put in wryly.

Priscilla smiled at him with sympathy. "Surely that sort of thing isn't permanent."

"I certainly hope not." He got up and began to wander restlessly about. "How could a person forget everything about his life? It doesn't seem possible, does it?" He stopped and gazed out the window, as if something in the garden might hold the key to his mystery. "I can understand forgetting a short while—the day it happened, say. But how could I possibly forget my own name? Or where I live?"

"Yet it happened. Papa found an article about it in one of his books. He read that the memory often comes back."

"All of it?"

"Yes, I think so. Sometimes only partially."

"Even that would be better than this blank I have now." He paused, still gazing out the window. "If only I had something with me—my clothes, a watch, anything that would jog my memory..."

Suddenly he straightened, his eyes narrowing. "Wait! I have it!"

"What?"

"What if I returned to that shack? Perhaps if I looked at it again, saw it from the outside, in the daylight, I would remember something about how I got there. How I got injured. Perhaps there might even be something of mine there."

Priscilla's interest was aroused. "It sounds reasonable. It would be worth trying, at any rate. The only problem is, how do we find the shack? Could you retrace your steps?"

He frowned. "No. It was dark, and I was running a lot of the time."

"How long did it take you to get from there to here?"

"I don't know. An hour or two, maybe. But I was so disoriented, I could have been running around this house in circles several times before I finally stumbled on it."

"Do you remember anything about the landscape that you passed through?"

"A lot of trees. That was the main thing. There was a patch of dense, thorny bushes that I skirted—that was when I stumbled on the path that led to your house."

"I know where that is," Priscilla exclaimed. "It's south of here. If you follow the path to Chalcomb Manor, you pass Wyfield Meadow. There's a thicket of thornbushes on the edge of the woods there." She jumped to her feet. "Let's go."

"What?"

"There's plenty of daylight left." Priscilla glanced out the window, as if to demonstrate her point. "It is not more than two or three o'clock. We can walk to the thicket, because I know where that is, and you can edge around it, going back the same way that you think you came the other night. We will have a much better idea where your hideaway was."

She started toward the hall to get her bonnet. Wolfe followed her, protesting, "No, wait. Don't go off half-cocked. I don't think you should go. It could be dangerous."

"Are you on about those men again? I told you, nothing happened to me on the way to the village, and I saw no sign of them."

"Yes, but you were not with me. They might not have been absolutely sure that I was at your house, and they didn't want to draw attention to themselves or get into trouble for accosting a genteel young lady. So they hid and watched. But we know that they suspect this house and that they are nearby, because they broke into the house last night. If they actually see me, they might be willing to risk harming you in order to get me."

"Mr. Wolfe, really…I think you overestimate your importance to these men, as well as their vigilance. Do you honestly think they are out there right now, hiding behind some bush or other, spying on our house?"

He shrugged. "It's possible."

"I think you are starting at shadows, Mr. Wolfe. If they were watching the front of the house, they could not see us leave by the back, which is the way we go to get to that path. Besides, I don't think they even come out by day. It is my guess that they are night creatures. That was when they came yesterday, and it seems much more suited to their way. Secretive and dark. Someone walking down the road or going into the garden might see them in the day. Besides, they have to rest sometime, if they're running about the countryside at night, chasing people and breaking into houses."

"I am not starting at shadows, as you say," he replied grimly. "You may be right that they are not out there watching the house. I don't know where they are or what they are doing. But I can hardly risk your safety on what I don't know."

"Then how do you propose to find this shack that you think will jog your memory? Sitting here wishing will hardly make it appear."

He flushed a little. "I am well aware of that, Miss Hamilton. I had no intention of staying here. I am merely saying that I will find the shack on my own. *You* will stay here."

Priscilla rolled her eyes. "Of course. That makes perfect sense. You, who are a foreigner and know nothing of this place, will go roaming about, trying to find something, whilst I, who was born and reared right here at Evermere Cottage, will sit at home and twiddle my thumbs."

He grimaced, recognizing the validity of her remarks, much as he disliked the thought of exposing her to danger.

Priscilla, seeing his indecision, pressed on. "Besides, you will be along for protection, will you not?" She cast a mock-innocent glance up at his face. "Or do you think you could not protect me?"

"You minx," he retorted, without heat. "Yes, in the normal course of things, I can protect you. But I'd feel a hell of a lot more confident if I had my gun."

"*Your* gun?"

He looked at her, his eyebrows rising as he caught her meaning. "I did say that, didn't I? My gun." He considered the thought for a moment. "I'm not sure. But I do feel as if I own one. Now, what it looks like, I have no idea—no picture comes to mind at the words."

"You sound as if you are indeed from the West. Perhaps you are a gunslinger."

"A gunslinger traveling through England? Sounds a bit unlikely."

"So does being hit over the head and imprisoned in a hut."

"You have me there." He grinned at her.

Priscilla gazed coolly back at him. "Well, shall we go, or do you plan to stay?

"All right, my dear Miss Hamilton, I concede. We shall find this thicket together."

She got her bonnet from the hall tree, where John was pleased to find a stout blackthorn walking stick. He weighed it consideringly in his hand and decided that it would do well enough for a weapon. Whistling cheerfully, stick in hand, he followed her through the house and out the kitchen door.

They wound their way through the garden and passed the small building where Florian conducted his experiments. It still smelled disconcertingly of sulfur. In only a few more yards, they came upon a barely discernible path. Priscilla turned confidently to the right and set out with a brisk stride. Her companion walked along just behind her, his eyes continually scanning the landscape around them.

Before long, they reached the thicket. John glanced

around, saying, "It seemed to take much longer the other night."

"I am sure so. You were exhausted and sick."

They walked along beside the thicket for a while, and even when the path turned toward the left, they continued to follow the line of the thicket. "I wish I was more sure of the time it took." He slowed, looking all around him. "I think it was about here somewhere. I came out of the trees, and there was a small clearing, with these bushes on the far side. "This looks like it might be the place."

He headed across the small clearing to the trees beyond, walking uncertainly back and forth. Finally he let out a low cry. "I think I came out here. Look."

Priscilla hurried toward him and looked at the trunk of the birch tree, where he was pointing. A brownish smear decorated its white trunk.

"I remember leaning against a tree, listening for their pursuit. This is blood. Remember the scratches on my arms and shoulders? I must have gotten blood on the bark when I leaned against it."

"Good. Then…straight ahead?"

"Let's try it."

They moved through the trees, looking for other signs of John's precipitate dash through the area the other night, but they found nothing else. After an hour's fruitless search, they moved northward for a while, then angled back toward where they had entered, hoping to find another mark, or something that looked familiar to John. They continued in this way, tracking out from the marked tree like spokes in a wheel, but finally gave up when it became too dark, as it did early in the woods.

They headed home in the twilight, agreeing to start again the next morning.

THERE WAS NO INTERRUPTION from their midnight visitors that night, though Priscilla lay awake for a long time, worrying about them. Despite the short sleep, she woke up early the following morning, excited by the continuing search and the possibility of solving John Wolfe's mystery—or at least part of it. She hurried through her dressing routine and breakfast, and skipped the morning's writing. The lure of a real adventure was far too strong to allow her to spend her day at a desk writing about an imaginary one.

They tramped along the path they had taken the day before, John cheerfully whistling and twirling the walking stick he held in one hand. Priscilla smiled, glancing at him, and said, "You seem well on your way to recovery."

"What? Oh. Yes, I am. Except for an occasional headache, I feel up to full strength." He grinned sideways at her. "Between your doctoring and Mrs. Smithson's food, I have recovered nicely." He nodded toward the picnic basket he carried. "Though I do think I could do with a little less of Mrs. Smithson's cooking today. It feels like she packed a roast in here."

Priscilla chuckled. "Mrs. Smithson believes in eating heartily. She's been thrilled to have you here. 'Someone who eats like a man, not like a bird,'" she said imitating the cook's low, accented voice.

"Is that what makes her like me—my appetite? Here I thought it was my charm."

"That, too," Priscilla assured him gravely. "She likes to be flirted with."

They reached the marked tree, and John set the food basket on a rock in the shade to wait while they explored farther. They struck out again, altering their course a little each time, as they had the day before. But this time, as they walked along, off to one side Priscilla noticed a small tree branch, broken and dangling, at about the height of Wolfe's chest.

"Look at this," she cried softly, going over to it, and Wolfe followed.

He lifted the branch and considered it. "It certainly looks as if something—or someone—barged through here." He glanced around. "It doesn't seem familiar. But these woods look so much the same. The only thing I remember that was unusual was a downward slope that led to a stream. I splashed through that. Well, let's veer off in this direction, then."

Priscilla marked the tree with a piece of yarn she had brought, taken from Miss Pennybaker's knitting bag. They had decided this morning that it would be wise for them to mark their trail today, in order to keep from getting lost or retracing their own steps. They continued to walk, going deeper and deeper into the woods.

"I wish we had Gid or Alec with us," Priscilla remarked, sighing, as they stopped once again and surveyed their surroundings. "They know these woods better than anyone. They always used to play in them. Maybe we should tell Alec the truth and get his help."

John shook his head. He was strangely reluctant to seek Alec's aid. It was related, he thought, to that unaccustomed spurt of jealousy he had experienced upon watching Alec's easy interaction with Priscilla, but he did not like to think about that. "We will find it eventually."

Priscilla shrugged and sat down on a large, moss-cushioned rock. "It wasn't far from here, you know, where they found Rose."

"Who?" He looked at her, puzzled, then his face cleared. "Oh, you mean the girl in your story? The one who was murdered by the heir?"

Priscilla nodded. "It was over in that direction. I'll show you."

She stood and began walking through the trees, curving around a rise in the ground. The ground sloped downward to a small clearing. Light filtered through the leaves, and vines surrounding the clearing, making it dim even in broad daylight and tinted faintly with green. A rock, half covered with lichen, formed a barrier on one side of the little glade, and the trees spreading over the clearing reminded one of a ceiling. But instead of seeming snug, the enclosed area, utterly silent, had an eerie quality to it.

Wolfe's eyebrow rose and he turned toward Priscilla. "This is it?"

Priscilla nodded, unable to suppress a shiver. "Yes. It seems a perfect spot for a murder, doesn't it?"

"But hardly what one would choose for a trysting place since it would be black as the pits of hell in here at night."

Involuntarily Priscilla looked behind her.

He grinned. "That is what I mean."

"Well, it is not what I would choose, certainly," Priscilla agreed. "But then, I don't suppose either of them was terribly sensitive to atmosphere. And it was far away from prying eyes. The sort of place where they would not be discovered."

"It's a wonder they ever discovered her body."

"He probably hoped for that. But she had told one of her girlfriends, apparently, that they met in Lady's Woods, which narrowed it down to this area."

He looked around him again, shaking his head. "It's a lonely place, that's for sure." He started to turn away, holding out his hand to her. "Come. Let's get out of here."

Priscilla slipped her hand in his, as naturally as if it belonged there, and they left the clearing. He turned to the left, holding up a branch for them to pass under. Priscilla started to point out that they were heading in the wrong direction, but something about the intent expression on his face stopped her.

"I hear water," he said, stopping and listening.

"Yes. There is a small brook over there." She pointed ahead of him and to the left.

He looked down at her. "I crossed a stream when I escaped."

"There's more than one. You remember, we came upon another this morning."

"Yes, but it wasn't right. It was too sunny, too open."

He strode in the direction of the water, and a few moments later they emerged at the edge of a brook. It ran clearly over mossy stones, and beyond it the land sloped upward slightly, thick with trees.

"This is more like the one I remember." He looked up and down the stream, frowning.

"The woods thin out in that direction," Priscilla noted. "Why don't we walk down this way?"

They did so, crossing the stream when they came to a natural bridge of stepping-stones. They continued to walk in the same direction the brook flowed, stopping to rest in a larger, more open clearing, where they sat upon a fallen tree trunk. They walked for a few more minutes after that, then Wolfe stopped suddenly.

"I think this is it. This looks familiar—that big rock there, with all the moss. I think I crossed right below it."

They hurried forward, and there, beside the mossy rock at the edge of the stream, was a footprint in the mud.

"Barefoot," Priscilla said excitedly, looking at him. "And large."

"The size of my foot," he agreed, and his eyes were sparkling with excitement. "Come on."

He hurried up the incline, towing her along as he followed the footprints until they disappeared in the leaves. They crested the rise, where the trees grew less thickly.

"There!" His voice was quick with excitement. "I went around that thick stand of trees. I wanted speed more than secrecy."

Priscilla squeezed his hand, excitement pounding through her, as well, and they hurried forward. They skirted the trees, and there, off to the right, ahead of them, stood a small brown hut. Priscilla started toward it, but Wolfe stopped, holding her back.

"Wait," he said in a low voice. "It's possible they might be here."

They stepped back into the cover of a low-hanging tree, and Wolfe scanned the area carefully. They waited, hearing and seeing nothing but the twittering of birds and the occasion rustle of an animal among the trees. Wolfe started forward quietly, pushing Priscilla behind him protectively. She gave him a poke in the back hard enough to make him grunt and moved around to his side again.

He gave her a sideways glance of irritation but did not try to make her follow safely behind him again. The hut and the land around it showed no signs of habitation as they approached, and they sped up as they came closer. With a final look around at the woods surrounding them, John reached out and pulled open the door. They peered inside.

The hut was quite small, barely long enough for a man of John's height to lie down in, and not tall enough for him to stand unless he was a little stooped over. It was dim inside, the only light provided by cracks between the boards and an occasional knothole; there was no window. The floor was hard-packed earth, and there was absolutely nothing inside the shack. But, despite the weathered look of the boards, it was solid and well put together. With the door barred from the outside, it would have been impossible for even a strong man to pound his way out of it.

"Oh, John!" Priscilla exclaimed feelingly. "You must have gone crazy in here."

"Just about," he agreed, eyeing the place with disfavor. "It is not a place I would want to visit again." He walked in, stooping over, and moved carefully around the small room, checking out the walls and floor. "There's nothing here," he said in disgust. "Not even a button or a piece of paper." He sighed and left the shack. "Not a clue as to who I am."

"Perhaps there is something out there," Priscilla suggested, making a wide gesture that encompassed all the trees around them.

"Perhaps," he agreed, though without much enthusiasm.

They began to circle the shack, moving in ever-larger orbits as they searched for anything unusual. There were a few scuffed footprints, this time obviously shod, but that told them little except the size of the men's feet.

Priscilla glanced to the side and stopped abruptly. "John! Look."

She pointed to a spot beneath a tree several feet away, where a small mound of freshly turned earth lay, darker than the land around it and rising in a hump.

"Something is buried there."

CHAPTER EIGHT

THEY HURRIED TO THE SMALL MOUND and dropped down on their knees beside it. The mound looked very much like a grave, except that it was far too short to be that of a person, only three feet in length and less in width.

"This has been dug recently," John said positively.

"I suppose someone could have buried an animal here."

"Why would anyone come all the way out here to bury an animal? Or who, walking through the woods and finding a dead creature, would have stopped to bury it? No, I don't think it's an animal."

He began to shove the earth away with his hands, then stopped and looked around for a better tool. He picked up a flattish rock to use, but paused and turned it from side to side.

"Look at this. I think someone's used it for the exact same thing. There's earth clinging to it on this end. I would say that means burying this was a hasty thing."

He began to dig. The earth was soft and moist, and the flat, wide surface of the rock made it a good tool. It was not long before the rock struck something besides earth.

"What is it?"

"I'm not sure," John said as he scooped dirt away in a wider area. "It isn't hard."

Priscilla joined him in scooping away the dirt, careless of her nails and hands. She was almost as caught up in the excitement of the moment as he was. Quickly the surface of the buried object emerged.

"It—it's leather," Priscilla said, puzzlement tinging her voice.

John plunged his hands into the hole, pulling and tugging, and the thing shifted and pulled free. It was a large brown leather bag.

"It's a traveling bag!" she exclaimed, and looked wide-eyed at John. "Is it yours, do you think?"

"I don't know. I don't recognize it. But it makes sense. They might have figured that burying it was the best way of hiding it." He stroked a hand across the side of the large bag. "It's good-quality."

He set it upright and reached for the clasp. It had a lock that had once required a key, but now it dangled uselessly, obviously broken.

"John, look!" Priscilla was peering into the hole left by the bag. "There's something else in here." She reached down and pulled up a shoe.

"My God." John forgot the bag and its clasp for the moment and grabbed the shoe. He brushed the clinging dirt away from its soft leather surface and held it beside his foot. It was the same size. He raised his eyes, and he and Priscilla gazed at each other for a long, silent moment.

He pulled off the shoe Lady Chalcomb had lent him and slipped on the one Priscilla had found. It fit perfectly.

"It must be mine," he said in a faintly awed voice. "It fits my foot as if it were made for it."

Priscilla dug into the hole again, pulling out the other shoe and a tied bundle of clothes. She tore at the knot, and the bundle separated, a wallet falling from it and bouncing on the ground. John pounced on it eagerly.

"Empty," he said in disgust.

Priscilla shook out the clothes, holding the various garments up one by one. There was a white shirt and trousers and a jacket. Even though they were muddied and crumpled now, the clothes were made of excellent materials and were extremely well cut. A silk handkerchief was still tucked into the pocket of the jacket. Priscilla pulled it out. In one corner was an elegant embroidered monogram.

She smoothed her thumb across the thread. *A,* she read. "There's an *A* initialed on your handkerchief."

He reached across and took the handkerchief in his hand, studying it thoughtfully. "*A.* Well, that's something, I guess. If these things are indeed mine, then my last name should begin with an *A.*" He gave her a rueful smile. "Leaves quite a bit open, doesn't it? What do you suppose I am, Adams? Aherne? Abernathy?"

"Abercrombie," Priscilla suggested. "Alden. Anderson. Aiken. Abbot."

"Allen. Lord, the list is endless. I wish one of them rang a bell." He pulled the sides of the bag apart and peered into it. "More clothes." He pulled out a small leather case and opened it. "A shaving kit." He pulled out brush, razor and mug, examining each in turn. "Nothing. Not even another monogram."

With a sigh, he closed the shaving kit and returned it to the bag. "It is obvious they took off with anything of value that was in there—and anything that might identify me."

"Do you suppose they meant to take what could identify you? Or were they just after the money and valuables?"

"I have no idea. Why would anyone want to hide my identity? And they could hardly count on my not being able to remember who I was."

"Yes, but if you had not escaped, you would not be able to tell anyone who you were, even if you did remember."

"And why did they go to the trouble of burying my bag? Why not just toss it aside somewhere after they'd stripped it?"

"Perhaps they were afraid someone might see it and wonder about it, might even begin hunting around to see to whom the bag belonged."

He shrugged. "I suppose so. Damn! It's so frustrating not being able to remember anything. I feel completely useless."

"Not at all!" Priscilla protested stoutly. "You are not useless. You found your way back here, didn't you? And discovered this bag?"

"Which doesn't lead us anywhere."

"It might. You can't know for sure. Maybe when you dress in these clothes, you will start remembering. You haven't gone through every single thing in that bag. There might be something in one of the pockets of some garment that will tell us who you are. We know more than we did—we know that your name begins with an *A*. And at least you have clothes and shoes that fit now."

He smiled faintly. "That's true. That will be a major improvement, believe me. I have grown quite tired of hearing threads rip every time I move. You are, as always, correct." He took her hand, lifting it toward his mouth as if to kiss it, but he stopped at the sight of her narrow fingers, liberally covered with moist earth, the fingernails broken and grimy. He chuckled. "My dear lady, I can see that you have made a supreme sacrifice in our pursuit." He made a show of twisting her hand this way and that until he found a clean spot on the back of it to press his lips against.

Despite the joking way he did it, Priscilla found that the touch of his lips upon her bare skin sent shivers through her. She could tell from the way his eyes darkened that the kiss had not left him unaffected, either. He held her hand for a moment longer as he looked at her. Their fingers twined together. Priscilla remembered the way he had taken her hand earlier as they walked, and how right and natural it had seemed to be hand in hand with him. She remembered their kisses the other night in her father's study.

"Priscilla..." He leaned forward, at the same time pulling her gently toward him. Their lips met and clung. They did not touch anywhere except their joined hands and mouths, but that contact alone was dizzying. It was as if their passion were so strong that they dared not press their bodies together. Their fingers gripped each other; their breath mingled hotly. Priscilla was aware of an ache deep in her abdomen, a pulsing, heated yearning that she had never felt before, a feeling so unaccustomed and stunning that it scared her.

John himself scared her—the sensations he could arouse in her, the power he could exercise over her when he chose, the way she melted at his touch. It made her feel weak, not in control of herself—and yet it was the most delightful thing she had ever experienced. When he kissed her, she wanted it to go on and on; she wanted more. She trembled, afraid, yet dizzy with excitement, eager and unknowing.

He pulled back first, drawing a long breath. "We cannot do this, not here."

Priscilla shook her head, agreeing with him, but she had to fight to keep her arms from going around his neck.

"God, I want you!" His voice throbbed with tamped-down desire. "But it is not safe. Who knows whether those two might be around?"

Priscilla nodded, struggling to control her thudding heart and rapidly pumping lungs. His hand came up and curved around her cheek; his thumb softly traced her lips. Priscilla's eyelids fluttered closed, and she drew a breath of such eager, innocent passion that it shook his control. He wanted nothing more than to pull her back to him, to kiss and caress her until those breathy little pants and hungry moans were tumbling from her lips.

He wished very much that they were somewhere else, somewhere safe and secure, where he could take his time, could kiss and caress and tease. He wanted to peel her clothes from her and gaze upon the creamy flesh beneath. He wanted to see her breasts, to touch them, to learn the exact tint of her nipples, to turn them into hard, pebbled points. Just thinking about it made him hot and hard. But he also knew that he would be a fool to expose her to the dangerous possibility that his attackers might return to this place and find them. Worse than a fool.

With a sigh, he forced himself to stand up, pulling her

with him. "We have to go." His voice was hoarse and short from the effort it took to restrain his passions.

They started back through the woods, with Priscilla, more familiar with the area, leading the way. John, walking along behind her, found his eyes drawn more to the movement of her hips beneath her dress than to their surroundings. He drew his eyes away from her time and again, forcing himself to be more alert to who or what might be in the woods around them, but his mind stubbornly returned to the thought of what she would look like naked. It was a difficult journey home.

Things did not improve much when they got there, for they walked in to find Priscilla's father and Miss Pennybaker taking tea with three men. Priscilla groaned under her breath when she saw them in the drawing room.

"Priscilla!" Miss Pennybaker cried, jumping to her feet. Her thin face was flushed and smiling. "Look who has come to tea."

"Hello, Reverend. Dr. Hightower." Priscilla greeted her father's two cronies, older men who regularly visited her father to discuss learned matters. But today there was a gray-haired gentleman with them, a large man with an upright carriage and piercing gray eyes whom Priscilla did not know.

"And this is General Hazelton," Miss Pennybaker went on enthusiastically. "He is a friend of the doctor's."

The general rose, as did the other men.

"I am so pleased to meet you, Miss Hamilton. I have been hearing wonderful things about you," the general said, turning to look at Miss Pennybaker, who blushed and glanced down modestly. "Miss Pennybaker has been telling me how accomplished you are. I am sure that is no small praise, for Miss Pennybaker is a woman of rare intelligence and taste."

Priscilla's eyes widened at that statement, but she managed to keep her mouth shut. Miss P. was a kind and well-meaning woman, and Priscilla was quite fond of her. But she would never have thought of describing the older woman's taste and intelligence in such glowing terms.

"Stop, please," Miss Pennybaker said coyly, letting loose a girlish giggle. "You will turn my head."

Miss Pennybaker and General Hazelton smiled at each other for a long moment, while everyone else looked on in varying degrees of amazement. Then the general turned back to Priscilla. Automatically Priscilla held out her hand to him, forgetting that she had not been able to wipe off all the grime and that her fingernails were still black with dirt. Seeing her hand as she held it out, however, she let out a little yelp at the sight of it and snatched it back, clasping it with her other hand behind her back.

"I'm sorry. I am afraid I'm not in fit shape to receive company right now. I was…ah, mm…working in the, ah, garden, you see. I must wash up."

She backed away hastily, and the general, giving her an odd glance, turned toward John, extending his hand to him and saying, "Terence Hazelton, Her Majesty's army, retired."

"John Wolfe," John answered, holding out his own hand, which was in much the same condition as Priscilla's. "I was helping Miss Hamilton."

"I see." The general's steely gaze went from one of them to the other; he was obviously forming his own opinion about the situation. Priscilla was furious to feel herself blushing, just as if she had done something wrong. Which she hadn't, she reminded herself. They had done nothing but kiss, and surely that was not a sin.

"Mr. Wolfe is a member of the family," Miss Pennybaker went on, to fill the awkward moment.

"Really?" Dr. Hightower turned toward Priscilla's father in surprise.

"Not *immediate* family," Florian corrected quickly. "A distant cousin from the United States."

"Ah," the vicar commented, understanding dawning on his face. Being from America explained all sorts of peculiar behavior, in his estimation. "I see."

"The United States, eh?" the general commented, beginning to smile. "I visited there once."

"Indeed?"

"Baltimore," he explained further. "Are you familiar with it?"

"No, I am afraid I don't live there," John returned quickly.

"Where are you from, then?" the doctor asked curiously. "I have been trying to place the accent. I'm usually good at that sort of thing, you see. Definitely American, but I think not from the South."

"No. I am not Southern." John strove to think of someplace he could remember anything about.

"I thought not." Dr. Hightower looked pleased with himself. "Let me think…. No, don't tell me, I'll get it in a minute. No swallowing your *R*s, so that lets Boston out." He closed his eyes in thought. "My guess would be New York or its environs."

"Quite right." John smiled, desperately hoping that the man would not start asking questions about the city. He couldn't think of anything he knew about the place.

The doctor beamed. "Told you I could guess it. Of course, I'm much better with British dialects. I can pinpoint a British speaker to within ten miles of where he was born."

"Remarkable," John responded lamely. "If you will excuse me, I must change."

"Of course, of course." The vicar smiled at him benignly. "We don't mean to interfere with you young people."

John left quickly for his room off the kitchen, and Priscilla seized the opportunity to start for the stairs. However, the vicar's fond voice caught her before she could get out of the room. "A finely setup young man, Priscilla," he commented cheerfully.

Priscilla turned back to him, pressing her lips together in irritation. Her father's friends were both kind and intelligent men, always trying to help people. But they had for some reason taken it upon themselves to be Priscilla's private cupids, and over the years they had tried to matchmake for her with a number of young men. They were not picky; any man of approximately the right age and with a decent family and sufficient intelligence was quickly maneuvered into meeting Priscilla. Priscilla had tried scores of times to get them to stop their well-meaning but misguided efforts, but she had finally given up and simply saw the young men that they proffered, then kindly, but firmly, sent them on their way.

"Yes, Reverend, he is. He is also related to me."

"Distantly, my dear, distantly. It means his family is good, which is something one can never be sure of with Americans, you know."

Priscilla sighed. "I suspect it was probably a more scandalous branch of the family that emigrated to the United States. Besides, I think it is a poor decision to marry within one's family, even when it's legal. I mean, look at the Hapsburgs."

"My dear, I wasn't suggesting that you marry the young man," the vicar protested. "I was merely saying that he is probably an agreeable companion for you. Of course, if something more were to develop...I wouldn't think you would need to worry about weak minds and Hapsburg chins. After all, that royal family intermarried far more often and more closely."

"True," the doctor agreed. "How many generations ago did his family emigrate?" When Priscilla merely gazed at him blankly, he turned toward her father. "Florian?"

"What? Heavens, it must have been a hundred years ago or so. I am not really sure of the relation. I think my grandfather was cousin to his great-grandfather, or something of that sort."

"You mean you haven't discussed his genealogy?" the general asked, looking disapproving. "How do you know he is really your relative? He could be taking advantage of your hospitality, you know. There's a sort of rascally look about his eyes, if you ask me."

"Well, no one did," Florian responded, looking disgruntled. "I didn't outline his family tree with him. Americans are not in the habit of that sort of thing. Not a bad way to be. A man's brains and abilities are more important than his family, don't you think?"

The general snorted and asked if he was a damned egalitarian, and the vicar jumped in to soothe the suddenly troubled waters of the conversation. Priscilla seized the opportunity to slip out of the room unnoticed and run up the stairs. Quickly she scrubbed the dirt off her hands and changed into a clean dress, then brushed out her hair and pinned it back into its usual tidy roll. She paused for a moment, looking at herself in the mirror. She had never been a woman who spent much time in front of mirrors, having always felt that there were more interesting things to do. She knew that she was not bad-looking, was even considered pretty by many men. Her figure was good, and her complexion was a creamy white. Her features were regular, and her gray eyes were large and dark-lashed. But her attractiveness, or lack of it, had never been her major concern. She had known that she was too smart and outspoken for most men, too poor for many others, and not breathtakingly beautiful enough to overcome such disadvantages. Suitors, she had found, were usually more trouble than they were worth in the long run.

But today she found herself lingering in front of the mirror, examining her reflection. Was her dress too plain? There was no decoration on it at all, not even a ribbon or ruffle. Was her coiffure too severe? It would flatter her more if her chestnut hair were fuller around her face. She wore it this way only because it took more time to do anything else to it.

Her hands went to her hair, starting to pull out the pins and start all over again, but she stopped herself. This was ridiculous. So what if she did not look as attractive as she might in front of John Wolfe? After all, there was no reason she should. She was not trying to get him to fall in love with her. It did not matter that he had kissed her passionately; he had no serious intentions toward her, no real feeling. He was obviously a very passionate man. She closed her eyes for a moment, re-membering the feel of his lips on hers, his arms around her. Anyway, she reminded herself, he had kissed her that way with her looking no better than she did now. She couldn't keep a little smile from curving her lips.

Then she shook herself sternly and started toward her door. She wanted to see if John had found anything after a further search of the traveling bag. She was not going to waste time primping.

Downstairs, she found him sitting at the kitchen table with a hot cup of tea in front of him, as well as a plate of tea cakes. He was talking with Mrs. Smithson while she bustled about, washing dishes and stirring various things in pots on the stove.

He stood up when Priscilla came quietly into the kitchen. She had managed to slip down the stairs and along the hall without being noticed by any of the people in the drawing room. Thank God the general had a loud voice.

She stopped, staring at John in his new clothes. If he had looked good before in Lord Chalcomb's old-fashioned, ill-fitting garments, he looked doubly hand-some now. The soft white shirt and brown trousers were perfectly fitted to his tall, wide-shouldered frame; there was none of the comical aspect that her brother's too-small garments or Lord Chalcomb's hopelessly out-of-date ones had given to him. He looked powerful and imposing.

For a moment Priscilla was tongue-tied, struck by his handsomeness. Then she cleared her throat and said, "I can see that the case was yours. Those clothes were obviously tailored just for you."

He nodded. "Yes. Not that it does us much good. I

practically took that bag apart, and I could find nothing that even hinted at who I am. The only thing the thieves left behind were a pair of cuff links, but they were plain, not even an initial on them. I may be dressed more comfortably, but I still know nothing about myself."

"That's not true," Priscilla said stoutly, crossing the kitchen to sit down at the table with him. "We know one thing—you must be a man of some substance. Those clothes are personally tailored and made of expensive materials. You must be well-to-do to dress like that."

"A well-off American," he said, encapsulating his knowledge about himself. "I could be thousands of people."

"A well-off American traveling through this part of England," Priscilla reminded him. "There must be some reason for your being here. Someone who is expecting you farther down the road. They will begin to search, surely, when you do not show up."

"That is provided that I really am expected by someone." He frowned. "I think my best chance is to find those men."

"The ones who kidnapped you?" Priscilla's voice vaulted upward. "But why? We've spent all this time trying to avoid them."

"I had no desire to be bushwhacked by them," he corrected her. "I want to meet them again, but on my terms. I want to be the one on the offensive. I shall have the element of surprise, not they."

"But there are two of them! Even if you do surprise them, you are still likely to get hurt."

"I will separate them if I can. Besides, I am almost back to full strength now. If I am prepared for them, they will not be able to take me down again."

"Just what do you suggest doing?"

"Going to town. I shall walk around and ask questions. See if I can catch sight of one of them. Or if anyone else has seen them."

"What good will it do you if you do find them?"

He smiled thinly. "I will persuade them to tell me who hired them. Once we find that out, I shall have a much better idea of who I am."

Priscilla scowled. His words made sense, but she did not like the idea of his exposing himself to danger that way. He might think, with his masculine pride, that he could take care of any number of men, but Priscilla was not so sanguine. These were wicked men, and they might have other cronies.

"You're right," she said finally. "That is our best option. We shall go to town."

"We?" he repeated. "I think not. *I* am going alone."

Priscilla sighed. He was the most stubborn man. "And how are you going to know where to go or who to ask in a strange town? Why, you don't even know how to get there."

He grimaced, crossing his arms across his chest and looking stubborn. "I am hunting for two rogues, Priscilla. I can hardly take a lady along with me."

"You need help, and I should think it would not matter if it came from a woman or a man."

"I refuse to expose you to danger. Why is that so hard for you to understand?"

"It isn't difficult to understand. I simply refuse to accept your decision. I intend to help you."

"Why are you so stubborn?" He glared at her.

She glared back. "Why are you?"

He ground his teeth noisily, and Priscilla thought for a moment that he might explode into shouting. But he contented himself with bringing his fist down with a loud thud on the table and saying, "Damn! It's a wonder no one has ever strangled you before now. All right; come with me."

If the truth be known, he really wasn't as furious with her as he made out to be, as he knew he *should* be. He enjoyed her company; he liked to hear her laugh, to hear her quick, intelligent comments, to look over at her as they walked along. It had been fun having her with him today, and even though he knew he was probably a scoundrel to let her endanger herself this way, he actually looked forward to having her accompany him.

"I don't suppose that it would stop you, even if I said you could not come," he said wryly.

Priscilla smiled. "That's true."

She could see Mrs. Smithson, over at the stove, shaking her head despairingly as she stirred one of the pots. Priscilla knew quite well what she was thinking—and would say, given the first opportunity:

"Why are you so terrible independent-acting? You'll never get yourself a husband that way, Miss Priscilla."

Her retort, always, was that she neither needed nor wanted a husband. But she found herself looking now at the man sitting at the table with her and wondering if that was still true. What if the husband was a man like John Wolfe? What if there was an aura of mystery and danger that clung to him? What if there was a wonderful zest to arguing with him—and the man didn't hold a grudge forever because you'd won? What if his kisses stirred her as John's did, and his merest touch made her tremble?

She was shocked at the course her thoughts were taking. She was *not* interested in marrying John Wolfe. There was no reason to change her vow not to marry just because this man had a charm and looks that other men had not. It was ridiculous even to be thinking about the subject. She was certain that he would not have any interest in marrying her, either. What *he* was interested in was an altogether different thing. Of course, she realized, if she was to be honest with herself, she was interested in that other thing, also. It was desire that drew her to John, not love or a yearning for marriage. Why, she barely knew the man. All it *could* be was pure animalistic passion. She was a freethinking woman, and she was willing to admit that women felt desire, too, without necessarily feeling any love or willingness to marry. It was a position she had argued many times. However, she had never really thought about such a thing happening to her.

She gave him a quick sideways glance, her heart speeding up inside her chest. His eyes met hers, and something changed subtly in his face. Priscilla looked away. She had the awful feeling that he knew what she was thinking. She sneaked another peek at him. He was still watching her, his eyes warm and searching. It was difficult this time to look away. She was certain now that his mind was on the same track as hers.

It was a relief to hear the visitors' voices in the hall as they left the drawing room. Priscilla jumped to her feet. "I—I should say goodbye to the vicar."

John rose more slowly, following her as she walked out of the kitchen and down the hallway to the front door. The older men turned to Priscilla with a smile, taking her hand as they said their farewells. The vicar patted her shoulder in an avuncular way. They nodded at John and said polite things about meeting him. Then they were gone, and Miss Pennybaker, giving them a final wave and smile, closed the door.

"Well!" Florian said, releasing a big sigh of relief. "Thank God that's over."

Priscilla and Miss Pennybaker looked at him in surprise. "I thought you liked the vicar's visits," Priscilla said mildly.

"I do. Nothing wrong with Whiting, except a liking for dreadfully sentimental poetry. But why did Hightower have to bring that army fellow?"

"General Hazelton?" Miss Pennybaker stared at him. "Why, he seemed like a fine man to me."

"What was wrong with the general, Father?" Priscilla asked, linking her arm through his and starting back with him toward the drawing room.

"Don't like military men, never have."

"But you approved of Gid getting a commission in the army."

He waved that idea aside. "Couldn't stop him. Nothing else to do there. The boy was dead set on it. I hope he will come to his senses one of these days. But that man chose to be military all his life."

"I see," Priscilla agreed gravely. "That would make a difference."

"He is not a scientist," Florian went on.

"He was quite intelligent, though," Miss Pennybaker protested mildly. "He sounded most knowledgeable regarding the habits of insects. You remember, when Dr. Hightower was discussing his butterfly collection."

"Yes," Florian agreed, although it seemed to Priscilla that he did so with some reluctance. "I suppose that is what Hightower sees in him. I personally was never that fond of insects."

"He was quite attentive to you, Miss P.," Priscilla pointed out, then smiled at the way her former governess fell into rosy blushes at her words.

Florian cast a look of irritation at Miss Pennybaker. "Made a cake of himself, is what."

Priscilla turned a speculative gaze upon her father. He sounded, well, almost jealous. She had long felt that her governess held an unrequited love for Florian, but he hardly seemed to notice her, except as someone who was willing to copy down his notes. Could it be that the general's fulsome compliments had awakened him to some feelings for Miss P.?

"Too lavish with his compliments, eh?" John asked, barely suppressing a quiver of amusement in his voice. Priscilla glanced over at him and saw that his eyes were dancing. He grinned at her, and Priscilla could not help but return it. "I hate it when a fellow is like that."

"Absolutely," Florian replied, looking pleased at their guest's understanding. "Never can trust a man when he's too flowery."

Priscilla chuckled. "And why is that, Papa? Because he gets all the ladies?"

Florian shot her a sour look. "It shows a lack of regard for the truth."

"Even when the compliments are true? I am sure he was speaking no falsehood when he complimented Miss P." She smiled at the older woman.

"Now, Priscilla, you don't know that," Miss Pennybaker told her modestly. "I am sure he was merely being polite." But Miss Pennybaker could not hide the pleased sparkle in her eye, or the glow that illuminated her face.

Priscilla pulled at her father's arm, slowing him down so that Miss Pennybaker and John walked on ahead of them. Going up on tiptoe, she whispered in his ear, "Looks like General Hazelton has stolen a march on you, Papa. You had better get started, or you will lose her altogether. You know, there's something very attractive about a man in uniform."

Florian gaped at her. "What in the world are you talking about?"

"It is obvious to me that you need help. Or else the general's going to sweep Miss P. away, right out from under your nose."

"Don't be absurd," Florian told her gruffly.

"Now, Papa…"

"I am going to my study. I have a great deal of work left to do. Their visit ruined the whole afternoon." He pulled away and stalked off down the hall to his study.

Miss Pennybaker and John turned and watched him. Miss Pennybaker asked puzzledly, "Now, what is the matter with Mr. Hamilton? You know, he did not seem himself today."

A smile curved Priscilla's mouth. "Perhaps he was not, Miss P. And that just might be a good thing."

She smiled and turned away, leaving Miss Pennybaker staring after her in confusion.

CHAPTER NINE

PRISCILLA AND JOHN KEPT UP A LIGHT CHATTER as they walked into the village two days later, trying to look as if they were doing nothing more than taking a stroll. After a few minutes of polite nothings, Priscilla was running out of things to say. Finally, she inquired mundanely how he had slept the night before.

"Well," he replied with a wry smile. "But none too long. I started reading one of your books."

"What?" Priscilla turned her head sharply. Her heart sped up. *How had he found out about her books?*

He gave her an odd look. "I said, I read a book last night. I picked it up in your library. I presumed it belonged to you, since it wasn't scholarly."

"Oh." Priscilla relaxed in relief. "I see. Yes, it probably did belong to me. What was it? How did it disturb your night?"

"It was an adventure story. *The Lost City of Lankoon.* Written by a man named Pruett, I believe. Quite an exciting yarn."

"Really? You liked it?" Priscilla smiled. Elliot Pruett was her pen name. He really *had* read one of her books, although, thank goodness, he obviously had no idea that she had written it.

He nodded. "Had trouble putting it down. That's why I didn't go to sleep till late." He did not mention that thoughts of their kisses the day before had kept him up, too; it was those thoughts that had driven him into the library, searching for something to take his mind off the erotic visions in his mind's eye.

"That's wonderful!" Priscilla beamed. "I mean, not wonderful that you didn't get enough sleep, but I am glad that you enjoyed the book."

"Got a bit wrong about Singapore, but—" he shrugged "—that doesn't matter. It didn't interfere with the story."

"What was wrong?" Priscilla bristled.

"Nothing much." He gave her a slightly puzzled look. "Misplaced the Market a little, that's all."

Priscilla started to protest the slight on her book. She had, after all, gotten all her information about Singapore from a very informative travel book written by the wife of a British sea captain. Then she realized how foolish she would sound to him. On the heels of that came another realization.

She came to a dead halt, staring at John. "Wait."

He turned and looked at her questioningly.

"Don't you see it? How did you know that the book was wrong?"

"Because I—" He came to a lame halt. "I don't know. I just knew. I—I can picture the city. The Market. Do you think I have been there?"

"How else would you know?" Priscilla's voice rose in excitement.

"You're right. I had not thought about it. How else could I be so certain?" They looked at each other for a long moment. "Well," he said finally, "then I am an American—with nice clothes—who is in England and who has once visited Singapore."

"A world traveler, obviously."

They began to walk again, quiet and thoughtful. After a few moments Priscilla said, "Perhaps you are a merchant who deals in goods from the Orient."

"Or a sea captain."

"Or simply someone of wealth who likes to travel."

"Perhaps I am an adventurer, like Mr. Pruett's Captain Monroe, who goes around the world rescuing orphans and saving young ladies while recovering vast treasures."

Priscilla chuckled. "Now why didn't I think of that? I am sure it must be so."

John assumed a wounded air. "Do you think I don't fit the mold?"

"Indeed, since I have never met a man like Captain Monroe, I am not sure what the 'mold' is."

"I would say 'uncommonly brave, unusually handsome and noble to a fault' would do."

"A perfect picture of you," Priscilla agreed with mock gravity. She hesitated briefly, then said, "You know, I think you spoke an Oriental name when you were in your fever."

He looked at her keenly. "What else did I say?"

Priscilla could not keep a blush from touching her cheeks. She was not about to tell him of the way he had fondled her—or the way she had shamelessly responded to it. "I—I'm not sure. It was garbled."

Something like relief flashed across his face. Priscilla wondered if he, too, had some memory of their kiss. Had he wondered whether it had been real or just a delirium-induced dream?

They walked along, neither of them speaking, until they came to the first straggling outskirts of the village of Elverton. Their first stop was the vicarage, a small gray stone house beside an old church built of the same material. The vicar's wife, a small, white-haired, tidy woman, greeted Priscilla with a smile and a quick glance of curiosity toward John.

"My dear, my dear, come in. I am so happy to see you." She took Priscilla's shoulders in her hand and leaned in for a quick peck on the cheek, then turned toward John. "And you must be Priscilla's cousin from America. Cyril told me all about meeting you the other day. Shame on you, Pris, for not telling me about him."

"I, ah… It must have slipped my mind," Priscilla replied lamely.

Mrs. Whiting gave her an admonishing look.

"Actually," John stuck in quickly, "you must not blame Cousin Priscilla. It was my fault. I was not presentable to meet anyone. I had nothing to wear, save the clothes on my back. The bags I was carrying were stolen."

Priscilla glanced at him, startled. She had not expected him to reveal the truth to the vicar's wife. She was reassured, however, by his next words.

"Ruffians, you see, waylaid me on the road here and stole my possessions. I had to wait until my trunk arrived by train."

Mrs. Whiting was quick with her sympathy, Priscilla's transgression forgotten at the prospect of more exciting gossip. "You poor thing," she said, leading them into the drawing room and ringing for tea. "You must tell me all about it. What happened?"

"They jumped on me from behind and struck me on the head. Took me completely by surprise. By the time

I came to, I was alone, my bags gone, and I had a large lump on the back of my head."

The vicar's wife tsk-tsked and opined that the world was coming to a sad state when a man was not even safe traveling the roads.

"I regret losing my bags," John went on sadly. "You see, they held pictures of my parents. I was bringing them to show my British cousins. They were of great sentimental value to me."

Mrs. Whiting drew in a quick breath. "How awful for you!"

"I wish I could find the men. I don't know where they went. Perhaps they came here to Elverton."

Mrs. Whiting looked thoughtful. "I haven't heard of any strangers in the area. Of course, men of that sort would not likely be ones I would see or hear about." She stopped, a look of realization dawning on her face, and turned to look at Priscilla accusingly. "So that was why you were here asking me all those questions about the most recent gossip! Honestly, Pris, why didn't you just tell me what you wanted?"

"I, well, I was afraid it would get out that—that Cousin John was here, and I, well, we didn't want anyone to pay calls. You see, he had no clothes fit for company, and—"

"What nonsense! As if I would tell anyone."

Mrs. Whiting looked indignant. Priscilla, knowing how eagerly the woman chatted to everyone about everything she heard, had to press her lips together to hide a smile.

"I am sure Cousin Priscilla thought no such thing," John assured the older woman smoothly. "She was quite worried, you see, about my safety. She feared the men might return to finish me off, to keep me from telling the authorities about them."

"Then you saw their faces!" Mrs. Whiting exclaimed. "That will make it much easier to locate them. What did they look like?"

"I am afraid I did not get the best look at them, actually. It was at night." He described both the short and the tall man.

Mrs. Whiting listened intently, but shook her head. "No…I have not seen them or heard anything about them, unfortunately. But I shall ask around for you. People do tend to tell me things, you know. Though, naturally, I would never tell anyone's secrets." She cast a wounded glance at Priscilla again.

"I am sure you would not," John agreed soothingly.

Priscilla squirmed in her seat. "Mrs. Whiting, I assure you, I did not mean that I thought you would reveal a secret. I simply thought that it was safer if no one knew about Cousin John…just in case something accidentally slipped out or…or someone overheard us." She smiled, pleased that she had come up with a reasonable excuse. "A servant, perhaps, or…or someone visiting Reverend Whiting. Someone without your discretion."

The older woman nodded sagely. "Very wise, I'm sure, my dear. One can never be too careful. That reminds me. I shall ask Cook if she's heard of anyone new in town. The servants have a tremendous grapevine of information."

When, a few moments later, her cook entered the room with a tray of tea, the vicar's wife, cheerfully disregarding her earlier promise not to tell anyone, related John's story, ending it by asking if she'd heard of either of the men.

The cook, a woman as dour and large as the vicar's wife was small and cheerful, looked at John and Priscilla glumly. "I'm sure as I don't know about such ruffians," she told them, folding her arms across her chest and giving them a stony gaze, as though she had been accused of being in cahoots with the men who had attacked John. "Where the likes of them 'd be, though, would be down by the river. Bad lot there. Taverns and such, where honest folk like me don't go. Inns, too, that cater to the lower sort."

"There. I knew Cook would have some knowledge," Mrs. Whiting said smugly as the other woman lumbered out of the room. "I am sure she is right. That is where one would find them. Not, of course, that it's the sort of place where you would go."

"No. Of course not," Priscilla agreed, and glanced at John, seeing in the twinkle in his eyes that he was as firmly resolved to go there as she was.

They drank a cup of tea and ate a few cookies, making their escape from Mrs. Whiting as soon as they could do so.

"Now, where is this river?" John asked as they turned right and walked alongside the churchyard to the quiet cross street in front of it.

"This way," Priscilla told him. "Across the road to Exeter. The rest of Elverton is set between it and the Bovey. That's the river the cook was speaking of."

"The road to Exeter?"

"Yes. It's the main thoroughfare through town. Just ahead of us." She pointed in front of them to a quiet avenue, down which a single cart was trundling along.

John's eyebrows rose. "Not exactly a thriving metropolis."

"No. That is why it should be easy to find out if the men we are seeking have been here. Even by the river, a stranger will stick out."

"Is it really the den of iniquity that the cook described?"

"I'm not sure." A faint blush stained Priscilla's cheeks. "I have never been there. It's, well…it is not the sort of place a woman can go alone."

"I see." He looked at her speculatively.

"No," Priscilla responded flatly, catching the look in his eyes. "I am not going to let you leave me behind, just when we are getting to the adventure part."

He grimaced. "It sounds as if it could be dangerous. You had better stay at the apothecary's while I go to the river area." A visit to the apothecary to buy supplies for Florian was their purported reason for the trip to town.

"Absolutely not!" Priscilla's eyes flashed. "I will be perfectly safe. After all, you will be with me."

"Priscilla…"

She stopped, hands on hips and glared at him. "John…"

They gazed at each other for a long moment, neither of them giving in.

"Oh, all right," John said at last, rolling his eyes. "I don't know how your father ever controlled you. You are the stubbornest woman I ever met."

"He didn't," Priscilla replied succinctly.

"I might have guessed," he muttered, falling in with her as she started walking again.

"Let's go to the apothecary's first. I had better leave him Papa's order. Then we can go about the rest of our business and return later to pick up his chemicals."

They turned the corner onto the main avenue of Elverton. It was as empty and lazy as it had appeared from the side street. A one-horse trap was coming down the road at a snappy pace, and nearer to them, an elderly gentleman was shuffling along. Across the street, a woman stepped out of a shop.

Priscilla turned into the low doorway of the apothecary shop, and John followed her, ducking to avoid hitting his head. Inside, the store was dim and small, stuffed with goods and smelling acridly of chemicals. The man behind the high counter at the end of the store looked up and smiled at Priscilla, adjusting his round spectacles.

"Miss Hamilton! It's a pleasure to see you. How is your fine father this morning?"

"Quite well, thank you, Mr. Rhodes. However, he is in need of a few things."

The apothecary chuckled. "I have no doubt of that. What shall it be this time?"

He took the list Priscilla handed him and studied it, murmuring under his breath as he read it. Priscilla told him that she would be back later to pick up the goods, and the two of them chatted politely about the apothecary's new grandchild for a few minutes. As Priscilla and John turned to leave, the front door opened again, setting a small bell atop it to tinkling, and a well-dressed man entered the store.

He appeared to be in his middle years; his brown hair was streaked throughout with gray. He possessed regular features, neither handsome nor unattractive, but the warm smile that lit up his face when he saw Priscilla transformed his face into one that was particularly pleasing.

"Miss Hamilton."

"Mr. Rutherford." Priscilla's smile was equally warm as she greeted the man, and John felt a flash of irritation, even anger. Who was this man whom Priscilla greeted with such pleasure?

Priscilla introduced John to the man and repeated her fiction that he was visiting her family from America. Rutherford looked at him with interest.

"America, eh?" he asked pleasantly. "I confess I've always wanted to visit there. Too much a homebody, though, I suppose, to take the chance."

John smiled noncommittally. Priscilla plunged into the story John had told the vicar's wife about the attack by brigands, and Rutherford was appropriately shocked.

"I say…what a shame. I hope you did not lose too much."

"Mostly sentimental things," John replied shortly, a little surprised by his immediate antipathy toward the man. He found he did not want Rutherford's help. "Don't worry about it."

Priscilla gave John a cross look at his lack of tact and proceeded to describe John's attackers to the other man, who admitted that he had seen no one answering their descriptions in town.

"I wish I could be of more help," Rutherford added, his brow knotting in a frown.

"I am sure we'll be able to find the curs on our own." John gave Rutherford a smile that was more like a grimace and steered Priscilla out the front door with a firm hand on her arm. As they stepped outside into the street, Priscilla turned to him, exasperated.

"What was that all about?" she hissed. "You were practically rude to Mr. Rutherford."

"Didn't like the fellow." He continued walking quickly, not looking at her, practically pulling her along with him.

"Why ever not? He is a very nice gentleman."

John made a disagreeable noise in his throat. "Looks can be deceiving."

"Are you daft? You do not even know the man." Priscilla came to a dead stop, jerking her arm out of his grasp. "Would you stop? I feel like a cow you're pulling to market."

He came to a halt and turned to her. "The way he looked at you was entirely too warm," he replied stiffly, thinking even as he said the words that he was making a fool of himself.

"Too warm?" Priscilla repeated, astonished. "You must still be suffering from the effects of the blows on your head. Mr. Rutherford is old enough to be my father. Besides, I think he's half in love with Lady Chalcomb."

"Oh." John found himself softening toward the other man.

"He has been a friend of our family's for years, ever since he moved here. He thinks of me as a…a niece."

"Oh." John felt even more foolish. "I…well…I am sorry if I was mistaken about his intentions. It appeared to me— That is, I thought—"

"Yes?" Priscilla had to fight back a smile. It was obvious that John was jealous. That was the reason he had reacted so peculiarly to Mr. Rutherford's quite ordinary friendliness. Now he was floundering around, trying to find some other excuse for his odd behavior.

It was quite amusing; she was not about to try to help him out of his predicament. She found it made her feel warm and soft inside, too. He cared for her; otherwise he wouldn't be so upset or so quick to assume that Mr. Rutherford's attentions were anything other than the natural liking of an old family friend.

"Oh, forget I ever said anything about it," John ended abruptly, and started to turn away.

But just then a man's voice sounded behind them, "Miss Hamilton! How delightful to find you in town."

A quiver of dislike moved across Priscilla's face. Then she set her face and turned around. "Mr. Oliver."

John noticed that she did not make any similar claim that it was nice to find him there. If there had been any doubt that Priscilla did not like the man, the stony set of her features would have dispelled it.

There was nothing about the man to explain her immediate and apparent unfriendliness. He was a strikingly handsome man, with thick, dark hair and compelling features. His eyes were large and soulful, a deep brown in color, and his lids drooped a little, giving him a sensual look. He was dressed quite well, and the smile he turned on Priscilla was charming.

Calculated to charm, John thought, but having been so wrong about Mr. Rutherford made him a trifle reluctant to make a snap judgment about this man.

Priscilla did not offer her hand to the man, but he took it anyway, raising it to his lips as he bowed. His lips lingered a trifle too long on the back of her hand, and John took an involuntary step forward. The other man released her hand and stepped back.

Ignoring John, he continued, "It has been so long since we've had the pleasure of your company at

Ranleigh Court. I am sure young Alec has been pining away for you."

"Alec knows where I live, if he wishes to see me. He is always welcome at Evermere Cottage." Her voice laid the faintest emphasis on the word "he."

John glanced at her in surprise. Priscilla was being overtly rude to the man. He wondered curiously what connection this Mr. Oliver had to Alec and to Priscilla, and why she was so clearly antagonistic to him.

Mr. Oliver, however, showed no surprise at Priscilla's words. He merely smiled and said silkily, "My dear Miss Hamilton, you wound me. One would almost think that you disliked me."

"No doubt one would," Priscilla agreed. "Now, if you will excuse me, I have several errands to run." She turned and put her hand on John's arm, pressing his arm significantly. John took the hint and immediately began to walk away with her.

However, Mr. Oliver was not so easily left behind. He hurried to catch up with them, saying, "Ah, then I will walk with you."

"Thank you, that is not necessary. Mr. Wolfe will accompany me."

"Indeed." Oliver looked over curiously at John. "You haven't introduced me to your friend, Miss Hamilton."

Priscilla stopped and faced the other man. "No, I did not. I saw no reason to, as I doubt the two of you will ever meet again. And it is not necessary for you to accompany us, Mr. Oliver."

For a long moment, they faced each other; then John stepped in front of Priscilla, facing Oliver, almost toe-to-toe with him. "I believe the lady said she would like you to leave her alone."

Oliver looked faintly surprised and confused. "I say—are you American?"

"Yes."

"How odd." He glanced at Priscilla, who regarded him stonily. "Wherever did you find an American champion, Miss Hamilton?"

"He is visiting my father," Priscilla replied. "Although frankly, Mr. Oliver, I don't see that it is any of your business."

"I am merely concerned for your well-being, Miss Hamilton. I should hate to think that someone is taking advantage of you or your…generous father."

"There is no reason to think that either of us is being taken advantage of, Mr. Oliver. Now, pray, excuse us, won't you?"

She turned and swept away. John remained for a moment longer, staring the other man down. Oliver glanced at Priscilla's retreating back, then at John. He doffed his hat and made an extravagant bow before turning away and setting off in the opposite direction.

John turned and hurried to catch up with Priscilla.

"What was that all about?" he asked.

Priscilla glanced at him. Her cheeks were flaming with color, and her eyes were bright. "That man makes me so furious!"

"I could see that. Why? Did he do something to you? Say something?"

"He's a low, filthy…" Priscilla stopped and drew a long breath. "He is the Duchess's paramour."

John's eyebrows vaulted upward.

"It's horrible. Poor Alec is utterly humiliated by the situation. His mother took up with Mr. Oliver after the

Duke died. The poor man was barely cold in his grave when Benjamin Oliver moved into Ranleigh Court."

"That blatantly?"

"She *claims* he is a dancing teacher. A tutor for Alec in the art of making one's way in polite society. But everyone knows that it is a polite fiction. Alec takes no sort of lessons from him. Why, Alec is barely civil to the man."

"I see."

"As if that were not bad enough, Mr. Oliver is not even faithful to her. He has made advances to Lady Chalcomb, and to me." Her mouth tightened at the thought. "He is disgusting. I could not believe it at first. It seemed beyond belief that he would dare to do so right there at Ranleigh Court—at one of Bianca's own parties!"

John's face darkened ominously. "Did he hurt you? Lay a hand on you?"

"He tried to kiss me. We were dancing—since then, I have never made that mistake, I can assure you—and suddenly he whisked me into an alcove and took me in his arms. I was so stunned, I didn't say anything. I couldn't even think. Before I knew it, he was kissing me!"

John stopped, his hands knotting into fists. "I shall go back and find that blackguard."

"What?" Priscilla looked at him, startled out of her unpleasant memories. "No, John. For pity's sake, do not start a brawl in the middle of the street. It was nothing, and it is long since over. I was able to take care of him, I assure you. I was not raised with two rowdy boys for nothing. I yanked his hair so hard he let out a yelp, and then I hit him in the stomach. Gid says I have a fair right, you know."

John let out a laugh, his body relaxing. "I should have known you got your own back. What did the fellow do?"

"Let go of me, of course. I let him know in no uncertain terms that I was not interested in being pawed by him. He hasn't tried anything like that again. But the man is a nuisance. He is always trying to charm me—as if I would have anything to do with him. But that does not stop him coming to call, or joining Alec or the duchess and me when I visit Ranleigh Court. I have almost given up going there, simply so I won't have to see him, and I have Penny tell him I'm unavailable whenever he comes to call. However, he is unbelievably persistent. Apparently he cannot believe that I am really not interested in him. Many women seem to find him attractive."

John smiled at her, aware that he was inordinately pleased that Priscilla was not one of those women. "Are you sure you don't want me to hunt him down? I guarantee he won't bother you again."

Priscilla smiled back at him. It seemed bizarre that a man's mere smile could affect her the way John's did. "No," she assured him, shaking her head. "Let him be. What we need to do right now is to find those two men."

It took a moment for it to register on him who she meant. "Oh. Them." He sighed. He rather disliked giving up the idea of finding Benjamin Oliver and setting him straight on his behavior around Priscilla. "All right. Let's go. Which way?"

"Frankly, we have been walking away from the river. I let Mr. Oliver get me off course."

They turned and retraced their steps to where they had encountered Oliver, then crossed the street and continued down a slight slope. As they walked, the buildings around them grew increasingly smaller and more dilapidated. The street narrowed, and there was a distinct smell of fish and other, more unsavory, things.

Finally they reached the last street before the river, unimaginatively named Water Street. They looked around. It was not a pleasant prospect. Upriver lay the mill, and down the street stood several dark warehouses. On the corner was an inn and beyond that, a tavern. A few men loitered about on the street, staring at them with a mixture of curiosity and defensiveness.

Priscilla swallowed. She was glad it was broad daylight; this place would be frightening at night. It was easy to understand why she had never been in this part of town; it was obviously not a place where ladies spent their time, even in company.

"Where shall we start?" she began, putting a good face on it.

Her companion looked dubious. "Nothing looks very hopeful." He glanced at the inn, then back at her. "I suppose I would try the inn first, but I am sure it is not the sort of place where you should go. Why don't we go back to Mrs. Whiting's, and you—"

"No," she replied firmly. "You are not going to leave me out of this." The area might make her uneasy, but she wasn't about to abandon their quest because of that. Nor was she willing to be thrust back into the parlor to mind her knitting like a good little woman while John did all the work—and had all the fun.

He glared at her, irritation written plainly on his face, and Priscilla crossed her arms and stared back at him. He sighed. "All right. Let's try the inn first."

When they stepped inside the inn, every eye in the place turned to look at them. The room fell silent. Priscilla swallowed and glanced around. It was a small room, dim despite the time of day. Priscilla suspected that this condition was because the windows were as grimy as the floor. Cigar smoke hung in the air, mingling with the odors of sweat and ale to create a foul miasma. It was all Priscilla could do not to pull out her handkerchief and cover her nose with it.

She glanced at John. She noticed that his face showed none of the surprise or repugnance she felt. It made her wonder whether he was used to such places, or merely more skilled at hiding his feelings. John took her arm and strolled across the room to the man behind the counter. The man watched them come, his arms folded across his chest, his face wary.

"Good day, sir," John began. "I am looking for a couple of men."

The man's only answer was a noncommittal grunt. John proceeded to describe the two men in a strong, clear voice that Priscilla was sure could be heard by every occupant of the room. The innkeeper listened, saying nothing, until John had finished his description.

"'N' wot'll ye be wantin' with 'em?" he asked finally.

"They've done some work for me in the past," John replied. He had guessed as soon as they came in that this was not the place to tell his story of kidnapping and robbery. Now he grinned knowingly. "A certain type of work, you understand. One that not everyone is capable of doing."

The man regarded John silently. "I ain't seen anyone like you're talkin' about." He shrugged. "But mebbe some'n like that'll come in 'ere one day. If ye want, I could give 'im your name."

"That would be very good." John smiled. "The name is John Wolfe. I can be found of an evening at the Sign of the Boar." He named a tavern he had seen closer to the center of town, one that he was sure was more respectable.

"I don't know as whether 'e'd go there."

"Well, if he does not, why don't I check back in with you tomorrow? Perhaps he will come in and you will have a chance to discuss it with him."

The man shrugged again. John pulled out a coin and flipped it to the man. The innkeeper deftly caught it in the air and pocketed it. With a nod, John guided Priscilla out the door.

"Whew!" Priscilla breathed a sigh of relief. "Do you think he will follow up on it? Did he believe you?"

"I have no idea. But I doubt that he wants to forgo the opportunity to make a little money. He will tell our friends, at least. They may be foolish enough to fall for it. But if his description of me is adequate, they will know it is a trap."

He walked down the street and stepped into the empty doorway of a warehouse, pulling Priscilla in with him. "Let's see if our bait brings any results."

"You think he will go find the men?" Priscilla's breath quickened in her throat, and she peered down the street at the door of the inn.

"It's possible. Worth waiting a little while to see, don't you think?"

Priscilla nodded, and they settled down in the shadow of the doorway to watch. They were rewarded a few minutes later when the door opened and the man they had spoken to stepped out. He looked up and down Water Street, as well as the side street; then, apparently satisfied, he struck off down the street in the opposite direction.

"How are we going to follow him?" Priscilla asked anxiously. "We stick out like a sore thumb in this area."

"I know. All we can do is give him a long lead and hope he doesn't look back too carefully."

John slipped out of the doorway, his hand in Priscilla's, and they walked swiftly after the distant figure of the innkeeper. They stayed far behind him, slipping into doorways now and then in the hope of staying hidden from his sight. The man turned up a side street, and John and Priscilla quickened their pace. When they reached the corner where he had turned, they stopped, and John peered cautiously around the corner of the building. He jerked back, looking amazed.

"What is it?" Priscilla asked. "Did you see the men we're after?"

"More than that. Look for yourself."

Priscilla edged closer to the corner of the building and looked around it. She could not suppress a gasp. The innkeeper was crossing the street, walking, more slowly now, toward a doorway where two men stood talking. One of the men was the short man who had come to the door looking for John. The man who was speaking to him forcefully, gesticulating for emphasis, was Benjamin Oliver.

Priscilla moved back and gazed at John. He nodded. "It's Oliver, isn't it? The Duchess's paramour?"

"Yes. But what on earth is he doing talking to your kidnapper? That *is* the fellow who was guarding you, isn't it?"

"Most definitely."

"Do you think that *he* was in on the plot to abduct you?"

John shrugged.

"What reason would Oliver have for wanting to kidnap you?"

"I have no idea."

"Do you think you know him? Can you imagine what a shock it must have been when he saw you?"

"He certainly hid it well. I never suspected that he recognized me."

"Nor did I. But then, he saw us before we saw him. Remember, he called to me, and then we turned and saw him? We don't know how long he was there. He could have had enough time to compose himself. And he was rather curious about you. He asked me to introduce you, and he wanted to know why you were here."

John nodded, frowning thoughtfully.

Priscilla peered around the corner of the building again. "Oliver is leaving now." She turned back to face John. "Shall we face your 'friend' now, or wait for the innkeeper to leave?"

John pulled himself back from wherever his thoughts had taken him. "Now. I don't want him to go back inside and join the other one. The innkeeper won't fight for him, I think." He paused, then said without much hope,

"I don't suppose I can persuade you to stay here and let me handle this."

Priscilla shook her head. John sighed and started off around the corner, with Priscilla right behind him.

CHAPTER TEN

JOHN MOVED ACROSS THE STREET ALMOST SILENTLY. Priscilla envied his quiet movement on even these old cobblestones. She had to walk on tiptoe to keep her heels from clacking on the stones. John, she thought, knew some rather unusual things.

Unfortunately, they had not yet reached the pair in the doorway when the kidnapper somehow sensed their presence. He looked up, eyes narrowed, then let out a noise when his eyes lit on John. Priscilla had expected the man to run away. To her surprise, he leaped forward, bellowing, "Will! Will!"

He startled Priscilla so much that she froze for an instant. John rushed forward to meet the man, and the innkeeper, after a hasty look around, took to his heels. John crashed into the kidnapper, but it was not enough to knock the sturdy fellow over. The short man wrapped his arm around John's neck, trying to choke him. John rammed an elbow into the other man's stomach. The man let go, staggering and trying to catch his breath. John gave him no opportunity to do so, but smashed his fist into the man's face. The man reeled backward, yelling "Will!" once again.

John started after him again, but at that moment, the door of the building flew open and the tall kidnapper ran out, launching himself at John. They fell in the street, rolling and punching. Priscilla stepped closer to them, wishing she had thought to bring her parasol. It would make a fairly decent weapon, although at the moment, given the way the two were thrashing around, she would not even be able to strike a blow for fear of hitting the wrong man.

The shorter kidnapper apparently thought the same thing, for he had moved closer to the struggling men, but was only watching them. Suddenly John was on top of the other man, his fist thudding hard into the man's face. The short man ran forward, clasping his hands together and raising them to bring his fists down with all his force against the back of John's head. Priscilla, shrieking, leaped onto the man's back. Wrapping one arm around the man's neck, she hung on tenaciously, and with her other hand she whacked her reticule down repeatedly on his head.

He let out a yowl and reached back for her, trying to pry her loose. His hand caught in her hair, and she shrieked again and boxed his ear. Clawing, hitting, kicking, they lumbered around in a clumsy, bizarre dance. Then a loud retort split the air, startling them all. The kidnapper froze, and Priscilla tumbled down from his back, ending up in an ignominious heap on the street. She looked over at John. He, too, was still, as was the man he was fighting.

Another man was standing over them, the end of a gun barrel pressed against the back of John's neck. "All right, now," the stranger said loudly. "You get up, mister. Slowly," he added, as John began to move.

Priscilla struggled to stand up, hampered by her petticoats and skirts. "Wait! You have the wrong man! It is these—"

The stranger favored her with a contemptuous glance. "You shut up there, missy. Less you want your fella's head taken clean off." At Priscilla's shocked expression, he chuckled. "Guess he wouldn't be such a handsome one then, would he? Now, the two of you get up and step back. I run a clean inn, and I won't have any rapscallions bothering my customers."

John stood up and stepped back, his mouth tight and his eyes flashing with anger. The tall man on the ground staggered dazedly to his feet, helped up by his shorter companion. The two of them hobbled off inside the building.

"You are letting them get away!" Priscilla exclaimed indignantly.

"Shut your trap, missy, or I'll do it for you."

"You don't understand," John told him. "It is those two men who are the villains. They kidnapped me and took all my money."

"Yes!" Priscilla agreed. "Call the constable, and you will see. I am Priscilla Hamilton. My father is Florian Hamilton. I am not whatever it is you think I am."

The man looked her over drolly. Priscilla was acutely aware of the fact that her skirts were twisted, her petticoats were showing and her hair had slipped out of its pins and was sticking out all over the place. Her hat had gotten completely knocked off and was dangling down her back, held only by the ribbons she had tied around her neck.

"Oh, yes, I can see you're a regular lady," the stranger agreed, chuckling. "Frankly, I don't care who you are, or this one, either. Those men are staying under my roof, and I won't have anyone bothering them. You understand? Now, get along, both of you."

"But—" Priscilla started again.

The man motioned threateningly with his gun. "Go on! I told you, I won't have anyone messing with my customers. Now get away with you. Go on."

Reluctantly John started away, taking Priscilla's hand and pulling her along with him. She shot one last fulminating look at the belligerent innkeeper and followed John.

"That man!" she fumed, twitching her skirt and petticoats back into place. "He let them get away. You would think he could at least listen to our story. He could have called the constable and let him straighten it out."

"I suspect he doesn't much want the police in his establishment." John rounded the corner and stopped. "Nor is he overly worried about who is in the right. All he wants is to protect his customers. No doubt that is very important to his business, given the nature of his clientele."

Priscilla made a disgruntled sound as she reached up and started untying the ribbons of her hat. They had been pulled into a knot as she fought, and she had a difficult time undoing them now. John's face softened into a smile as he gazed down at her, and he smoothed a piece of hair back from her face.

"What a fierce one you are."

Priscilla grimaced. "You needn't laugh at me. I know I look a perfect mess. Oh, why won't this stupid thing come undone?"

"I am not laughing at you. You don't look like a mess. You look…utterly adorable."

He bent, taking her chin between his fingers, and kissed her. Priscilla's knees went weak suddenly, and she leaned forward, holding on to his jacket for support. All thought of the two villains fled her mind, and she was aware of nothing but the feel of John's mouth moving on hers. She moaned softly, and his arms went around her, pressing her to him. His kiss deepened; his breath was hot against her cheek. Priscilla clung to him, kissing him back fiercely. Desire flooded her, leaving her weak and trembling.

"Oh, God." John raised his head, gazing down into her eyes. "I did not mean to do that. I don't know how— I must be mad to be doing this here. Now."

"Yes." Priscilla nodded dazedly. "I think that I have been a little mad ever since you came here."

"I want you so much." His voice was dark and husky with passion. "I have never wanted a woman like this. But you—"

He drew a long breath and stepped back, holding her at arm's length, as if he were setting her away from him. "We cannot do this."

"I know." With a sigh, Priscilla tore her gaze from his and began to smooth down her skirts and fuss with her hair—small, meaningless gestures to distract herself, to make her keep her eyes off him. But that was the only place she wanted to look.

John turned away, clearing his throat, and walked back to the corner. "The landlord is no longer there with his trusty gun," he commented. "But no doubt that means that those two have safely cleared out. Either that, or they have barricaded themselves inside. Either way, I have little chance of getting to speak with either of them now."

"We can get the constable and come back."

His face changed subtly, and he looked away. "I'm not sure that's a good idea."

Get 2 Books FREE!

GET 2 BOOKS

We'd like to send you two novels, from the Harlequin® Historical series, absolutely free. Accepting them puts you under no obligation to purchase any more books.

HOW TO GET YOUR
2 FREE BOOKS AND 2 FREE GIFTS

1. Return the reply card today, and we'll send you two books, from the Harlequin® Historical series, absolutely free! We'll even pay the postage!
2. Accepting free books places you under no obligation to buy anything, ever. The two books have combined cover prices of $11.98 in the U.S. and $13.98 in Canada, but they're yours to keep, free!
3. We hope that after receiving your free books you'll want to remain a subscriber, but the choice is yours— to continue or cancel, any time at all!

EXTRA BONUS
You'll also get two free mystery gifts!
(worth about $10)

"Why not?"

"If we show up with the constable, I can guarantee that they will be out the back door, if they haven't left already. No, I think we have no more hope of catching them today. Perhaps another day, if I come back disguised and loiter around the area."

"But the constable could be on the lookout for them." When he did not reply, Priscilla went on, "John? What is the matter? Why are you looking like that?"

"I…" He rubbed his chin, then sighed. "I'm not sure I will like what the constable finds out. What if I am involved with them somehow? I mean, what if I'm like that fellow Oliver? Some sort of scoundrel or cheat? Maybe I am just as wicked as they, and they are only after me because I stole something of theirs?"

"Oh, John, no! You could not be. Why do you even consider such a silly thing?"

"Because I know nothing about myself!" he blurted out. "I have no idea what I am really like. If I associated with people like these, what is to say I was not like them? It would stand to reason."

"It is just as obvious that you are their enemy," Priscilla pointed out. "If someone wicked hates you, it is more likely to mean that you are a good person than a bad one."

He gave her a sideways glance, a smile quirking the corners of his mouth. "You have an answer for everything, don't you?"

"Yes, I do. And don't you forget it." Priscilla smiled back, relieved to see the darkness gone from his face. She knew, with everything in her, that he could not be a bad person. Even if it turned out that he had done some things that were wrong, he could not be, deep inside, a bad person.

"Now," she went on briskly, taking his arm and starting down the street. "We know they are in Elverton. We can return another day and start looking for them all over. If we found them once, surely we can do it again. Why do you suppose they are remaining here?"

"They must want something from me pretty badly. Since they went through all my possessions, it must be something I hid somewhere, or it's something in my head."

"Something you know." Priscilla nodded. "That makes sense. Otherwise, why wouldn't they have killed you and been done with it? They do not seem the sort who would hesitate at murdering someone."

"I imagine you are right about that. The larger question, though, is what do they have to do with our Mr. Oliver? Why would a man who is cozily installed as a duchess's favorite be fooling around with these two?"

"I have no difficulty believing that *he* was involved with criminals in his past. I have always thought he was a snake."

"Still, it is a risk for him to associate with them. After all, the Duchess might find out."

"It might be even worse if she learned whatever it is you know." Priscilla brightened. "That's it! Oh, this explains it all! You know something very detrimental about Mr. Oliver, and you were coming here to inform the Duchess of it. Oliver knows, as do you, that she will toss him out when she finds out this thing, whatever it is, so he and his cronies try to stop you."

"Why not just kill me?"

"This close to where he lives? No, it would be a

scandal. Nobody would talk about anything else but the murder for months. Why, people still speculate on that killing thirty years ago in Lady's Woods. There would be an investigation, and it might easily turn up the fact that you were somehow connected to Oliver. He would be terrified of that. No, the best thing would be to hold you, to keep you from getting to the Duchess."

"I will grant you that. But he could not expect to hold me forever. What was he planning to do?"

Priscilla waved that objection away. "I don't know. Maybe he is going to leave soon anyway—rob her or cheat her out of some large amount of money. After that, it wouldn't matter what you told her. He just wants you out of the way until then."

He nodded. "It makes sense." He smiled. "You're quite good at this, did you know that?"

"People say I have a good imagination." She looked at him. She wanted, in that moment, to tell him about her writing. She wanted him to know that she had written the book he enjoyed last night. More than that, she wanted him to know her, to know everything about her. He would not be horrified, she thought; after all, he was worried that he had been a criminal of some sort. Her vocation of writing would probably seem quite innocuous compared to that. He did not seem to have the usual prejudices and entrenched beliefs.

Priscilla hesitated, on the verge of telling him. Then she pictured the shock that might appear on his face, the disbelief. He would never look at her in the same way again; she could not call back her words or make him forget them. If she was wrong, it would be disastrous. Anxiety clutched at her, paralyzing her. She swallowed and did not tell him.

Instead, she said, "The Duchess is having a party Saturday evening."

"Really?"

"Yes. She should, not because they are still in mourning, but they have always had a large party in the spring at Ranleigh Court, and she says she does not want to break tradition. Personally, I think it is more that she loves parties. I think it would be just the thing for you to accompany us."

"Indeed?"

"Yes. I would like to see what Mr. Oliver does when he sees you arrive. Maybe he will make a mistake and let out who you are. Or perhaps you could question him in private."

"Yes. Perhaps I could." He smiled. "An excellent idea, my dear Miss Hamilton. Excellent." He paused. "Now, if only I can remember how to dance."

"Don't worry." Priscilla smiled up at him, dimpling. "I shall teach you."

PRISCILLA SLEPT LATE THE NEXT MORNING. They had tried out John's dancing skills in the drawing room after dinner, with Miss Pennybaker providing the music on the piano. It turned out that John remembered quite well how to dance—so well, in fact, that they spent the rest of the evening dancing. He had even twirled Miss Pennybaker around the room while Priscilla played the piano. Miss Pennybaker's face had flushed pink with pleasure, and even Florian had been drawn from his study by the sounds of their gaiety and stayed to listen to the music, tapping his foot. By the time she finally went up the stairs to bed, Priscilla had been quite happily exhausted.

This morning, when she awoke, she found herself bursting with ideas, and she sat down immediately at her small desk and began to write. She did not even change out of her nightgown, simply threw a light dressing gown over it. She scribbled away without stopping for almost two hours, and when at last she set down the pen, her hand was cramped. She got up, smiling as she rubbed her aching hand. She had been worrying over this scene, between the hero and the woman he had saved from certain death for some time now. She had rewritten it twice, but she had never been satisfied with it. This morning, however, it had come to her, perfect and complete, and writing it down had been like opening up a dam and releasing the water. It was wonderful when it came like that.

She dressed and went downstairs, humming contentedly and wondering what she and John would do today. There was something very pleasant in the idea of having someone with whom to share her day—no, if she was honest, it was in having *John* with whom to share her day.

However, when she got downstairs, she did not find him in the sitting room or in her father's study, nor even in the kitchen, flirting shamelessly with Mrs. Smithson. When she asked Mrs. Smithson if she had seen him, the cook replied, "Why, yes, he headed off to the village this morning. Said he had some things he had to do and would be back as soon as he could."

The day suddenly seemed not nearly so bright. "Oh, he did, did he?"

"Yes. I told him to look out for those villains, for Miss P., she told me what ye said about what happened yesterday afternoon. But ye know that lad. All he said was, 'Now, Mrs. Smithson, me love, don't you know it's those villains that better look out for me!' He's a sight, that one."

"Mm… A sight. He certainly is."

"It's past noon, Miss Priscilla. Won't ye be wanting yer meal now?"

"What? No. Yes. I don't know. I am not feeling very hungry."

"Well, ye should eat anyway. Can't have you turning into skin and bones."

Priscilla sat down distractedly at the table while Mrs. Smithson bustled around, dishing up a plate of meat and potatoes and setting it down on the table in front of her. At first Priscilla felt only deflated by the fact that John had taken off for the village without her. Why had he denied her a part of the fun? Did he simply not want her with him?

But she knew that was not it. He was doubtless protecting her, keeping her out of danger. The more Priscilla thought about it, the more irritated she became. She'd thought he had reached the point where they were sharing things together equally, both danger and fun. She'd thought he had grown to understand that she did not want to be left out, did not want to be swaddled and smothered with patronizing concern. She wanted to participate, to take part in it all. *She wanted to be with him!*

Priscilla frowned at her thoughts. She sounded pitiful, even to herself, and she did not like that. She straightened up and began to eat, forcing down mouthfuls of meat and potatoes, even though they tasted like sawdust to her. She thought about what she ought to do. One thing she would not do, she was certain, was sit meekly here in the house. Nor was she going to chase after John into Elverton. But she could think of no way she could further their hunt for the two men. Finally she decided that it would be a good day to go visit Lady Chalcomb. It would not accomplish much, but she liked Anne, and at least she would not be sitting here, quietly tending to her housework and waiting for him to return. She could take her drawing pad and pencils and consult with Anne on the needlepoint pattern she had been planning for the new dining room chair cushions.

A short time later Priscilla tied her bonnet on her head and set out along the path toward Chalcomb Hall, pad and pencils in hand. It was not a long walk, and it was one she usually enjoyed, winding as it did through broad meadows. At this time of year everything was green, and flowers dotted the meadows. A few puffy white clouds floated in the sky, and a faint breeze kept the temperature pleasant, despite the sun. Today, however, Priscilla paid little attention to the scenery.

She hardly looked to left or right as she plowed along the path, her head down, a frown furrowing her brow. She considered whether she should be angry or freezingly polite when John returned—or pretend she had not even noticed he was not there. She reminded herself of all the reasons John Wolfe was nothing to her, and mentally cursed herself for being worried about what might happen to him. Priscilla was not used to feeling such a jumble of emotions concerning any man—or at least not since she was fourteen years old and had had a severe crush on the vicar's new assistant—and she did not like feeling this way now.

By the time she reached Chalcomb Hall, she was in a thoroughly foul mood, and Anne Chalcomb, upon seeing her face, jumped to her feet and came forward, saying with concern, "Priscilla! My dear child, what is the matter?"

"Nothing," Priscilla replied gruffly, and when Anne looked taken aback by her answer, she sighed and went on, "I'm sorry. I should not have come here in this mood. I apologize."

"Never mind that. What's wrong? Let me help." The other woman's kind face was creased with worry. "I have never seen you look so black."

"It's nothing important. I don't know what is wrong with me. It is just that…" She hesitated, looking at her friend, and suddenly the whole story came tumbling out of her mouth.

Anne listened, her brown eyes wide, as Priscilla described the manner in which "John Wolfe" had arrived at her home and the events since then, as well as all the things about the man that irritated her and the many times when he had been overbearing, foolish and stubborn.

When at last Priscilla wound down, Anne drew a deep breath and said, "Oh, my." She put a hand to her head. "I can hardly take it all in."

She turned, leading Priscilla to the sofa. "I think we had better sit down." They did so, and Anne turned so that she faced Priscilla, her hands folded in her lap. "Now, let me get this straight. John Wolfe is not your cousin, nor is his name John Wolfe."

Priscilla nodded. "Yes. And he is the most aggravating man I have ever met."

"Yet you are furious because he went to town without you."

"I know that sounds foolish…." Priscilla began unhappily.

"Only because it is," Anne put in, a twinkle in her eye. "But I think there's far more going on here than a man merely going into Elverton by himself." She gazed at Priscilla steadily for a long moment. "It seems to me that this young man, whoever he is, is terribly important to you."

"He is a complete stranger."

"That makes it even more obvious. A complete stranger, and you are worried, upset, angry…. Priscilla, dear, I think you have rather deep feelings for this man."

Priscilla grimaced. "That is impossible."

"Is it?"

"Of course. I barely know him. Why, it has been only a week or so since he banged at our door."

Anne smiled, lighting up her face, and Priscilla thought that she must have been considered a great beauty in her day. One could see it clearly in her now, when she smiled like that, even though crow's-feet nestled at the corners of her large, expressive eyes and lines bracketed the corners of her mobile mouth. Mrs. Smithson had once told Priscilla how amazed everyone had been when Lord Chalcomb brought home his lovely young wife. "A right beauty, she was," Mrs. Smithson had said with a sigh and a mournful shake of her head. "All wasted on that old roué."

"Is that the way it was with you?" Priscilla asked quietly. "Can it happen that way?"

Anne nodded, and Priscilla thought she caught a glimmer of tears in her friend's light brown eyes. "Yes. I saw him on horseback. The sun was on his hair, and his shirtsleeves were rolled up. His arms were browned by the sun. He looked so…so elemental, so powerful. He dazzled me." She turned aside, closing her eyes.

Priscilla felt painfully as if she were intruding. "I—I'm sorry."

"No." Anne blinked a little and turned back, forcing a smile onto her face. "You have nothing to be sorry for. I am foolish to be thinking of things that happened so long ago. It doesn't matter now. I only meant—well, that I know love can happen so fast it takes your breath away."

"He more often takes my breath away with fury," Priscilla replied lightly. She wasn't in love with John Wolfe. She *wasn't*.

Then she thought of the way she trembled when he laid his hand on her arm, and the way she seemed to melt when he kissed her, and she was no longer so sure. "But it is only…only lust!" she protested. "That is not the same as love. Is it?"

Her friend smiled wryly. "Sometimes it is hard to tell the difference."

"Then how do you know?" Priscilla wailed.

Anne's smile grew smaller and sadder. "I suppose… all you can do is wait and see. When it doesn't go away, you know it was love."

Priscilla was even more dissatisfied with this answer. "Anne! That's hardly very helpful now."

"I don't know what to say. I think…if your heart swells up as if it is about to burst whenever you see him, or if, when he enters the room, you can hardly sit still and you want to jump up and run away or else run straight to him, when you can't think of anything or anyone else, and you don't care a flip what happens so long as you can be with him, it is love."

"Even when you disagree about everything?"

Anne chuckled. "I'm not sure. I guess it depends on whether you find it exciting to disagree with him."

Priscilla stared at her. She had never thought about it before. But it was exciting to disagree with John. Feelings boiled up in her until she thought she would explode...and yet, oddly, she found herself looking forward to those arguments. She would never think of trying to avoid one.

Her thoughts shook her. She rose restlessly to her feet and crossed the room to the window. "This is nonsense," she declared stoutly. "I am *not* in love with that man. He is completely aggravating. I am merely curious about who he is and why he is here. That is all. And it was foolish of him to go out alone."

"You are out alone," Anne pointed out calmly.

Priscilla looked at her. She had not thought about that fact until this moment. It gave her a shiver of apprehension. How blithely she had walked over here, not looking about her or even thinking about the two men who had assaulted John.

"I was careful," she replied by way of an excuse. "And at least I am knowledgeable about the countryside."

"Yes, but you are not six feet tall, with great muscles in your arms, as he is," Anne pointed out.

"All right. I am being unreasonable, I admit it." She sighed and resumed her place on the sofa.

After that she settled down to talk to Anne about the purported reason for her visit: the design for new needlepoint covers on the cushions of their dining room chairs. Later, Anne invited her to stay for tea. The whole time, Priscilla did not think about John Wolfe, or his trip to the village of Elverton without her—at least, not more than once or twice.

It was late in the afternoon when she left Chalcomb Manor. This time she was more conscious of the landscape around her and the possibility of someone lurking in the bushes, but she reminded herself that the men had probably fled the area, and, if not, they would be in the village, not out here in the countryside. Still, the thought of them made her quicken her step.

She had just passed the huge oak tree that was almost halfway between the two houses when she heard a noise. She whipped around to see what had caused it, and a fist came down hard on her back, knocking her to the ground and forcing all the air from her lungs. Her pad and pencils went flying. As she struggled silently for breath, two men pounced on her and dragged her to her feet. Air was finally returning to her lungs, and she gulped it in. It felt as if she were breathing fire.

Before she could turn and look up to see her captors, one of them threw a large dark cape around her, covering her from head to foot, and in only seconds she was wound up in it and secured as tightly as if she had been bound, and she could see nothing but darkness. She began to scream and struggle, but by then it was too late. Her struggles only made it more stifling inside the heavy cloak, and when one of the men tossed her casually over his shoulder and began to stride off with her, jarring her with every movement, she felt sick and faint. Panic set in. She was helpless, and she was certain that some terrible fate awaited her. She began to writhe and struggle frantically. The tightly wrapped cloak felt as if it were smothering her. Redness swam before her eyes, and there was a buzzing in her ears, and in another instant she was aware of nothing at all.

WHEN SHE AWOKE SOME TIME LATER, Priscilla had no idea where she was or what time it was. For a moment she could not even recollect what had happened to her. Everything was dark and hot, and it was hard to breathe. Then she remembered what had happened, and she realized that she was still encircled by the dark, heavy garment. She was not, however, still being jounced along on someone's shoulder. Rather, she was lying on some hard surface.

She continued to lie still, gathering what little information she could. There was such a penetrating silence all around her that she soon became convinced that she was alone. No one could remain this quiet; there would bound to be a shuffle, the scrape of a heel, or a breath, a cough or a sigh.

Cautiously she sat up. Nothing happened. There were no shouts, and no one knocked her down again, further proof that she was alone. The cloak sagged open a little at the top, and a bit of light seeped in. Priscilla jiggled and shook, writhing until the cloak loosened further and she was able to bring her arms up and pull it open.

She shrugged it off and rose to her feet, looking around her. It was still quite dark, and she was sure she was inside a building. There was not even the twinkle of stars or the light of the moon. She extended her arms on either side of her and felt nothing, then squatted and touched the floor around her. It was hard-packed dirt. She was beginning to suspect that she was in the same cabin in which John had been locked up.

By standing still and looking long and carefully about

her, she was able to make out a few faint streaks of… not quite light, but paler darkness. These, she thought, must be cracks between the boards of the shed. There was in one wall a definite thin line of paleness that ran in a rectangular shape. Priscilla made her way carefully toward the traces of light, holding her hands out straight in front of her and sliding her steps across the floor. When at last her hands made contact with the wooden wall, she felt her way along to a corner and an intersecting wall. She continued, turning corners and groping her way along, until she was certain that she was in a very small room and that there were no windows.

She was trapped in the darkness, she realized, unable even to alleviate it by opening a window. Panic began to rise in her, clawing its way up her throat. Priscilla clamped her mouth shut on the scream that wanted to come out. She clenched her hands into tight fists and shoved the panic back down.

It was night, that was all, she told herself. There was nothing to fear here in this small hut. In the morning, the sunlight would come through the cracks, and she would be able to see better. She would simply have to wait. In the meantime, her family would have realized she was missing. John would know about it…if he had returned from the village. *What if they had gotten him, too?*

No. She forced herself to calm down. She refused to think that way. They could not have gotten John, or else there would have been no need to take her. No doubt they hoped to bargain with him, to get him back in exchange for her. They would have perceived that it was too dangerous for them to try to take John once they could not surprise him. That was doubtless why they had come after her.

John was free, and John would guess what had happened. He would search for her. Would he guess that she was at the same hut? Would he be able to find it?

It never occurred to her to wonder whether he would make the effort. She knew him better than that.

He would come for her. And that thought was what enabled her to remain calm in the small, dark hut as she waited for him.

CHAPTER ELEVEN

JOHN RETURNED FROM ELVERTON not long after Priscilla left for Lady Chalcomb's. He grimaced when Mrs. Smithson told him where Miss Hamilton had gone, but he was not surprised. He was sure that she was angry at him for having left her behind when he went into the village this morning. He could understand that, too, but there had been no way he could go into the rough taverns and housing that he had visited today with a lady on his arm. And it was in that sort of place that he would find his quarry—or news about them.

He had found news, too, which was pleasing, but it had been of little use. The two men had been staying in rooms above a dark and dirty tavern, where they had been serviced frequently by the women who worked the streets outside. He had found three girls who got over their disappointment that John was not a prospective client and were happy to talk about the two men from London who had hired them, one of whom had blacked Maisie's eye. John had heard more than he had wanted to about the pair's sexual habits, and he had also learned that the men had cleared out of their room this morning, taking their belongings with them.

They were gone, had no doubt hurried back to London when they saw him yesterday in the village, scared that he would turn them in to the constabulary.

Now he would never find out why they had seized him or who he was. He had turned back, failure grinding at his soul. He was not used to not getting what he wanted. He was sure of that. He hated failing, and he hated the thought of facing Priscilla and telling her that he had failed. It was not that he thought she would upbraid him for it—no, the scolding would doubtless be reserved for the fact that he had gone without taking her along on the adventure. It was simply his pride; he hated to have her think he was not capable of capturing two buffoonish ruffians. It was bad enough to be penniless and nameless, to be completely dependent on Priscilla's generosity, without showing that he was incompetent, as well.

Disgruntled, he had sat down to wait for Priscilla, sure that she would take her sweet time about the visit. She would want to make sure that he returned before she did; otherwise, there would be little point in going. At first he read, but as the afternoon wore on, he became less and less able to keep his mind on the story. By tea-time he had abandoned the book altogether, and when it grew dusk, he was pacing back and forth across the sitting room like a caged animal.

Florian looked up from the book he was perusing with a pained expression. "I say. Whatever are you doing?"

"Don't you realize that she has not come home? Don't you realize how late it is?" John turned on the man with a growl.

Florian blinked, taken aback by John's ferocity. "Why, yes, it is a quarter till seven. But what has that to do with—"

"She hasn't come back yet!"

"Who?"

"Who?" John repeated in amazement. "Your daughter, that's who. Priscilla! She has been gone since early this afternoon, and she has not returned yet."

"There is nothing unusual in that." Florian waved away the problem. "You know how it is. You are going somewhere. Then you sit down for a spell, and pretty soon you are thinking about something, and before you know it, several hours have passed."

John gazed at him blankly. "No. I don't know how that it is."

"Oh." Florian looked surprised. "Well, perhaps you aren't like that. I am. Priscilla is. She likes to daydream, think up stories, you know. She will be back before you know it. Is there something you want her to do?"

"No. But a young girl out like that for hours…there's no telling what might happen to her."

"I shouldn't think anything would happen to her." Florian's brow wrinkled with thought. "Pris is quite careful, you know. Never knew her to break a bone or anything. That was Gid. He was a daredevil, forever coming home with bruises and broken bones and all."

"Other things can happen to a woman by herself." John grated the words out through clenched teeth.

Florian looked at him in amazement. "Here? In Elverton? I wouldn't think so. It is different here, you see."

"Different from what? The rest of the world? Have you no crime here? No assault? No—"

"My dear fellow!" Florian turned pale. "You cannot be suggesting that someone would…would… No. It's unthinkable. Everyone knows Priscilla. She is very well liked."

John groaned at the older man's naiveté. "Priscilla is a very attractive young woman. There is always the possibility of someone passing through. I did. Those men who kidnapped me did." He stopped, his stomach turning to ice. "Those men…"

His increasing fear had been only a general one before, the idea that something must have happened to keep Priscilla so late. But as he mentioned his kidnappers, his fear coalesced into a very real, very possible, form. The men had left their inn. But that did not necessarily mean that they had left the area. Perhaps they had moved into the woods, even taken up residence in the very shack where they had put him. One of them had seen him and Priscilla together yesterday in the village. What if they were not simply cowards who had run when they knew he had discovered them? What if they had decided to hide and catch Priscilla alone, then hold her to force him to give himself up to them?

"What are you talking about?" Florian asked, his brow now furrowed with worry. "Do you really think that Priscilla is in danger?"

"Yes. Yes, I really think so." He turned to the older man. "I am going to look for her."

"I will come with you."

"No. Just get me a lantern. You stay here in case Priscilla should come home. If she does, make sure she stays put—tie her up, if you have to."

Florian goggled at him. "I shouldn't think there would be any need for force. Priscilla is eminently reasonable."

John grimaced. "I have no time to discuss that now. If anyone shows up with a message for me, say I went to town today and have not gotten back yet. Don't let anyone know I am out looking for Priscilla."

"But I don't understand…. I would think the best thing would be to enlist all the help we can."

"No. Not yet. If I can't find her, we will get out a search party and comb the woods. But I have a fair idea where she is, if *they* have taken her."

"Who! If *who* have taken her?" Florian's voice rose in frustration. "Good Gad, man, you are talking in riddles. What the devil is going on?"

"I'm not sure. I will explain when I get back. Just do as I asked you. Please?"

"If you really think it's so important."

"It is. I promise you. It could mean your daughter's safety."

Florian nodded. "All right, then. I will do as you say. Take a message, say you are in town. Keep Priscilla here if she returns."

"Right."

"Let me get the lantern for you." Florian turned and led him through the house to the back door, surprisingly brisk and silent. The older man opened a cabinet door and pulled out an old lantern. Raising the side, he lit the wick, then handed the lantern to John. "Take care."

"I will. And I hope, when I return, I will bring Priscilla with me."

He strode out the door and through the backyard to the path behind the house that he and Priscilla had taken the day they went exploring. Priscilla had said that it was the path that led to Lady Chalcomb's manor house. He held the lantern up, looking carefully from side to side as he strode along, his long steps eating up the ground. He forced himself not to think about what might be happening to Priscilla right now, if she was indeed in those men's hands. He had to think, had to concentrate on what he was doing, if he expected to get Priscilla back. He could not let himself be distracted.

Before long he passed the point where he and Priscilla had turned aside into the woods that day. He had not yet seen any footprints but Priscilla's. The earth was hard, and the path did not provide good tracks, but every once in a while he ran across the partial imprint of a woman's shoe. He had not yet seen the sign of any larger boot or shoe.

He hesitated, thinking of plunging into the woods to seek the shed right now, but he continued along the path. There was always the possibility that Priscilla had not been taken, but had somehow fallen and hurt herself. If she had indeed twisted an ankle, it would be no help to her if he went haring off through the woods looking for the hut. He walked on, alert to every noise in the night, to every deviation in the path. He was beginning to think that he might have to walk all the way to Chalcomb Manor when something on the path before him caught his eye.

The earth in front of him, unlike the rest of the trail, had been disturbed. The ground had been stirred up, scuffed and kicked, and the grass on either side looked as if it had been trodden on. A long, narrow rut made him think of the heel of a woman's shoe being dragged across the ground, and in the softer earth beside the trail, he could make out almost a whole bootprint, clearly large enough to be a man's. Most damning of all, a set of colored pencils lay scattered on the grass, along with a small drawing pad. Mrs. Smithson had said that

Priscilla had gone to Chalcomb Hall to copy a design for her needlework.

John's heart thudded in his chest, and for a moment he was gripped by a fear so great he could hardly move, hardly breathe. *They had seized Priscilla!* Somehow, he had hoped deep inside that his fears would turn out to be foolish, that he would find Priscilla still deep in conversation with Lady Chalcomb, or even that he would find her furious and frustrated, sitting on a rock beside the road, nursing a sprained ankle or a broken bone. But there had obviously been a struggle here, and he knew that the worst had happened. The men—his enemies, for whatever reason—had taken Priscilla.

He had to get her back.

John turned and left the path, heading straight into the trees that grew close to the path. He remembered that he and Priscilla had left the trail and headed in a northeasterly way the other day. He thought that if he walked straight ahead, he would probably intersect the path they had taken then. It would be much quicker than going back to the place where they had left the path; he only hoped that he would not be thrown off by the different angle and be unable to find the shack.

Finding the small hut in the woods was not, he knew, a very viable proposition, anyway. He had been there only twice, and he was not familiar with the area. However, he was not about to wait for morning to start searching, nor was he about to waste time raising a search party of locals. He could not bear to think what might happen to Priscilla while time went by.

He was rewarded—and relieved—a few minutes later when the light from his lantern picked up a small scrap of material caught on a thornbush, stirring in the faint breeze. He reached out and plucked it from the thorn, rubbing it between his fingers. There was no way of telling whether it had been torn from Priscilla's dress. He did not even know what color dress she had worn that day. But this did mean that someone had passed here, and, judging by the condition of the material, it had been recently. It gave him hope, and he pressed on, on the lookout for any other signs that people had gone this way.

He found several such signs as he made his way through the dense darkness: the imprint of a man's boot in the mud, a snapped branch dangling from a tree, still moist inside with sap; another bit of cloth. And where there were no such signs, he struggled on through the trees and underbrush, hoping he was continuing in the right direction. There was a long period where he could see no sign of anyone's having passed that way, and he became certain that he had wandered from the correct path, but then he came upon a small glade that looked familiar. He sank down gratefully on the fallen tree trunk. He was certain that he and Priscilla had passed this trunk on their way to the shack.

Placing the lantern on the ground in front of him, he looked around, trying to get his bearings. He could see above him only a tiny slice of sky, where a few stars twinkled. He walked slowly around the clearing, cudgeling his brain for memories of the clearing and the way he and Priscilla had gone from there the other day. It seemed to him that they had walked into the clearing facing the fallen log, then walked out past it, whereas tonight he had walked in much closer to the log and to one side of it. Finally, without much confidence, he picked up the lantern and strode out past the log.

It was some time before he came upon the stream, and he could tell that he was farther downstream than he and Priscilla had been the other day. He walked along the bank of the small stream, shining the lantern on either bank, looking for footprints in the muddy area beside the creek. His pulse sped up when he saw a small trampled place on the other side of the stream. He leaped over the stream and held the lantern close to the ground. There were several prints, all of men's shoes, mingling and smeared, as if the men had slipped and struggled to regain their footing. There were no signs of a woman's shoes anywhere about.

But that, he told himself, made sense. They would have had to carry Priscilla; she would have fought too hard if she was on her feet. He surged forward through the trees with renewed strength. He was close; he was sure of it. Priscilla must have been taken to the hut. He would find her there. *And he would find the men.*

His fist knotted into a ball, and a certain gleam came into his eyes. If he found the men, he would make sure that they regretted this encounter. He wished he had brought a gun; even Florian's ancient dueling pistol would have been good for whacking someone over the head.

He was sure that he must be nearing the shack. It had not been far from the stream. He brought down the panels of the lantern on all sides except the one facing him, reducing the lantern's glow to the smallest amount he needed to see his way through the darkness. His pace slowed, and he took careful steps, so that his passage through the trees was almost silent. All the while, he looked about sharply. If he were the one hiding someone in the shack, he would have one of the men sleeping and the other keeping guard, hidden in the trees so that he could see anyone who approached the cabin.

It seemed to John that the area in front of him was faintly lighter than the darkness around him. He slowed his steps even more, then stopped and brought down the final panel of the lantern, plunging himself into darkness. Slowly his eyes adjusted, and he could make out the shapes of trees in front of him. He was right. There was some small amount of light somewhere. He moved forward carefully and stopped beside a tree. In front of him lay a long, narrow clearing. The faint light came from the stars and moon that streamed into the clearing, not blocked by tree branches. It was not much, but it was enough for him to see the small, square mass of the hut sitting in the clearing. No light gleamed inside it.

They had her in the darkness. That fact made him burn with anger, but at least it meant that there would be almost no light to give away his presence as he approached the hut. He waited, half hidden by the large tree, and made a slow survey of the trees around the clearing. He could see no sign of a person standing or sitting anywhere among them. But he knew that did not mean there was no one. They would be as difficult to see as he was.

He moved through the trees to his right, on the lookout for guards, until he was positioned straight across from the door of the hut. There was an odd, shapeless bulk at the bottom of the door, and John stared at it for a long moment before he realized that it must be one of the men, sitting on guard outside the door—probably sleeping, judging from the way his form was sprawled.

It was possible, of course, that this was a trick, that

the man's alert companion was hiding in the trees, watching to see if anyone would come and take the bait of the sleeping guard. John hesitated for a moment, looking around the edge of the clearing again.

He found it difficult to believe that either of these two had the mental capacity to think of a trick such as that. This, after all, was how they had guarded him, one there and one away, presumably sleeping in the comfort of a bed. He doubted that they would think a woman was worthy of another guard, even if he had demonstrated that they had been foolishly lax with him.

Or perhaps the other one was inside with Priscilla.

He hurtled forward at that thought. Even though he knew it was probably untrue—the man would have had some light with him, surely, and Priscilla would be screaming if anyone was hurting her—he could not stop himself from rushing forward. Propelled by the anxiety and fear of an entire evening, he charged the recumbent form and, dropping the lantern, he grabbed the man by his clothes and jerked him to his feet.

"Wha—?" The man's eyes flew open, and he gaped at John, but before he had time to even get a question out, John's fist smashed into his face.

The man lurched backward, letting out a cry of astonishment and pain. John went after him, hammering him with his fists. The man fell to the ground like a rock. He lay limp. John halted, frustrated. He would have liked to vent all his anger and fear on the man, but the damn fellow hadn't put up enough of a fight.

He swung around and went to the door of the hut. It was fastened crudely but effectively, with a bar of wood across it. John jerked the bar up out of its slot and pulled open the door. He bent into the low doorway and peered inside. "Priscilla?"

A huddled heap in the corner launched itself at him, but even as John instinctively took a step back, Priscilla flung her arms around his neck and clung to him. "John! Thank God! I knew you would come!"

"Priscilla." Her name was a sigh of relief this time. His arms went around her, and he pulled her close, burying his face in her hair. For a long moment he luxuriated in the sheer sensation of holding her, murmuring soft endearments into the silken mass of her hair.

Priscilla turned her face up to look at him, caressing his cheek with her fingertips. "I was so scared. I told myself you would find me, that you would know that they had taken me here. But I was so afraid that you wouldn't be able to find it in the dark."

"I would find you anywhere," he murmured, gazing hungrily into her face, and then he bent to kiss her lips. As soon as his mouth touched hers, the pulse of fear that had been driving him turned into passion. Heat flamed between them, fiercer than any fire.

He pulled her into him, his arms tightening around her, as if he could pull her into his body until she became part of him. He made a noise deep in his throat, a sound of pure animal desire. Priscilla clung to him, as suddenly, overwhelmingly, alive with passion as he was. It was as if the emotions of the last few hours had stripped away all pretense, all trappings and teachings of society, and there was in them now only the elemental reality of their hunger for each other.

His hands moved eagerly up and down her back, smoothing over the curve of her hips, as they kissed again and again. Lips clung, tongues twined, fingers pressed into flesh. They were giddy and greedy, incapable of speaking, even of thinking.

He slipped a hand between them, curving it over her breast and cupping it, delighting in the exquisite softness, the contrasting hardness of the small pointing nipple in the center. Priscilla gasped at the sensations that flooded her at his touch. He rubbed his thumb over the hard little bud, and it tightened eagerly. Warmth flooded Priscilla's abdomen, and she was aware of a curious moisture between her legs. She squeezed her legs together tightly, wanting something, though she was not sure what. A pulse began there and grew as he stroked her nipple with his thumb, his hand gently cupping and squeezing her breast beneath the cloth of her dress.

His lips left her mouth and trailed down her neck, arousing the gentle flesh with hot, velvety kisses. Priscilla let out a soft mew of desire and leaned back against his arm, soft and pliant, her head drooping back, exposing more of her throat to his mouth. He took advantage of the mute invitation, raining kisses down her throat. His hand moved to her other breast, arousing and caressing it the same way. All the while, the heat built low in Priscilla's loins, pulsing and aching, turning her to fire.

Impatiently John pushed up her skirts and petticoats, delving beneath them to find her leg, clothed only by her soft cotton stocking. His breath came out in a groan as he caressed her thigh, sliding upward and over her garter to the bare skin above it. A shudder ran through him, and he raised his head and pressed his lips into hers once again. His tongue plunged inside her mouth, fierce and demanding, as his fingers teased her flesh.

His hand moved upward, under the loose legs of her underwear, until it reached the hot, damp source of her passion.

Priscilla gasped, the sound swallowed by his mouth on hers, and jerked in surprise. He murmured to her soothingly, soft, meaningless words, and kissed her cheek and eyes and ears, until she relaxed again. Then he returned to the long, drugging kiss on her mouth, and his fingers crept up to the joinder of her legs.

This time Priscilla did not jump, only quivered at the unexpected pleasure that rushed through her. It was startling, embarrassing, and yet it was incredibly exciting, as well. She wanted it to continue, wanted to follow this passion wherever it might lead.

Gently his fingers probed, separating the slick satin folds of flesh and sending exciting shivers through her. He caressed her, and her knees went so weak that she was afraid they would give way and she would fall to the ground. She trembled, feeling as if she were on the edge of a different world. Her breath rasped in her throat, and her hands dug into the front of his shirt, holding on for dear life.

And then there was a groan outside the cabin.

CHAPTER TWELVE

PRISCILLA AND JOHN FROZE. There was another groan.
They remembered then the man who had been standing
guard outside the cabin, the man John had knocked down
and left as he rushed to open the door of the shack.

John let go of Priscilla and stepped back, aghast at
his own loss of control. He had been so caught up in
his passion, so blind to the outside world, that the guard
he had knocked unconscious earlier could easily have
awakened and come in and struck both of them down.
It was sheer luck that the man had started groaning as
he returned to consciousness.

He ran outside to where the man lay. Behind him,
Priscilla hurriedly adjusted her clothing, a blush spreading over her cheeks. She had never in her life experienced anything like the past few moments, not even
when John had kissed and caressed her before. She had
been flooded with desire then, but that had been nothing like the all-consuming passion, the greed to couple
with him, that had overtaken her tonight. It had been as
if nothing in the world existed except the two of them.
Her limbs were still weak and trembling, her skin was
tingling, and her blood was pulsing through her like
mad.

A little shakily, she followed John out of the hut. She
glanced around and found his darker form in the dim

landscape. He was kneeling beside the tall guard, and he hauled the man up into a sitting position as Priscilla came up behind him. Blood trickled from the villain's nose and smeared his chin. His eyes rolled vaguely. He moved his arms and legs a little, as though not quite sure where they were or what they were supposed to do.

"I am glad to see that you're coming to," John said conversationally. "I was wanting to have a bit of chat with you."

The other man let out a snuffle that conveyed surprise.

"You thought I wouldn't? Oh, no, I am most eager to talk to you. Or, I should say, to hear what you have to say."

"Won't tell you nothin'," the man mumbled.

"You think not?" There was a dangerous quality to John's voice that Priscilla found rather chilling. "Somehow I think you will change your mind. Priscilla, dear, does that dress of yours have a sash?"

Priscilla blinked. "Uh, yes."

"Good. Then may I have it?"

Priscilla began to untie the sash, asking uneasily, "What are you planning to do?"

"Just tie up our friend here," John replied, whipping the man over onto his face and pulling his arms behind him before he could even begin to struggle. "Thank you."

He took the sash from Priscilla's hand and proceeded to tie the man up efficiently, knotting the fabric around his hands, then pulling the long strand of cloth down to tie it around the man's ankles, so that he lay awkwardly, his hands drawn back and down, and his feet up behind his back.

"'Ey!" the man protested.

"What? Are you uncomfortable? How unfortunate. Of course, I could have tossed you into that cabin and left you there in the dark for a few days, the way you did Priscilla and me. Until I brought back the constable. How long do you suppose you will get in prison?"

It occurred to Priscilla that John was talking this way in order to scare the man so that he would talk freely. But his voice and face were so cold, so suddenly foreign to her, that it frightened her a little. She went on hastily, "I think that getting the constable is an excellent idea. Why don't you put him in the shack and let's go?"

"The English are very law-abiding people, I find," John remarked. "I admire that in them. Of course, in America, we are not quite so particular. There's not always law around in the wilds, you see, and we are more apt to mete out our own justice. They hang men, you know, just for thievery." He lowered his voice, saying, "Worse than that, when it comes to harming a woman."

He hunkered down beside the man's head, staring down steadily into his eyes. "I don't take kindly to man-handling women. Especially when it is a woman who belongs to me."

Normally Priscilla would have bridled at the way he had referred to her, but she was too worried now about what his intentions were to bother with such niceties. She laid a hand on John's shoulder, softly saying his name.

Without moving his gaze from the other man's face, John patted her hand and said, "It's all right, Priscilla. Maybe you should go back into that little cabin, or over on the other side of it."

"Why?"

"So you won't have to hear or see anything that would offend you," John replied. "A slow death is not a pleasant thing to watch."

Priscilla's jaw dropped. The captive's eyes widened, the whites of his eyes glistening in the dark.

Priscilla stared at John, then said firmly, "No, thank you, I shall stay right here. John, what are you planning to do?"

"I wanted to ask this man—Will, your partner called you, wasn't it?—I wanted to ask Will some questions. For instance, who his partner is and why they attacked me. Why they kidnapped you. How they know Benjamin Oliver. That sort of thing. The only problem is, he said that he was not going to answer."

Priscilla went a little weak with relief. He *was* trying to frighten the man into answering questions. It had been foolish of her to suspect anything else. However, she was careful not to let her feelings show. It would ruin John's plan if she acted as if she didn't believe him.

"Oh, dear. Well, he might talk to you, you know. Perhaps he has changed his mind." She turned toward the ruffian on the ground. "Won't you reconsider?"

"I ain't no bleeding ratter," the man named Will responded, but his voice was less sure than it had been earlier.

"See? I told you. I will try to make him talk, of course. There are several things I learned from the Indians. Not many men can stand up to them."

Will's face turned a paler color, but John went on, oblivious, "But in the end, I imagine I shall have to kill him. Give him the death he deserves for hurting you."

"I'm not sure that it is worth *killing* over, you know," Priscilla suggested.

"We handle things differently in the United States. You can't let anyone get away with harming you or yours, or people will think you're weak. It's a hard land. Fortunately, living with the Indians those two years toughened me up."

"I—I've read of the sort of things they do to their captives. It's horrid, barbaric," Priscilla said, putting a quaver into her voice.

She was certain now that he must be putting on an act. But even so, she could not suppress a little gasp when he reached behind him and pulled a large knife from his belt. "John!"

"Did you think I would go out without a weapon when I came hunting for you? A knife is better than a gun in many ways, when you know how to use it. It's quiet, and it's better for what I need to do now."

"What are you going to do?" she asked dutifully, sneaking a glance at the other man's face. Beads of sweat had popped out on Will's upper lip and forehead, and she could see his throat bob as he swallowed nervously.

"I'm not sure. I thought of cutting out his tongue, but that would be defeating my purpose, now, wouldn't it? Staking him out on an anthill would take too long. Besides, I haven't got the equipment I'd need. I saw the Apaches skin a man alive once. It would probably be most effective."

A choked noise came from Will, and John glanced at him indifferently.

"I do know what I will do when I have finished with him. I am going to scalp him. Start cutting right about there." He leaned over and touched the edge of the man's hairline. "Then peel the skin right back."

"John!" It did not take much acting for Priscilla to sound appalled.

"Don't worry, Pris, you don't have to see it. That's why I told you to move away. It isn't a sight for a fine lady like you."

"No! I won't let you do this!" Priscilla exclaimed.

"You don't have any choice."

Priscilla swung agitatedly to the man on the ground. "Please! Tell him what he wants to know! You can save yourself."

Will was sweating profusely now; the front of his shirt was soaked. He licked his lips, his eyes darting to the large knife in John's hand.

"Well, I might as well start." John moved closer, the knife glittering in the moonlight. Will tried frantically to wiggle back from him, but John rolled him over and planted a foot firmly on his chest, pinning him to the ground. He leaned closer and placed the knife between the edges of Will's shirt. Slowly he drew the knife downward, and the fabric parted like melting butter beneath the sharp blade, leaving a thin line of blood down the front of the man's chest.

Priscilla jumped, her stomach turning, and let out a cry. Will yelped.

"Guess I better gag you," John said, whipping his handkerchief out of his pocket. "Can't have you making too much noise."

"John! You cannot! You must not!" Priscilla ran forward and dropped down on her knees beside Will. "Please, you must tell him what he wants to know."

"Step aside, Pris."

"Please! Tell him! Where is your partner? What is his name? How do you know Benjamin Oliver?"

John leaned over him with the gag, bringing the cloth down toward Will's mouth.

"All right! All right!" Will burst out. "I'll tell ye everything I know. Just—just don't let that madman loose on me."

"Excellent." Priscilla settled down on the ground beside Will. "Now, let us begin with Benjamin Oliver. Who is he?"

"I don't know. I never seen the bloke 'fore 'e 'ired Mapes 'n' me!"

"Then you were not cohorts of his?" Priscilla asked.

"I don't know what that is, but we wasn't nothin' to 'im. 'E's some bleedin' gen'leman, 'e is, always puttin' on airs and actin' like some ladies' man. Bleedin' pouf. 'I paid you good money,' 'e says, 'and now you say you've lost 'im. Well, find 'im, man.' As if it was that easy. I'd like to see 'im keep 'is 'ands on that one. I'd like to see 'im duke it out with 'im."

"Believe me, I'd like to see it, too," John put in dryly. "But why is Oliver so concerned about keeping hold of me?"

"'Ow should I know? The likes of 'im don't confide in the likes of me. Ye'll 'ave to ask 'im that yerself."

"I suppose I shall. Did he tell you to kill me?"

"No. It'd of been a lot easier, I can tell ye that, but 'im, 'e's all squeamish about blood, ye see. 'E says as we're just to lock you up in that cabin and keep ye."

"But why?"

The man attempted a shrug. "I told ye, 'e didn't let us in on 'is plans. 'E just said follow ye, and knock ye on the 'ead right before ye get to Elverton. 'E paid us 'alf before, and 'e was goin' to pay the other 'alf when the job was ended."

"And when was that to be?"

"I don't know. 'E said 'e'd get to us if we 'oled up at the Dolphin—that's where ye found us. Only 'e came stormin' in right before ye came, jawin' at me 'cause 'e'd seen ye in town. 'E wanted to know why we 'adn't told 'im we'd lost ye—and I'd like to know 'ow we could, when 'e 'adn't ever showed up there before. Wot was we supposed to do, I'd like to know? 'E told us we'd better get ye back if we wanted our money. I told 'im we was tired of playing cat 'n' mouse in the wilds. It ain't right to live out 'ere with all them trees and the like. Everybody watches ye when ye walk down the street, 'n' there's no place to hide. We just wanted to go back to London, and that's the truth. Only 'e said 'e'd 'ave our 'ides if we did that." Indignation filled his face. "'E said as 'ow 'e'd bring us up afore the constable and tell 'im we'd stolen from 'im. So if we wanted to stay out of jail, we'd better find you. And that's when ye and yer lady friend showed up, and we figured we could get ye back if we took 'er. Mapes, see, remembered 'er from when we was lookin' for ye, and she said she hadn't seen ye."

Will shot a resentful look at Priscilla. "Ye lied to us."

"Well, yes, I did," Priscilla admitted.

"Damn!" John sat back on his heels. "So we still have no idea why Oliver would want to get rid of me. Or why he wanted me held and not killed."

"Maybe it was what this man said—he was squeamish about killing someone."

"'E said as 'ow 'e'd talk ye into leaving. 'E thought if you were 'ungry and scared enough, ye'd take off if 'e let you go."

"Or maybe he hoped you would die from exposure and starvation, and he could pretend he was not responsible," Priscilla said. "That would fit Mr. Oliver's personality exactly. He's cowardly and sneaky."

"The only thing to do now is to confront Oliver." John looked down at Will with narrowed eyes. "And what am I going to do with you?"

"Let me go?" the man suggested hopefully, trying what Priscilla assumed he must think was a winning smile.

"To run around trying to kidnap me or Priscilla again? I think not."

"We wouldn't!" Will assured him. "I swear, we wouldn't. We'd shake the dust of this bleedin' place off our feet in a trice. All we want is to go back to London, and that's the truth."

"So I should let you return to London to rob and kidnap people there? I don't think so. No, I'm afraid that Priscilla is right. I must take you and your accomplice to the constable. However, if you were to tell him your story about Mr. Oliver, you might have an easier time of it. They usually enjoy catching the bigger fish more than the small fry."

"'E wouldn't believe me, not against a gen'leman like Oliver."

"Ah, but Priscilla and I can testify that we saw him talking to you. I think the constable will believe you. Besides, I hope to get a little information out of Mr. Oliver that might help your story make more sense. Anyway," he pointed out practically, "look on the bright side of it.

I am not going to scalp you now, or any of those other things, since you told me about Oliver. Now, where's Mapes?"

"Mapes?" Will replied, looking blank.

"Yes, Mapes. Your partner. Where is he?"

"'E's out in the woods. That's where we been stayin' the past days, on account o' ye seein' us in town. It's a fearful place, too, I'll tell you. All sorts of noises; things rustlin' and birds 'ootin' and such. I couldn't sleep at all last night."

"Mm… Dreadful, I'm sure. I am going to untie you and let you take me to Mr. Mapes at your campsite."

John went behind him and began to untie the sash from his ankles. When that was done, he stopped. "Wait. I have a better idea. When is Mapes going to come to relieve you?"

"'Bout 'alfway through the night. That's what we agreed—if 'e don't cheat me on it."

"That sort, is he?"

Will gave him an odd look. "Ain't everybody?"

A faint smile touched John's mouth. "Apparently everyone you know is. Well, my good man, I have decided to put you in the cabin, where you so recently kept Miss Hamilton. I shall retie your legs, but more comfortably, and I fear I shall have to use the gag this time. We can't have you alerting your partner, now can we?"

The man rose to his feet and shambled docilely in front of John to the cabin. There John rebound his ankles and gagged him, then left him in the shed, pulling down the heavy wooden bar. He turned, scanning the trees and bushes behind them.

"Come on." He took Priscilla's hand and led her to a spot behind a small bush, where they were well hidden in the dark but had an excellent view of the door of the cabin.

"We are going to hide and ambush Mapes when he comes to change the watch?" Priscilla asked.

"Yes. It seemed unlikely that we could get Will to lead us to the correct spot or, if he did, not to make too much noise and give us away. Plus, his feet would be untied, and I would have him on my hands, as well as Mapes. This way is easier, though I'm afraid it will leave your papa in worry a little longer."

Priscilla quirked an eyebrow. "Papa noticed I was gone?"

"I brought it to his attention," John admitted apologetically. "I'm sorry. I am sure he would have realized soon."

"Mm-hmm… When he couldn't find something, or when Miss P. pointed it out to him." She shrugged. "Don't worry. It doesn't matter. I know Papa better than anyone else. He is a kind and loving man, but not the sort you want to have with you in a bad spot."

She did not add that John was precisely the sort of man she *would* want to have with her in such a situation. She sneaked a sideways glance at him. He was watching the area around the cabin steadily, relaxed, but with his eyes never ceasing to roam in front of the cabin and off to the shadows on either side. He felt her watching him and turned to look at her. He raised an eyebrow quizzically.

"Did you mean any of what you said back there…to Will?" she asked.

"What? Oh…to make him talk?" He chuckled. "No. I have never met an Indian in my life, much less lived with them. Nor have I ever tortured anyone. Or, at least,

I don't think I have. It's very strange, not knowing yourself. But those things I talked about—I felt that I was
making them up, not talking about something I actually
knew."

Priscilla let out a little sigh of relief.

"I thought you realized that. I thought you were going
along with me."

"I was. I did. When you started talking about the
Indians and all, I thought surely, if you *had* remembered
things like that, you would have told me. But…at first…
well, I wasn't quite certain. You sounded so cold and
hard, as if you were capable of anything."

"I felt cold and hard. After all, the man had abducted
you. I had been stumbling through the dark for hours,
praying that you were all right and that I was going the
right way. Then, when I found you locked in that little
dark place and thought about you being in there, scared
and alone—" His jaw clenched and his eyes narrowed
as he remembered the emotion that had swept him. "I
was in a rage. I was determined to make him talk, to
find out what was going on. To stop those two before
they could actually harm you."

"Oh, John…" Priscilla breathed, stirred by the fierce-
ness of his anger and his fear for her.

He smiled a little at her and reached out with one arm
to pull her close. He bent his head to hers, murmuring,
"I don't know what I would have done if I had not found
you. Or if they had hurt you. When I was searching
through the woods, I kept thinking about you—what
they might have done to you. How you might be lying
hurt, even dead, somewhere. It nearly drove me crazy
with fear. If I had found you like that, then I might have
killed him. I am not sure I would have been able to stop

myself, or to even think." He paused. "Thank God you were all right."

"Thank God you came after me."

"You knew I would."

Priscilla nodded. She had never doubted him, only whether he would be able to find his way there again at night. She leaned against him, enjoying the warmth of his arm around her and his hard chest against her shoulder. She had never felt this way before about any man—the surety, the passion, the completeness she felt when she was with him, the emptiness when he was gone. For some time now—ever since he had arrived, in fact—she had been fighting the feelings she had for him. She was not sure why she fought them, or why it was this one particular man who could bring them out in her. She did not know him at all in the way she knew everyone else in her life. But, she realized, she knew who he was in the most important sense.

He was the man she loved.

The thought startled her, and she drew back mentally to examine it. She loved him? It seemed wrong—absurd, even. She hadn't known him long, and it seemed as if they had spent most of their time bickering. Surely people did not fall in love that quickly; surely what she felt was merely an unseemly lust for him.

Yet even as she marshaled her arguments against the idea, she knew deep down that none of them mattered. She had been trying to hide it from John and from her family, and most of all from herself, but the truth would not stay submerged. She loved John Wolfe, and it did not matter that most people would say he was a virtual stranger to her. Her heart had given itself to him.

She knew it in the way her heart leaped whenever he

came into the room, in the way she trusted him to rescue her, in the way she feared for his safety or waited for his smile or melted in his arms. There was no way she could reason herself out of that surety. She found that she did not even want to.

Not, of course, that she would tell him so. It was far too soon, and their relationship was far too unsteady. A declaration of love would be more likely to make him turn and run than to induce him to offer his love in return.

"What are you thinking?"

"What?" Startled from her thoughts, Priscilla looked up at John. "Why?"

"You were smiling," he explained. "This little secretive smile. It made me wonder what mischief you were brewing."

Her smiled broadened. "No mischief. But it is a secret. I shall tell you someday."

"That's guaranteed to arouse my curiosity."

"When do you think he will come?" Priscilla asked, changing the subject.

John raised an eyebrow, just to let her know that he was aware of her maneuver, but followed her lead. "Our friend Will said in the middle of the night. Exactly what that means, I'm not sure. Nor am I sure that Mr. Mapes will, either."

Priscilla stiffened, and she gripped John's arm hard. "Look!" she whispered urgently, pointing a finger.

He looked in the direction she indicated, at first seeing nothing. Then he realized that there was a flash of light somewhere in the trees, then another. It grew gradually steadier and brighter until it resolved itself into a bobbing glow. John took his arm from around

Priscilla and moved into a low crouch, leaning forward a little and staring, poised for action.

Finally the edges of the moving light reached the small clearing, and a moment later Will's squat companion came into view, carrying a lantern. He moved without caution, striding forward quickly and even whistling a bright little tune.

"Whistling in the dark," John murmured beneath his breath. "I wonder—is he confident, or trying to frighten away the shadows?"

Given Will's citified account of camping in the woods, Priscilla was willing to bet that his friend was more scared of the woods and what was in them than he would like to admit.

"Will?" Mapes called as he headed toward the front door of the shack. He lifted his lantern higher and peered at the door, which the glow revealed to be empty of any sort of guard. "Will? Where are ye?"

He walked closer to the door, his back square to John and Priscilla now. Like a flash, John was on his feet and around the bush where they had been hiding, racing toward the man. Mapes heard his approach and swung around. His eyes widened with astonishment, and he froze for an instant, barely getting his fists up before John was upon him.

The fight was brief. Mapes was a bullish sort, accustomed to head-butting and plowing his opponent down to the ground, where his lack of stature was little detriment and his heaviness and muscle were an advantage. Unfortunately for him, however, John was a precise, almost professional, fighter. He stopped just before the man, his long arm flashing out and jabbing the shorter man in the eye. Mapes's head snapped back, and he staggered. John came in with a blow to his midsection, followed by a solid right fist to Mapes's chin. The man's eyes rolled up, and his body went limp. He weaved and crashed to the ground.

"Good," John said to Priscilla, who had followed on his heels. "The extra lantern will come in handy."

He picked it up and handed it to Priscilla, then pulled up the wooden bar across the door. He opened the door cautiously, just in case Will had managed to get free of his bonds. He relaxed when he saw the man still lying bound and gagged.

He turned back and grabbed the limp Mapes under his shoulders and began to drag him into the shed. Priscilla hurriedly set down the lantern and moved to pick up the man's heels. They pulled the heavy weight into the shed and left him on the earthen floor beside his friend. Quickly they went back out and pulled the door to, dropping the heavy wooden bar across it to secure it.

"There. I think that takes care of those two until we get back." John turned and held out his hand toward Priscilla. "Shall we go?"

Priscilla glanced at the shack. "I— Do you think we should leave him bound like that? Mightn't it cut off his blood?"

"Now you're worried about your kidnapper's health?" John shook his head, amused. "My dear girl, you are going to have to become more callous if you keep hanging about these types."

Priscilla made a face at him. "May I remind you that it was not *I* who brought those two here?"

"Mm… Fair hit. Well, do not worry. Mapes is unbound. Presently he will come to, and can untie his friend's bonds. Then they can wait and think about how much they have lost through associating with a 'gentleman' like Benjamin Oliver. By the time the constable comes to get them, I warrant they will have remembered every possible sin they know about him."

He picked up the lantern that Priscilla had set aside and relit the one he had brought. They started back the way he had come. As they walked, their steps grew slower. John slipped his arm around Priscilla to help her, and she leaned into him, sighing.

"Tired?"

"Mm-hmm… Are you sure this is the way back?"

"Yes. There's that little glade ahead of us. See?" He held the lantern higher, partially illuminating the small clearing cut off on one side by a large fallen tree overgrown with moss.

"Oh, yes. We came through here that first day, when we found the hut."

He nodded and guided her over to the large log. "Here. Sit down and rest a little."

Gratefully Priscilla sank to the ground and leaned back against the tree. She sighed. It had been a long and tiring day.

"I should not have gone to call on Anne," she said quietly. "I didn't think about Will and Mapes being about. I was simply so irritated with you…"

He looked down at her. "I know. When I got home, I wasn't sure whether to strangle you or run out looking for you. Then, when you didn't return…" He pulled his features into a frown. "Don't do that to me again. Do you hear?"

"I won't—as long as you don't cut me out of all the fun."

"Fun? It was anything but. It was boring and tiresome and utterly useless. Besides," he admitted, "it was no fun without you."

"There. You see?"

"I was trying to protect you. To keep you safe. I didn't want you there if I ran into Will and Mapes again. I didn't want you to get hurt."

"You see how well going without me ensured that," Priscilla pointed out sarcastically.

"Only because you were so damnably stubborn that you went sailing off somewhere by yourself, just to spite me."

"I wanted to visit Anne."

"Why? What was so urgent that it couldn't wait until I could escort you?"

"Escort me? You think I cannot go anywhere without your escorting me? I should sit in the drawing room twiddling my thumbs until you are available to take me where I want to go?"

"Only until those men were put away. Now they will be, so it will be perfectly all right."

Priscilla gave him a long, cool look. "Men!" she commented, but her pose of regal indignation was spoiled by the long, jaw-popping yawn that seized her.

John chuckled. "Here," he said, leaning forward and taking off his jacket. He folded it up and put it down on the ground for a pillow. "Lie down and rest. You are exhausted."

"But it is so late. Papa will be frightfully worried."

"I don't think it will harm your father to spend a few hours inhabiting the world the rest of us do. You are so tired you will never make it all the way back to your house if you don't rest. A little nap will refresh you." He patted the ground beside him. "I shall wake you before long."

"All right." Priscilla could see the force of his argument. She felt as if she could not take another step. Even the invigorating little discourse with John had not revived her enough to set out walking again. She slid down until she was lying on the ground and turned onto her side. Then she closed her eyes and fell immediately asleep.

John sat gazing down at her. He brushed his hand across her cheek, easing a strand of hair away from her face. She stirred in her sleep and squirmed backward, until her back was flush against his legs. She snuggled into him. Heat flooded him at the feel of her, warm and pliant, against him.

He told himself that he was a cad for thinking the things he was thinking, especially after the ordeal Priscilla had been through. But then he remembered the way she had kissed him in the shed, when their passion had overflowed its bounds and swept them away. He found that once he started thinking about that moment, it was difficult to think about anything else.

John stirred restlessly, shifting his position. He wondered what it would be like to have Priscilla lying beside him every night, to wake up to her each morning. It sounded like heaven to him. He wanted her, and he was beginning to realize that he wanted her always and forever, not just for the moment, not just to satisfy the lust that gnawed at him whenever he was around her. The more he thought about it, the less sure he was that his lust for her could be satisfied so quickly and easily. He suspected that it might plague him for the rest of his life, that as soon as his thirst for her was slaked, it would spring up again.

It struck him that what he was thinking about was marriage. What else lasted for a lifetime? The thought was amazing. He had known Priscilla for such a short time. Yet he could not deny that the thought of being married to her was quite pleasant. They must give it a little time, he supposed, must make sure of their feelings. He might know what he wanted, but he knew he could not assume that Priscilla felt the same way about him. After all, she was a gently reared girl, not used to… He frowned. Not used to *what?*

He did not even know what sort of life he could offer her. He did not know whether he was a pauper or a robber baron. He did not know if he had a home or, if he did, where it was. He had no family, no ties, no past. Hell! He did not even have a name to give her! John was damned if he would marry her as Mrs. John Wolfe. Worse than that, for all he knew, he already had a wife or fiancée waiting for him somewhere, worrying about him and wondering where he was.

No. He could do nothing. He should not even think of Priscilla or a future together until he had solved the mystery of who he was. He had to have a life to give her. Until he did, no gentleman would even speak to her about the possibility.

He frowned, crossing his arms over his chest, and leaned back against the log, thinking about Priscilla. Thinking about the future—or his lack of it. Probing the black recesses of his memory, hoping for something that would make sense, that would spark some bit of understanding in him. Slowly his eyes drifted closed. His breath shifted into a deep, slow rhythm. He was asleep.

CHAPTER THIRTEEN

PRISCILLA OPENED HER EYES AND BLINKED. It was dark all around, with only a faint light far above her. She was on her side, something heavy lying over her arm and chest, and there was a soft warmth all up and down her back. She felt deliciously enveloped by heat. A long, mournful noise sounded, and she knew that it was what had awakened her. Just an owl, she thought, and closed her eyes, snuggling back into the warmth behind her.

An owl? Her eyes opened again, her foggy mind stirring. *Where was she?* She was lying on something very hard. Hazily she tried to turn over, but she could not; the weight was heavy.

As she moved, a voice mumbled in her ear, and the warmth behind her shifted. She remembered then that she was lying out in the woods with John. She turned her head, and as she did, her hair brushed against his face. She found herself looking straight into his eyes as they opened. His gaze was as vague as hers had been, but he smiled at her, and his arm moved, his hand sliding possessively over her breasts and down to her waist. Priscilla could feel the sudden heat that emanated from his flesh. The combination of heat and the touch of his fingers made her own body come immediately alive, aching with desire. Sensations and emotions overwhelmed her mind, which was not yet functioning fully.

"Beautiful," he murmured huskily, continuing to explore her body, and he began to nuzzle the side of her neck, his lips gently nibbling and kissing the sensitive flesh into arousal. "Priscilla…"

His fingers fumbled at the buttons of her dress. Priscilla hastened to help him, unbuttoning from the bottom until their hands met in the middle. Then he slid his hand beneath the cloth, onto the soft cotton chemise, caressing her stomach and breasts. One tug at the ribbon across the top of the undergarment and it came undone, loosening the chemise all the way down. His sensitive fingertips slipped beneath the loose cloth and onto the orb of her breast, stroking the supremely soft skin. Priscilla moaned, thinking vaguely that she should not be doing this, but she found it far too difficult to think *why* she should not.

Had it been another time, had John not awakened to find Priscilla warm and willing in his arms, he would have tried to stop the course they were taking. He had decided, just hours ago, before he slid into sleep, that he should not even think about making love to Priscilla, knowing that he could offer her nothing until he regained his memory. But hazy with sleep, coming awake with her mouth only inches from his, his hand on her body, John did not even think. He only acted on the hot, hard desire that was coursing through him.

He dragged down the top of her chemise, revealing her soft white breasts. The globes quivered faintly, the pink-brown nipples tightening in the cool air. Passion slammed like a fist down through him at the sight of them, budding eagerly. He let out a groan as he cupped one breast in his hand. It filled his palm, heavy and soft. He stroked his thumb across her nipple, as he had done last night through her dress, and watched the swift response. His hand roamed her breasts, taking each nipple and rolling it gently, caressing and teasing them so that they pebbled, loving the feel of them growing harder in his hands.

He glanced up at Priscilla's face. She was flushed, even in the dim light, and her eyes were closed, her lips slightly parted as she breathed in heavily. She was the very picture of a woman in the grip of desire, and the sight stirred John even more. He bent and kissed her nipple. She jerked, moaning, in response. Smiling faintly, he kissed the other one and looked back up at her. Her tongue crept out, wetting her lips, and her breath came faster.

Cupping her breast, he took the nipple between his lips, rubbing and pressing it with velvet pressure, then lazily wetting it with his tongue. He heard Priscilla's quickly indrawn breath and felt her arch beneath him, startled and aroused. He traced the nipple with his tongue, licked and circled it.

Priscilla was flooded with wild, delightful sensations as his mouth worked its magic on her breasts. Her hands clenched into fists, and her heels dug into the ground, tension building in her with each movement of his hot, wet tongue. She let out a choked moan as he pulled the nipple into the damp heat of his mouth and began to suckle it. It seemed as if a cord ran directly from her nipple, so amazingly alive and sensitive, straight down through her into the core of her being. With every pull of his mouth, every stroke of his tongue, the cord tugged and pulled, sending bursts of flame into her loins.

She reached out, her hands digging into his hair and clenching frantically with each new wave of delight. By the time he moved to her other breast, she was almost sobbing with passion. Her legs moved restlessly, the ache between them growing and throbbing. She squeezed her legs together, moaning, and her hands moved down his neck and onto his shoulders, caressing and exploring, seeking something she was not even aware of. Her hand slipped inside the collar of his shirt, touching his hot, damp skin, and she knew that that was what she wanted. She yearned to have his firm flesh beneath her fingers, to explore and arouse.

She made a wordless noise of frustration, and he sat up. His face was stark with desire, and his eyes were dark, molten pools. He ripped off his shirt, heedless of the buttons, and threw it aside. He sat like that for a moment, looking down at Priscilla, eating her up with his eyes, studying the soft curve of her breasts, the nipples proudly pointing and damp from the ministrations of his tongue, darkened with desire.

Priscilla felt the stir of the cool night air on her damp nipples, felt them tightening even more. She was also aware of the damp heat pooling between her legs, of the empty ache there that desperately sought fulfillment. She wanted to wantonly spread her legs, wanted to pull up her skirts and feel his hands, his eyes, on her there. She blushed even at the thought. But even her embarrassment and her unsureness could not keep her from reaching out and putting her hands upon John's chest. His skin seared her hands. She moved them over his chest, exploring the layering of bone and muscle, the hard, masculine nipples, the crisp, curling hairs that grew there. His flesh grew even hotter, and sweat popped out on his upper lip. He closed his eyes, a groan escaping his lips.

Panting, John reached down and took her by the shoulders, lifting her up and pushing the sleeves of her dress down her arms with fingers made clumsy by desire. When Priscilla realized what he was doing, she moved quickly to help him, twisting out of the bodice of her dress and leaving it on the ground behind her. Her fingers trembled as she reached around to her side and began to undo the hooks of her skirt. She glanced up at John once and saw him watching her, his glazed eyes fixed on the movements of her breasts as she twisted and pulled. Then she lay back down atop the bodice and began to push the skirt and petticoats down onto her hips.

John was quick to help her, hooking his hands in the waistbands and drawing everything, petticoats, skirt and underpants, down to her knees in one swift movement. Priscilla kicked them off as he knelt there, drinking in the sight of her completely naked before him. His eyes roamed over her breasts and down to the plain of her stomach and abdomen, taking in the sharp thrust of her pelvic bones and coming to rest on her legs and the soft thatch of hair that lay between them.

"You are so beautiful," he said huskily. "I could look at you forever."

Priscilla lay quietly beneath his gaze, stirred by the heat in his eyes. He reached out and laid his hand upon her chest, skimming it down over her breast and stomach in the same way that his eyes had touched her. Her flesh quivered under his touch, exquisitely sensitized, so that she felt the texture of his skin as it moved along hers. Priscilla jumped a little when his hand touched the thatch of hair, and he paused. He traced his forefinger over and down onto her leg, then back up and across to the other leg. Gently he moved up the inside of her legs, teasing them apart.

Priscilla stirred under the sweet torture of his fingers. She wanted him to do more; she wanted him to touch her at the center of her heat. Yet the thought of it frightened her, too. Tension built in her as his fingers teased her, advancing and retreating, until before long she was so aching for release that she arched her pelvis upward, silently seeking him.

At that moment, he slid his fingers down into the crevice between her legs, threading through the soft, curling hair and onto the slick, hot flesh. Priscilla shuddered at the touch and bit back a groan, aroused past anything she had ever known could exist. Gently his fingers worked between the folds of flesh, down and up, grazing over a little nubbin and making Priscilla twist and moan in response. She clenched her fists on the ground beneath her, digging into the soft moss. Unconsciously she opened her legs wider, giving him greater access to the deep recesses of her femininity.

John sucked in his breath at the silent invitation. Passion pounded in him until he was almost dizzy with it, hard and aching for a release that he knew must be delayed for Priscilla's sake. He forced himself to continue to probe softly, instead of plunging himself deep into her, as he wished. Stripping off the remainder of his clothes, he lay down on his side, letting his fingers roam and explore while he took her mouth in a kiss. Priscilla quivered at the double delight. As his tongue came into her mouth, he slid a finger gently into her. Startled, she stiffened, but he slowly stroked his finger in and out, matching the movement with that of his tongue. She felt filled by him everywhere, and the feeling was almost unbearably arousing.

He kissed her again and again while he opened her wider, filling her now with two fingers, stretching her pleasurably. His mouth left hers, trailing down her neck and to her breasts. He sucked at her nipple, flicking it to life, and as he did so he moved his fingers rhythmically in and out, and his thumb located and caressed the hot button of flesh. Priscilla whimpered at the wild sensations. She felt filled and possessed, as if he had taken control of her senses, and yet the sensation was not frightening, but delightful. There was such passion building in her that she thought she might explode at any moment.

Then he moved between her legs and, raising her hips, he began to probe at the gates of her femininity. Priscilla gasped at the unfamiliar touch, strange, yet curiously exciting. He moved slowly into her, stretching and filling her, and she wrapped her arms around him, urging him closer. He panted, sweating with the effort of restraining his passion so that he did not frighten or hurt her.

Priscilla was aware of a startling flash of pain, and then he was deep inside her, filling and fulfilling her in a way that she had never imagined. She wrapped her legs around him convulsively and held on, trying to absorb all the sensations bombarding her. He began to move within her, stroking forward and backward in a primal rhythm that left her trembling and breathless. She moved with him, taking in the slow, deep thrusts, her fingers digging into his shoulders. A moan escaped her as the tension built in her again, screaming along her nerves and tightening the knot in her abdomen.

Soon it seemed as if there were nothing to her but the yearning ache deep in her loins, the hunger that grew and expanded, sweeping her along toward some future she could not envision, yet wanted desperately. Then the knot within her exploded, hurling her into a velvet oblivion. She let out a soft cry of delight and surprise, and her body shuddered. John answered with a hoarse groan, pumping wildly into her. Priscilla clung to him, lost in a swirl of pleasure.

He collapsed upon her, sweating and spent. Slowly, blissfully, she floated back from the far reaches of pleasure. John kissed her neck and rolled off her onto his side, still cradling her in his arms. Priscilla snuggled into him, too filled with joy to speak or even think coherently. And soon they slid back into sleep.

THIS TIME, WHEN THEY AWOKE, the pale light of dawn was filtering down through the filigree of the tree branches above their heads. John opened his eyes, aware of nothing for a moment but a deep sense of contentment. Then the full understanding of what he had done the night before jolted him. He jerked upright, startling Priscilla.

"What?" She blinked up at him. Her mind was still fogged by sleep, though she was aware of a deep sense of happiness inside her. The world looked brighter this morning, more beautiful.

"My God." He gazed down at her blankly.

"What?" Priscilla struggled to sit up on her elbow, alarmed at his expression, and as she did so, she became aware of the fact that she was lying there naked. She woke up completely then, memories of the night before flooding in on her. Oh, dear heaven! Had she been mad?

John's eyes went to her bare breasts, which were swaying with her movement, and desire snaked through him, despite his horror. He groaned, reaching out and grabbing one of her petticoats and wrapping it around her, hiding her from his eyes. Priscilla took it gratefully. It felt so strange to be sitting there unclothed with a man. And yet... She could not help but remember how wonderful last night had been, how beautiful. She had felt something she had never even dreamed of, and though she knew that others would probably condemn her, Priscilla found herself unable to regret it. Whatever might happen, last night would always remain in her heart.

"I am so sorry. I never meant—" John began, then stopped. "I mean, I thought I had better control of myself. If I had not been half-asleep— But when I woke up, there you were, and so desirable. I didn't think."

"You regret what happened?" Priscilla tightened, her voice cool.

He stared at her. "No. I don't regret what we did. It was the most wonderful thing I have ever experienced."

"Really?" Priscilla's expressive face lit up. "It was for me, too, but I didn't think it would be like that for you."

He pulled her to him impulsively, wrapping his arms around her and burying his face in her hair. "It was beautiful," he assured her. "And you were wonderful... indescribably wonderful."

Priscilla released a small sigh of satisfaction and snuggled against him. The doubts she had been feeling were dissolving quickly. She loved John, and last night had been a perfect expression of that love. Though he might not realize that he loved her yet, his words indicated that he had at least found last night to be just as wonderful as she had. "Good. Because I liked it exceedingly."

Again he felt his response shooting through him like fire, and he knew he was already growing hard, wanting her.

"Priscilla…" he groaned, releasing her. He smoothed his hands down over her hair, pulled loose from its pins and flowing everywhere. He twisted his fingers into her tresses. "You are so beautiful, so utterly desirable… God, I want to make love to you again."

Priscilla smiled back at him. "Then why don't you?" she asked provocatively.

His mouth went dry at her words, his heart picking up its beat. He could not keep from thinking about lying back down on the ground with her and making love again. He remembered her passionate response the night before, and wondered what she would be like when there was no newness, no pain.

He swallowed hard and stood up, turning away. "You know why not. It would be madness. You don't even know who I am. I could be married and have seven children, so that I could not give you the protection of my name. I could be a scoundrel, so that my name would be a scandal itself, not a protection."

"It is not your name I am asking for," Priscilla replied evenly. What she really wanted was his heart, she knew, but for now his lovemaking would be enough for her.

"It is not just my name. It is what *I* am that worries me. I can't help wondering why Benjamin Oliver knows me and why he wants me shut away. I keep thinking—what if I am a crook, too?"

"You are worrying about nothing." Priscilla refused to believe that he was married, telling herself that surely he could not forget a wife and a family as if they were nothing. Besides, he wore no wedding band, and, while Mapes and Will might have stolen it, there was also no whiter band against his tanned skin where a wedding ring would have been. As for his other worries, that he might be a scoundrel, Priscilla dismissed them as rubbish. She *knew* he was a good person. Others might balk at the idea that he was an American and that one did not know who his family was, but Priscilla did not care about such things. It was what a person was that was important, not whether his family went back to the Conquest or not. Her own family was quite genteel, but where had that ever gotten them? It was all silly pride, she thought.

John took another tack. "Your father and Miss Pennybaker will be worried about us, you know."

Priscilla's eyes flew open wide, and her hand came up to cover her gasp. "Oh, no! You're right. This is dreadful."

She began to pull on her clothes, castigating herself for having fallen asleep last night. It did not speak very well for her, she thought, to have forgotten her father and her governess because she had been swept away by her own passion. She had been thoughtless and selfish.

Priscilla finished dressing and brushed the leaves and twigs from her clothes as best she could, running her fingers through her hair in lieu of a brush. She realized what a mess she must look. Thank heavens there would be no one to see her come in except her family.

Looking at her, others would probably suspect that she had been—well, doing exactly what she *had* been doing. Still, she didn't want the whole village of Elverton knowing it.

"Do I look all right?" she asked anxiously, giving her skirts a final shake.

"You look beautiful," John replied, smiling, and leaned down to kiss her on her forehead.

"You know what I mean."

"Yes, you look fine. Alive and healthy and like someone who had to spend the night in the woods, but none too worse for wear for having been kidnapped."

"I suppose that will have to do."

They left the clearing, heading back the way John had come last night. It was much easier going in the daylight, and they were able to see where to turn to take the more direct path to Priscilla's home. Soon they were able to see Evermere Cottage ahead of them. Their steps sped up. As they reached the rear yard, the kitchen door burst open and Mrs. Smithson rushed out, arms wide open.

"Priscilla! My little love!" she sobbed, then tossed back over her shoulder, "Miss P.! Master Florian! It's her! She's home safe!"

Priscilla flew into the other woman's motherly arms. Mrs. Smithson patted her, crying, taking her by the shoulders and shaking her, telling her fiercely that she ought to know better than to go off like that, then pulling her back to her massive bosom for another bone-crushing hug.

Behind them, Florian ran through the door. His white hair was flying every which way, and he wore no jacket, only his shirt, one sleeve rolled up and the other still fastened by a cuff link, and a waistcoat, which hung open and flapping. His disarray was normal, but the lines of worry in his forehead were not, nor were the tears of relief in his eyes.

"Priscilla!" He crossed the last few steps and pulled Priscilla out of Mrs. Smithson's arms, which was no small feat. He looked at her and started to speak, but then just crushed her to his chest, saying her name again.

"Oh, dear! Oh, my!" Miss Pennybaker came out the door and fluttered across the yard, followed by the vicar, Dr. Hightower, the general and Alec.

Watching them, John groaned inwardly. So much for their hopes of keeping Priscilla's abduction quiet.

"Dear girl!" the vicar exclaimed, shaking his white head as he hobbled across the yard, using his cane.

The general and the doctor quickly outstripped him, but stopped a few feet from Florian and his daughter. Mrs. Smithson stepped aside, beaming at her employers, and Miss Pennybaker fluttered around agitatedly, touching Priscilla's hair or arm or back.

"Oh, dear! Oh, my!" she kept saying. "I was so afraid. Oh, Priscilla, it is so wonderful. A miracle! That's what it is. Wouldn't you say so, Reverend?"

"Yes, indeed…" the small man began, smiling, but Miss Pennybaker did not wait for an answer to her question, but hurried on.

"All night long we waited. We were so worried about you. All of us." Her hands fluttered toward the rest of the group. "It is so wonderful to see you alive and well and— You are well, aren't you, dear?"

She stopped fluttering for a moment and began twisting her handkerchief in her hands instead, watching Priscilla anxiously.

"Yes, I am quite all right," Priscilla reassured her, giving her father a final squeeze and stepping back. "Nothing happened to me. I mean, well, obviously something happened, but I was not hurt. Honestly. You must not worry, Miss P."

At that the governess burst into tears. Priscilla went to her and pulled her into her arms, patting her back and murmuring comforting things. "Hush, now, Miss P. I am all right. I promise you. And I'm back, and—"

She stopped, for the first time catching sight of the other men. "Alec! What are you doing here? And Reverend Whiting. Dr. Hightower. General. I—I am surprised to see you all here."

"Do you think we would stay home, knowing that you were in danger?" the vicar chided her gently. "When Florian came to my house last night to tell me the news, of course I came back here with him. I could hardly let him go through such a time alone."

"I happened to be at the vicarage when your father came," Alec put in. "I had driven the trap over with a few things from my mother for the charity bazaar. So I offered to bring the vicar and your father back here in the trap."

Dr. Hightower said heartily, "They thought my services might be necessary, though you look well enough…." His last words ended on a questioning note.

"Yes, I am fine. I was not hurt. Well, I did lose consciousness for a little while, when they put that cloak over my head. He slung me over his shoulder, you see, and it was hard to breathe, what with being jounced…." Priscilla stopped, realizing that she was rattling on nervously. "Really, I am fine. You were sweet to worry, but it's over, and nothing worse happened to me than being locked in a hut."

"Locked in a hut! Oh, my dear!" Miss Pennybaker put her hand to her heart and looked as though she might swoon. At that, the general moved forward quickly and placed a strengthening hand under her elbow.

"There, there, Miss Pennybaker," he told her with bluff concern. "It's all right. It's over now. No need to be upset."

"But the scandal!" Miss Pennybaker wailed, bringing her handkerchief to her nose and sniffing. "She has been out alone all night! Worse—with a man. And everyone will know! Her reputation is ruined. She will never marry now."

John started to speak. He wanted to tell the woman that Priscilla had no need to worry about that, that he was going to marry her. But he stopped; he could say nothing, and he knew it. He did not even know whether Priscilla would want to marry him. And until he knew who he was, he had no right to ask her.

"For God's sake," he said as he moved forward, his inner frustration making him irritable and impatient. "What a thing to worry about! She could have been raped or killed, and when you find out she was not, all you can say is that her reputation is ruined."

"Oh…" Miss Pennybaker moaned. "Don't say such things! I feel faint."

The general cast John a baleful look and patted the woman's arm, saying, "Don't mind him, my dear lady. He simply does not understand. American, you know. He would not understand a woman of your fine sensibilities."

Alec, who had been quiet throughout all this, took a

deep breath and stepped forward, with the expression of a man going to the guillotine. "Priscilla, I will marry you. You won't have to worry about your reputation or what people will say. You will be a duchess."

"Oh, Alec…" Priscilla smiled at him. "You are very sweet to offer, but, truly, it is not necessary. Miss P., please stop worrying about my reputation." Why had she said that right here, in front of everyone—especially John? Now he would think that it was his duty to marry her, that she would expect him to. And forcing John into marriage was the last thing she wanted. "I have no intention of marrying anyone. I am sure we can count on the discretion of our friends to keep the matter quiet." Her eyes swept over Mrs. Smithson and the men.

Everyone hastened to agree, assuring Priscilla that no word of what had happened, either her kidnapping or her rescue, would escape their lips. Frankly, Priscilla had her doubts, especially when it came to the vicar keeping silent in face of his wife's questions. He was the dearest and kindest of men, but he was no match for his wife.

Someone cleared his throat loudly, and all of them glanced in that direction. A middle-aged man with a full walrus mustache stood in the doorway, arms crossed, looking uncomfortable.

"Ah, perhaps I should not be here," he began. "If it has turned out to be merely a case of getting lost or—" his eyes flickered over to where John stood, looking as disheveled as Priscilla "—or something," he finished lamely.

"Constable Martin!" Priscilla gaped. "I—I'm sorry. I did not realize that you were here."

He gave her a small bow. "Miss Hamilton. I am glad

to see that you are all right. Yes, your father sent for me. He was quite worried about you."

"And well he should have been," John said forcefully, coming forward. "Miss Hamilton was seized by two ruffians, the same two men who attacked me."

"Attacked you?" the constable frowned. "Did you bring a complaint against them?"

"No. I did not. I should have, I realize, but…well, frankly, I assumed that they had left the area after they robbed me, and…"

"And who are you, sir?"

John looked at him for a moment. Finally he said, "Well, there you have me. That is another reason I was reluctant to come to you. You see, I—I don't know who I am. I have no memory."

"What?" The word came as a chorus from the general, the doctor and the constable. Alec said nothing, simply gaping at John.

The vicar, who was a little hard of hearing, looked from one to the other of his friends, saying, "What did he say?"

"I have no memory, Reverend." John spoke directly to the man. "I am sorry that I lied to you, to all of you. You see, I did not know who I was. And I was not sure who would be my friend and who would not."

"No, it was I who made up the lie," Priscilla said. "You must not take the blame."

"Lie?" the constable looked from one to the other of them, as if he thought they might both be a little mad. "What lie? That you were seized by brigands?"

"No, that was the truth," Priscilla assured him earnestly. "The lie was that I told everyone that John was my cousin from America. I mean, he obviously was from America, but I had no idea who he was. We had never seen him before the night when he came to our door. He had been attacked, you see, by the two men who kidnapped me."

"Mm-hmm…"

"I thought it would be better if no one knew who he really was. Of course, none of us *did* know who he really was, but what I mean is if everyone thought he was a different person altogether."

"I see." The constable's expression belied his words.

"I am making myself very unclear. I realize that, and I apologize. I've had a difficult night."

"Of course you have, my dear," the vicar reassured Priscilla, patting her arm. "You need not apologize to us. I can understand why you would want to keep his identity a secret…I mean, until you found out what his identity was. That is… You are right. This is a very confusing subject."

"We thought we would see if anyone was expecting an American or had heard of one coming through Elverton. We wanted to discover who John was, but we did not want everyone to know that he had no memory."

"Quite right," the general agreed. "Not good strategy to let the whole world know what you are doing. But I do wish you had confided in me. We could have drawn up a plan of action."

"I am sure we should have, but, you see, I didn't even know you when John first came here."

"Why do you keep calling him John?" the constable blurted out impatiently. "I thought you didn't know who he was."

"I don't. We have no idea what his real name is. But

we had to call him something. So we made up the name John Wolfe."

"When were you attacked?" the constable asked, trying to bring the subject back to something he could deal with.

John described his coming to in the hut, and how long it had been since then, ending by saying, "But as I don't remember the attack, or anything before I woke up, I have no idea when it happened."

The constable shook his head, looking grave. "Odd business, this, very odd." He turned his gaze on Priscilla. "When did these men attack you, Miss Hamilton?"

"Late yesterday afternoon. I was walking home from visiting Lady Chalcomb, and they leaped on me. I struggled, but they threw this mantle over my head and lifted me, and I had a great deal of difficulty breathing. And after that I don't remember anything until I came to consciousness in the shed."

"Those blackguards!" Alec burst out. "I'd like to get my hands on them!"

"The same shack that Mr.—that *he* was in?"

"Yes. I'm sure it was. It is this side of Lady's Woods, not far from a brook."

"I know the place you're talking about!" Alec said, looking pleased. "Gid and I used to play there. But, I say, how did they keep you in there? The door had no latch."

"It does now. And a rather heavy bar on the outside to keep it shut."

The constable cleared his throat. "Why did they attack you?"

"They didn't hit me or hurt me, really. I think they wanted only to hold me there. I think they must have wanted to use me in some way against Mr. Wolfe. I know I heard one of them say that this would bring him now. I assume they meant Mr. Wolfe."

"Yes, the villain told me so himself," John supplied. At the constable's surprised look, he went on, "I talked to him, you see. After I found him at the cabin and got Miss Hamilton out, I, um...had a discussion with Will before I locked him and Mapes up. I can take you to them."

"You locked them in the shack?" the constable looked dumbfounded. "You overcame two of them and locked them up?"

"Well, it was one at a time," John admitted modestly. "Shall I show you the way?"

"I can," Alec said eagerly, coming forward.

"I am rather tired," John agreed readily. "If you can find it, you are more than welcome to take the constable."

Alec went off with the constable, looking thrilled to be a part of the adventure, and the others went inside to have a cup of tea and listen to Priscilla's story in detail. There was much oohing and ahing as Priscilla and John described what had happened. When they reached the end—the tale having been drastically expurgated—where Will confessed that he was working for Benjamin Oliver, the doctor brought his hand down on the table with a thump, nodding triumphantly.

"I always knew that fellow was a rascal," he declared. "Jolly good, I say. Now maybe we shall be rid of him. That would certainly be a boon to Alec."

The vicar nodded sagaciously. "Poor boy. He's had a great deal to bear this past year."

"That may take care of *him,* but what about you?"

the general asked John. "You still don't know who you are."

"That's right. I have to talk to Oliver. He is the only lead I have. If the constable locks Oliver up, I will never get to find out anything."

"He will move slowly on it," the general told him. "They always do when they suspect a gentleman, and since the scoundrel is a friend of the Duchess's…he'll want to make dead sure before he does anything. Look for substantiating evidence, that sort of thing. My guess is you will have several days before he arrests the man."

"Then I would say we had best stick with the original plan," Priscilla proposed. "Talk to Mr. Oliver at the party. It is only two days away, and it will be your best chance of getting close to him. I am sure he would refuse to see you if you tried to call on him at Ranleigh Court."

"Excellent suggestion." The general nodded his approval. "We are going to the party, also." He turned and smiled at Miss Pennybaker. "Miss Pennybaker has done me the honor of accepting my escort to the event. You can come with us in my carriage."

Priscilla's eyes widened a little at this news. She glanced at Miss Pennybaker, who was blushing and dimpling coyly, then over at her father, who wore a disgusted expression.

"Why, yes," Priscilla agreed. "That sounds wonderful. But no doubt Papa will be coming, too. Is there room for all of us?"

"Yes, of course," General Hazelton responded graciously, although his face grew a trifle stiffer. "If Mr. Hamilton is going. I was not aware that he was."

Florian snorted. "I am sure there are many things of which you are not aware, General. Of course I am going."

Priscilla struggled to hide her smile. "How nice. Thank you so much, General. Mr. Wolfe, is that agreeable to you?"

John nodded. "Yes. Fine."

He looked at Priscilla. He had to know who he was before he could have anything with her. Friday could not come soon enough for him.

CHAPTER FOURTEEN

"QUIT SQUIRMING, MISS P., or I will never get you finished in time." Priscilla frowned at her former governess in the mirror.

Miss Pennybaker nodded, folding her hands and sitting very erect, like a child who had been scolded. "I will. I promise."

Priscilla relented and gave her a smile. "You are going to look just beautiful when we get through."

The older woman giggled excitedly. She had been on pins and needles the past few days, waiting for the Duchess's ball. Now that it was here, she literally could hardly sit still.

She did look much better, Priscilla thought. Her usually sallow cheeks were high with color, and she was wearing an attractive dress in a dusky rose hue. Priscilla had persuaded Miss Pennybaker to wear something more flattering than her usual browns and grays, though the woman had stubbornly insisted that all of Priscilla's clothes were much too young-looking for her. Finally Priscilla had remembered her mother's clothes, locked away in trunks in the attic, and they had found this muted rose gown in soft velvet. It had taken some tucking and hemming to fit Miss Pennybaker's thinner, smaller figure, as well as several stylistic changes to make it look less outdated. But the change it made in Miss Pennybaker was well worth it. As a crowning touch, Priscilla had decided to arrange Miss Pennybaker's hair.

She rolled the last lock of hair around the hot curling iron and waited, counting under her breath. She pulled the iron away and carefully brushed the curl around her finger, letting it lie beside the others. As a last touch, she tied a small ribbon at the top of the curls and stepped back.

"All done."

Miss Pennybaker stared at herself in the mirror. "Oh, my…"

Priscilla grinned. "You look perfect, Penny."

"Oh, my," the other woman said again, fascinated by her image in the mirror. The arrangement of curls and the short fringe of bangs that Priscilla had cut to soften her forehead enhanced her looks considerably, but it was the glow in her face that really worked the magic.

She stood up, smoothing down the skirt and turning this way and that to get a good look at herself in the mirror. "I have never worn anything so pretty."

"The general will pop a button, he'll be so proud to escort you."

Miss Pennybaker giggled. "Oh, Priscilla, you say the silliest things."

"Tell me something, Penny. Do you like the general?"

"Oh, yes. He is an excellent man and most gallant. Of course, he is not the intellect that your father is. Few are. But he is very pleasant to be around."

"He seems quite taken with you."

Miss Pennybaker blushed and waved her hand in negation. "Nonsense; he is simply polite."

"He doesn't have to be *that* polite. Why, even Papa has noticed." Priscilla watched the other woman narrowly after she spoke.

"He has?" Miss Pennybaker's color rose even higher, and she turned to Priscilla with some excitement. "What did he say?"

"A few uncomplimentary things about the general. How bold he was, something like that. I think he was jealous."

"Mr. Hamilton? Oh, no, I don't think so."

"Maybe not. But you had better look out, or you will have those two fighting over you."

"Priscilla!" Miss Pennybaker tittered. "You say the most outlandish things!" But there was a decided lilt to her walk as Miss Pennybaker left the room.

THEIR ENTRANCE DOWNSTAIRS was all that Priscilla could have hoped for. Florian rose to his feet, staring openmouthed at Miss Pennybaker, and the general was long and effusive in his compliments. For her own part, it took only one look at John's face to see how Priscilla's outfit affected him. The heat from his eyes was almost tangible as his gaze swept down her body, taking in the full swell of her bosom above the neckline of her deep blue dress, and the narrowness of her waist.

Priscilla hoped that meant that tonight he would have trouble sleeping. She had been having enough trouble herself the past two nights.

She had lain, tossing and turning, waiting for him to come to her room. Hoping. But he had not visited her, and Priscilla was not bold enough to go to a man's room uninvited. She had told herself that he was not avoiding her, that he was simply wary of Miss Pennybaker, a notoriously light sleeper—or that he respected her too much to put her in a compromising position in her own home. But she had had difficulty believing her words, given the stiff and remote way he acted toward her during the day. Their easy friendliness seemed to have vanished with the night they had spent in the forest. It seemed to Priscilla that John made every effort not to be alone with her, and when they did happen to be without companions, they sat in awkward silence and John soon made some excuse to leave the room. She was beginning to think that the vicar's wife had been right that time when she had told Priscilla that a man wanted only one thing from an unmarried woman, and that once he got it, he was no longer interested in her.

But the look that had flamed in John's eyes tonight was not that of a man who was no longer interested in a woman. It had been a hot, devouring gaze, as if he could barely keep from reaching out and taking her in his arms. Priscilla smiled in acknowledgment—a slow, sultry smile that was guaranteed not to reduce the heat in a man's blood the least bit.

"Ah, Miss Pennybaker!" the general said, moving forward to take that lady's hand and gallantly kiss it. "You are a vision. And Miss Hamilton. I can tell that the pupil took after the teacher." He let out a short blast of laughter. "Ha-ha!"

Florian gave him a sour look. "Are we leaving, or are we going to stand here all day oozing compliments?"

The general cast him a quelling look and offered Miss Pennybaker his arm. They swept toward the front door, followed by a grumbling Florian.

"Priscilla…"

"Yes?" Priscilla turned and looked up at John, forcing herself to appear innocent and unconcerned.

"I... That is, you..."

"Yes?"

"Nothing." He held his arm out stiffly, and Priscilla laid her hand on it. It gave her another little burst of satisfaction to feel that his arm trembled slightly beneath his coat.

She knew that she looked her best in this striking blue gown. The color and the shimmering satin did wonders for her skin and eyes, and the heart-shape neckline of the dress exposed the quivering tops of her breasts, pushed up by the stiff corset she wore beneath. Priscilla remembered how John had kissed those breasts, laving and caressing them until she was at a fever pitch of desire. The memory made heat flood her abdomen. She glanced over at John, wondering whether he remembered it, too. From the stiff way his jaw was set, she had a suspicion that he did.

All the way to the Court, John said almost nothing, although Priscilla caught him sneaking a look at her now and then. She pretended not to notice, and maintained what she hoped was an indifferent silence. Florian, scrunched in the corner of the seat across from the general and Miss Pennybaker, crossed his arms and glowered at them. That left Miss Pennybaker and her swain to carry the conversation, which they seemed to have no trouble doing. He complimented her, and she giggled; he whispered into her ear, and she waved her fan coquettishly; he made jokes, and she tittered, declaring him "too wicked for words." Even Priscilla, pleased as she was for her friend, felt that she might be ill if she had to ride much longer with them.

Ranleigh Court was impressive. Built of massive gray stone in the shape of an E, a conceit popular in the Elizabethan times, it loomed at the end of a long drive. An Aylesworth of the eighteenth century had ordered all the trees along the drive cut down, so that nothing would obstruct one's view of the huge house as one approached it.

John, looking out of the carriage, let out a low whistle. "That's what Alec stands to inherit?"

Priscilla nodded. "Along with quite a bit of land."

"Looks like a lot for that runaway heir to give up."

"It *is* something to behold," Priscilla admitted. "But Alec says it is a monstrosity to maintain."

"I can imagine."

They emerged from the carriage at the front door and walked in through the front doors, opened by a pair of footmen. The receiving line was at the head of a grand staircase, where the Duchess waited, Alec restless at her side. Alec greeted Priscilla joyously and John with some reserve, then passed them along to his mother.

The Duchess was an attractive woman still. She had married the old Duke when she was only seventeen, so that despite having a grown son, she was still a year or so away from forty. She had fought approaching age with such fury and dedication that she managed to look even younger than that. Her hair was blond and arranged in such a way that feathery curls framed her face, softening the rather sharp set of her features. Her eyes were a lovely blue, and she had darkened the pale lashes around them, so that this, her most attractive feature, dominated the remainder of her face. Her mouth, however, was small, and her nose sharp, and because she tried her best to keep her face free of lines by rarely smiling or frowning, there was an unnatural stiffness to her expression.

She beamed at Priscilla as she greeted them, startling Priscilla, who had long felt that the Duchess disliked her. Then Priscilla realized that it was not she who was the object of the smile but rather John, standing just behind her. The Duchess ran her eyes over his tall form, a spark of appreciation in her eye, and said gaily, "Priscilla, how wonderful to see you. Pray, tell me, who is your friend?"

The look the Duchess gave John was almost blatantly leering. Priscilla suppressed a quiver of distaste and forced herself to smile, stepping aside so that John could move directly in front of the other woman.

"Your Grace, this is John Wolfe, who is visiting with us. Mr. Wolfe, allow me to introduce you to the Duchess of Ranleigh."

"I hope you are having a pleasant visit," the Duchess said, dimpling and looking up flirtatiously through her lashes at John.

"All the more pleasant, Your Grace," John said with smile, "now that I have met you."

Priscilla would have expected Bianca to preen at the obvious compliment, to giggle and bat her eyelashes. Instead, she looked startled. "I— Ah, you are an American?"

"Yes, I am. Pray do not hold that against me."

"No. Of course not." Bianca continued to stare at his face. "It is just, well…it surprised me. We are not used to such distant travelers here, are we, Miss Hamilton?"

"No. Not usually." Seeing the Duchess's expression, Priscilla felt a sudden urge to see her reaction to John's story. "In fact, Mr. Wolfe would merely have passed through here—if it had not been for what happened to him."

"Happened to him?" The Duchess's voice rose almost to a squeak, and she glanced apprehensively at John.

"Yes," Priscilla went on earnestly. "Mr. Wolfe was attacked by ruffians."

"Attacked? Here?" Bianca's skin had taken on an unhealthy pallor, and Priscilla noticed that her hands were clenched tightly around her delicate ivory fan. "But how dreadful!"

"Yes, wasn't it?" Priscilla agreed. "It seems as if it is becoming positively unsafe to travel the roads anymore."

"Yes." Bianca looked distracted, and repeated in a faint voice, "How dreadful. What—what did they want?"

"My valuables, of course. They took my wallet, my pocket watch, all my cuff links," John told her.

Priscilla saw the other woman's shoulders sag a little in seeming relief. "That was all they wanted? Your valuables?"

John raised his brows. "I presume so. What else could they have wanted? I don't know anyone here, so they could hardly have done it out of animosity toward me."

Bianca smiled, and this time Priscilla was certain that it was relief she saw on the Duchess's face. "Of course. How silly of me. I am sure you are right. It was simply a random theft. It is so distressing how crime runs rampant these days." She cast a quick glance around. "If you will excuse me, I must attend to my guests. It was ever so nice to meet you, Mr. Wolfe."

She flashed a bright, meaningless smile at him and

Priscilla, then turned to the general and Miss Pennybaker, waiting behind them. "Ah, General, how wonderful to see you."

Priscilla and John moved several steps away from the Duchess and stood watching her, pretending to be in idle conversation.

"Well, my presence certainly seemed to cause some distress to the Duchess," John said dryly.

"Yes. I would say that Bianca was not entirely ignorant of Oliver's plan to kidnap you."

"Do you suppose she merely knew of his plan, or that she, too, wanted to be rid of me?"

"I don't know. Did you notice that she did not recognize you by sight? It was not until she heard your voice that she began to act strangely. It seemed to be because you were an American."

"I cannot imagine sheer xenophobia setting one to hire thugs to beat up all Americans."

"No. I admit it seems unlikely. Let's see what she does."

They moved over to the wall, casually hanging about behind a large potted palm and watching the receiving line through the palm fronds. As they watched, the Duchess gave a dismissive smile and nod to the general and Miss Pennybaker and turned away, looking all about the room. Finally she spotted what she was seeking, and headed in a determined manner across the room. Priscilla and John followed at a discreet distance. Finally she came to a stop beside Benjamin Oliver, who was in conversation with another woman. Bianca flashed a quick, dismissive smile at the woman and tugged urgently at his sleeve. He gave the woman an apologetic bow and went with Bianca.

The couple came straight toward Priscilla and John, who quickly turned and began to admire an alabaster statue a short distance from them.

"What the devil do you want?" they heard Benjamin snap as the couple passed behind them. The Duchess's reply was muffled by the sound of her rapid steps on the marble floor.

Once Oliver and Bianca were past them, Priscilla and John turned and sauntered after them, doing their best not to look as if they were following. They need not have bothered with the subterfuge. Neither Bianca nor Oliver looked back. They were too busy glaring at each other to notice anyone else.

Bianca led Oliver out a side door, and Priscilla and John slipped through the same door a moment later. They saw their quarry halfway down the hall. The couple turned left and disappeared into a room. Priscilla and John hurried quietly down the hall, slowing down when they grew close to the room. The closed door muffled the sound of the voices inside, so that they could tell little, except that a high-pitched woman's voice was shrieking. Priscilla motioned to John to follow her and ducked back into the room they had just passed. She pointed to a door in the side wall of the room.

"A connecting door," she whispered. Carefully they eased the hall door closed behind them and made their way to the connecting door. Here, sound escaped much more freely around the edges of the door.

"...could you have been such a fool?" they heard Bianca snap.

"Would you quit storming about and tell me why you are so furious?" a man's voice lashed back. "You sound like a sea gull."

"Don't try to draw me off the subject by insulting me. It won't work. You have ruined everything. Bungled it all."

"What do you mean?"

"There is a man with that nasty little Priscilla Hamilton. Didn't you see him?"

"No." Oliver's voice grew wary. "Why? Who is he?"

"I don't know who he is. I never saw him or heard of him in my life. The point is that he is an American! And he told me that he had been attacked and robbed a few days ago."

"No! It's impossible." They heard a thud as Oliver hit something. "God damn them! They swore to me that they would get him this time."

"This time?" Bianca said dangerously. "*This* time? What do you mean by that? What other time was there?"

"He got away." There was a surly tone in Oliver's voice. "But they promised that they would get him back. I offered them money, threatened them, everything I could think of, and they promised."

"Why didn't you tell me this? Did you think I didn't need to know? Why did you leave me to find out from this perfect stranger, to run into him and hear…" Her sentence ended in a wordless shriek of rage.

"It is all right, my love. Calm down. I will manage it somehow."

"Why isn't he dead? I told you to kill him! Why couldn't they manage to kill him? Did you hire utter idiots? What am I thinking? Of course you did. You are an utter idiot yourself!"

"I— Well, it did not seem entirely necessary to kill

him. I thought perhaps he could be reasoned with, made to see that it would be better for him to go back to the United States."

"You coward! You were too scared to kill him—even to hire someone else to do it for you!"

"Well, it was not you whose neck was on the line," Oliver told her petulantly. "Those two fellows never met you. You are not the one they could inform on to the police. Easy for you to be so brave, when I was the one doing the dirty work."

"A duchess can hardly go about hiring ruffians," Bianca reminded him haughtily. "What good are you to me, if you can't do even something as simple as this?"

"I will do it. Right now, this very evening. I shall snatch him as he leaves the party."

"He is with friends. What do you plan to do, whisk away the entire carriage?" Bianca's voice dripped sarcasm. She walked away, and they could not hear the first few words she said, but then she turned back and said, quite clearly, "Besides, he is not the one."

There was a moment of stunned silence. Priscilla and John looked at each other in equal amazement.

"What?" Oliver finally squeaked out.

"You got the wrong man," she replied wearily. "That man isn't Lynden. He could not possibly be. He is far too young. Have you no sense? How could he be Ranleigh's son?"

"Alec is Ranleigh's son," Oliver said defensively. "He is younger than this Wolfe fellow. This man was the one at the solicitor's office. The clerk sent me a note when he came in, and I went to the office, and that was the man who came out. The clerk said it was he."

"Then the clerk is as great a fool as you. Or else he

was lying and pocketing your money. Lynden was practically a grown man when he left Ranleigh Court, and that was thirty years ago! He has to be middle-aged now. I told you the entire story. It all happened long before I even met Ranleigh. Lynden is old enough to be Alec's father, even if he is his brother. And you follow a young man, thinking he's the new duke!"

Priscilla and John turned toward each other, eyes wide and faces blank with astonishment.

There was another long silence on the other side of the door, then a rustle, followed by the crack of a slap. "Get your hands off me, you dolt! Lynden's out there somewhere, and I have no idea where or when he will show up. You have ruined my life, and you think you can make it up to me by playing the adoring lover? Get away!"

Her heels clattered across the floor, followed by the outer door slamming. In the room behind her, there was the sound of glass hitting the floor and breaking. It came again and again, until Oliver had apparently exhausted either himself or his supply of breakable objects. Then he, too, stormed out of the room.

Priscilla sagged against the wall. She felt as if her legs would hardly support her. "My God!" she breathed. "They thought you were the missing heir! The Duke! That is why they attacked you!"

John scarcely heard her. He was focused on what was most important to him. "It was a mistake. It was all by chance. They don't know me. And I still have no idea who I am!"

Hearing the distress in his voice, she turned, reaching out to him. "Oh, John! I'm sorry. I didn't even think... how awful this must be for you."

"God, Priscilla, I had hoped! I wanted to find out so badly." He went into her arms, pulling her close to him and burying his face against her neck. "I wanted to lay it to rest, to find out what I am and whether I am free."

"I know. I know." Priscilla rubbed her hands soothingly over his back. She ached for him, but even so, it felt wonderful to feel his arms around her again. She had never before realized that a person could actually feel starved for another's touch. But she had been starved for John the past two days. "I am so sorry. But it will happen. I am sure of it. Don't worry. One day you will remember."

"But when?" Despite his despairing question, his voice had lost much of its strain. Her soothing touch was drawing the anguish and frustration from him.

"Don't worry about it. Just believe. It will happen. It has to."

They stood for a long moment, arms around each other. Then his arms tightened around her. Priscilla could feel tension, a different sort of tension, growing in him.

"God, you smell good," he murmured.

"Thank you." She tilted her head back to look up at him, smiling.

Her lips were soft, and faintly moist. John gazed at them, his heart beating faster in his chest. "You are so beautiful tonight. It took my breath away when you came downstairs."

"Did it?"

"All I wanted was to kiss you. And keep on kissing you. Never stop." Unconsciously, he bent his head toward hers.

"Then why don't you?"

"I can't." His voice was barely more than a breath.

"Yes, you can." Her eyes began to dance. "Look. I'll show you." She stretched up on tiptoe, raising her delectable lips to him.

He bent. Their mouths met and joined sweetly. For an instant he drank her in, his breath searing her cheek. Then he jerked back abruptly.

"No." His voice was harsh, and his breath came fast in his throat. "I must not. I cannot."

Priscilla went back flat on her feet, disappointment written on her face. "John! What is the matter? For two days you have avoided me. Why? I thought the other night—"

"No!" He turned away. "I was a fool. I should never have allowed it to go so far. It would not have happened, except that I was hardly awake, and I did not think, only did what I wanted."

"I had something to do with that, too, not just you," Priscilla pointed out reasonably.

"But I should have been more in control." John set his jaw. "You are young and inexperienced. It was wrong of me to take advantage of that."

"You did not. I offered freely."

"I still was a cad to take what you offered," he responded shortly.

"You regret what we did?" Priscilla asked, her voice shaking a little.

"No! Never. I told you that. What we did was…was heaven." He let out a groan and ground his teeth in frustration. "But I cannot let it happen again. I would be a coward, a scoundrel. Until I know who I am, and whether I have a wife, it would be very, very wrong of me. Priscilla, please…do not tempt me."

She drew back, irritated, and yet somehow pleased, as well. He would not hold back, denying his own desire, simply for the sake of convention. She was sure of it. His reluctance must mean that he cared for her. "Is that why you have avoided me ever since? Scarcely talked to me or looked at me?"

He nodded. "Yes, I— It is very awkward. I don't know what to do or say. It is so difficult to be around you and not to be able to take you in my arms and kiss you. I am afraid that when I look at you, everyone will see how much I want you."

Priscilla's breath caught in her throat at his words, and she felt a flush of pleasure rising in her cheeks. "Then you do not dislike me now, because we did—what we did? I know Mrs. Whiting has told me that a man no longer likes or respects a woman if she lets him 'have his way with her.' I thought perhaps that was how you felt, that you—"

"No!" He grasped her arms and pulled her back against his chest, wrapping his arms tightly around her. "God, no, don't think that." He rained kisses over her hair and face and neck. "I want you with every fiber of my being. I respect you, like you, I—"

Priscilla ended his words by throwing her arms around his neck and kissing him. He groaned deep in his throat and kissed her back, and by the time they emerged from their kiss, they were beyond words. They kissed again—a light, sealing touch—then moved apart.

Priscilla smoothed her hair and skirts, buying herself time to recover, then said, her voice a little shaky, "We ought to return to the party, I suppose. Miss Pennybaker may come searching for me if she can't find us."

"Not tonight, I think," John responded, offering her

his arm. "She has a little romance of her own to tend to tonight."

Smiling and talking of Miss Pennybaker and her romantic triangle, they walked back down the hall and into the party. The dancing had started it, and they joined it.

After that they strolled through the large room, talking to people they knew and introducing John to those he did not. Lady Chalcomb was there, looking quietly lovely in a blue-gray satin gown, and as they stood talking to her, they were soon joined by Mr. Rutherford. As they talked, they became aware of a stir near the stairs, a faint susurration of whispers and the rustle of movement. Priscilla and John turned toward the noise as the crowd parted slowly. A man came into view, striding slowly through the people. He was middle-aged, with sharp wings of white slicing back through his dark blond hair, but he was still an attractive man. Tall and broadshouldered, with a firm jaw and prominent cheekbones, he exuded power and confidence. Priscilla was certain that she had never seen him before, yet there was something familiar about him.

But before she could consider what that familiarity was, she was distracted by a sharp hiss of indrawn breath from Anne, beside her. Priscilla turned to look at her and was amazed to see that the older woman's face had drained of all color, and she was staring fixedly at the new arrival, her mouth open and her fingers clenched tightly around her fan.

At the same moment, on the other side of Anne, Mr. Rutherford spoke, staring at the late arrival. "My God! It can't be!"

"Who is—?" Priscilla started to ask, but she was

interrupted by the aging butler of Ranleigh Court, Oaksworth, who came tottering after the newcomer.

The butler's face was all smiles, even as he trembled with what looked to Priscilla like distress. "Your Grace," he called out to the Duchess, his aging voice quavering with emotion. Bianca turned to look at him, frowning slightly at the almost rude way he spoke. She glanced behind him at the large man outstripping the butler.

"Oaksworth?" she said icily to the butler.

Oaksworth stopped, thrusting out his chest proudly, and announced, "His Grace, the Duke of Ranleigh."

There were gasps from among the crowd, but Bianca could do nothing more than stare at the man, her breath frozen in her lungs. She gaped at him, as did everyone else on the floor, trying to take in the fact that the long-lost heir had returned.

The large man bowed elegantly, saying to Bianca, "I am pleased to make your acquaintance, madam. I hope it is not too much of an inconvenience, my showing up this way."

Bianca's eyes rolled up. She let out a quavery sigh and fainted.

Those closest to Bianca caught her as she fell and supported her, then wrestled her up and carried her to the nearest couch. The new Duke straightened from his bow, his eyebrows going up lazily as he watched the men cart away the Duchess. He glanced around him, and his eyes fell on John, who had moved forward slightly, away from Priscilla, and was staring intently at the new Duke.

"Ah, Bryan, there you are. I was beginning to worry about you," Ranleigh said.

John took another step toward the man, saying calmly, "Hello, Father."

CHAPTER FIFTEEN

FATHER?

Priscilla watched, mouth open, as John Wolfe strode across the floor of the ballroom without hesitation. The Duke of Ranleigh threw his arms around John, and the two of them laughed and clapped each other on the back. John knew who he was, Priscilla thought in amazement—and that person was the son of the Duke of Ranleigh.

Anger swept over Priscilla. It was obvious that he had known all along who he was. He had answered the man easily, promptly, without hesitation or stumbling. He had lied to her, deceived her. Priscilla thought of her earnest efforts to find out his identity; she remembered the ingenuous way he had asked about the long-lost heir to Ranleigh and the way she had repeated the local gossip to him. And all the while they had been talking about his father! He had encouraged her to make a fool of herself in front of him!

Fury and bitter shame swelled in Priscilla's chest in equal parts. She did not know why John had acted out that charade of losing his memory—whether he had been acting as a scout for his father, to check out the locale and the people before the Duke himself actually arrived, or he had been afraid to admit who he was after he had been attacked. That was reasonable, she

supposed. But he could at least have told *her!* He could
have trusted her enough to let her know who he really
was. Instead, he had treated her like a stranger. She felt
an utter fool.

Priscilla glanced at Mr. Rutherford. He, too, was leaving them without a word, walking toward the Duke as
if in a trance.

"Sebastian!" Ranleigh called out heartily. "Is that
you? Come here and let me see you."

Priscilla turned to Anne and said abruptly, "I have
to leave." She noticed then that Anne looked the color
of parchment. "Anne? Are you all right?"

Anne shook her head. "I never thought…" She gazed
at Priscilla, her eyes huge in her face. "It has been thirty
years. I thought—I was sure he was long since dead."

"As was everyone else," Priscilla commented dryly.
Anne seemed terribly shaken by the Duke's arrival.
She didn't understand why it should affect her so, but
she was too upset herself right now to try to delve into
Anne's actions. "I'm sorry; you must excuse me. I have
to leave."

"But why? Where?"

"I am going home." Priscilla's voice was grim, and
her jaw was set. She could not bear to see John turn
and smile at her, to hear him laugh and say that he was
sorry, that it had all been in a good cause. "I cannot stay
here."

She started toward the door so rapidly that Anne,
following her, almost had to run. "Wait!"

Priscilla turned. Color was high in her face, and her
eyes were overly bright.

"I am leaving, too. Let me offer you a ride."

Priscilla nodded, relieved. She had come in the

general's big, antiquated coach, and she hated to make all the others leave the party early, simply because she was miserable. "Yes, thank you. Just let me tell my father where I am going."

It took her some time to track down Florian, but at last she found him downstairs, near the refreshments table, with Dr. Hightower, busily scribbling away on the tablecloth. "Yes, but look, Reginald, the equation can't be right. It breaks down when you get to—"

"Papa!" Priscilla looked down in exasperation at the once sparklingly white cloth. "You've ruined the tablecloth!"

"What? There you are, my dear. Having a good time?"

Dr. Hightower gazed in some dismay at the tablecloth. "Oh, I say. I didn't even notice."

"No paper, you see," Florian explained, then frowned. "Damned nuisance to write on— Wouldn't you think people would have paper around?"

Priscilla's lips twitched, but she refused to smile. "Not at a ball, usually."

"I daresay it will wash out," Dr. Hightower put in reassuringly.

"I am going home now, Papa. Lady Chalcomb kindly offered to take me."

"Are you?" Florian's face lit up. "Excellent! The doctor and I shall accompany you. It will be far easier to show him what I am talking about in my own study."

Florian rose to his feet, and the doctor followed more slowly. Florian saw nothing odd in his daughter's wanting to leave a dance early, but the doctor frowned in concern.

"But, Priscilla, dear girl, isn't it rather early to be leaving a ball?"

"Nonsense," Florian told him. "Deady dull thing, anyway. I can't think why we ever came."

"Young girls usually enjoy them, Flo," Dr. Hightower pointed out. "They like to dance, and that sort of thing. Dress up, you know."

"Yes, I daresay." Florian tightened his lips grimly. "Not just young ones, either, I find. Miss Pennybaker was making a cake of herself on the dance floor tonight."

"Papa!" Priscilla cried at this injustice. "She was not. She was merely dancing. I thought she and the general looked quite good together."

"Too old for that sort of thing. Both of them," Florian grumbled.

"You are never too old to dance. *You* ought to try it sometime. Perhaps then Miss Pennybaker wouldn't resort to going out on the floor with the General."

"Me? What nonsense. Besides, what do I care whether she dances with that old fool?"

Priscilla shrugged. "I am sure *I* don't know, Papa. *You* were the one who was complaining about it."

Her father glowered at her for a moment, then started away, saying, "What are we standing here for? Let's join Lady Chalcomb."

When they got outside, they found that Lady Chalcomb had not brought the cumbersome old coach that her husband had been wont to rattle around in, but merely a light trap pulled by two horses.

"I'm sorry," she said apologetically as they all squeezed into the small conveyance, clearly not meant for more than two or three people, and certainly none with the bulk of Dr. Hightower. "I am afraid I haven't the team any longer for Lord Harry's coach."

A blush rushed into her cheeks; she knew that everyone was aware of her straitened circumstances, but that scarcely made them less embarrassing. She had sold all her husband's expensive horses and hunting dogs after his death, as well as the best artworks at Chalcomb Hall, in order to pay off the bulk of his debts. Even to one as unknowledgeable as Priscilla, it was obvious that these two horses, not a matched pair, would have been gone, as well, except that they were too old for anyone to want.

"No problem," Florian told her cheerfully. "I shall stand on this step here." He followed his words with action, standing on the small metal stepup and hanging on to the pole supporting the right side of the trap. "That way, I will counterbalance the doctor. It should ride better that way, too."

So off they went in the shabby little trap behind the aging horses, Florian hanging off the side like a schoolboy hitching a ride on a delivery wagon. Their progress was little faster than walking on foot would have been, but none of them seemed to mind. Anne and Priscilla were silent with their thoughts, and Florian and the doctor continued their discussion of equations.

Finally, about halfway back to Evermere Cottage, the doctor and Florian decided to postpone the conversation until they had adequate paper and pencil. For a few moments, they rode in utter silence. The doctor looked from Anne to Priscilla and back again, then up at Florian. He raised his eyebrows questioningly, but Florian simply shook his head. He had never attempted to understand his children's moods, and especially not his daughter's.

"Interesting, wasn't it, about Lynden showing up?" the doctor said, making a stab at conversation.

Anne's hands tightened on the reins, and the horses came to a dead stop. Priscilla shot him a look, as if he had said something indelicate.

His eyebrows rose. "Oh. I'm sorry."

"Sorry?" Florian replied. "What for? The Marquess coming back? I mean the Duke, I suppose, now."

"How did you know about it?" Priscilla asked stiffly. "You two were downstairs."

"We saw him when he came in—before old Oaksworth saw him and started crying. I recognized him, of course, though it took a moment. He was only a stripling when he ran off, tall, but thin. He's fleshed out a good bit since then. And browned, of course. Been out in the sun in the New World. Wonder if he killed that girl. Never seemed the sort to me, really."

"Of course he did not," Anne said in a strangely choked voice.

Everyone glanced at her, surprised at her vehemence. She blushed again and said, "He was not the sort. He wouldn't have killed a woman. He wouldn't even have been dangling after a woman like that."

"Well, uh, that's not the sort of thing one would tell a lady," Dr. Hightower pointed out mildly, looking a trifle red-faced himself.

"True," Florian agreed, though he himself rarely paid attention to what one should or should not tell a delicate female. "Still, he always seemed a good enough lad. No doubt he sowed a few wild oats at school. But that's hardly the same as strangling a girl. I am inclined to agree with Lady Chalcomb."

"John Wolfe is his son," Priscilla said flatly. Her words were followed by a stunned silence.

"Who? Oh! Wolfe, yes, of course." Florian frowned thoughtfully. "Hmm, well, yes, now that you mention it, I can see it. Has the same sort of build, you know, though more muscled than his father was as a lad. Darker, too. But then, that's the sun in the colonies."

"John Wolfe?" the doctor repeated, confused. "The lad who doesn't know who he is? How can he be Ranleigh's son?"

"He *claimed* he could not remember his name or his past."

"Why do you say 'he claimed' like that, Pris? You think he was only pretending not to remember?"

"He recalled his past quickly enough tonight. The minute the Duke walked in, he called him 'Father.' There was no hesitation. No confusion. He walked right toward him." *And away from her.*

Florian nodded. "I can see the wisdom of keeping it quiet. He may have been attacked because of who he was, in fact. He wouldn't have known for certain that he could trust us. Smart to keep his knowledge to himself."

"He is crafty enough," Priscilla agreed bitterly.

"Don't be hard on the lad," Florian advised her. "He had his reasons, I'm sure. He's not a bad sort."

Priscilla had some difficulty agreeing with her father's assessment. All she could think of was the fact that she had given herself to John, body and soul, not caring that he had no name, that he did not know who or what he was, even whether or not he was married or engaged. She had loved him for himself alone.

And now he turned out to be a marquess! Not a rankless American, not an adventurer, but a member of the nobility. It had been easy enough for her to disregard his lack of rank, but it was far more difficult when the opposite was true. He was no one whom she could possibly marry; he was a future duke, and he would have to marry accordingly. In one instant, he had passed beyond her, out of her reach forever.

She was certain he had known about it—though perhaps not when he first arrived at their house. That might have been a legitimate reaction, a moment of stunned confusion and memory loss. But sometime, somewhere along the way, the truth had settled in on him. It was no wonder he had been so interested in Alex and the Duchess, or in the story of why the Marquess had fled the country! He had probably been waiting for his father to make his grand entrance at the party tonight before he revealed his identity.

And while he was waiting, lying low and pretending he was a nobody, had he decided to amuse himself by seducing a country girl? The thought burned through her. If she had known that he was the heir to Ranleigh, she would have been more on guard with him. She would have realized that there was no future for them. She would have done her best to hold on to her heart and not to give it where it could never be returned. Could he have been so selfish and heartless, to use his ruse to win her body?

Priscilla could not bear to think so. She reminded herself that during the past few days he had held back from taking her, even when she had more or less thrown herself at him. He had been the one to resist, and she had been the insistent one. It had not always been that way. When he first came to the house, he had kissed her eagerly, caressed her, wanted her. Then, at some point, he had changed. Now she realized that it was probably because he had remembered who he was. He had realized that a future duke could not get entangled with a nobody. No wonder he had regretted bedding her. No doubt when Penny was talking about her reputation he had been struck with fear, thinking that she might try to force him to marry her because of the night they had spent together. *As if she would do such a thing!* She would not marry him for love nor money, Priscilla told herself.

When the trap reached their house, Priscilla got out quickly and hurried inside. She ran up the stairs and into her bedroom. All the way home, her chest had felt as if it were swelling with anguish, filling up until she was about to burst. Now, finally, she was alone. She threw herself on her bed and let the bitter tears flood out.

BRYAN AYLESWORTH STEPPED BACK from his father and looked at him. He felt stunned, as if someone had punched him in the stomach. His memory had rushed back in on him in an instant. He had seen his father, and suddenly he had known who he was. It left him feeling faintly dizzy and sick, as if he had been whirled around wildly. Added to that strange feeling was the fact that, though he suddenly knew who he was, his father seemed to have become an entirely different person.

"Where have you been, lad?" his father was saying. "I didn't know what to make of it when I arrived at the inn in Elverton and they said they had seen no sign of you. I was beginning to worry. I knew you had reached London before I did. That sobersides lawyer told me you had come to his office, just as I'd told you to, and he had given you the information about Elverton and the inn and all." He made a vague gesture around him.

"I—I was delayed." Bryan glanced around him. "Priscilla? Where is she? She was right here a moment ago."

"Who was?"

His son grinned. "A woman. Priscilla Hamilton. Your future daughter-in-law, I believe."

The Duke's jaw dropped. "You're joking. Are you serious? You have been caught at last? Is that what delayed you?"

"Not exactly. I shall explain it all to you in a moment." His brows drew together darkly. "We have quite a number of things to discuss, in fact. But first I have to find Priscilla. I have to tell her who I am."

"You have to *what?*" Ranleigh repeated in astonishment, but Bryan had already turned and was walking away, searching all around him.

It took him a good fifteen minutes of fruitless searching before he found someone who remembered seeing Priscilla and Lady Chalcomb going down the stairs right after the new duke walked in. He headed downstairs, as well, only to find no trace of either of the two women. Finally he went outside, where a footman told him that Miss Hamilton and her father had left the party with Lady Chalcomb and Dr. Hightower.

"What the devil—?" Bryan murmured, confused. Why would Priscilla have left so suddenly? Especially after the strange and startling things that had occurred?

He stood for a moment, gazing out into the dark night, faintly troubled. He could not understand Priscilla's disappearance, and he wanted to go running after her. But if she was with her father and Lady Chalcomb, surely she would be all right…and, first, he had a mystery right here that needed to be resolved. He turned around and went back to the party, looking for his father.

It was not hard to find him. There was a huge knot of people clustered around him, all eager to reacquaint themselves with the new Duke of Ranleigh. His father was chatting happily with Mr. Rutherford. The man who had saved him from being a suspect, Bryan realized with some amazement. He found it hard to connect his father with the lad Priscilla had said had run off years ago, under suspicion of murder.

Bryan, taller than most of the people surrounding his father, was able to look over their heads and catch his father's eye. He jerked his head emphatically, indicating that they should leave the room, and Ranleigh, with a knowing grin, nodded back and began to make his way through the crowd around him. Bryan waited impatiently for him by the door. Even after Damon had succeeded in working his way free of the clot of well-wishers and curiosity-seekers, he could not seem to take a step without someone else coming forward to greet him.

Finally he reached Bryan and took his elbow, saying, "Come along. I know where we can escape them all."

He led his son quickly out into the same hall that Bryan and Priscilla had taken earlier. However, he took Bryan past the room where they had eavesdropped on the Duchess and down a set of stairs to a large room. In the dim light cast by the wall sconces in the hall,

Bryan could see that it was a library, with shelves of books lining the walls and a massive desk squatting in the center of the room. The wall opposite the door was a bank of windows, their drapes now drawn against the night.

Ranleigh went to the desk and lit a lamp, and the room was suffused with a golden glow. Bryan watched his father as he looked slowly around the room. The older man shook his head. "Exactly the same," he said, his voice hoarse with emotion. He cleared his throat. "Father always was one for tradition. I remember he sulked for a month when my mother redecorated the dining room."

He turned back to Bryan, who was watching him, arms crossed over his chest. "I presume you have some questions for me."

"A few," his son retorted sarcastically. "Mainly, when in the hell did you become a duke?"

"When my father died, a year or so ago," his father replied calmly, and walked over to a large wingback chair by the fireplace, motioning to Bryan to sit in the chair across from it.

Bryan sat down with ill grace. "Then you really are the Duke of Ranleigh?"

"Of course. Did you think I was deceiving those people out there?"

"I don't know what to think. Why did you never tell us? Does Delia know?"

"She does. I told her as soon as I heard of his death. You, as I recall, were in Malaya at the time."

"That's where I was when I got your telegram telling me to go to the attorney's office in London. They refused to tell me a damn thing except to come here to Elverton and wait for you."

"I thought it was something that needed to be explained by me in person, not by a set of strangers."

"Why did you not explain it some time ago?"

The older man shrugged. "I'm not sure. When I first left England, I was so furious with my father, so…unhappy, that I wanted nothing to do with my family or this house or the title. I washed my hands of the whole thing, started a new life. My title didn't help me much in the United States. It seemed pretentious to use it. It was strange when I arrived in New York. For the first time, I was on my own, without my father or his title to pave the way for me. It was hard. I had no skills to speak of, no idea how to take care of myself. I didn't even have a valet. It was frightening…but it was freeing, as well. When I married your mother and had you and Delia, well, I didn't see any reason to burden you with the family heritage. I thought it was better for you to grow up an American, to make your own way, not to have everything planned out for you as I had. I had made a good life for myself and my family. It seemed to me that the name Aylesworth was enough. I never even told your mother about it. She accepted me as I was, without a past. I had no intention of coming back and taking over the title."

He paused and leaned forward, bracing his elbows on his knees and his chin on his hands. He gazed down at the floor for a long moment, then went on. "But a few years ago, after your mother died, I began to think about things here…about Ranleigh Court, and my father, and…people I had left behind. Finally I engaged a solicitor in London, and he made inquiries for me. He wrote me that my father was still alive, that he had remarried and had a child. I decided then that I would forget about the title and the estate, just let the boy have it. Still, I could not stop thinking about Ranleigh Court, and my father, and…the cloud I had left under. I hated knowing what my own father thought about me, what everyone who had known me thought. I told myself it did not matter, but I couldn't get it out of my brain."

He sighed and gazed at the drapes, as if he could see through them to the landscape beyond. "It was odd. I realized that I missed Ranleigh Court. Without your mother, New York no longer felt like home. I wanted to come back. I wanted to make my peace with my father. Then my solicitor informed me that Father had died. I realized how foolish I had been to hold off returning. Now I can never make things right with him. But I could come back. I could at least clear my name, and maybe that would make it up to him a little. It occurred to me that I had been wrong all these years to deny you and Delia your true heritage. You had a right to know, to be the Duke of Ranleigh when I'm gone. It was selfish and unfair of me to decide for you. So I had my solicitor contact my father's solicitors, and I wrote to you to join me here."

Bryan gazed at him for a long moment. He shook his head in amazement. "I find all this hard to take in at one time. What did Delia say? Did she come with you?"

"No. She laughed and said that her friends would be green with envy now that she could be called 'my lady,' but she is far too interested in her babies and Robert to think of coming here. Her life is in the United States."

"So is mine."

"Is it?" Ranleigh smiled quizzically. "I had gotten

the impression that it was all over the world for the past ten years."

Bryan smiled, admitting, "I suppose it has been. But…Father, I am no English gentleman."

"I know. Neither am I, anymore. However, one doesn't have a choice about one's name or family. It is something you will have to learn to accept."

Bryan looked down at his hands. There was a long silence, then he said quietly, "I've heard that the Marquess left England because he had killed a girl." He looked up squarely into his father's eyes. "Is that true? Did you kill Rose Childs?"

CHAPTER SIXTEEN

HIS FATHER STARED BACK STONILY AT HIM. "You have to ask me that?"

"I cannot believe that you would kill anyone, let alone some girl whom you had…been intimate with. But, you see, the man I know is Damon Aylesworth. Not the Marquess of Lynden. Were you a different man then?"

"No. I was the same. I ran away because my father and I quarreled bitterly. He believed that I had committed murder, and I could not bear knowing that. But I did *not* kill her. Nor had I had an affair with Rose. I barely knew who she was."

"Were you with Rutherford that night? Playing cards, as he said?"

"No. He came forward and said that simply to save my hide. I had no alibi."

"Why not?"

"I was out of the house. One of the grooms had seen me ride my horse out earlier. That was one of the more damning things against me. I was not at home, and I could not say where I was nor who I was with."

"You were alone? Did no one see you at any time?"

"No. I was not alone. That was the problem."

"You're not making sense. Who were you with? Why did they not speak up?"

"I cannot say. It concerns someone's honor."

Bryan quirked a brow. "You said you wanted to clear your name. How can you clear your name if you cannot prove you were elsewhere?"

"I will have to do it some other way. I'm not sure how. But revealing who I was with is not an option."

"Father! You cannot even tell me?"

"It concerns a lady. I could not compromise her."

"You were meeting a woman? Someone other than Rose?"

"Of course someone other than Rose. I told you, I barely knew her. She was just one of the chambermaids. And I was in love with someone far more beautiful, far more..." He stopped. "She was married, Bryan. I was a lad head over heels in love with a married woman. It would have meant the ruin of her reputation if I had revealed I was with her. Moreover, her husband would have beaten her if he had found out about it. I could not do that to her. She wanted to tell the authorities where I had been, but I would not let her."

Bryan stared at him. "You were having an affair with a married woman? Who was it?"

Ranleigh quirked an eyebrow at him. "You think I am going to tell you that? No. Not even you."

"You must have loved her very much."

"I did." His words were a heavy sigh. "I loved her more than anything."

Bryan sat still for a moment, trying to absorb yet another secret he had learned about his father. "I am beginning to think that I don't know you at all."

"What a man does as a barely grown lad is rarely part of the stories he tells his children. It was a different life. It had nothing to do with you."

"Did you love her still when you married my mother?"

"Yes. I won't try to deny it. I loved her long, long after I knew her. Your mother was a good woman, and I loved her. Don't think I didn't care for her. But…it was not the same way that I loved—the other one."

"I see. Did Mother know?"

"I did not tell her. She may have guessed. I don't know. She was always a canny one. But she did not ask about the women in my past. She told me that she preferred not to know. She knew that I was never unfaithful to her."

"Except in your heart."

Ranleigh sighed. "I suppose so, if you want to look at it like that. But your mother was content. She was happy. She knew that she had all the love I had to give. I did not sit around and pine after…her. I didn't compare your mother to her. I did my best to be a good husband and father."

Bryan looked away, shaken by his father's revelation.

"Bryan, it was your mother's choice. She was happy with what she had. I was happy, too."

"Without the woman you really loved?"

"I could not have her. She was married." His face darkened. "She would not leave him. Should I have spent the rest of my life mourning her?"

Bryan shook his head, studying the pattern of the rug beneath his feet. "No. But if you loved this woman, how could you bear to leave her? How could you live without her all your life?" His mind went involuntarily to Priscilla; he thought of how empty he would feel at the thought of never seeing her again, never again tasting the sweet pleasure of her body.

"I didn't feel I had any choice. You don't understand, and, frankly, I hope you never do. There is such frustration in loving a woman you know can never be yours. No matter how much you love her, no matter what you would do for her, she is another man's wife, and will remain so. Strong as the love is, there is an anger, a bitterness, too. Sometimes, lying in my bed alone at night, thinking about her with him, I hated her for being married to him—even while I was aching all over to touch her. I felt as if I paid in blood for every bit of time I spent with her. Every minute of joy had hours of pain to counter it."

"I'm sorry." Bryan surged to his feet. He hated hearing the pain that lay in his father's voice. "I did not mean to criticize. You don't have to explain or justify anything to me."

"No. It was a legitimate question, one I would probably ask in your place. Believe me, there were more than a few miserable nights aboard ship and in America when I cursed myself for having left her, when I called myself all kinds of a fool and told myself that it would have been worth anything—all the pain, all the jealousy, even living with my father's lack of faith in me and the hounds of the police baying at my heels, anything!— just to lie with her again." He let out a short, humorless laugh. "Indeed, if I had not been thousands of miles away and practically penniless that first year, I would probably have run straight back to her."

"Fortunate for Delia and me that you could not, I suppose."

"Humph. Fortunate for me, too. That kind of loving

is a living death. It saps a man's pride, his strength, his honor. She was not a wicked woman—don't think otherwise. She was good and kind and wonderfully gentle, and she was married to a brute who did not deserve her. But what we did was wrong, and we knew it was wrong, and it tainted our lives. If we had gone on, I think it would have blackened my soul eventually."

Bryan was silent for a moment, then asked quietly, "Will you try to see her again? Now that you are back?"

His father looked at him for a long moment. Finally he said, "Yes. Though I don't even know if she is alive or lives here still." He stood up and walked over to the bookcase, staring blindly at the books' bindings. "After you went off tonight to seek out your 'future wife,' I looked all around for her. I couldn't see her anywhere. She was not in the throng of people who came up to talk to me. And I didn't want to make it obvious by asking about her first thing. But I *will* ask. If she is alive and here, I shall have to see her again, if only to find out what has happened to her, how the years have dealt with her. I have to know." He turned and faced his son, and there was a bleakness in his eyes that Bryan had never seen there before. "Beyond that, I do not know. But I must see her."

A heavy silence fell upon them. Finally the Duke turned away from the windows. "Enough of the past. Now, tell me what has happened to you. And what is this about a woman you want to marry?"

Bryan grinned. "She is a very special woman."

"Beautiful?"

"Very. Well, perhaps not in the common sense. But her eyes—gray as the sea, and she can fix you with a gaze that looks straight into your soul. The first time I saw her, I was on my last legs, and when she opened that door, with the light glowing behind her, she looked like an angel to me. The next time I saw her, she damn near blew my head off."

His father's eyebrows vaulted up. "Indeed."

"Well," Bryan explained, "I was holding a knife to her throat, you see, so she had to defend herself."

"Of course," the other man murmured, his eyes dancing. "It makes perfect sense now."

His son had the good grace to grin. "I know; it sounds like a madman's story. But, you must remember, neither one of us knew who I was."

"I understand why she did not, but how could *you* forget your identity?"

"It was the rogues who whacked me on the head and abducted me. That was how I met Priscilla to begin with."

"She was one of the ones who abducted you?"

"No. Of course not. Priscilla would never be involved in something like that. I met her when I escaped."

"Of course. Silly of me."

"She is the most exasperating person I have ever met. Stubborn, pigheaded, absolutely refuses to listen to reason."

"That explains why you have decided to marry her, no doubt," his father inserted dryly.

"No. I decided I wanted to marry her the other day, when she was kidnapped, and I was afraid I might not ever be with her again. I realized how awful life would be without her."

"*She* was abducted? I thought it was you."

"It *was* me—the first time. But this time the rogues

took *her,* thinking to force me to surrender myself to them."

"Your life seems to have been rather active the past few weeks."

"It has. I had no idea why any of it was happening. I understand it far better now."

"I am glad someone does. *I* haven't understood any of it yet. I am afraid that blow on your head must have affected you more than you realize."

"Let me go back to the beginning. When I got your telegram, I set sail for England at once. I was fortunate to find an English ship leaving the next day. No passengers. I had to sign on as a crewman, but it was a fast trip. When I got to London, I went straight to the lawyers, and they gave me instructions to travel here, to Elverton, and meet you at the inn. When I was almost to Elverton, two men stopped my horse. A robbery, I thought. But when I got down, they did not ask for my money. They simply knocked me over the head, and the next thing I knew, I woke up in a hut, stark naked and with absolutely no idea who I was."

His father stared at him. "Bryan… Good Lord."

"Yes, I know. A bit bizarre, isn't it?"

"More than that, I should say."

"After a while I escaped, and that is when I met Priscilla. She and her father took me in. By that time, I had a fever, as well, and she nursed me back to health, in addition to concealing me from the two thugs who were looking for me."

"I have much to thank this girl for."

Bryan nodded. "But even when I recovered, I had no idea who I was. We have spent the past weeks trying to find out."

Ranleigh scowled. "We have to find those men."

"I took care of that. They are currently in jail. And I found out who hired them—the current Duchess of Ranleigh."

"That bit of fluff downstairs? The one who fainted when I showed up?"

"Exactly. Apparently she did not take kindly to the real heir coming back." Bryan quickly explained what he and Priscilla had learned tonight of the scheme to get rid of the Duke, and the mistaken capture of a different American, himself.

"I'll be damned." Damon shook his head. "I would say we have found ourselves with some villainous relatives, son."

"Bianca's not blood kin to you. I don't think there's any harm in her son. He knew nothing of the plot. It was all a scheme of his mother's…and her lover."

"'Tis certainly an interesting household we have stumbled into here," Ranleigh mused.

Bryan nodded. "Do you plan to stay here?"

Ranleigh shrugged. "I'm not sure. 'Tis odd to be back here. Everything looks so much the same, it is almost as if I had never gone…and yet it has been so long, and there has been so much in between. I wonder myself what I will do. I would like to live here, at least for a time. I would like you to, also. It seems important to me that you come to know the land, the responsibilities you will inherit someday." He looked at his son questioningly.

Bryan gazed back at him blankly. "I have never thought of being a duke—or even this other thing I seem to be now, a marquis, or whatever it is."

"Marquess."

"Marquess, then. It doesn't suit me. But I will stay—because you ask, and because…"

"Of the lady?"

"Yes. Because of her." His brow knit in a frown. "I cannot imagine why she left tonight."

"Perhaps she had grown tired of the excitement."

"Priscilla?" Bryan looked skeptical. "You don't know her. I would have thought she would have been right on my heels, wanting to know who you are and how I remembered you and…oh, a thousand other things. She is a great one for questions."

"I should very much like to meet this woman."

"You will. Believe me. Once you do, you will realize why I must marry her." He smiled. "It is amazing, when I think about it. How could I have found a woman so perfect for me, when I wasn't even myself? She is the only lady I can imagine traveling around the world with me."

His father's brows rose. "You plan to take her jaunting about with you?"

"Of course. I couldn't leave her home all the time. Besides, she will enjoy it."

"Most women would prefer a home and children."

"Perhaps she will someday, and then I guess we will settle down. But you should have seen the sparkle in her eyes when we were talking about Singapore. She has read all those travel books written by some Englishman bringing 'civilization' to some remote part of the world. It may be quite likely we will take the little ones with us."

"A remarkable woman, indeed, if she agrees to this."

Bryan nodded, smiling. "There is no question of

that." After a moment, his smile faded away, and he sat forward earnestly. "Father...there's another reason I'm staying."

"And that is?"

"To help you clear your name."

His father smiled to himself. "I suspected that you might."

"But if you refuse to reveal the identity of this woman, then how do you plan to do it?"

"By trying to find the person who did kill her."

"How? Obviously the police could not."

"They gave up after I left the country. Sebastian had given me an alibi, and I was gone, anyway. But I think they still believed that I was the killer, so they never looked any further. They closed the case. I, however, have one advantage over them. I *know* that I did not kill her. So I am able to have a more open mind about the evidence."

"And?"

"Well, we know three things about the killer. He was someone whom Rose would have spoken of as a wealthy, high-class gentleman. Either he *was* one, or he was posing as one. He had to live within a close enough distance that he could meet her in Lady's Woods frequently. And he had to have access to our safe. Now, who are the gentlemen in this area? Myself, my father, Lord Chalcomb and my cousin Evesham."

"Evesham? I haven't met him."

"It's no loss. He was always a sneaky sort. I find it hard to believe that even a naive girl would have believed that Chalcomb would have married her, which she boasted her lover would do, since he was already married. My father was a widower, but...I don't think he was so skilled an actor as to have killed her and then had the scene with me over my killing her. Besides, neither he nor Chalcomb could remotely have been considered a 'young' gentleman. My choice for a suspect is Evesham. He frequently visited in our house; he was Father's brother's son, and close to my age. Father always fondly believed we were like brothers to each other."

Damon quirked an eyebrow. "But only if the brothers he was speaking of were Cain and Abel. Evesham and I never liked one another. He was forever stealing my things or doing something that I got blamed for. Anyway, he was here often, so he would have seen Rose and been able to seduce her. He could have met her in the woods even when he was not staying here, because his house isn't all that far away from here—and it is closer to Lady's Woods than it is to Ranleigh Court. *And* Evesham was always a great one for the ladies. No, I shouldn't say that, for it was usually a lower sort he was after. His mother had had to get rid of any housemaid under forty, because he was always chasing them. Even tried to seduce his little sister's governess once. He was definitely the sort to go after Rose and tell her anything to get her into his bed."

"Sounds like a villain to me."

"He was."

"But what about your other point? Did he have access to the safe?"

"Yes. He was here during the school holiday. He could easily have taken the rubies then. Father did not open the safe every day. Nor would it have been difficult for him to have found out the combination. Father never could remember the numbers, and he kept them on a paper in that unlocked drawer. Everyone in the family knew it. Foolish, but he was rather arrogant. He thought the only people to worry about were burglars from the outside, and he presumed they would not think of looking in the desk to find the combination."

"So what we need to do is dig up some evidence on dear old cuz."

"I realize it is a rather vague task."

"Mm-hmm..."

"But I have plenty of time to work on it."

"I don't," Bryan responded, rising. "You forget, I intend to get married before too long, and I don't wish to have my father's reputation as a killer hanging over the nuptials."

Damon smiled faintly. "That would be a bit awkward. Then we shall have to wrap it up quickly, won't we?"

His son grinned back, and the resemblance between them, masked by differences in coloring, was suddenly startling. "That is my intention." Bryan started toward the door.

"Now what are you doing? Where are you going?"

"I thought I would let you get reacquainted with your old friends—and your new family. I am going to find Priscilla and find out what the devil's going on."

ANNE HANDED THE REINS OF HER PONY to the aging groom who had waited patiently for her, sitting on a bale of hay and dozing, his back against the stable wall. She lifted her skirts and hurried across the yard to the kitchen entrance of the house. It was dark inside, lit only by the banked fire in the huge, old-fashioned fireplace. In the hallway beyond, a sconce burned here and there along the wall, left to light her way. She took the snuffer and put them out as she went along, well used to the economy.

No servant waited up for her. Her personal maid had long since gone on to better employment, and she made do with a housemaid when she needed a gown buttoned where she could not reach. Tonight she was very glad that she did not have to face anyone, not even a maid. It had taxed her skills to their utmost to appear normal on the ride home with the Hamiltons and the doctor. Had they suspected? Had they noticed her pallor and jittery inattention?

She reached her room and went inside, shutting the door thankfully behind her. She began to shiver. Though it was always a little bit cool in this old manor house, even in the summer, it was not really the chill in the air that set off her shudders. It was simply a release for her raw nerves, held in check for the last hour.

He was here! He had returned! She did not know what to do or what to think. Why had he returned after all this time? She had been telling the truth when she said she thought he had long since died. She had told herself that he was gone forever, that she would never see him, and the years had helped convince her of the truth of it. And then…there he had been, handsome and smiling, looking so much like the boy she had known, and yet so different, all at the same time. It had been all she could do not to faint right there on the spot, as that silly Bianca had.

Anne stripped off her gloves and threw them on the dressing table, then began hurriedly undoing the buttons down her front. Had he seen her? Would he have recognized her if he did? She gazed anxiously into the mirror above her dressing table, seeing the gray hairs sprinkled among her blond ones, the wrinkles fanning out from her eyes and framing her mouth. It had been thirty years, and she was afraid that every one of them showed on her face. She was hardly the girl she had been then, when he had called her the most beautiful woman in England.

Her dress had fallen open, exposing her chemise. One hand went to the tops of her breasts, running lightly across the swell. She remembered how firm and full they had been when she was young, how their creamy tops had practically spilled out of her ball gowns, full and luscious. She cupped her hands beneath her breasts, closing her eyes, as she remembered how he would caress them, almost in awe, praising her beauty.

Tears brimmed beneath her closed lids, and she dashed them away in irritation. What a fool she was! He would have no interest in her. He had come back here to claim his title, not to see her. He probably did not even remember the brief time when they had been in love. Obviously he had married; he had a son. No wonder her heart had stuttered when she first saw the young man sitting in Priscilla's kitchen. For just a split second, he had looked so much like Damon, until her mind had registered the obvious differences in coloring and features and she had told herself that she had been crazy to think he was Damon.

It had been the frame, the posture, the way he held his head, the shape of his jaw and chin, that had been like Damon. She remembered them all so well.

With a little sob, Anne tore off her dress and tossed it on the chair, quickly following it with her petticoats and other undergarments. Usually she was far more careful with her clothes, but tonight she could not bring herself to care. She wanted only to get into bed and lose herself in sleep, to forget what had happened tonight—and so long ago. But even after she pulled on her nightgown and hopped into bed, pulling the covers up tightly around her to combat the shivering, she found that sleep would not come to ease her mind.

Instead, all she could think about was him. He had looked very much as he had thirty years ago. The years had added character to his face, not taken away from the handsomeness. Even the wings of white in his hair were attractive.

She remembered how she used to wait in the gazebo, down by the pond, her nerves leaping in anticipation. She would sit on the west side because she knew he would come from the east, and soon she would see him, a dark figure on a horse, lithely at one with the animal, coming across the field. He would turn before he reached her, going into the wood to tie his horse where it would not be seen. And then he would come across the grass to the white gazebo, almost running, his eagerness as great as hers. She could remember the clutching in her stomach as she watched him approach, the combination of desire and guilt and love, spiced with the fear that Chalcomb might return early from the tavern that night.

She remembered, too, that last night. Chalcomb had gone hunting for the week, and they had seen each other over and over again. They had wanted to sleep together, to lie beside each other all night long, and that last night she had daringly crept downstairs and opened the door to let him in, sneaking upstairs with him to her bed-chamber. Her heart had been in her throat, for she had been sure that some servant would see them, yet her desire had been even greater than the fear. She could feel again his large hand in hers, the palm hardened from years of riding, could feel his tall body close beside hers as they rushed up the darkened staircase, could hear his breath, fast from his dash across the yard. His heat, his smell...

Anne groaned and turned over, burying her face in the pillow. *Why was she doing this to herself?* She could not remember how many nights she had lain awake, torturing herself like this, recalling every last moment with him, every word, every gesture, every caress.

Their coupling had been wild and furious that night, as it always was. They had been young, and their passion had run in them like wildfire. Just the touch of his hands had always ignited her. His mouth could drive her to the brink. And when he came inside her, driving deep into her softness, it had always felt as if a missing part of her had been returned, as if for those few moments she was whole again.

But afterward they had lain together quietly, whispering and giggling, laying foolish plans for the future, reveling in the luxury of having a night together. And soon they had made love again, slowly, leisurely, exploring every facet of their desire. That time had been closer to heaven than anything Anne had ever known, before or since.

He had left just before dawn lit the sky. The next time she saw him, he had been accused of murder and in a rage over his father's lack of belief in him. He had wanted her to flee with him, to leave Chalcomb and begin a new life with him. But she had been too afraid, too guilty, too full of doubts. He had gone, his face white with fury and shock. He had gone on to that new life; he had married, had children. And she had remained here, bearing with Chalcomb's temper and relieved by his infidelities, doing her duty, stitching her embroidery and watching her life drain out of her, bit by bit.

She wondered what would have happened if she had gone with him. She had thought about it many times, imagining their children, their cozy home, their love. And as many times she had told herself that it might just as easily have been fights and woes, bitter regrets and gnawing guilt. Tonight, however, seeing him again, she knew that it would not have been. She would have had a son with him, perhaps, a man like John, and they would have shared each day of his growing up, knit together in happiness. Instead, he had shared those days with another woman. And she had lived her life in emptiness.

Tears flooded her eyes and began to pour down her cheeks. She had had her chance, and she had not taken it. She would never get it again. He was married. And he would not look at her twice now, anyway. He was a handsome and powerful man, a duke, and she…she was but a dried husk of a woman, her youth and beauty gone, wasted on an old roué. Anne turned on her side and gave way to her tears, sobbing as years of regret and loss poured out of her and were soaked up in the sheets of her empty bed.

CHAPTER SEVENTEEN

PRISCILLA WAS IN THE SITTING ROOM, pretending to work on the mending, the next morning when a heavy knock sounded on the door of Evermere Cottage. She knew immediately that it was John—no, not John, Bryan. *The Marquess of Lynden*. He had come by late last night. She had lain in bed and listened to him pounding on the door, calling out her name, but she had stubbornly refused to get out of bed and answer him. Miss Pennybaker had not gotten back from the ball yet, and Florian was in his workshop out back, too immersed to hear anything. So no one had ever opened the door. But she had known he would come back. He was not the kind of man who gave up easily.

Since she had gotten up this morning, Priscilla had been dreading his call. She had tried to compose herself so that she could speak to him, holding cold compresses to her eyes to hide the puffiness of crying and reminding herself over and over that she was strong. On the one hand, she wanted to see him again, so that she could storm at him and tell him what she thought of his lies. On the other hand, she was afraid that she would simply burst into tears and be unable to say anything. Now that he was actually here, she froze, unable to move.

She heard Miss Pennybaker going to the front door and opening it. "Oh, my lord! How kind of you to drop by!" The governess's voice managed to be both giggly and awed. "Isn't it remarkable? I was struck dumb last night—utterly dumb—when His Grace came into the party. And then to find out that you are his son— Well! It was almost beyond belief. To think that we have been harboring a marquess under our roof and didn't even know it!"

Miss Pennybaker, to no one's surprise, had been swept away by the romance of the news last night. She had prattled on about it all morning, much to Priscilla's annoyance, commenting on how it was just like a novel, the way Ranleigh had swept into the room. The Duchess's fainting had added to the high drama. But the crowning touch, of course, had been the discovery that their own guest, their patient, the unknown John Wolfe, was in fact the son of the Duke! Miss Pennybaker's cup of joy had run over. Priscilla had replied shortly to the woman's questions and comments, but Miss Pennybaker had seemed to take no notice of her mood. Priscilla had been deeply grateful when Florian asked Miss Pennybaker to help him with his article.

There was the rumble of a deep voice outside; then Miss Pennybaker went on gaily, "Of course, my lord. She is in the sitting room. Let me show you the way."

As if he didn't know exactly where the sitting room was, Priscilla thought sourly. He had, after all, lived here for two weeks. She got to her feet, thinking of fleeing, but there was really no way out of the room without going into the hall, where she would run right into them. She considered the windows, but she knew that by the time she opened one and started to climb out, they would have reached the room, and she would only look quite ridiculous, halfway in and halfway out the window.

She clasped her hands together and attempted to look cool and uncaring as Penny came into the room, followed by Bryan. "Priscilla, look who's here!" Miss Pennybaker exclaimed brightly, then added, as if Priscilla could not see him, "It's Lord Lynden."

"Bryan," he said to Miss Pennybaker, smiling sheepishly. "Please, it's just Bryan. This 'my lord' business is too strange for me."

"So modest." Miss Pennybaker beamed at him.

She looked over at Priscilla, waiting for her to greet the new, romantic lord. Bryan, too, looked at her expectantly. Priscilla could think of nothing to say, so she merely stood, stonily gazing back at him. Miss Pennybaker began to frown and make strange grimaces at Priscilla, tilting her head toward Bryan.

"Miss Pennybaker, is anything wrong?" Priscilla inquired.

The gentle woman glared at her, then simpered up at Bryan. "You must forgive her, my—I mean, Bryan. Priscilla hasn't been herself since last night. She was stunned by your news. All of us were stunned."

His easygoing grin lightened his face. "Including me." He glanced back at Priscilla, then said in a low voice to the former governess, "Miss P., do you think you could let me speak to Priscilla for a few minutes... alone?"

"Of course, my— I mean— Well, of course." She tittered nervously, covering her mouth with her hand.

Priscilla stared at her, astounded. Was this the same woman who had warned her all her life against spending even a few minutes alone with a man? Who had managed to pop into the room at some point whenever Priscilla and Bryan happened to be by themselves?

"Miss P.!" she protested. "What about my reputation?"

"I am sure a few minutes won't harm your name, my dear. After all, it is the Marquess of Lynden." The older woman scurried from the room, looking as if she were a conspirator.

"You have certainly won over Miss Pennybaker," Priscilla commented sourly.

"I think it has more to do with my new title than with me." Bryan looked at her quizzically. "Just as obviously, I seem to have offended you."

"Offended me, my lord? Why would you say that?" Priscilla's voice was coated with ice.

His mouth twisted in a wry smile, and he gave her a long look. "Perhaps because you are calling me 'my lord' instead of Bryan."

"I do not know you well enough to address you by your first name."

"Priscilla! What is the matter? You think that after what we have felt, have done, that you do not know me well enough to use my name?" He came toward her, one hand outstretched, his face lined with confusion and frustration.

"I know no one named Bryan."

"You knew me well enough when my name was John."

"I thought I did." She could not keep from adding bitterly, "But obviously I was wrong."

"Priscilla! What are you talking about? Why are you angry with me? What have I done?"

"What have you done?" she repeated, aghast. "You

can stand there and ask me that, knowing that you have lied to me for two weeks? That you have let me believe that you were unaware of your name, of your home, of anything about you, gaining my sympathy, taking my—"

"Priscilla! You think I knew who I was? That I was only pretending not to remember?"

"Of course I think that. Who wouldn't? The Duke appeared, and immediately you stepped forward and said, 'Hello, Father.' You did not have to think or have your memory jogged. You didn't go blank. As soon as he arrived, you were able to drop the charade, to admit who you were. I don't know why you felt you had to pretend before. Perhaps you thought it would be safer. But could you not have trusted *me* not to tell anyone? I feel like such a fool—only a naive country miss like me would have believed that you could remember nothing. Why did you have to go through all that nonsense about trying to discover who you were and why anyone would try to kidnap you?"

"Priscilla! Wait—"

"It was obvious," Priscilla rushed on heedlessly. "No wonder Oliver followed you. You really are an heir, even if you aren't the Duke himself. I don't know why I didn't see that—an American going to the Aylesworths' solicitors, then riding to Elverton. I was as stupid as the Duchess, thinking that because you are too young you could not be the Duke, but not realizing that the Duke could have had children, *American* children. I didn't think. I was too caught up in a mystery that didn't exist…too given over to the *romance* of it all—"

"No!"

"How did you keep from laughing when I told you

that I did not care that you didn't know who you were, didn't care if you were a thief or a married man or lowborn—when all the time you knew you were a marquess! Did you think that when I found out the truth I would be so dazzled by the title that I would not mind? That I would fall down at your feet and be thankful that you had made me your mistress? Well, I am not! I feel cheap and despoiled. Used. And I wish you had gone to any other house than this one to play your little game!"

As she talked, overriding his efforts to speak, the color first drained from his face, then returned in a bright red flush, and by the time she finished, he looked as if he might burst. He waited for a long moment, visibly struggling to restrain himself.

Tightly he said, "Priscilla…sit down."

"I will not! I prefer to—"

"I said, 'Sit down,' damn it!" he roared.

Priscilla dropped into a chair, wide-eyed.

"I have stood here and let you revile me long enough. Now you are going to listen to what I have to say."

Priscilla lifted her chin, but said nothing.

"I never lied to you. Not once. I did not know who I was. I could remember nothing about myself before I woke up in that miserable hut. I was completely in the dark until my father walked into that room. When I saw him, my memory returned. I was not even aware of it. I saw him and started toward him, and suddenly, the word *father* tumbled out of my mouth. It surprised me as much as you. Then I realized— I remembered him. I remembered it all. I knew who I was, where I came from—New York City, by the way. What I do for a living—we are in shipping. I represent the business.

That's why I have been to Singapore and Canton and those other places. I go around the world, dealing with foreign merchants. I have a younger sister named Adelia, whom everyone calls Delia. My mother died two years ago. I know it all. I remembered it all, as if some part of my brain had been taken out, then suddenly replaced." He paused and said grimly, emphasizing each word, "*But not before my father appeared in that room.* I swear it to you. I did not lie."

Priscilla stared at him. She wanted to believe him. She *did* believe the sincerity in his firm voice, in the set of his jaw, in the glint of his eyes. Yet, somehow, there was something in her that wanted *not* to accept it. "How could you remember it so suddenly? How could it come back to you like that?"

"I don't know. I lost it just as suddenly. Maybe I would have remembered sooner if I had seen someone who was familiar before that. But I was so far from everything and everyone that I knew. I had never even heard of Elverton or the Duke of Ranleigh."

"What?" Priscilla gaped at him.

He nodded emphatically. "Yes. It is true. Even if I had recovered my memory, I would not have known that my father was the Duke. My name is Bryan Aylesworth. Father never told us that he was a marquess in England. Hell, I couldn't have told you what a marquess was."

"You're joking."

"I'm not. He never talked about England or his life here. I could not even have told you when he came to the United States." Bryan shrugged. "It never occurred to me to ask him why he emigrated. I guess I assumed that he was looking for a better life, a chance to make a fortune, or whatever. I am not sure that my mother even knew."

He smiled faintly. "It must have given my father a secret laugh—my mother's family looked down on him, said he was 'parvenu rich.' They were always going on about how they were Van der Beecks, one of the first families in the state, back when New York was New Amsterdam, and he was just a poor nobody when Mother met him. They liked to say it was Mother's connections that had brought him most of his business. When Mother would fire up in defense of him, he would smile and say that it didn't bother him, that family names didn't count for much."

"This is all so...so..." Priscilla brought her hands to her head, as if pressure would somehow put all her thoughts in order.

"Bizarre?" He let out a grunt. "You can imagine how I feel. One minute I didn't know who I was, and the next I not only remember my past, I find out I am someone other than what I have always thought."

"And to add to it, I accuse you of lying."

"Then you believe me? You know I wasn't lying to you?"

Priscilla sighed and nodded, sinking back into her chair. "I believe you. It's too absurd not to be the truth."

"Thank God! I knew someday my sheer absurdity would be of some benefit to me." He grinned, coming toward her, his hands outstretched to take hers.

Quickly Priscilla stepped away. "No, wait. John—I mean, Bryan—we cannot."

"Cannot what? Kiss? Why? Don't marquesses do that sort of thing?" His expression was slightly puzzled, but still amused and cheerful.

"No. I mean, of course they do. But, well, not you and I. There is too much between us."

"Whatever are you talking about? The only thing between us is the space that you are creating." He was frowning in earnest now. "Everything is cleared up. I know who I am, and this title apparently even makes me respectable in Englishmen's eyes. The two ruffians who abducted you are in jail, and shall be for years. And I understand that they are ratting on our friend Oliver in great detail. He has already taken to his heels. Father knows about Bianca and what she tried to do to him and me. The only thing left to resolve is that murder thirty years ago, to prove Father was not the one who killed her. But that doesn't mean that you and I cannot be together." He paused, then added quietly, "Or does it? Is that what is troubling you? That I am his son? Do you think he is a murderer?"

"No. I mean, well, honestly, I have no idea whether he is or not. But if he is your father, I find it hard to believe that he could be."

"Then is it the reputation?" His face was hard. "Do you not care to be with a man whose father is under a cloud?"

"No! Honestly, John—*Bryan*—how could you think that of me? You are not your father, and even if he did do it, that doesn't make you bad."

"Then what? Why won't you marry me?"

"Marry you?" She stared at him, stunned.

"Yes. What did you think I was talking about?"

"I—I'm not sure. I didn't think. But I did not hear you ask me to marry you."

"I probably didn't. I am not very good at this sort of thing—never done it before, you see." He cleared his throat, "Miss Hamilton, will you do me the honor of marrying me? Or do I have to be formal and ask your father for your hand?"

"No. Of course not. But this is all so sudden. I'm not prepared."

"It doesn't take preparation. I am not asking for a speech. A simple yes will do."

"I cannot!" she cried out, twisting her hands together. "It is impossible. We can't be married."

"Why not?" He frowned impatiently. "Damn it, Priscilla, it isn't like you to play games."

"I am not playing games! Honestly. But I cannot marry you. You are a marquess now. You will be the Duke of Ranleigh someday."

"So?"

"So you have to marry according to your station. You cannot marry some little nobody with no money. You have to marry as befits a duke."

"I don't have to marry in any way except as I choose," he retorted. "What a load of hogwash. You told me you did not care about rank or title or any of that stuff."

"That was when I thought you didn't have one! It is all different now. You are a marquess."

"Would you quit saying that? You make me feel like I'm a disease or something. It doesn't matter whether I have a fancy title. I am still me."

"You don't understand. There is a great deal of responsibility that comes with a title. Responsibility to your family and your name and your land. To all the generations of dukes who have gone before you."

"What does that have to do with my marrying you?"

"You have to marry someone worthy of being a duchess."

"You are more worthy of it than anyone I know. You are smart, beautiful, generous, brave…."

"No, I don't mean worthy in qualities. I mean worthy in name. My family is genteel, but we are not nobility. Oh, scattered here and there among the family tree may be the odd knight, or even a baronet, but there are no earls or viscounts or dukes."

He shrugged. "That doesn't bother me."

"I told you. You are not the only one you have to consider. You have a duty to your name."

"Blast my name. My name isn't marrying you, *I* am."

"No one is," she replied firmly. "Bryan, be reasonable. If I were wealthy, perhaps a respectable family would be enough, but you know that we are merely genteel *and* poor."

"Somehow, marrying a person because she is rich does not sound very noble to me."

"It's more practical than noble. It is the sort of thing that one has to do sometimes in order to save the…the family traditions."

"What?"

"Ranleigh Court," she said bluntly. "It is falling apart, and the Aylesworths don't have enough money to repair it adequately. Everyone knows that they shut up the east wing years ago because they could not afford to keep it up. It needs money spent on it—lavishly. And the lands are in need of improvements. The family is not penniless; it is just that they haven't nearly enough to devote to the estate. That's what I mean about responsibility to the family. Someone who is heir to a dukedom has to think of things like that, has to put that before everything else."

"Well, I don't," he retorted bluntly. "Father has enough money to refurbish the old place."

"What do you mean?"

"He didn't come back here for the rents, or however the dukes make their money. I told you we were in shipping. He has enough money to repair Ranleigh Court, or rebuild it, or what*ever* he wants. I have no need to marry for money. And I certainly am not going to marry some girl because she has a name that pleases you or my neighbors or even my father. I intend to marry you."

Priscilla blinked, stunned. She wanted to throw her arms around his neck and say yes. She had done more than enough, she told herself, to make him see reason. If he still insisted on marrying her, then it was not her fault that he married beneath him or that other people might talk. But it *was* her fault that he did not know that she wrote adventure stories under a man's name. And if word of that were ever to leak out—as it doubtless would, if she were to become a marchioness and be subjected to the ruthless scrutiny of Society—it would be a terrible scandal. The proud Aylesworth family would be humiliated, and it would be because of her.

"No," she said reluctantly. "There is— It's just— Well, there could be a terrible scandal if you married me."

"What are you talking about?"

"I mean, if I were to marry you and go into Society, everyone would poke into everything I have done. The gossips would be looking to find some scandalous tidbit about this country nobody who snagged the Aylesworth heir."

"And have you done something reprehensible?" His eyes danced with amusement. "What? Danced too many times with a man at a ball? Or, let's see, maybe you didn't write a thank-you note soon enough?"

"I am perfectly serious!" Priscilla snapped, annoyed at his laughter. It was killing her to turn him down, and she thought she was displaying great honor and nobility. And he had the temerity to laugh at her! "There is a scandal…. In the past, I have done some things, and… and if that got out, it would humiliate your family."

"Something worse than being the prime suspect in a murder? We already have that little scandal in our family."

"Of course not. But it would make it worse. One scandal is one thing, but then, to marry a nobody, that's a second one, and then if they found out about me, it would offend everyone, and—well, it would be a mess. And I don't want to be the one who embroils your family in it."

"You are not joking, are you?" He regarded her seriously. "You have actually done something scandalous? Something that would get you tossed out of Society?"

"Yes, by quite a few members of it. And there would be gossip. Awful gossip."

"What is it? I cannot imagine you having committed any serious sin."

She looked at him, agonized. What if she told him her secret and he was repulsed by it? What if he was relieved that she had not accepted his proposal? What if he found her unfeminine now, and turned away from her in disdain? She had considered confiding her secret to him a few times, particularly when he had been worrying about what he might have been in the past and she had wanted to comfort him. But she had always held back for fear of what his reaction might be. He seemed a forward-thinking sort; he disdained many of the hidebound British ideas and traditions. But what if that was because he was an American? It did not mean that he was a proponent of women's rights, or that he would not be shocked by the idea of a woman doing something like writing a book, and particularly the kinds of books that she wrote. She had heard even some of her father's intellectual friends talk with great contempt of women trying to step into things that had always been a man's province. She had never even told the vicar, whom she loved and respected, about her writing, because she had heard him remark with great sorrow on other women who had deviated from God's design by taking on a man's work.

"No, Bryan, please do not ask," she murmured.

Bryan was thoroughly curious now. He could not imagine what Priscilla could have done that would be so scandalous. "Did you kill someone?" he asked, joking.

"No! Bryan, please."

He frowned, thinking. "You—you've been married. And you got a divorce."

"Bryan!"

"You had an affair."

"No! Is that what you think of me?"

"No, of course not. I am just trying to think of what you could have done."

"Well, stop. You know, I think, that it would be impossible for me to have been married or had an affair," she told him pointedly.

"Oh." He could not keep from smiling sensually as

he thought of the time they had made love. "Of course. You're right."

"Stop smirking," she snapped. "I am not answering any more of your questions. Please, just go."

"Not until you give me a good reason why you will not marry me."

"I can't. Bryan, please, just trust me. Believe me. It would be impossible. Ask your father. He will tell you how a duke must marry."

"I don't think you will get the answer you want from him. Remember, he married a titleless American."

"Why must you make this so hard for me?" Priscilla cried out, tears welling up in her eyes.

"I must," he answered simply, coming forward and taking her hands in his. She tugged, trying to pull her hands out of his grasp, but he would not let her go. "Don't you see? I cannot let it be easy for you to send me away. You will have to want me gone more than I want you for my wife. That is the only way you can get rid of me."

"I have refused you. Can't you accept that?"

He shook his head, smiling as he raised each of her hands to his mouth in turn and laid a soft, lingering kiss on it before he set it free. "You know I am far too stubborn for that."

Priscilla's insides went as soft as mush as he brushed his mouth against the backs of her hands. She thought of his lovemaking and the way his lips had caressed her body all over. That was what she was giving up, she thought: a whole lifetime of Bryan's caresses and kisses. A whole lifetime without his smile, his laugh, his wit. She bit her lower lip, forcing back the acceptance that tried to leap from her throat.

"You will have to say yes to me eventually," he said. "I intend to keep on trying."

She shook her head, but he disregarded it.

"I will take my leave now," he told her. "But I promise you that I will be back. I will not quit until I have the answer I want."

Then he turned and strode out of the room. Priscilla stood silently, listening to his footsteps in the hall outside. When the front door closed behind him, she collapsed onto the chair behind her and gave way to a torrent of tears.

CHAPTER EIGHTEEN

THE DUKE OF RANLEIGH STRODE into the dining room. "Ah, good morning," he said politely to the two other occupants of the room, the Duchess and her son, Alec.

"Good morning, Your Grace." Alec jumped to his feet to greet him. He had been impressed by the other man's stature and demeanor last night at the party. He looked the part of a duke, Alec thought, and, frankly, he was relieved not to have the burden of the title. He was now only a younger brother, third in line for the title, and once John—no, Bryan—got married and had a son, he would be even farther away. Alec could see all the advantages of the freedom that offered. His mother would no longer be able to bind him with the responsibilities of being a duke, and he would be off to the army, somehow, some way.

"Good morning, Alec," Damon responded. "I am glad you decided to join me."

"Did we have any choice?" the Duchess asked sourly. She was not used to arising so early, and she would still have been sound asleep if her personal maid had not told her that the Duke had requested that she join him at breakfast. It was a polite way of saying the Duke demanded it, she knew.

"Mmm... I suppose one always has a choice," Damon replied, sitting down at the head of the table.

The footman standing by the silver-laden sideboard immediately stepped forward to fill his cup with coffee.

"What may I get Your Grace?" he asked, but Damon impatiently waved him away.

"I shall get it myself," he told the man. "You may go back to the kitchen. We will manage by ourselves, I think."

Bianca arched an eyebrow. Personally, she did not like to get anything for herself. However, she did not have the nerve to say so. She and Alec watched as the new Duke filled his plate from the sideboard and finally sat down again. He took a sip of the coffee.

"Not the best," he commented. "I shall have to change that." He glanced around the table casually. "Well, I see that we have one less houseguest this morning."

Bianca compressed her lips. Benjamin had taken off last night, shortly after Damon arrived. When she had been supported back to her room last night to recover from the shock of Damon's return, she had found the coward packing. He had heard, he told her, that the two men he had hired were in the custody of the town constable. It did not surprise her that the rat was leaving the sinking ship. He would know that, now that Alec would no longer be the Duke, she would no longer have any real power or money. She would be almost entirely dependent on the new Duke for her support, except for the pittance that was her dower. And she would probably not be able to save him if his cohorts decided to reveal his part in their crime. Well, at least she had been clever enough to have *him* deal with the crooks; they would not be able to trace the scheme back to her.

Alec, across the table from her, did not attempt to

hide his glee. "Yes. The scoundrel took off. Thank God."

"I hope the Duchess will not miss him too much."

Bianca shrugged and took a casual sip of her coffee. "He was nothing to me," she replied brittlely.

"Good." The Duke turned his attention to his food for the next few minutes. Bianca toyed with her toast, and Alec merely waited, watching the Duke.

"Ah…" Damon said at last, pushing aside his plate and taking another drink of his coffee. "Nothing like an English breakfast." He paused, his gaze going from Bianca to Alec and back. The tension rose in the room with every passing tick of the clock.

"Well, Alec," he said at last, "I am looking forward to getting to know you. I must say, it is a trifle odd to find out one has a brother after thirty years. Especially one who is more the age of my son than me. I suppose it must be as peculiar an experience for you."

"Yes, Your Grace."

"Oh, please, none of that between us. We are brothers. Call me Damon."

"Thank you…Damon."

"Good. My son tells me that you are eager to join the army."

Predictably, Alec's eyes lit up. "Oh, yes! It's what I'd like more than anything!"

"I see no reason why you should not. The military's always been an excellent career for a younger son. I have no problem with that."

"No!" Bianca cried out. "He cannot! I refuse to allow it."

Damon turned his eyes on her, the pale blue orbs

devoid of emotion. "I believe I am head of the family now, Bianca."

"He is my son!" Bianca retorted. "I will not let him do it."

"He will be twenty-one in a few weeks, and I am afraid that you will no longer have any control over him. Of course, if he would rather stay with you, he is certainly welcome to. However, I would think a young man would find life at the Dower House rather dull. Yorkshire is somewhat isolated. Fine for a widow, of course, but—"

"The Dower House!" Bianca exclaimed, her eyes opening wide and her nostrils flaring. Her concern over her son's departure for the military was quickly replaced by this daunting vision of her own future.

"Why, yes, I believe it is customarily where the Duke's widow retires after her husband's death." He paused, then added, "It makes sense, too. I might marry again, and if I don't, I understand that my son has intentions of doing so."

"Priscilla?" Alec asked eagerly. "Are he and Priscilla going to get married?"

"Oh, Alec, do shut up!" Bianca snapped. "What does it matter whether he marries that stupid Hamilton girl? This man is kicking me out of our home! Why don't you do something about it?"

Alec shifted uncomfortably. "Well, ah, Mother, I—I don't know what I *can* do. It *is* his house."

"Don't plague your son. He is quite right. There is nothing he can do. Nor is there anything you can do. There are other reasons, very good reasons, why you should live there. After all, it is a much smaller house and will more suit your income."

Bianca's jaw dropped. She had not expected him to cut off all her funds. "You expect me to live on that... that pittance?"

"It is your inheritance."

"It is nothing. All the real money is tied up with the title!"

"I am afraid there is not really all that much of it anymore, particularly at the rate you have been spending it the past few years. The solicitors showed me the accounts. At any rate, your inheritance is quite adequate, I believe, to maintain the dower house and even have a few weeks in Bath, say, every year."

"Bath!" she spat out with loathing. "With all the old ladies? I think not!"

"You might be able to rent a house in London for a couple of weeks a year."

"I won't go!" Bianca returned shrilly.

"You cannot stay here." There was steel in his voice.

Bianca and Alec simply stared at him in amazement for a long moment. Though the Dower House was traditionally the home to which the ducal widow retired, it had not been used as such for the past two generations. The dowager duchesses had preferred to remain at Ranleigh Court, and their sons, the new dukes, had not wanted to force them out.

"I shall tell everyone what you have done!" Bianca was seething. "You may have the power to throw me out of here, but everyone in the country will know what a cruel, heartless bastard you are!"

Damon regarded her coldly for a long moment. "I would suggest that you think long and hard before you do such a thing. It is sometimes better for all concerned to keep silent on a subject."

Bianca blinked. "I—I don't know what you mean!"

"Don't you? Then let me spell it out for you—though I had hoped to spare your son learning this about his mother. For the good of the family, I had decided to keep silent about what you have done to my son and tried to do to me. I wanted to spare your son the embarrassment, as Bryan assured me that Alec had no part in your schemes."

"What schemes?" Alec asked, his voice rising. "Mama, what is he talking about?"

"You are bluffing!" his mother told Damon boldly, ignoring Alec.

"Am I? You think I don't know all about it? You think I won't let it out? Believe me, I will, if you even once spread gossip about me or my family. Tell your friends, if you want, how I refused to let you stay at Ranleigh Court, and I will tell them how you hired killers to get rid of me. How you had my son kidnapped and beaten up."

"Mother!" Alec sat back in his chair, aghast, staring at her.

"You cannot prove it!" Bianca jumped to her feet. "They never dealt with me! They do not even know my name!"

"Perhaps not, but your lover knows. You think he cannot be tracked down? You think he wouldn't be glad to tell us all about how he acted on your command when he hired those two ruffians—when he is facing long years in jail? Think well, madam, before you open your mouth. You could go to jail for this, not simply be banished to the Dower House in Yorkshire. At the least, you will never be received in any decent house in this country again."

Bianca stood still, staring at him, her mouth opening and closing as she struggled to say something that would overcome his argument. Alec, his face as white as paper, had also risen to his feet and now stood facing her across the table.

"Mother?" he asked, his voice strained. "Is this true? Did you try to harm Damon and Bryan? Mother, answer me!"

She turned on him then, her eyes narrowed to slits, her frustration and rage at the Duke slipping out against her son. "What do you think? I couldn't just sit by and let them come in and seize your inheritance, not when I had worked so hard to get it! Do you think it was easy living with that old man for twenty years? I thought he would die within two or three years after I married him, but he lived on forever! Do you think it was something I enjoyed, enduring his wrinkled old hands on me? His kisses, his— Ohhh!" She let out an inarticulate cry of anger. "I did it for you! All of it was for you! So that you could have your rightful inheritance. So that you could have the title, the land, the money. It should all have been yours. I could not let them spoil that!"

"Alec…" Damon made a move toward the boy, whose face was so white and shocked it almost frightened Damon.

"No." Alec held up a hand. "I am all right." He stared straight at his mother. "Did you ever think to ask me if I wanted it? You did not do any of that for me. It was for yourself. I was not even born when you married 'that old man.' You didn't endure that for my sake, but from your own desire for wealth and power. I didn't even want to be the Duke of Ranleigh. I just wanted to join the army with Gid, you know that. Yet you kept forcing me into the mold of the Duke, making me feel guilty for wanting to leave you, telling me that I would not be meeting my responsibility—even when you knew that I was not going to inherit the title! That old man you hated so much was my father. The men you tried to kill are my brother and nephew. How could you say you were doing it for me? I don't want any part of it." He drew a deep breath. "I don't want any part of *you*."

Bianca let out a noise like a hiss and swung around, running out of the room. Alec looked after her, his face a study of pain. Damon walked around to him and laid a hand lightly on his shoulder.

"I am sorry you had to learn this way."

Alec turned to look at him with confused blue eyes. "How could she have done that? I— She's my mother...."

"I know. Nothing will ever change that. Maybe, after a time, you can reconcile what she did with who she is to you."

"No! I can't even bear to think of it! It was bad enough when she was living with that—" his lip lifted in a sneer "—that cur, Oliver. There were times when I hated her almost as much as him. But this is ten times worse. To find out that she is capable of killing someone, much less a member of my own family!"

"She saw only a threat to her child and herself. You have to remember that. Have you ever seen a lioness protecting her cub?"

"She wasn't protecting me," Alec told him bitterly. "If she had been interested in protecting me, she would never have taken up with Oliver. No, she was interested in protecting her own income, her own status. You were perfectly right about that. It is just… that it is so hard to accept what she's really like."

Damon patted his shoulder again, wishing he knew the right words to say. It was too bad Delia was not here. Women always seemed to be so much better at these things than he was.

"Look," he offered, "I was about to go for a ride, look over the countryside now that I'm back. Why don't you come with me?"

Alec gave him a brief smile. "Thank you. That is very kind of you. But I think right now I'd rather be by myself." He forced another smile and walked out of the room.

DAMON HAD FELT SORRY FOR ALEC, but he was glad that the boy had turned down his offer to go riding. He had planned to call on Anne Chalcomb this morning; it had been on his mind ever since he had arrived last night and not found her at the ball. Indeed, if the truth be known, it had been on his mind long before that, before he'd ever set foot on board the ship to England.

As he rode along the familiar path, memories flooded in on him. So little had changed in thirty years—a large tree that had been cut down here, a hedge of bushes that had sprung up there, a new fence in another place—that he felt almost as if he were eighteen again and riding to meet the woman he loved. He remembered well the anticipation growing in his chest, the strumming of his nerves, taut with eagerness and danger, the desire pushing him onward.

At last he topped a rise and looked down on Chalcomb Manor. The yards around it seemed to have shrunk, the fields encroaching upon them. To his right lay the road and the driveway leading to the front. To his left was the small pond and the gazebo where they had usually met. Damon gave in to impulse and turned his horse's head in the direction of the gazebo. As he drew near it, he could see that the little wooden building, with its gingerbread trim, had not been painted in a long time; the pristine white had faded to a dirty gray. Up close, he could see, too, that several of the boards had broken. Even the pond beyond seemed scummy and stagnant.

He turned away, feeling faintly troubled. He admitted to himself that one of the main reasons he had come back after all these years was to see Anne. Now he was beginning to wonder if the love affair he remembered would have grown shabby with time, as the surroundings had. Would he find Anne nothing like the girl he had loved? Would he see that what he had thought was grand passion had been only fleeting lust?

For a moment he was tempted to turn back, but he urged his horse forward, skirting the edge of the manor's yards and coming out on the cobblestoned drive. He felt odd as he dismounted. He had almost never come in this way, except once or twice before he had fallen in love with Lady Chalcomb. Somehow, he still felt a little furtive as he looked around.

No groom came running to take his horse, so he tied it to a post and went up the front steps. He knocked at the door and waited, and after a few moments it was opened by Anne herself. Damon had expected a maid or a footman to open it, so he was caught off guard when Anne appeared. He stood for a moment, staring, unable to say a thing.

She had aged, but gracefully. Her red-gold hair,

arranged neatly on her head, was streaked with strands of white, and her skin had softened with time. Tiny lines from smiling fanned out from the corners of her eyes and mouth. But her form was slender and graceful, and the girl she had been still shone out of her clear amber eyes.

Damon swallowed, finding himself too choked with emotion to say anything. It was Anne who was the calmer one, who said quietly, "Damon. I wondered if I would see you again." She stepped back, adding, "Would you like to come in?"

He nodded, wordlessly following her through the high, old-fashioned entryway and into a sitting room a good distance back from the door.

"I'm sorry," Anne told him with a polite smile. "I am afraid I haven't kept the front drawing rooms open since Henry died. I so rarely get formal company these days."

"I would not have thought I was formal company," he said, his throat freed at last from its paralysis.

She smiled faintly, sitting down and motioning him toward another chair. Anne hoped he would not realize that she had rehearsed this little scene throughout last night, all the while telling herself that there would be no opportunity, that he would not come. Yet here he was. As tall and handsome as ever.

Her eyes ran over him as she tried to look as if she had not been inspecting him, taking in the breadth of his shoulders, the shape of his face, the sharpness of his pale blue eyes. There was little of her slender, lithe boy in him; this was a man who had lived and worked hard. Yet here, too, was all the promise that the nineteen-year-old boy had held: the power and strength, the assurance, intelligence and maturity. Was there kindness there, as well? She was not sure. She wondered, too, what he saw when he looked at her, whether he saw a weathered, dried-out old woman in place of the girl he had loved.

"Well," she told him in reply to his comment, "it has been thirty years. People change in that time."

"You think I have?"

"Of course. I am not sure exactly how. One thing has changed, certainly. You are a duke now."

He shrugged. "I am less of a nobleman than when I was a marquess, I assure you. Thirty years in the United States tends to knock a little snobbery out of one."

"You were never a snob."

"No? I think I was often arrogant."

She remembered his arrogance well—in the tilt of his head, the way he carried his shoulders, the smile that flashed across his face. "You were merely aware of your position in life."

"Too certain of it, I think. I've learned how little it matters when one is struggling to survive."

"Was it…very hard after you left here? I mean, living in the United States, working and…all that."

"The work was the least of it. I got used to hard physical labor rather quickly. I found it was something even a lord could easily do, if he was young and strong enough. The brains took a little more oiling to run smoothly, but eventually I managed."

There was a small silence. Anne looked down at her hands. "I see you have a family. I met your son."

"Yes, Bryan is a good lad. Not a lad, anymore, though. He's twenty-eight now."

"He reminded me a little of you when I met him. But I thought I was imagining things."

"I have a daughter, also. Delia. She is in New York. She has a husband and two children."

"So you are a grandfather?"

He chuckled. "Yes, I have to admit, I am. Devilishly cute rascals. But they make me feel old."

"You must have married young."

He nodded. "I was always in a hurry."

"I remember." There was another long pause. Anne hesitated, but she had to ask. "And your wife?" she asked quickly, not looking at him. "Did she accompany you?"

"No. She died two years ago."

"Oh. I'm sorry." A knot in her chest loosened, though she told herself that she was foolish to care.

"She was a good woman. But," he added softly, "she was never you."

Anne glanced up at him quickly, then away, afraid that the instant delight she felt at his statement probably shone in her eyes. "But I'm sure you did not expect her to be."

"No," he agreed. "Fortunately for my marriage, I did not. I realized that that kind of love happens only once… if you're lucky."

"Oh, Damon…" Her voice choked. "I am so sorry for what happened."

He frowned. "You mean my leaving? Going to New York?"

She nodded. "It was my fault. It never would have happened if it had not been for me. You would have been at home. Your father would have known where you were. He would have trusted you. You should have let me tell them where you were. I should have gone to the authorities even though you did not want me to."

"It is not trust when he sees it with his own eyes. What was important to me was that he believe me even though he had no proof. That was what cut—that he did not." He stood up and began to pace, too restless and pent-up to sit still. "You are not responsible for the fact that my father and I could not get along. We could not before I ever met you. We were like oil and water, always had been. Until I had Bryan, I thought that was the way it was supposed to be between father and son. Anyway, no one was responsible for my being accused of murder. It was sheer circumstance."

"I am responsible for what happened between us."

"No." He turned and faced her, his eyes boring into her. "No more responsible than I."

"I was older."

He smiled fractionally. "A year."

"I should have been wiser. I was married. I should have held off…."

His smile turned grim. "Do you honestly think that you could have? That I would have let you? That first day, when I saw you, sitting there so serene and lovely, so beautiful that it made my insides ache, I knew I had to have you. I knew that there was nothing and no one else for me."

Anne's breath caught in her throat at his words. "Damon…" Her eyes shone, their amber light glowing. She rose slowly, as if pulled up by some outside force. "It was that way for me, as well."

She could remember vividly the way he had looked, wild and young and full of strength, sitting on his magnificent bay, sweat plastering his shirt to his chest and dampening his hair. He had been out riding and had met Lord Chalcomb, who had invited him home. She had been in the garden, picking flowers for a table arrangement, and she had walked over toward the horsemen when they arrived. She had been unaware of the way the sunlight played upon her hair, tousled by the breeze, and caught the unusual color of her eyes. She had not realized the picture she presented, flowers held to her chest, a spill of color beneath the creamy perfection of her face, her light spring dress caught by the breeze and flattened against her form.

Damon strode over to her in a rush and took her hands. Old feelings pushed up in him, fierce and chaotic, as if the past were at once immediate and yet strangely long ago, part of a different life. "Why would you not go with me?" he asked harshly, his eyes searching her face. "Why did you stay here with him? Why wouldn't you go with me to a new life and forget all this?"

Her hands trembled in his; his touch made her tingle, as if she were coming alive once more after years of a sleeping death. Her eyes filled with tears. "I don't know!" she cried softly. "I was such a fool. I cursed myself a thousand times after you left. I was too scared. I felt guilty about what we had done, about betraying my husband. No matter how awful he was and how much I regretted letting my parents push me into marrying him, he was still my husband. And I was committing adultery. Sometimes I felt so wicked and guilty. When you came and told me about the fight with your father and him thinking that you murdered that girl, I was so confused and frightened. I didn't have your courage, to throw everything aside, to say that my vows didn't matter, to give up everything and start a whole new life."

The tears spilled out from her eyes and down her

cheeks. "I'm sorry, Damon," she told him shakily. "I made such a mess of everything, of both our lives. I have lived with such regret."

"Don't." His voice was soft as he wiped her tears from her cheeks with his hands. "Don't be sorry. You did not ruin my life. And it was not courage that made me run. It was because I was too weak to stay and watch you as his wife. I couldn't give you up. I couldn't let you go. When you would not come with me, it seemed the only path left to me, to get as far away from this pain as I could. People thought I ran because of the murder charge, but that was never it. It was not even because of the fight with my father, not really. We had quarreled countless times. It was because I wanted you and knew I could never have you. I could not face that."

He caressed her face with his fingers, outlining her cheeks and jaw and forehead. "We did the best we could, Nan. It's pointless to have regrets."

She smiled tearily. "No one else ever called me that."

Damon brought her hands up to his lips and kissed them tenderly. "Do you think it is possible to start again? Do you think that after all this time, there might be a chance for us?"

"I don't know," she answered shakily. "Perhaps we're too old for all this."

He bent, and his lips brushed hers, then lingered. Her arms crept around his shoulders, and their kiss deepened. And all time was lost.

CHAPTER NINETEEN

PRISCILLA FOUND THAT BRYAN was a man of his word: He spent the next two weeks taking every opportunity to woo her. He seemed to regard her refusal as only a minor setback. He came to call on her, bringing flowers and candy. He appeared at almost every function she attended, even church, and he always found an opportunity to sit with her and be quite obvious about paying attention to her. When the new Duke sent the Hamiltons an invitation to a small dinner in honor of Alec's birthday, she seriously considered not going. Bryan would probably be by her side all evening, making it extremely difficult for her to stick to her resolution. However, Miss Pennybaker felt she could not attend unless Priscilla went, also, and it seemed rather unfair to Alec not to go to the party celebrating his twenty-first birthday. He had been far less cheerful than usual since the Duke's arrival, even though he was getting his dearest wish, to join the army. Priscilla suspected that it had something to do with his mother's hasty departure from Ranleigh Court only two days after the Duke arrived. However, Alec had never said anything about it, and she did not wish to pry.

So, in order not to disappoint Penny and Alec, she told herself, she went to the dinner at Ranleigh Court. It was a rather small group, just as Alec had said it would be—only Lady Chalcomb, Mr. Rutherford and a few other guests in addition to the Hamilton party and Alec's new family. Bryan greeted her with a polite bow over her hand, brushing his lips across the back of her hand in a way that made her flesh tingle, though she struggled not to show it. He had managed to arrange the seating so that she was next to him during the meal, flirting with her so outrageously that it was almost impossible not to flirt back.

She was somewhat distracted, however, when she glanced up the table and saw Anne and the Duke talking together in an almost intimate way, their voices low and their heads close together. It surprised her. She had not known that her friend even knew the Duke of Ranleigh. Anne had never spoken of him before. And he had been here only a couple of weeks! Of course, she reminded herself, it had not taken her any longer to fall in love with the Duke's son. Still, it seemed odd to her. She continued to glance back at them from time to time throughout the meal. She generally found them conversing or smiling at each other. Even if they were talking to the people on their other sides, they would glance back at each other now and then, exchanging a look that Priscilla could only describe as loverlike.

After dinner, Priscilla managed to escape Bryan's attentions, finding an unoccupied room on the first floor where there was a large window seat in which she could sit almost hidden. However, it was probably not more than twenty minutes before Bryan stuck his head in the room and saw her.

"Hello. I wondered where you had gotten to," he said cheerfully, coming across the room toward her.

"Would you stop it?"

"Stop what?" he asked innocently, glancing around as if to see what he had done.

"You know what," she snapped. "Following me around. Showing up everywhere I go. Talking to me. People have noticed and commented on it."

"Have they?" He sat down beside her companionably on the window seat. "People love to gossip, you know."

"It is because you are paying such particular attention to me."

"That is usually the way a man acts when he wants to marry a woman," he pointed out reasonably.

"Bryan…please. I have told you time and again that I will not marry you."

"Not that many times. Haven't you noticed that I have ceased asking? I decided I was making a nuisance of myself."

"You are."

"So I haven't asked in some time. But can we not be friends? Can I not enjoy your company?"

Priscilla looked at him a trifle warily. She was not sure that mere friendship was something she was capable of sharing with Bryan. Besides, it seemed highly suspicious that he was suddenly willing to give up his campaign to convince her to marry him.

"I suppose we can," she said slowly. "What does that entail?"

"Doing what friends do, I suppose. I have tried to woo you, and that obviously is not working. You seem unusually immune to charm, and flowers appear to move you not at all."

A small smile played about her lips. She could rarely

keep from being charmed by Bryan, however well he might say she hid it.

"I am a hard woman," she admitted.

"I have something better to offer you than flowers. A mystery."

"What mystery?" Then she thought of his father. "Oh. Rose's death?"

"Father and I have been mulling over ways to discover whether his cousin Evesham actually killed that woman thirty years ago."

"And?"

"And we have not come up with much of anything. Father has talked to the constable about the case. It is not even the same constable, after all this time, and the case was filed away unsolved. Father finally got him to open up the file and let Father look at it. But it did not do much good. What little evidence they had all pointed to Father."

"Why is the Duke convinced that it was his cousin?"

Bryan explained his father's theory, and Priscilla listened, nodding now and again. Finally Bryan stopped abruptly and said, "You don't believe it, do you?"

"What?"

"That my father did not do it."

Priscilla shrugged. "I do not know, Bryan. I know very little about the case, really, only what gossip has said for thirty years, and everyone seemed pretty convinced that he did it."

"He could not have. I know it."

"He does not seem the sort who could commit murder," Priscilla admitted.

"He is not. It is absurd. He can be tough sometimes,

but I have seen him sad because he had to fire one of his workers, even though the man was a well-known drunk and egregiously bad at his job. But the man was supporting seven children, and Father hated to do it."

"However, I suppose that even good men can be goaded into killing."

"Not Father."

"Because he is your father, and you love him, you would feel that way. I understand that. I would never believe such a thing about Florian, either."

Bryan had to chuckle at the thought that Florian could ever be distracted from his chemical equations long enough to even think of killing someone.

"All right. 'Tis a poor example, I know. However, I am inclined to believe him simply because he is your father. It seems unlikely that he would be that different from you. You would not murder someone, especially, I think, if she was carrying your child."

"Good God, I should hope not. It sounds even worse, doesn't it, when you look at it that way? He not only killed her, he killed their child."

"Nor, I think, would you have led the poor girl on, making her think there was a possibility that you might marry her when you knew that you could not."

He glanced at her suspiciously. "Is that just a remark, or are you trying to make a point?"

Priscilla shrugged.

"It is a far different case from you and me, if that is what you mean. But you are right, I would not try to make a woman think I would marry her if it were not possible. But there is no impediment in our case. When I say it will happen, it will. There is nothing to stop it."

"I should not have spoken of this." Priscilla turned

away, starting to rise, and Bryan grasped her wrist, holding her down on the window seat.

"What holds you back?" he rasped. "Damn it, Priscilla, there is nothing against this match except your stubbornness. Why, even this precious 'reputation' that seems to mean so much to you would demand that we marry. We did, after all, spend that night together in the woods."

Priscilla whirled to look at him. "Is that why you pursue me so? Because you think you have to? Because my reputation is ruined?" Her heart ached. It seemed the worst that could happen that she should want him so much and have to refuse him, and all the while he was pursuing her only out of duty.

His mouth twisted bitterly. "Of course that is not all. But that seems to be the only thing that matters to you. You think only of appearances and nothing of substance."

Priscilla recoiled. "That is not true!"

"No? Then why do you hold back?"

"You don't understand…."

"No. How can I, when you won't tell me anything?"

"I cannot. I fear you would hate me." She looked at him, wanting to tell him, aching to unburden herself and hear him say that it did not matter. But what if it did? He had not spoken of love. In all the times he had asked her, though all the cajoling and demanding, he had not said the simple words "I love you." He wanted her; she knew that. She could tell that from the way he watched her whenever they were together. But that was not the same as love, real, abiding love. Desire could easily be destroyed.

He made a frustrated noise and jumped to his feet. "Damn it! What could be so awful? Is your grandfather mad? Locked up in an attic somewhere?"

"No. Don't be silly."

"Then are you actually somehow related to me?"

"Bryan…"

"You wrote a feminist tract—or you have been arrested parading for women's suffrage."

"That is ridiculous."

"This whole situation is ridiculous."

Priscilla drew breath to answer him. It was at that moment that they heard the shot.

PRISCILLA AND BRYAN BOTH FROZE. In the next instant, he was tearing out the doorway, with Priscilla right behind him. He headed for the main stairs, but Priscilla grabbed his arm.

"No, this way!" she called, and ran down the hall to their left. A small servants' staircase there led up in a steep, rather dizzying way to the floor above, emptying out into a back hall.

Furiously they ran down the hall toward the sound of voices—no, a single voice, raised in anger, and, unless Priscilla was mistaken, more than half drunk, as well. They crept around the corner, moving closer to the blue room, a formal room where most of the guests had gathered this evening after dinner. They stopped beside a massive mahogany breakfront decorated with porcelain figures, squatting down so that it concealed them from view.

The wide double doors of the drawing room were open, and a roughly dressed man stood just inside them. He was weaving a little on his feet, waving a large revolver around wildly. All of the guests stood across the room from him, white-faced, watching him with great concentration. The Duke stood, with his friend Mr. Rutherford and Lady Chalcomb, in front of the mantel. The others had drawn a little away, for it was to Ranleigh that the pistol kept returning. A large Chinese vase beside the fireplace was shattered, mute testimony to the man's poor aim.

Bryan looked at Priscilla, his brows rising in an unspoken question. She leaned closer and whispered, "Rose's brother."

"God."

"What did you care?" the man was now ranting. "You had money, you had power. 'Course you got away with it. And now you're back, never a lick of punshi—punch—punishment for what you done to Rosie. She never hurt nobody. Nobody. Just fell in love with the likes of you."

"I assure you, Childs, Rose was not in love with me. I had nothing to do with her death. Whoever she was talking about, it was not I."

"Sure," the man returned scornfully. "There bein' so many 'gentlemen' around here. 'Twas one of the others."

"Or someone who convinced her that he was."

Childs snorted. "No. It was you, all right, and I'm going ta see that ya pay for it. My Rosie's been lying in her grave thirty years now, cryin' out for justice. And I'm goin' to get it for her."

"This is not the way," Sebastian Rutherford began. "You will only get in trouble yourself. Think, man. What will happen to your mother and your farm if you get arrested for murdering a peer of the realm? Do you think they will go easy on you?"

"Not likely," Childs snorted. "The likes o' me they'll throw in jail, good and proper. It's only high-and-mighty ones like 'im what get away with it."

"That is my point exactly. It will do you no good."

"It will ease my mind!" he roared back at Rutherford. "It will bloody well ease my mind."

As the two men talked, Bryan bent and whispered in Priscilla's ear, "When I give you the signal, pick up a figure and crash it on the floor, then duck down immediately behind the breakfront." He jerked his head toward the massive piece of furniture beside him, on which stood various ornamental figures and vases.

She nodded her understanding. He slid silently down the hall, creeping behind the man until he was past the door. For an instant, Ranleigh's eyes flickered past his accuser to his son, then immediately back.

Childs raised his other hand to the one that held the pistol, steadying it as he took aim. Ranleigh faced him expressionlessly.

"At least do not put these other people at risk, Childs," Ranleigh said. "You cannot want to murder innocent people. Let them leave."

"And have them walking between you and me to the door? I ain't as stupid as you think, Your Grace."

"Then allow Mr. Rutherford and Lady Chalcomb to move away from me."

"All right." Childs jerked his head to the side. "You can move, my lady. You, too, Mr. Rutherford. Neither one of ya deserve to die, and he's right. My aim ain't too good tonight."

"Certainly not," Rutherford retorted. "I am not budging. Although Lady Chalcomb should—"

"Wait," that lady said firmly, stepping forward. "Mr. Childs, I cannot let you do this. You would be making a grave error."

"Anne!" Ranleigh snapped. "Don't say anything else."

"I am not going to let this man kill you just to save my reputation, Damon," the lady replied coolly, all the while keeping her eyes on the man with the gun. "Mr. Childs, do you know me to be a truthful woman?"

"Why, yes, my lady," the man answered, looking thoroughly confused. "Everyone knows that. There is none better than you."

"Thank you. Then will you believe me when I tell you that I know for a fact that Ranleigh did not kill your sister?"

His mouth twisted into a grimace. "How could you know that, my lady? You wasn't there."

"No, I was not there when your sister was murdered. But I was with Ranleigh. At my home. The whole evening and night."

Priscilla stared, her mouth dropping open, and the porcelain figure she had picked up from the breakfront slid nervelessly out of her hand.

The resulting crash startled everyone out of their immobility. Childs jumped and whirled, the pistol dropping from his hand. It went off with a loud retort, sending a bullet straight into the massive breakfront beside Priscilla. Bryan, who had been listening with the same attentiveness as everyone else to Anne's confession, cursed and jumped forward, grabbing Childs and bringing one of his arms up sharply behind his back.

"Damn it!" Bryan barked at Priscilla. "I didn't give you the signal."

Priscilla came out of her shock and sent him a withering glance. She walked forward and bent to pick up the pistol from the floor. "Apparently it was not necessary."

The drawing room was filled with a babel of voices as Damon strode forward and clasped Anne in a long embrace.

"QUITE A GIRL, BRYAN," Ranleigh said sometime later, after most of the other guests had left. Even Alec was not there, having gone with the general to take Mr. Childs to the constable. Only the Duke and his son, Anne, Rutherford and Priscilla were gathered in the smaller, less formal drawing room.

The Duke raised his snifter of brandy to Priscilla in a salute, then took a drink and said in an aside to Bryan, "I approve of your choice."

Priscilla felt too giddy with relief and the aftermath of the excitement to even summon up a twinge of anger at Bryan for having told his father she was his choice for a wife.

Damon then looked at Anne, standing beside him, and hugged her to his side. "And this dear lady here rather took away the surprise from the announcement we had planned to make. Lady Chalcomb has consented to be my wife."

"Oh, Anne!" Priscilla went to her friend and hugged her as Bryan and Rutherford offered their congratulations to the Duke. "I am so happy for you. You look absolutely radiant."

She spoke the truth; she *was* very happy for Anne.

But she could not help but wonder about Mr. Rutherford, whom she had often thought had more than a little interest in Lady Chalcomb. It must be hard for him, but she could not tell it from his face.

Anne answered with a smile that demonstrated the truth of Priscilla's compliment. "Thank you. It is a dream come true—something I had no hope of ever doing."

Damon went on grimly, "That's why it is even more important to me to prove that I did not kill Rose Childs thirty years ago. I don't want Anne to have to reveal the truth in front of the whole county—any more than Bryan wishes to marry that way."

"Uh, excuse me, but Bryan is not—" Priscilla began.

Bryan broke into Priscilla's words, drowning her out. "Priscilla and I were talking about your investigation earlier this evening, Father. Weren't we, Priscilla?" He raced on without giving her a chance to respond. "How you plan to prove Evesham did it."

"Evesham!" Rutherford exclaimed. "That popinjay? You think he killed Rose?"

"Who else?" Damon pointed out. "There are not many choices. Evesham would certainly be the type to woo an innocent servant girl, hinting at marriage."

"He *is* low," Rutherford agreed. "Still, it sounds too forceful for Evesham."

"You know this Evesham?" Bryan asked Rutherford.

"Oh, yes, we all went to school together. In fact, I believe Evesham was here with us that holiday from school, was he not?"

Damon nodded. "Yes. He had the opportunity."

"But why do you have to find out who killed the poor girl?" Rutherford asked. "Now that Anne has...revealed where you were."

"I am hopeful that the people who were here tonight will not spread that fact around. They are good people, our friends, and I think they will not use it as gossip fodder."

"But if we tell them it is all right to reveal it—" Anne began.

"Do you want your name bandied about all over the county? I do not. It is not my wish to rescue my name by having yours trampled in the mud. I *don't* want them to spread it about. If it did get out, there would still be those who will say you lied because you love me. After all, we will be married soon. Or they will say that I bought your lie by promising marriage. The only way to completely clear my name is to find the real killer." He sighed. "Besides, that poor wretch who came here tonight deserves to have the murder cleared up."

"He tried to kill you!"

"He was distraught...and drunk. Obviously he loved his sister, and it must have been a torment all this time to think that his sister's murderer got away with it. He deserves to know the truth. And Rose—don't you think it would only be fair to Rose to expose the real killer?"

Anne sighed. "I suppose. But I am afraid you will put yourself in danger, looking for him."

"What if you could find the rubies in Evesham's possession?" Priscilla asked. It was a subject she had been thinking about for some time.

Rutherford looked startled. "You think he would still have them? Wouldn't he have gotten rid of them?"

Ranleigh shook his head decisively. "I don't think

so. They would have been hard to sell. They were quite well-known. It was a very old and distinctive piece. He could have taken the gems out and sold them to be cut up into smaller pieces, but it would have meant a huge loss of money. I think he would have decided to wait and let it die down, then someday sell the necklace as a piece. Or simply keep it. After all, at that time, he was thinking that he would be the next heir if I were executed for murder. A Duke of Ranleigh would never sell that piece. I'm not sure that any Aylesworth would, even Evesham. He was quite proud, you know. By the same token, I am certain he could not have borne to throw it away. All that wealth? All the family ties? I think he would have kept it."

"Evesham likes beautiful things," Anne put in.

"You know him well?" Damon asked.

She shook her head. "Not well. I have seen very little of him the past few years. But he and Lord Chalcomb were friends. They had…certain interests in common. I saw him now and then when my husband was alive. He admired some of the old tapestries at Chalcomb Hall and some ornamental pieces that had belonged to Lord Chalcomb's mother. In fact, I believe he purchased a chess set done in black and white marble from me after Harry's death."

"If he kept the necklace, it would be proof that he was the one who committed the murder, would it not?" Priscilla asked, bringing the conversation back to her original question.

Damon nodded. "I think it would certainly cast suspicion on him. The problem would be proving that he has it."

"We would have to search his home. That is the only method I can think of," Priscilla said.

"Sneak in in the middle of the night?" Anne asked, looking shocked. "Priscilla—that is a crime!"

"Of course it is, but it is hardly as bad as murder. Besides, we won't sneak in in the middle of the night. What I propose is to do it in the evening. The servants will be down in the servants' quarters, because their work will be finished. There will have been no dinner for Evesham that night, because he will not have been there."

"And how have you determined that, Miss Hamilton?" Bryan asked her, his eyes twinkling, enjoying the faintly bemused expressions on his father's and Mr. Rutherford's faces.

"Why, because he will have been invited to dinner here."

"Indeed?" Damon murmured.

"Yes. You will invite him over—a gesture of friendship, reconciliation and so forth. He is bound to accept. If nothing else, he will be curious about what you look like and what kind of life you have led since leaving England. Bryan—that is, the Marquess—and I will enter his house very quietly and search it. You will keep Evesham here all evening, even ask him to stay the night, because of the lateness of the hour."

"An excellent idea," Bryan agreed. "How soon can you invite him, Father?"

Damon stared at him in amazement. "As soon as I write a note to him, and he accepts. I can invite him for…say, next Saturday. That should give him enough time to reply. But, Bryan, surely you are not going to agree to Miss Hamilton doing something so dangerous as breaking into his house with you?"

"Oh." An odd look crossed Bryan's face. He was frankly looking forward to the idea of going there with Priscilla. He had not even thought about the danger to her any more than he would have for himself. "Well, uh, Father, Miss Hamilton is different from most young ladies. She will be a help, not a hindrance, and...um, I am not sure I could keep her from going, anyway."

Priscilla nodded, satisfaction warming her at Bryan's acceptance of her competence. "He's right. He could not. He will need me to take him to Evesham's house. Also, I can identify the necklace if we find it. I have seen it in paintings. Bryan, on the other hand, has no idea what it looks like."

"Alec can go with him. He knows those things, too," Damon responded, in a voice that usually meant the end of any discussion.

Priscilla seemed not to notice the authority in his voice. "Alec is young and impetuous, far more likely to get all of us in trouble. Anyway, he is departing tomorrow for the army."

Damon frowned, silent for a moment. "Yes, you're right. The logical thing is for me to go. Neither Bryan nor you should be placed in jeopardy."

"Then who is going to invite your cousin over for dinner? It would look rather odd for Bryan to do it and for you not to even attend."

The Duke's jaw set in irritation. "Forget the dinner invitation. I shall simply enter his house one night and search it."

"No!" Anne cried, stepped forward and putting her hand on his arm. "I won't let you do that. It is far more dangerous. Priscilla's plan is the best, and I am sure that she and Bryan will do an excellent job. Why, you were telling me just this afternoon of all the adventures Bryan had gotten into and out of."

"I know, but placing a girl in danger…it doesn't set well with me."

"Nor me, Damon," Mr. Rutherford added. "The whole thing strikes me as too dangerous."

"I will take care of Priscilla," Bryan assured the older men, his eyes twinkling.

Damon sighed. "All right. That is our plan, then. I will write to Evesham tonight and invite him for dinner this Saturday. Sebastian, you come that night, also, and we shall keep him occupied all evening with billiards or reminiscences about the old days. And you two will find whatever evidence you can."

"Agreed." Bryan smiled down at Priscilla, thinking of the hours he would get to spend alone with her.

THE PLAN PROCEEDED SMOOTHLY. Ranleigh wrote a note of invitation to his cousin, and Evesham replied quickly that he would love to attend. On the appointed night, Bryan left the Court before Evesham arrived and rode across the fields to Evermere Cottage, leading a horse for Priscilla. They had decided that riding would be the faster way to Evesham's house, and if they happened to cross his path on the road as he was going to Ranleigh Court, it would be less likely that he would recognize Bryan, whom he did not know at all, and Priscilla, whom he knew only slightly, than that he would recognize the ducal carriage, if they went in that. Priscilla, who had never ridden much, dug out her mother's old habit, which did, she had to admit, look quite dashing on her, and hoped that Bryan would be true to his word and bring her a gentle mare.

The ride over was uneventful, though rather long. They passed by Evesham's house and left the road to disappear into the trees a short way past the drive. They wound their way through the trees until they were almost even with the house, then hobbled their horses and walked under the cover of the trees to the house. They were lucky in that, while an empty field lay on the other side of the house, on this side the trees grew down almost to the garden.

It was dusk when they reached the edge of the trees, and they sat down just within the wood to wait for dark to settle completely. It was difficult to wait with patience. Priscilla felt as if excitement were fizzing inside her. She glanced over at Bryan and saw the same excitement reflected in his eyes. If there was anything better than having an adventure, she thought, it was having it with the man you loved by your side.

Was this what marriage with Bryan would be like? He had told her that he traveled to places all over the world, solving problems for his father's business. Would she get to help him solve them, get to travel to all those places she had always yearned to see and had resigned herself to never getting an opportunity to visit?

She thought of being with him, sharing not only his bed but also his adventures, and suddenly it seemed too great a sacrifice to make to refuse to marry him. Perhaps, if she gave up writing, no one would ever find out that Eliot Pruett, who had written only two books, since forgotten, was the same person as the future Duchess of Ranleigh. But that, too, seemed an unbearable thing to have to give up. Besides, what kind of marriage would it be if they started it out with such a lie between them?

Bryan reached across and touched her arm, startling her. He pointed toward the house, a dark shape in the even darker night, and said in a low voice, "Time to go."

Priscilla nodded and put aside her thoughts as she followed Bryan out of the trees. They hurried across the open space and into the garden that lay beside the house. They threaded their way through the crushed-rock paths of the garden and up to the side of the house. Most of the windows were dark. Bryan tried each one; all of them were locked. They slipped around to the front of the house, then the other side, and there they found a French door unlocked. Turning the knob, Bryan stepped inside, then motioned for Priscilla to follow him.

They stood for a moment, waiting for their eyes to adjust to the room, which was even darker than the outside. Finally they saw a faint light beneath the doors on the other side of the room. It was a large room, floored with stone, and there were dark shapes all around them that Priscilla finally realized were plants. They were in a conservatory, it seemed.

Making their way cautiously around the plants, they reached the door, and Priscilla eased it open. Beyond lay a hall, dimly lit. It appeared to be empty, so Priscilla opened the door farther and stuck her head out. They were about halfway down the hall. At the rear end was a small staircase, obviously a servants' stairway. The hall ran in the other direction, toward the front of the house. Priscilla thought that the back of the house was more dangerous, for it was there that they were most likely to run into a servant. With the master out and the day over, the servants should be congregating in the kitchen or the housekeeper's sitting room, and the front of the house should stand empty.

She slipped out of the door and made her way along the hall toward the front, walking on tiptoe to avoid making any sound on the wooden floor. She felt extremely exposed; her heart was pounding in her chest. The only thing that kept her from turning and fleeing was Bryan's presence right behind her. She couldn't let him see how scared she was.

They made it to the front of the house and up the grand staircase, which was even more frightening, to the second floor. It was there that the bedrooms lay. Priscilla and Bryan had discussed what they would do at some length, and had decided that they would search Evesham's bedroom first, as it seemed the most likely place for a person to hide something.

Upstairs, they checked several doors before they found one room that was larger than the others and appeared to be lived in. They closed and locked the door behind them, and Priscilla felt far safer. Curiously, it was then that she felt as if her knees might give way beneath her. Bryan wrapped an arm around her waist, steadying her, and leaned down to kiss her head.

"The worst is over," he whispered.

Priscilla smiled back gratefully, wondering how he had known the way she felt. They lit a candle and began a thorough search of the room in the dim light. They went through every drawer, careful not to mess up the neatly folded articles of clothing. Priscilla found two promising boxes, but there turned out to be a diamond stickpin in one and several loose calling cards in the other. Bryan opened the small jewelry box on the highboy and searched through the tie pins and cuff links on the off chance that Evesham had been brazen enough to hide the jewels there. He also looked under the bed and behind the various pictures, searching for a hidden safe, then checked out the small attached dressing room, while Priscilla rifled all the drawers. Bryan even tapped softly along the walls, looking for a spot that sounded hollow.

"What are you doing?" Priscilla whispered. "Stop knocking on the walls. Someone will hear you."

"Father told me that he faintly remembered Evesham bragging when they were children that he had a hiding place in the house. He thought that if it were true, it might be where he hid the jewelry."

"Then the most likely place for that would be in the nursery, wouldn't it?"

Bryan shrugged. "Father couldn't remember him mentioning a location. The nursery doesn't seem likely for a hidden room, does it? Father recalls him describing it as being a large enough space that he could get into it, like a priest's hole or something. He thought it could be almost anywhere in the house."

Their search of the rest of the second floor was cursory, but they did go up to the nursery on the third floor. It was more dangerous, as the maids' quarters were up there, also, and any who were already in bed might hear them. They moved very quietly, only whispering to each other now and then, but the largely bare rooms yielded no evidence of a hiding place.

They made their way quickly downstairs. Time was running out, and they were becoming somewhat discouraged. They had already decided that the most likely of the formal rooms to hide anything in was the study, for that was the most personal of the downstairs rooms. After a quick check of the sitting and drawing room walls for safes, they locked themselves in the study and lit a candle. One wall held books, all of them perfectly aligned and looking unused. A large set of glassed-in shelves stood against another wall, each glass front locked. This place intrigued Priscilla the most, for it was filled with beautiful objects, small vases, glass miniatures, little carved Oriental scenes and other such things. However, since all the contents of the shelves could be clearly seen and there were no rubies among them, she soon left the shelves and went to the desk. This yielded nothing; most of the drawers were not even locked.

"Hello," Bryan said quietly, breaking the stillness, and Priscilla turned.

"What?"

"This panel of the wall," he said. "Listen." He knocked on the wall on one side of the fireplace, then on the wall on the other. The second piece of wall sounded peculiar.

"I think it's hollow."

Excitement flared in Priscilla, and she hurried over to where Bryan stood. "You found it? The hiding place your father talked about?"

"Maybe." He ran his hand over the wall. "I can't feel a crack. How do you get into it? That's the problem."

"Try the mantel," Priscilla suggested. "It is carved with all kinds of curlicues and knobs and such. That's always where they put the release mechanism."

"You have a wide experience with hidden doors?"

"In books, I mean."

He made a face. "I am talking about reality, not books."

At that moment, the knob he touched moved. He twisted it, and the panel of wood beside the fireplace slid open.

CHAPTER TWENTY

PRISCILLA LET OUT A LITTLE SQUEAK, immediately stifled, as the door slid noiselessly into its pocket, revealing a dark space behind it.

"It really exists!" Bryan breathed, amazed, and held up the candle to illuminate the room.

Their hearts immediately fell. The "room" was not as big as the inside of a wardrobe. As tall as the rest of the room, it was barely wide enough or deep enough to hold more than one person. Bryan moved the candle up and down, illuminating it from ceiling to floor. It was absolutely bare.

"Not much of a secret room, is it?" Priscilla commented in disappointment.

"Maybe something in it opens up," Bryan said, and felt the walls and floor for a crack or a sound that indicated another empty space behind it. Nothing moved or looked as if it ever would.

"I pity the poor priest who had to hide in there."

Bryan stepped back out and twisted the knob on the mantel. The door moved back into place. They continued their search of the room, feeling even more downhearted. Finally they had searched every inch of the place, even turning up the corners of the Oriental rug to see if there might be an opening for a safe beneath it. They walked to the door and unlocked it. Bryan leaned his head against the wood, listening for any sound of a person outside. Then he turned the knob and eased the door open an inch.

At that moment the knocker on the front door crashed down hard. Priscilla jumped, clapping her hand over her mouth. Bryan stiffened, closing the door to a mere crack and putting his ear to it.

They heard the measured steps of a footman crossing the marble entryway, then the sound of the door opening.

"Good evening, sir. We hadn't expected to see you back so soon."

"Quite right. However, I decided to return early."

Priscilla's eyes went wide. *Evesham!* She and Bryan looked wildly at each other. Quickly Bryan eased the door to and, taking her hand, hurried across the room to the mantel. He pressed frantically on the ornate carving. They could hear steps on the marble of the entryway and muffled voices.

For one breathless moment Priscilla thought that the strange door would refuse to open, or that Bryan had gotten the wrong rosette, but then the panel in the wall slid open. Bryan reached out for her hand, but she hesitated.

"It's too small!" she hissed.

Bryan stepped into the space and unceremoniously jerked her in after him. The panel was still open, however. The voices were closer, right outside the door. Panic gripped Priscilla. Then she noticed the small button on the inside of their box, beside the open panel. She punched it, and the panel closed.

The space was indeed too small. Priscilla found herself pressed against the wall in front, and Bryan was

so close behind her that she could feel his body all the
way up and down her back. It seemed hard to breathe,
and she wondered about the amount of air there might
be in this upright coffin.

There was a click as the study door opened, and then
a loud, familiar voice, "But surely you don't keep your
objets d'art in here. I would think they would be on
display in the drawing room."

Ranleigh? Priscilla glanced back up at Bryan in
amazement. What on earth was he doing here? And
with Evesham!

Bryan raised an eyebrow and shrugged. Outside,
Evesham's silky voice replied, "What? To let the masses
see? Oh, no, dear boy, I keep them in here, where only
I can look at them."

"But where's the fun in that?" another voice asked.
It sounded very much like Mr. Rutherford's.

"I say, why are you speaking so loudly?" Evesham
asked petulantly.

"Am I?" Rutherford returned blandly.

"Yes. Both of you."

"Oh, sorry." That was Damon's voice again. "Guess
I'm used to speaking on board ship. Hard to hear on the
open sea, you know."

Priscilla had to smother a giggle. It was obvious that
the two men were trying to warn them of Evesham's
presence as best they could. She doubted that they suspected that Priscilla and Bryan were in the very same
room with them, but no doubt they hoped that their loud
talk would reach them wherever they were searching.

Outside, in the room, they heard the sounds of
Evesham opening the glass display case into which

they had gazed earlier. Rutherford and Damon began to exclaim over the miniatures within at great length.

Priscilla realized that the Duke and his friend might keep Evesham talking in here for some time. Since it was apparent that Bryan and Priscilla were not in this room, no doubt they would assume that the couple were escaping from some other room. They would want to give them plenty of time in which to do it. She leaned against the wall in front of her, suppressing a sigh.

Now that her heart had subsided a little and her nerves were no longer standing on end, she began to think about how close Bryan was to her. His front grazed her back, and she could feel the heat of his muscular body through their clothes. She looked up at Bryan, and in the faint light seeping in through the cracks around the secret door, she found him gazing back at her. Blood flooded her cheeks; she was glad that he could barely see her.

She glanced immediately away. But it was too late; the sexual awareness was there, and with every passing second it grew, seeming to feed on the silence and awkwardness. Outside, the three men continued to chat. Priscilla wondered impatiently if they would ever shut up.

Bryan touched her hair. Priscilla flinched, barely suppressing a gasp—less of surprise than of pent-up desire. It had been only a few weeks since she had felt his intimate touch, but it seemed as if it had been forever. He smoothed his hand over her hair, then delved into the knot in back, pulling out pin after pin. A shudder ran through Priscilla, and she pressed her lips together to hold back a moan. His hands felt so wonderful in her hair; it turned her knees to butter. She flashed him an admonishing look, trying to appear stern and forbidding, but she knew inside that what she really wanted was to feel his hands all over her.

Bryan grinned at her, his eyes alight with deviltry, obviously reading her mind. She dared not speak, and there was not enough room in the hidey-hole to pull away from him. She could only glare at him, but he ignored her, continuing to take down her hair until at last it tumbled freely over her shoulders. Then he combed his fingers through it, fingering the silken locks. Priscilla leaned her forehead weakly against the wall in front of her.

His hand went to her face, and his finger traced over her brow and cheeks as if he were a blind man. He ran his forefinger slowly across her mouth, and it was all Priscilla could do not to take it between her lips. His finger trailed down over her chin and onto the soft flesh of her throat, delving beneath the collar of her riding habit.

Priscilla's eyes fluttered closed, and her breath came more quickly. Bryan's hand moved to the long row of buttons down the front of her jacket, and he began to unfasten them. Her eyes flew open, and she turned her head to glare a warning at him, but he paid no attention to her, just gave her a bland look and continued working on the buttons. She could say nothing, for fear of being heard by Evesham, outside in the room. Bryan's hand slipped inside the bodice and under her chemise, and further efforts to stop him went right out of her head. Her breast fit perfectly into his hand; Priscilla quivered at the feel of it there. His other hand came up, and took possession of the opposite breast.

He bent and began to nuzzle her neck, his hands busy teasing her nipples into hardness. Priscilla went weak at the knees. Her head lolled to the side, giving him freer access to her neck. Taking her nipples between his forefingers and thumbs, he rubbed and tweaked and caressed them into thrusting out. His fingers explored her breasts and delved down beneath her chemise as if he had all the time in the world, as if they were not stuck in a hidden space, perhaps to be discovered at any moment.

Now his fingers left her breasts and went to the fastenings of her skirt. Deftly he disconnected the hooks and eyes, then slid his hand beneath her petticoats and undergarments, finding bare skin at last. Priscilla was startled from her haze of desire, and she craned her neck to look up at him. He met her gaze this time, his hot eyes boring into hers, and she felt herself melting all over. This could not be happening, she told herself.

He rucked up one side of her skirt and moved his hand up under it, smoothing it over the sensitive skin of her inner thigh. Priscilla jerked convulsively. But there was nowhere to go and nothing she could do. Desire rushed in on her like a freight train. His fingers went between her legs, and she had to clap her hand over her mouth to keep from crying out. He stroked her there, and she labored for breath. His hand came out and around to the back, moving down inside her pantaloons and over her derriere, squeezing the firm flesh there. Then his fingers found her soft inner passage from the back.

Her hands came up, elbows resting against the wall. She was so caught up in passion that she could scarcely breathe; it seemed as if every fiber of her being were centered in the heat in her abdomen right now. It was all she could do not to groan or cry out as Bryan's fingers worked new delights on her tender flesh. He buried his finger deep within her, while with his other hand he continued to caress her breast. He stroked in and out, arousing her, as he nibbled at her neck.

She could feel his maleness hard and stiff against her bottom. He pushed her hips back against him, making it even more obvious, and rubbed them back and forth across him. Priscilla took her lip between her teeth, clamping down on it to keep from making any noise.

His hand found the tiny button of pleasure that lay between her legs, hard and aching. He teased it gently, gliding over the slick flesh again and again. Priscilla began to rotate her hips involuntarily. Desire was building in her, making her desperate. She wanted to beg him to take her farther, higher, faster, to the pleasure she knew awaited her. She buried her face in the crook of her arm to stifle the sound of her quick breath.

His finger pressed harder, instinctively answering her mute plea. The pleasure was swirling in her, moving inexorably to its goal, and Priscilla trembled, poised on the brink. Then, suddenly, she was falling over its edge, warmth flooding through her. She moved her hips, biting her lip till it bled to keep from letting out a moan.

At long last she came back to her senses, floating down from the blind pinnacle of pleasure. She leaned against the wall, struggling to control her breathing. At last it reached her consciousness that there was no longer any sound from the room beyond them. She glanced back up at Bryan questioningly.

"I think they have left," he whispered in her ear. His face was flushed, his eyes were glittering, and she could feel the insistent throbbing of his aroused manhood against her.

They waited for another moment, and when there

was still nothing but silence, Bryan pushed the button. The door slid open, revealing an empty room. Priscilla stumbled out of the small space, feeling as if her legs would barely support her. Bryan came after her and twisted the knob on the mantel to close the door.

He reached out and whirled Priscilla around, pulling her to his chest and sinking his lips into hers. They kissed forever, their mouths fused. Priscilla, languid in the aftermath of her own passion, could feel the heat rising in her again.

"What about Evesham?" she whispered.

"He won't come back," he answered, his lips trailing down her throat to the open neck of her riding habit. "And I don't give a damn if he does."

He picked her up, his hands beneath her buttocks, sliding her up his body. For a moment he fumbled with her skirts and his own clothing, and then he was inside her. Priscilla made a noise, startled, but she was quick to catch on, and she wrapped her legs around his waist as she wiggled a little, moving down more fully over his stiff maleness. He let out a groan at the sensations her movements generated. Then he was moving inside her, his head buried in her neck, his breath rasping harshly in her ear.

He moved blindly back to the wall, partially supporting Priscilla against it as his hips drove into her, setting up a primal rhythm of lust. Priscilla tangled her fingers in his hair and leaned her head back against the wall, lost in their mutual passion. Any number of people could have come in at that moment, and she would not have noticed.

Bryan thrust into her deeply, his fingers digging into her crumpled skirts, and muffled his groan against her skin. He shuddered, pouring his seed into her, and Priscilla tightened her legs around him as if she could hold him closer, pull him inside her even more deeply.

With a sigh, he relaxed against her, his breath coming in short pants. She brushed her hand over his neck; it was damp with sweat cooling in the air.

"Am I still alive?" he murmured.

Priscilla chuckled softly. "Yes." She kissed the top of his head, caressing his hair with her hand. "But neither of us may be much longer, if we stay here."

"I don't think I can move."

But he did, stepping back and letting her slide down his body to the floor. His eyes took in her tousled hair and her swollen lips, the slackness of her face, the disarray of her riding habit. Her appearance sparked his desire again, despite what they had just done. She looked like a lass who had just taken a hasty tumble in the hay with her lover, a woman well loved and passionate.

"God, Priscilla," he said impulsively, "you have to marry me. I do not think I can live without you another day."

Priscilla, who had begun trying to straighten and refasten her clothes, looked up at him in surprise. His words struck her as all his fanciful wooing had not. His need was real and deep; it fairly vibrated from him, touching a chord deep within her. She opened her mouth, but could not speak.

He looked away, pulling his clothes back in order. The moment passed. Priscilla hastily finished buttoning her bodice and straightened her skirts, shaking them and her petticoats into some semblance of order. As for her hair, there was nothing she could do with that. The pins were scattered all over the floor of that little room, and she certainly hadn't the time to pick them up.

They glanced around the room to make sure they had left nothing incriminating behind, then went to the door and eased it open. There was no one about. The house stood empty and still. Above them, somewhere, a door closed. Evesham's bedchamber, Priscilla hoped. That would mean he was not anywhere about down here, about to jump out and apprehend them.

Bryan looked longingly at the front door. It was not far away, but the great lock on it had been turned, and he could imagine the sound it might make were he to turn it. Also, in the entryway, they were completely exposed, with no place to hide. He turned back to the room and walked over to one of the windows. Pushing the heavy curtain aside, he looked out. It was only a short distance to the ground, and the window was wide and tall, with a single lock. He tried the lock, and it slid open easily. The window, too, slid up with little effort. Once they were outside, he thought he could close it again. It would be impossible for him to relock it, of course, but perhaps no one would notice, or perhaps no one would think anything of it if they did. An unlocked window would not implicate him or Priscilla, anyway.

He helped Priscilla out, then crawled through himself, reaching back up to pull the window down. When it was closed, he and Priscilla navigated their way through the dark garden. He did not look up to see if anyone was watching. If they were, he didn't want them to get a good look at their faces. Soon they were past the edge of the garden, and they ran full tilt across the small open space to the woods beyond. It wasn't until they reached the trees that they stopped and turned around, panting, and looked back at the house. It appeared as dark as it had before, except for the dim light that shone in Evesham's bedroom windows. However, the windows were only rectangles of vague light. That meant the drapes were closed, and it was unlikely that Evesham or his valet had looked out and seen them running away from the house.

Bryan threw his arms around Priscilla and hugged her, picking her up off the ground. His heart was pumping wildly, and though they had found nothing to help his father in the house, he was filled with jubilation. It seemed to him that Priscilla had told him clearly, without words, what she felt for him.

"Marry me," he said, setting her down. "No more of this dancing around, no more playing games. Marry me."

"Did you mean what you said back there?" she asked, looking up at him seriously.

"What? About not being able to live without you? That is true enough."

"You have talked about marrying me. About saving my reputation. About wanting me. But you have not talked to me about love."

He gazed at her blankly. "Love? Are you asking if I love you?"

She nodded. "I do not want to be an obligation to you. I do not want to be a burden, a regret."

"I would never regret marrying you. Never." He seized her hands and held them between his earnestly. "Priscilla, I love you. I have loved you for a long time now. Why else would I have asked you to marry me? I don't feel obligated to marry you. And I would never, never consider you a burden. Don't you understand? I don't care that I am to be a duke. I don't care if your blood is not blue enough. I don't care what you have done in your past that you think is so terrible. Hell, I don't even care that you have a father who regularly blows up his workshop! I love you, and I want to marry you. Will you marry me?"

"Yes!" Priscilla threw her arms around him, beginning to weep. "Yes, I will. Oh, Bryan, I love you. It hurt so much to refuse you. I have loved you for weeks now. For— I don't know, I think I have loved you since I first saw you."

"Then why have you held back?"

"I don't know. I was so afraid…." She paused and looked away. Now was when she should tell him about her writing, let him know the scandal that might await them. Let him decide whether he really loved her enough to accept her, to accept what she did.

"Of what?"

Her nerve failed her. "I'm not sure. Of your not understanding who and how you should marry, of your regretting it years later."

"I promise you, I will not regret it." He pulled her to him and kissed her soundly on the lips. "Now, get on that horse, and let's leave this place."

She nodded, grateful not to have to elaborate on her words. They mounted up and made their way through the trees and out to the road, where they kicked their horses into a trot. After a few minutes of riding they rounded a corner and discovered two men on horseback waiting for them.

Priscilla started and reined in, realizing belatedly that it was the Duke and Mr. Rutherford.

"Father!" Bryan burst out.

"Bryan! And Miss Hamilton. Thank God! We weren't sure whether to wait for you or if you had already gone."

"We were in that damn study with you the whole time you were jawing with Evesham," Bryan told him.

"What?"

"How could you have been?" Rutherford asked in amazement.

"There is a secret room—more like a closet, really, just as you said there might be. It happens to be in the study. Luckily, we had found it earlier, or you would have walked right in on us."

Ranleigh groaned. "I had no idea where you were. Sebastian and I were making fools of ourselves, practically shouting our sentences."

"I know. We heard you. What the devil were you doing there, anyway? Your aim was to keep Evesham *out* of his house, not bring him right back there."

Rutherford gave Ranleigh a fulminating look. "Damon took it into his head to start talking about Evesham's damn-fool collection of knickknacks."

"Well, I couldn't converse with the fellow. By the time dinner was over, I had pretty much run out of anything to say. He doesn't even play billiards. I was desperate for something to keep him talking so he would not leave early. I remembered Anne saying that he collected things." Damon paused and glowered at his friend. "Anyway, it was you who had to blurt out that you would love to see his collection sometime."

"How was I to know the fool would take it into his head to show me right then?" Rutherford shot back.

The two men looked at each other and began to chuckle. "Lord," Ranleigh said, "we looked like idiots all the way over here, riding like old men and talking about every damn fool thing we saw along the way."

They laughed, their relief turning them giddy, and the four of them turned and started back along the road to Elverton. As they rode, Bryan told them of their failure to find the necklace in Evesham's house.

"He has thrown it away by now," Rutherford said gloomily. "I am sure of it. It was a wild-goose chase the whole time."

"So what do we do now?" Bryan asked.

"Talk to the Childses," Priscilla answered promptly.

The other three men turned to look at her, perplexed. "But they think *I* did it," Ranleigh reminded her.

"Yes, I know. But if I could talk to Childs and get him to tell me exactly what his sister said, not what he interpreted it to mean, we might get some clues as to who it really was. Maybe he or his mother heard something that meant nothing to him but will mean something to you or Mr. Rutherford."

Damon was silent for a moment, then said thoughtfully, "Yes. I suppose so. I know that Alec said on the way to the constable's the other night Childs kept raving about having proof, said there was something he found in Rose's room afterward. Some frippery thing her lover—he said me, of course—had given her."

"What?" Rutherford asked, intrigued. "You didn't tell me about this."

"I didn't remember it earlier. It just flashed into my mind when Miss Hamilton said that. It would be bizarre, wouldn't it, if she'd had in her possession something that would point to the real killer after all this time?"

There was a moment of stunned silence at his words.

Finally Bryan said, "You mean he assumed it was yours, this thing? And never brought it forward? But why?"

"I'm not sure. All I know is what Alec told me the other morning. I think he found it after I was already gone. He probably figured there was no point to showing it."

"Then I would say it is very much worth a talk with our Mr. Childs," Bryan said. "Is he still locked up?"

"I think so. Serving a couple of weeks for being drunk and disorderly. But I am not pressing charges on the other things."

"You are going to let them set him free?" Bryan asked, appalled. "After he tried to kill you?"

"He's had enough misery in his life without being sent to prison, don't you think?"

Bryan seemed flabbergasted, but Priscilla said, "I think you are a very warm and generous man, Your Grace. And I am sure that Mr. Childs will be more willing to talk after this. It sounds hopeful."

"It's worth a try, anyway," Damon agreed. "I confess that if that doesn't work, I am a little stumped. The only thing I can think to do is choke a confession out of Evesham."

Rutherford spoke up. "After spending several hours in his company tonight, I will be happy to do the choking myself."

They rode on through the night, the three men dropping Priscilla off at Chalcomb Manor to spend the night. Because of the presence of his father and Rutherford, Bryan's farewell to Priscilla was necessarily quite chaste, but his eyes spoke volumes as he bent over her hand and kissed it.

"The wedding date must be soon," he murmured.

Priscilla nodded and smiled, though inside she was already beginning to worry and doubt her decision. She knew she should have told him about her writing tonight; it had been cowardly of her to back away from it. She would have to tell him, she told herself as she opened the door and walked inside the manor, and soon, before he had a chance to spread the word that they were getting married.

PRISCILLA ROSE LATE THE NEXT MORNING and breakfasted with Anne, who was eager to hear all the details of the night before. Priscilla gave her a very much expurgated account, telling of their failure to find anything, but added that they planned to question Tom Childs further about what his sister had said about her "gentleman," as well as the object he had given her.

"Damon didn't tell me about that!" Anne exclaimed, grimacing. "Men! They think a woman is too fragile to hear anything. Sometimes it is exceedingly annoying."

Priscilla thought, a little smugly, that Bryan was no longer that sort. He had shown no qualms about her participating in their adventure last night.

After breakfast, Priscilla dressed in the clothes she had brought over the night before, chatted for a while with Anne, then started home. She was somewhat surprised, when she arrived at Evermere Cottage, to see the vicar's small gig in front of the house. She walked inside and found the vicar in the cozy sitting room with her father and Miss Pennybaker. Miss Pennybaker's cheeks were flushed, her eyes were bright, and she looked far prettier than Priscilla had ever seen her, even the night of the ball. Her father, too, looked different, though at first she could not place why. Then she saw the bandage on her father's forehead.

"Papa!" she exclaimed. "What happened? Did another experiment blow up? You ought to be more careful, you know."

"What? Oh, no. How was the evening with Lady Chalcomb?"

"Quite pleasant. But first, tell me about your injury. If it was not an experiment, what did you do?"

"Well, I, ah, actually, it was— Well, I think I shall let the vicar tell you about it. Right now, I have work to do. Isabelle?" He turned to Miss Pennybaker, holding out his hand and smiling in a way that Priscilla had never seen him do before.

"Papa?" she asked, wondering if the injury to his head had damaged the inside, as well. He was wearing a grin that was positively foolish. And why had he called Penny "Isabelle"? It *was* her first name, Priscilla thought, but she had never heard anyone use it, and it seemed rather rude of Papa to speak to her so familiarly.

"Yes, Florian." Miss Pennybaker rose, all smiles, reaching out to clasp Mr. Hamilton's hand. She glanced over at Priscilla and hesitated. "But, Florian, don't you think we ought to tell Priscilla the news?"

"What news?" Priscilla asked, feeling as if she had walked into a house she did not know. Everyone looked the same, but they were all acting so strange.

"Well, my dear..." Florian paused, and Miss Pennybaker blushed, tittering behind her hand. "Miss Pennybaker has done me the honor of consenting to be my wife."

Priscilla gaped.

"I see we have taken you by surprise," Florian went on in masterly understatement. "Well, not such a surprise, really. Bound to happen one day, I suppose."

"But how— When—?"

Florian waved an airy hand. "The vicar will fill you in on all the details. Isabelle and I have work to do now."

With that, he turned and left the room with his fiancée, his head close to hers in talk. Priscilla stared after them, then swung around to the innocent vicar.

"What in the world is going on?" she exclaimed. "What happened? When I left, everything was as usual."

"Well, we had a meeting last night. You know, your father, Dr. Hightower, the general and me. Miss Pennybaker was there, too, for she brought us the tea and all, and then she found your father's notes for him. We were talking about Mr. Edison's experiments in the United States, and then…well, I am not sure exactly how it happened. But the general addressed some remark to Miss Pennybaker, and your father took exception to it."

"Why?"

"I am not entirely sure. As I remember, it was an innocuous remark, something about wanting to show her an experiment *he* had been working on. Then Florian got quite upset and declared that the general was making *warm* remarks to her. Well, the general, of course, said that he was not. He called your father a 'dog in the manger,' I believe. And, well, it went rapidly downhill after that. Miss Pennybaker kept fluttering back and forth between the two men, trying to persuade them to stop their foolish argument. But no one would listen to reason. Finally the general said that he was going to ask

Miss Pennybaker to marry him, whereupon that good lady gasped and fainted dead away on the sofa. Florian got enraged and jumped up and popped the general right on the nose. The general got up, shouting and swinging at your father, all the while trying to hold his handkerchief to his nose to stop the bleeding. He chased Florian all around the room, and finally Florian fell backward over a footstool and knocked his head on a chair leg. That is the injury on his forehead.

"At that point, Miss Pennybaker came to and saw your father struggling to sit up, looking rather woozy and bleeding from his forehead. She rounded on the general like a tiger, telling him that he was arrogant and bellicose and, oh, I don't know what else. She said he should not have attacked your father, and the general, needless to say, felt somewhat wronged by this statement. She went over to help Florian up, and was holding her handkerchief to his head and asking if he was all right. That is when both the general and your father realized that she loved your father. So your father asked her to marry him, she said yes, and the general went off in a huff."

"My," Priscilla responded inadequately. "I can hardly believe it. I always suspected that Miss Pennybaker was half in love with Papa, but he never seemed to know she existed."

"Apparently he discovered her."

Priscilla chuckled. The vicar smiled back.

"Now, tell me—how are things going with that young man of yours?"

"We have been trying to prove that his father did not kill Rose Childs, but it has been very difficult. It was so long ago. Ranleigh was talking about questioning Mr. Childs."

"I wouldn't think Tom is very interested in answering any of the Duke's questions."

"No. Although the Duke thinks that something new has turned up, something that might point to another man."

"You know, I have been wondering something about that night. At first, like everyone else, I more or less assumed that the Marquess was guilty of it. It did not look good, especially after he ran away. But now, since he has come back, and you seem convinced that he really was somewhere else that night—"

"I am sure of it. I have the word of someone whom I trust implicitly. He was with…that person. He could not have been in Lady's Woods."

"What I wonder is, where was Mr. Rutherford during that time that he said he was with Lynden?"

Priscilla simply stared at him. "What? What do you mean?"

"Well, Rutherford came forward and said that Lynden was with him, but obviously Lynden was not. He was with…this other person. So if Lynden was not with Rutherford, who was? And where was he?"

Priscilla blinked. "Yes, I see. Obviously, his alibi for Lynden was an alibi for himself, as well. If Lynden was not with him, then he did not really have an alibi."

The vicar nodded.

"But, Vicar!" Priscilla breathed, aghast. "Surely you don't suspect Mr. Rutherford!"

The older man shrugged. "Frankly, I don't know who I suspect or don't suspect. Only God and the killer know for sure who he is. But now that you have convinced me that the killer was not the Marquess, it makes me doubt all the notions I held as truth about the matter. One was that the young Mr. Rutherford was covering up for his friend. What if, in doing so, he was really covering up for himself? Mr. Rutherford would, after all, qualify as a 'young gentleman.' To a naive young serving girl, he probably would have appeared wealthy. He was living at Ranleigh Court during the time of the affair and the murder. What if he knew that Lynden was out visiting this person whom he could not acknowledge he was seeing? And what if he realized that by giving Lynden an alibi, he was also guaranteeing that Lynden would alibi him, even though Lynden had no idea where his friend was at that time."

Priscilla stared. "Reverend Whiting, I never realized that your mind could work in such a devious way!"

"Frankly, neither did I," said a masculine voice from the doorway.

Both Priscilla and the vicar whirled around, startled. Sebastian Rutherford stood there, hat in hand, watching them.

CHAPTER TWENTY-ONE

PRISCILLA BLUSHED BRIGHT RED. Rutherford had obviously heard them speculating about the possibility that he could have been the murderer.

"Oh, dear," the vicar commented weakly.

"Yes. Oh, dear."

"I am terribly sorry that you heard that," Priscilla began in embarrassment.

"I am sure you are."

"I hope you won't be angry with us. We were simply trying to think of any and every possibility, you see."

"No, I am not angry with you, my dear Miss Hamilton. I am merely regretful." He raised his hand, which he had been holding by his side and slightly behind him, and pointed the pistol in it straight at Priscilla.

"Oh, dear, oh, dear," the little vicar began to say in a breathy litany of fear. Priscilla merely felt cold all the way down to her toes.

"I didn't believe it," she said in amazement. "Even after what the vicar said, I was so certain that it was wrong that all I felt was embarrassment when you came in and found us talking about it."

"I am pleased to find that you hold me in such esteem. Unfortunately, I doubt that Bryan or Damon will be quite so reluctant to accept the possibility. Even before I overheard you and the reverend speaking, I saw how this thing was going. I knew that once you started snooping around, checking out Evesham and talking to Rose's family, it would soon be the end of my masquerade. I tried to scare you off by encouraging Evesham to come home early, but it did not seem to deter you at all. Instead, you decided that you would talk to Rose's family! And they have whatever Damon was talking about yesterday. When he sees it, he is quite likely to realize to whom it belongs. I think it is best if I make my move before you and the vicar have the opportunity to talk to everyone about his little theory."

"What do you plan to do?" Priscilla asked. "Kill us both to silence us? That is bound to cast suspicion on you. There must be someone who saw you riding over here or will see you riding away. It is broad daylight outside."

"I realize that. But I don't plan to kill you. That is, unless I am forced to. I am afraid I am not very good at such things. I didn't even do a very good job the first time."

"I don't know. You certainly managed to cast suspicion on the man who thought you were his friend," Priscilla responded acidly.

"Do you think I intended to do that? I did not. I had no idea where Damon was or where he had been going all those nights. I had simply been glad he was gone, because it had allowed me to pursue my dalliance with Rose. It never occurred to me that he would be unable to tell where he was at the time Rose was killed. Well, frankly, I didn't think about it one way or another. I didn't intend to kill her. It just happened."

"Is that what you are going to do now? Just let murder happen again?" Priscilla asked sarcastically.

"Priscilla," the vicar murmured anxiously, "do not antagonize him."

Rutherford's face darkened, and he started toward them, saying, "Yes, my dear, do not antagonize me. I might forget how much I detest bloodshed, if you push me."

"You are quite brave when you are facing a woman— with a pistol in your hand."

Rutherford's jaw tightened, and for an instant Priscilla thought he was going to break and fly into a rage. She braced herself, not sure what her needling would incite. But he visibly forced himself to calm down. In a level voice, he said, "Priscilla, come here."

"No." The frail vicar stepped in front of her. "I will not allow you to carry her off."

"*You* are going to stop me?" Rutherford swept a scornful look over the small white-haired man.

"I am going to try. I will not let you take this young, innocent girl out and kill her—not as long as there is breath in my body."

Rutherford sighed. "Don't force me to hurt you, Reverend. I am not going to kill Miss Hamilton, or even hurt her, no matter how annoying she can be. She is my asset, the chip that I will trade to the Aylesworths in return for my freedom."

"What?" Priscilla looked at him, puzzled.

"I told you I saw the impossibility of remaining here. It is only a matter of time until all of you figure out the truth. Unfortunately, I haven't the means to leave the country. That is what I will get from Damon, and in return I will spare the life of the woman his son loves. I think he will make the trade."

"You're joking. You threw suspicion of murder on

Ranleigh thirty years ago, so that he fled his home and country, and now you expect him to finance your flight from justice?"

"It will be a small price to pay, actually, for proving that Damon did not commit the murder. He might give me the money in return for that. But I would rather not count on it. Damon tends to hold a grudge. So I think it best that I give him more incentive, such as his son's future happiness."

He moved toward them again. The vicar braced himself, lifting his fists in a move that would have been ludicrous, had it not been so touching. Priscilla put her hand on his arm.

"No, Reverend Whiting. Do not put yourself in harm's way on my account. I believe him. I don't think he means to kill me, merely to use me to get away himself."

"Quite smart, Miss Hamilton. You obviously have a good head on your shoulders."

"Besides, you must stay here to tell my father what happened."

The vicar nodded. "You are right. I am a witness to what happened to you." He fixed his gaze on Rutherford. "Everyone will know that you have her. I will make sure of that. If you hurt her, you won't stand a chance of getting away."

Reluctantly he stepped aside, and Priscilla walked across the room to Rutherford. He took her elbow, placing the gun directly against her spine. "All right, Miss Hamilton. Let us go now."

They took the vicar's small trap, which was sitting in front of the house. Rutherford tied his horse to the back of the trap and climbed into the small seat beside Priscilla. Priscilla drove, and he held the gun to her waist the whole way, concealing it behind her back whenever they chanced to come upon anyone on the road.

Fear had left Priscilla sometime back in her father's house. She was certain that Rutherford would not harm her as long as he got what he wanted out of Ranleigh. But she burned inside with a determination to see that he would not get away with it. He had murdered that girl! Had seduced her and gotten her pregnant and then killed her when she confronted him with it. It made Priscilla see red just to think of it. As if that were not bad enough, he had implicated his own friend in the murder—no matter how much he protested that he had not intended for Damon to be blamed, the simple truth of the matter was that Damon *had* been blamed for it. The fact that he had given Damon an alibi did not relieve him of that guilt; it had been an alibi for himself, as well. Then he had lived among them all these years, accepting everyone's friendship and liking. He had fooled them all. He must have laughed at them secretly. He must have thought they were all fools for believing in him, trusting him, liking him—when all the time he was guilty of murder!

While Damon had been as good as exiled to another land, parted from the woman he loved…

Priscilla had to swallow back her rage. She could not let it cloud her thinking. She did not want this man to get away, and she must be clearheaded, so that she could seize whatever opportunity arose to escape from him.

Before long they pulled up in front of Ranleigh Court and got out of the trap. A groom ran to get the pony, and Priscilla walked to the front door with Rutherford following, carefully concealing his gun behind her. The footman who answered the door, used to seeing both of them, ushered them in and showed them to the informal drawing room. It was only a few minutes before the Duke entered the room, saying jovially, "Sebastian! Priscilla, my dear. It is so nice to see you."

He stopped short as the pair turned toward him. It was immediately apparent from their stiff demeanor that something was wrong. His eyes dropped to Priscilla's waist, and he saw the gun. His face seemed to age years in those seconds.

"So it *was* you." He shook his head in a dazed way. "When Bryan told me his suspicions, I couldn't believe it."

"Bryan knew?" Priscilla exclaimed in surprise.

Damon shook his head. "He didn't *know*. But he had suspicions. He was the only one who came into this from the outside, who didn't already have an opinion of Sebastian. He saw the holes, I guess, and he asked me questions that I could not ignore. I kept thinking about it. And then, Sebastian, you were a little clumsy about maneuvering us into going to Evesham's home. It made me wonder all the more. That is why I planted that seed yesterday, the little story about Rose having left something of her lover's behind."

"What?" Rutherford looked stunned. "You mean, there isn't any memento?"

"I know of none. I just made it up. I wanted to see if you would react to it, if it would make you do anything. Unfortunately, it never occurred to me that you would react by seizing Miss Hamilton." Damon sighed heavily. "Oh, God, Sebastian, why did you do this? I was always so certain that you were my friend."

"I *was* your friend, Damon. You have to believe that. I never intended to hurt you. I didn't know it would happen that way. I just—I saw Rose, and she was quite available, always flirting and smiling. It was obvious that she was experienced. Everyone acts as if she were some innocent child, but she knew what she was doing. I didn't realize that she would try to take advantage of the situation. When she told me that she was pregnant, I was flabbergasted. And she acted as if she expected me to marry her! A chambermaid! I assumed that she wanted money, but I hadn't much. You know the shape I was always in. I could barely stay in Oxford. I tried to give her what I had, but she was scornful of it. So I decided to take some jewels from your father's safe in the library. I had seen him open it. I knew where he kept the combination. It was dead easy. I grabbed the first thing I saw. I didn't know it was a special necklace, that everyone could identify it. I knew nothing about jewelry. I didn't even realize how valuable it was. It was wrong of me; I admit it. But, please, absolve me of malicious intent."

"Lord, man, why are you worrying about your thievery?" Ranleigh asked, amazed. "You killed a girl!"

"I didn't mean to! I keep telling you—I didn't mean to do anything terrible. I just wanted to give her a piece of jewelry that would be worth enough to keep her quiet, to get her to leave me alone. But when I gave it to her that night, she had a fit. She was screaming and crying, saying I had to marry her, that she would tell your father and everyone else. We struggled, and somehow the necklace got broken. She kept going on and on about it, and how I had to marry her, and then... I don't know how it happened. I wanted her to shut up, and I put my hands on her neck, and I shook her. And the next thing

I knew, I was standing there, and she was lying on the ground. Dead. I didn't mean to."

"Things like that tend to happen when you're squeezing someone by the throat," Priscilla remarked dryly.

He jabbed her with the gun. "Keep quiet. I have no need for your opinion." He looked back at Ranleigh, appealing to him. "I didn't dream that they would think you had done it! I didn't know the silly chit had told her family she was seeing a 'gentleman.' Or that they would be able to trace those damn rubies back to your family. It all…just happened."

Ranleigh nodded. "Things seem to do that with you."

Rutherford nodded eagerly, not noticing the sarcasm in the Duke's voice. "It's true! I don't know why. But when I realized that they were trying to put the blame on you, I came forward and said you were with me. So they wouldn't arrest you."

"And very conveniently providing an alibi for yourself, as well. One that I could not refute, if I wanted to save my own neck." Ranleigh made a disgusted noise. "I cannot believe I was so completely taken in. I really believed that you were acting as a friend. It never occurred to me to wonder whether your lie covered up something you needed hidden, too."

"I was thinking of you," Rutherford insisted. "You can believe what you want, but I acted as a friend. I could not let them accuse you of murder. I needn't have done anything, you know. No one suspected me."

"Yet. But what if the woman I had seen that night had come forward and revealed that I was with her and couldn't have committed the murders? Then what? They would have started looking around again. And how many other 'gentleman' would there have been around to lay the blame on? Evesham? Lord Chalcomb? You? The list is short."

"I did it for you, damn you! Why do you persist in misjudging me?"

"Perhaps because I have already misjudged you so—in the opposite direction." Damon sighed. "All right, Sebastian. I believe that you did not mean to harm me. But—" Ranleigh spread his hands in a gesture of appeal "—what are you hoping to accomplish now? Do you think that killing another young woman will make anyone go easier on you?"

"No. I don't plan to kill her—not unless you give me no other choice."

"What can *I* do?"

"You know I'm not flush with money. I never have been. It has been easier, with that house your father gave me, but still, I haven't any money saved. And obviously I cannot stay here anymore. I have to get away—go to America, as you did. Or Australia. But I need money for that, for the ship fare and for getting started in a new land."

"God forbid that you should have to work," Priscilla put in scathingly, earning herself another jab in the back.

"Shut up, I said!"

"All right, Sebastian. I will give you money. Come into the library. It is where I keep it."

He started out the door, and Rutherford propelled Priscilla after him, staying a cautious distance behind the Duke and keeping his gun pressed into Priscilla's ribs. Priscilla glanced around but could see nothing out of place. Rutherford was twisting and turning nervously, checking out every nook and cranny.

"Where is your son?" he asked finally. It was something Priscilla had been wondering, also. She would have thought that Bryan would come down to see her, yet he had never come into the drawing room. Had he heard them talking? Hope began to rise in her. Perhaps he had heard them and had realized what was going on. He might have gone to get the authorities— No, not Bryan. He would more likely have decided to hide until they came out, then jump Rutherford himself. At any moment, he might come out of nowhere and—

Her hopes were dashed by Ranleigh, who said, "He went out riding this morning. I am afraid I don't know where he is."

Rutherford nodded, obviously relieved at the news. The Duke opened the door to his library and walked in. It was a large, elegant room, not the jumbled study that her father's library was, but a well-proportioned chamber lined with gilt-lettered leatherbound books. One wall was all books from floor to ceiling, with a tall ladder on rollers that moved along a track. The wall adjacent to it faced the front of the house, its long casement windows providing a view of the rolling green lawn that stretched out before it.

Ranleigh walked over to his desk, with Rutherford and Priscilla close behind him, and unlocked the center drawer. "Let's see." He pulled out a small flat metal box and opened it. "Here are some bills." He started to count them out, then paused, glancing over at the windows. "Trifle stuffy in here, isn't it?"

He turned and started toward the windows.

"What the devil are you doing?" Rutherford snarled. "I hope you don't think you can escape that easily."

"Of course not." Ranleigh turned back, looking affronted. "Do you think I would try to escape, leaving Miss Hamilton in your hands? It is warm. I thought I would open a window."

"Well, don't. Come back here."

Ranleigh shrugged and started back toward the desk, but Priscilla turned to Rutherford, saying, "Please, let him open one. I am feeling quite faint." She did not know why Ranleigh wanted to open a window, but because of its very oddness, she felt it must be part of some plan he was cooking up.

Rutherford frowned, looking undecided.

"For pity's sake, Sebastian," Ranleigh snapped. "You can come with me, if it bothers you. I give you my word of honor that I will not try to escape."

"Oh, all right. But I do wish you would get on with it. I need to leave."

Rutherford accompanied Ranleigh to the window, dragging Priscilla along with him, and he watched suspiciously as Ranleigh cranked out the window.

"There, that's better," the duke said, breathing in the cool air. "Are you all right, Miss Hamilton?"

"Oh, yes, I feel much better," Priscilla answered, taking a deep gulp of air, too. Ranleigh smiled at her, and there was a twinkle in his eye that made her wonder more than ever if he was planning to use the open window somehow.

Ranleigh returned to the desk, and Rutherford and Priscilla turned to follow him. As she did so, Priscilla caught a glimpse of the large bush to the left of the window. It trembled suddenly, and it wasn't until after she had turned and taken a step away that she realized that a few branches of the bush had moved and that there had been a hand, a human hand, on one of them. She nearly stopped, but she caught herself, turning it into a stumble.

"I'm sorry," she murmured. "I am afraid I felt a little dizzy for a moment."

Her mind was racing. There was someone out there, waiting for a chance to jump in and wrestle the gun away from Rutherford. It might be a servant who had overheard the conversation, but her heart told her it was Bryan. No doubt his father had been lying when he said he was out riding. He had known Bryan was in the house and would be maneuvering into position to take care of Rutherford.

"Be careful," Rutherford returned irritably. "You will make my finger twitch on the trigger."

"Yes. I know. I'm sorry."

Ranleigh began to count out the money in his cash box. Then he handed it to Rutherford. Rutherford grabbed it out of his hand, saying, "But that's not nearly enough! I cannot even get to America on this!"

"I'm sorry. I am not in the habit of keeping large sums of money around the house. I would have to go to the bank to withdraw a larger amount."

"Damn it, Damon, are you playing with me?"

"No! I swear it. It's the truth. Why would I keep enough money here for a man to go to the States and set up a new life? It would be foolhardy of me."

"Open the safe. There is bound to be some in there."

Ranleigh shrugged. "If you wish. But it's mostly jewelry and some stock and bonds, debentures."

"Just open it."

"All right." He went around the desk and over to the small safe in the wall.

Rutherford started to follow, but Priscilla sagged against the desk. She didn't want Rutherford going very far from the window, nor did she want him turning and perhaps catching a glimpse of Bryan climbing in. She grabbed Rutherford's arm, saying in a dying voice, "Please, I feel quite ill. This is too—too much excitement."

Rutherford let out a curse, struggling to hold her up as Priscilla let the full weight of her body sag against him. "Bloody hell, woman!" he began, bringing the arm that held the gun up to catch her under the shoulder.

At that instant, there was an earsplitting yell from behind them, and before Rutherford could even turn, a heavy weight thudded into him from the rear. He staggered forward, carrying Priscilla with him, and they crashed into the desk. Priscilla, as soon as she heard the noise, grabbed for Rutherford's gun hand with both her own hands, and she hung on even when they fell against the desk. Her breath was knocked out of her, but she clung to Rutherford's arm like a limpet.

She could see nothing but darkness as the three of them struggled. There were curses and grunts as the men grappled atop her, driving the last of the air from her lungs. The gun went off with a loud bang, and something crashed across the room. Sparks danced before Priscilla's eyes, and she was certain that she was about to faint when suddenly there was a loud crash much closer by, as a stick slammed into the desk, not far above her hands—and right across Rutherford's arm.

Rutherford let loose an inhuman yowl, and suddenly

the two bodies were off her. Priscilla looked up to see Bryan lifting Rutherford from the floor and throwing him against the bookcase.

"Careful, Bryan. I may have broken the man's arm," the Duke said calmly behind her head.

He reached down and slipped an arm under Priscilla, lifting her up into a sitting position on the desk. Priscilla looked up at him. In the other hand he held a long stick with a clamp at the end, useful for getting down hard-to-reach books. Rutherford's gun was lying useless on the ground at his feet.

Bryan, who had just slammed his fist into Rutherford's gut, let out a growl to the effect that he really did not care about the other man's arm. He followed his words with an uppercut to Rutherford's chin. Rutherford's eyes rolled up in his head, and he slid to the floor in a heap. Bryan looked down at him, clenching and unclenching his fist.

"Don't," his father told him calmly, bending down and picking up Rutherford's gun. "It's unsportsmanlike."

Bryan cast him an expressive look. "You forget. I'm not English."

"True. But you are not entirely a savage, either."

Bryan sighed regretfully. "I suppose you're right."

He turned away, and his eyes went to Priscilla, who was sitting on the desk, still trying to recover her breath. He was at her side in one quick stride, pulling her off the desk and into his arms, burying his face against her neck.

"God, I was scared to death. I thought he would make a mistake and the gun would go off. Or I wouldn't hit him right and he would have enough time to shoot."

Priscilla smiled brilliantly, surprised to find tears

suddenly coursing down her face. "You did it exactly right."

"No, it was you who made it work." He kissed her again and again as he spoke—quick, eager kisses. "You are so damned clever, getting him to open the window. And then to grab for the gun. You are a jewel. A woman in a million."

Priscilla giggled through her tears, returning his kisses.

"No, wait, sir, wait!" came the agitated voice of the Ranleigh Court butler.

A moment later Florian Hamilton burst into the room, brandishing the large dueling pistol that had belonged to his father. "Damn you!" he shouted. "Release my daughter."

Right behind him were Miss Pennybaker, clutching her parasol in a death grip and looking as if she were ready to dispatch a scoundrel or two with it, and the vicar, carrying no weapon and looking anxiety-stricken.

"Release her, I said!" Florian raised the old gun and pointed it straight at Bryan.

Bryan groaned. "Not that damnable pistol again!"

"No, Florian, wait," the vicar exclaimed. "That isn't the one who dragged Priscilla off. It was Mr. Rutherford. Where is he?" He looked over at the person in question, who was lying on the floor, clutching his arm and groaning. "Oh. My. I—I guess the situation is in hand."

"Yes, Papa. I am fine. See?" Priscilla slid out of Bryan's embrace and went to kiss her father on the cheek. "Thank you for trying to rescue me, though. It was very sweet."

"Well, you are my daughter," Florian replied

reasonably, setting the dueling pistol down on the nearest table. He peered across the room at Rutherford, adjusting his spectacles. "I say, what happened to him?"

"Bryan saved me from him," Priscilla explained.

"I see. Handy fellow with his fists, Bryan." He came over and shook Bryan's hand. "Good work, lad. I'm proud of you."

"Thank you," Bryan returned. "I am glad to hear that, since I intend to marry your daughter."

"Do you, now?" Florian looked faintly surprised, but not concerned. "Lot of that going on these days, isn't there?"

"I beg your pardon?"

"Marrying. Seems to be an epidemic of it."

"Papa and Miss Pennybaker have decided to tie the knot, also," Priscilla explained to Bryan.

"Ah, I see."

"Your father, too," Florian pointed out. "Well, that's good. Priscilla's a trifle bored at home, what with the boys gone and all. And now Isabelle can do my copying, so it will work out nicely." He nodded, satisfied.

"Wait." Priscilla turned to Bryan. "I…I'm…you must not go about telling everyone that we are getting married. Not until…"

"Yes? Until what?"

"Until I tell you my…the secret. The scandal. I cannot in good conscience marry you unless you are aware of it."

"All right." He looked unconcerned. "Then tell me."

"I—I am Elliot Pruett."

He looked at her blankly. "Pardon?"

"I am Elliot Pruett. I mean, that is my nom de plume."

When Bryan still said nothing, she went on, "I write books."

"Yes. And...?" Bryan said encouragingly.

"And what?"

"The scandal. I thought you were going to tell me what the scandal was."

"That's it. I write books. Not just books. I write adventure stories."

"Really?" Bryan looked intrigued. He glanced over at the Duke. "Did you hear, Father?"

"Yes. It's rather unusual."

"You wrote that book that I read," Bryan went on in a tone of discovery. "That was good. Well, no wonder you always want to be in on the adventure. It gives you something to put in your books."

"I had never been on any adventures until I met you."

"You hadn't?"

"No. I think the adventure arrived with you."

He grinned. "Well, you performed admirably your first time, then."

"Bryan...aren't you even going to get upset?"

"No. Should I?"

"If it ever got out that I wrote adventure novels, it would be a terrible scandal, and the scandal would be far worse if I were the Duchess of Ranleigh."

"And that is why you refused to marry me? Because of the scandal of your writing books?"

Priscilla nodded. Bryan threw back his head and laughed. He laughed so hard tears came to his eyes. Priscilla, watching him, began to grow a little aggravated.

"Bryan! Would you stop? This is serious. Everyone else will take it seriously. They will talk. There will be gossip. I don't know how we could possibly keep it a secret forever, not when I am married to you."

"I'm sorry." He tried to calm down. "But I can't be serious about this. You think I should worry because a bunch of people I don't know and couldn't care less about will gossip and be offended if they find out that my wife writes novels?"

Priscilla hesitated. "Well, yes, essentially."

"Priscilla…when are you going to believe me? I don't give a damn about the British people, most particularly the peerage. They could talk about me every day of the week, and I wouldn't much care. I won't be here to hear them most of the time, and when I am, I still won't care. As for their talking about you, I think I can guarantee that they won't do it long."

Priscilla looked aghast. "Bryan, you can't go around threatening everyone with all that Indian talk."

"I shall use a different tack." He reached out and took her hands, pulling her closer. "You silly goose. Did you honestly think I would care? That it would bother me that you wrote books?"

"It would many men."

"I am not 'many men.' I liked your book. And it fits in perfectly."

"With what?"

"With our life. We will be at sea a lot, and writing will give you something to do to pass your time aboard ship. You can see all the exotic locales you want to, write stories set there…."

Priscilla's stomach quivered with eagerness. She squeezed Bryan's hands hard. "Tell me this is not a dream."

"No one ever accused me of appearing in their

dreams. Nightmares, perhaps. No, I would say that this is utterly, completely real."

"Oh, Bryan." She threw her arms around his neck. "I love you. I love you."

He turned his face into her hair, kissing it. "I love you, too."

Priscilla leaned back and looked up into his face, smiling. "Do you know what I've learned?"

"What?"

"You just never know when something wonderful is going to show up on your doorstep."

Bryan smiled and bent to kiss her.

* * * * *

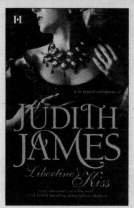

REQUEST YOUR FREE BOOKS!

2 FREE NOVELS
FROM THE ROMANCE COLLECTION
PLUS 2 FREE GIFTS!

YES! Please send me 2 FREE novels from the Romance Collection and my 2 FREE gifts (gifts are worth about $10). After receiving them, if I don't wish to receive any more books, I can return the shipping statement marked "cancel." If I don't cancel, I will receive 4 brand-new novels every month and be billed just $5.74 per book in the U.S. or $6.24 per book in Canada. That's a saving of at least 28% off the cover price. It's quite a bargain! Shipping and handling is just 50¢ per book.* I understand that accepting the 2 free books and gifts places me under no obligation to buy anything. I can always return a shipment and cancel at any time. Even if I never buy another book, the two free books and gifts are mine to keep forever.

194/394 MDN E7NZ

Name _____ (PLEASE PRINT) _____

Address _____ Apt. # _____

City _____ State/Prov. _____ Zip/Postal Code _____

Signature (if under 18, a parent or guardian must sign) _____

Mail to **The Reader Service:**
IN U.S.A.: P.O. Box 1867, Buffalo, NY 14240-1867
IN CANADA: P.O. Box 609, Fort Erie, Ontario L2A 5X3

Not valid for current subscribers to the Romance Collection
or the Romance/Suspense Collection.

**Want to try two free books from another line?
Call 1-800-873-8635 or visit www.morefreebooks.com.**

* Terms and prices subject to change without notice. Prices do not include applicable taxes. N.Y. residents add applicable sales tax. Canadian residents will be charged applicable provincial taxes and GST. Offer not valid in Quebec. This offer is limited to one order per household. All orders subject to approval. Credit or debit balances in a customer's account(s) may be offset by any other outstanding balance owed by or to the customer. Please allow 4 to 6 weeks for delivery. Offer available while quantities last.

Your Privacy: Harlequin Books is committed to protecting your privacy. Our Privacy Policy is available online at www.eHarlequin.com or upon request from the Reader Service. From time to time we make our lists of customers available to reputable third parties who may have a product or service of interest to you. If you would prefer we not share your name and address, please check here. ☐

Help us get it right—We strive for accurate, respectful and relevant communications. To clarify or modify your communication preferences, visit us at www.ReaderService.com/consumerschoice.

MROM10R